Tatty pushed the door open. Siren let out a frightened squawk and launched itself into the air. Daisy grabbed Tatty by the collar and pulled her to the side an instant before a semi-circular blade flashed down from the ceiling, swinging from a cable-like pendulum. It swept back and forth through the doorway as Tatty clutched her doll to her breast, taking deep breaths. A lock of her blond hair floated down through the air – the blade had a keen edge. Daisy picked up her broom handle and used it to stop the swinging blade.

'That would have cut your head right down the middle,' she muttered. 'Your nanny should have taught you some caution.'

She stepped across the threshold, peering into the darkness and the floor suddenly gave way beneath her. Tatty caught her friend's flailing hand as she fell, but it took all of the girl's strength to stop Daisy from plunging down onto the spikes lining the bottom of the pit fifteen feet below . . .

Also available by

Oisín McGann

Small-Minded Giants
'A debut novel so powerful it all but explodes off the page
. . . This book isn't content to sit on your shelf; it's too
busy screaming at you to pick it up and READ IT!'
SFX

Strangled Silence
'His most accomplished young adult novel to date . . .
an impressive and highly intelligent political thriller'
IRISH TIMES

THE WILDENSTERN SEQUENCE
Ancient Appetites
'A pacy, bloodthirsty story . . . a Godfather-style Mafia
family fighting and infighting; social deprivation
of the past; a Pullmanesque blend of history and
fantasy; the age old battle between good and evil.
And it's great fun . . . I'd certainly look forward
to reading another book about the Wildensterns'
Jill Murphy, *BOOK BAG*

The Wisdom of Dead Men
'An explosive fantasy read, set in the Victorian era.
It opens with a gripping spontaneous combustion
and the action never lets up'
IRISH INDEPENDENT

www.oisinmcgann.co.uk

Merciless
REASON

Oisín McGann

CORGI BOOKS

MERCILESS REASON
A CORGI BOOK 978 0 552 56485 4

Published in Great Britain by Corgi Books,
an imprint of Random House Children's Books
A Random House Group Company

This edition published 2012

1 3 5 7 9 10 8 6 4 2

Text and inside illustrations copyright © Oisín McGann, 2012
Cover illustration © Steve Stone, 2012
Cover design by James Fraser

The Random House Group Limited supports the Forest Stewardship Council (FSC®),
the leading international forest certification organization. Our books carrying the FSC
label are printed on FSC®-certified paper. FSC is the only forest certification scheme
endorsed by the leading environmental organizations, including Greenpeace. Our paper
procurement policy can be found at www.**randomhouse**.co.uk/environment.

Set in Bembo

RANDOM HOUSE CHILDREN'S BOOKS
61–63 Uxbridge Road, London W5 5SA

www.**kids**at**randomhouse**.co.uk
www.**totallyrandombooks**.co.uk
www.**randomhouse**.co.uk

Addresses for companies within The Random House Group Limited can be found at:
www.**randomhouse**.co.uk/offices.htm

THE RANDOM HOUSE GROUP Limited Reg. No. 954009

A CIP catalogue record for this book is available from the British Library.

Printed and bound by CPI Group (UK) Ltd, Croydon, CR0 4YY

For Inga, Danu and Oscar – three wonderfully mad kids,
who keep me sane in a nutty business

Acknowledgements

My first thanks, as ever, must go to my family. It takes a fair bit of nerve to spend months pouring the contents of your imagination into a document, to turn it into a book and then expect people to pay good money for the pleasure of reading it. I don't know if I'd ever have had the confidence – or indeed, the ability – to do it if it weren't for the belief and support (and critical faculties) of my family. What my mother and father started off, my brothers and sisters contributed to, and now my wife, Maedhbh, and my children help me maintain my reason and bring their spirit to this way of life I love so much.

My brother, Marek, makes sure my website (www.oisinmcgann.com) keeps on ticking and responds with equanimity to my sudden notions, odd requests and any number of run-of-the-mill questions that he has answered more than once before.

A quick note of appreciation to all the people in the children's book crowd, in the UK, but particularly in Ireland. This is a bit of a crackpot industry, but its effects are tempered by the passion, warmth and enthusiasm of those who work in it, help to promote it and those who take part in so many different ways. It's a pleasure to be part of this community. Please support your local library! But even more importantly, get in there and take advantage of it – it has a thousand and one uses!

Thanks to my agent, Sophie Hicks, as well as Edina Imrik

and everyone at Ed Victor Ltd, who apply the firm hand of reason to a shifting world of rights, contracts and percentages and who keep a watchful eye on a business environment that is going through some major changes. I'm grateful to the team at Random House for their continued support and for the quality of their work, and for being understanding with a writer whose fickle choice of genre and subject matter must cause the occasional pounding headache for marketing. Cheers, too, to designer James Fraser, for staying in touch.

And finally a special thanks to my new editor, Lauren Buckland, for her deft hand in fine-tuning the story and to Sue Cook, for adding the finishing touches in the copy edits.

Thanks to all of you.

Oisín McGann

THE WILDENSTERN FAMILY
The Rules of Ascension

With the intention of encouraging the qualities of aggression, strength and ambition, the family will sanction the act of assassination of one family member by another, under eight strict conditions – the Rules of Ascension. They are as follows:

Number One: The Act of Aggression must be committed by the Aggressor himself and not by any agent or servant.

Number Two: The Act must only be committed against a man over the age of sixteen who holds a superior rank in the family to the Aggressor.

Number Three: The Act must only be committed for the purpose of advancing one's position and not out of spite, or because of insult or offence given, or to satisfy a need for revenge for an insult or injury given to a third party.

Number Four: All efforts should be made to avoid the deaths of servants while committing the Act. Good servants are hard to find.

Number Five: The Target of the Aggression can use any and all means to defend themselves, and is under an obligation to do so for the good of the family.

Number Six: Retribution against the Aggressor can only be carried out after the Act has been committed. Should the Aggressor fail in his attempt, and subsequently escape to remain at large for a full day, only the Target of the Aggression and no other person will be permitted to take Retribution.

Number Seven: No Act of Aggression or Retribution must be witnessed or reported by any member of the public. All family matters must be kept confidential.

Number Eight: Any bodies resulting from the Act must be given a proper burial in a cemetery, crypt, catacomb or funeral pyre approved by the family.

A COMPENDIUM OF THE CHARACTERS

Edgar Wildenstern (deceased) – Patriarch of the family and Chairman of the North American Trading Company. Murdered at the dinner table not long after the death of his eldest son.

Miriam Wildenstern (deceased) – Wife to Edgar and mother to Marcus, Berto, Nathaniel and Tatiana. Committed to a mental asylum, then later imprisoned in the house until her death.

Marcus Wildenstern (deceased) – The eldest of the Wildenstern siblings, murdered while in the process of planning his father's assassination.

Berto Wildenstern (deceased) – Next in line after Marcus; served briefly (and reluctantly) as Patriarch before his own untimely death.

Nathaniel Wildenstern – Eldest surviving son of Edgar Wildenstern and rightful Patriarch of the family. Now missing, presumed to have taken leave of his senses.

Daisy Wildenstern – Widow to Berto. De facto managing director of the family business, despite her disadvantages as a woman.

Gerald Gordon – Nathaniel's cousin. A scientific prodigy, acting as Patriarch in Nathaniel's absence.

Tatiana Wildenstern – Nathaniel's high-spirited younger sister. The youngest of the Wildenstern siblings and Daisy's closest friend and ally.

Cathal Dempsey – A recently discovered young cousin of the Wildensterns, now living with them. Gerald's protégé, but close friend to Daisy and Tatiana.

Clancy – Nathaniel's former manservant.

Lieutenant William Dempsey – Cathal's father.

Elvira Gordon – Edgar's sister, Gerald's mother. Oldest living Wildenstern female.

Gideon Wildenstern – Edgar's younger brother.

Oliver Wildenstern – Gideon's son.

Elizabeth Wildenstern – One of four ancients raised from the dead some years ago. Her brothers, Hugo and Brutus, and sister, Brunhilde, died in the conflict that followed.

Leopold Wildenstern – Illegitimate son of Elizabeth and Nathaniel.

Detective Inspector Urskin – Police officer with the Royal Irish Constabulary, tasked with combating Irish revolutionaries.

Eamon Duffy – Irish revolutionary and self-made businessman.

Red – Career criminal and Gerald's chief enforcer.

Thomas 'Harmonica' Radigan – A bounty hunter from the United States.

The Irish Republican Brotherhood (the Fenians) – Irish revolutionary group.

Prologue

THE LEVIATHAN

Then, as if things weren't bad enough, a storm struck. The ship's timbers groaned as the vessel clambered through the growing banks of water. Heavy waves slammed against the tired, wooden hull and crashed across her decks. Men were swept off their feet, only their lifelines saving them from being carried overboard. It was next to impossible to keep your footing on the heaving deck, the sickening motion made worse by the sudden, jarring impacts of the waves.

Bushnell, her black-bearded captain, bellowed for more sail. Clinging to the wheel, the first mate, Pollard, automatically passed on the order at the top of his voice, the shout faltering as he realized what he was ordering. Able Seaman Jim Hawkins heard the shout with a sinking feeling in his gut. The rain glued his blond hair and beard to his lean, sombre face.

1

The ship was already taking on water, creaking ominously under the strain brought on by its current speed. Trying to catch more wind was madness. As it was, the gales were threatening to rip the sails from the masts.

The *Odin* was a three-masted Yankee whaler out of New Bedford, Massachusetts. She was a tough old ship, purpose-built to be fast, rugged and self-sufficient for voyages of up to four years. She carried five longboats for hunting the whales, all equipped with Greener guns for firing harpoons. The ship had her own try works – a brick furnace just behind the foremast, for processing the oil from the blubber cut from the carcasses of the great beasts after they were caught and killed.

But the fire in the furnace had long gone out. The huge casks in the ship's hold were empty of oil. Her maintenance had become neglected as the captain had grown more and more irrational. Jim swore bitterly as he scrambled across the slippery boards of the deck, making for the bow. They had not caught a single whale after months of hunting. It had taken the crew a while to realize that Bushnell had no interest in running down the sperm whales that were their normal prey. He had spun them a yarn that there were rich pickings out in these dangerous Atlantic waters off the coast of New England. The rumours of sea monsters in this area were just fairy tales for scaring children to bed, he'd said. Pay them no mind.

The first mate had whispered one of those stories to Jim

one evening, when they were both on watch. Word was, Pollard said, that Captain Bushnell's son had been on board a whaler sunk in these waters. She went down with all hands, watched helplessly by the crew of another ship. And she was sunk, Pollard added, by a monster of enormous size. His ruddy, broken-veined face betrayed his anxiety. Sneaking gulps of rum from a flask, the *Odin*'s first mate told Jim the story because he feared they were being led to their deaths. He was certain that the old man was out for vengeance.

Now, after months of fruitless searching, they had found it. Or rather, it had found them. The first they knew of it, the creature had run up against their starboard side and stove in the timbers just aft of the surgeon's quarters. The carpenters were struggling frantically to stem the leak as others pumped and bailed the water out. Even so, the ship was listing to starboard, leaning into the wind.

It took courage to be a whaleman, and only the toughest dared to hunt the sperm whale, the most dangerous of all. But this creature was like nothing they had ever seen – a true leviathan.

The captain ordered them to give chase even as the storm descended on them.

Bushnell's roars were drowned out by the howl of the wind; it shrieked through the rigging, filling out the sails with a noise like giant doors slamming. Raindrops fell like bullets, sweeping down off the sails in wide sheets. Jim was thrown against the gunwale as the bow pitched into another wave, the water hitting him with the force of a predator, ice-cold jaws closing around him, swallowing him and gargling him in its throat. He felt the rope pull taut around his waist, grabbed it and reefed it in, pulling himself in against the foremast. Gasping for air, he was back on his feet even as the water washed away. He staggered towards the ratlines, the web-like rigging strung to the top section of the mast. It was lunacy to let out more sail, but the captain would not be defied. The scars on Jim's back were still healing after the last flogging he had received.

The desperately unhappy lookouts clung to their perches at the tops of the masts. They had lost sight of the leviathan in the squall. If it escaped them, there would be hell to pay. Jim started climbing, his cold, numb hands clutching at the wet ropes. Looking across, he saw Zachariah, the boatswain, scaling the ratlines on the other side. One of the thousands of freed Negro slaves who had flocked to the whaling industry, Zachariah was a loud-mouthed bully, but a sound whaleman and utterly fearless. He let out a raucous laugh as he raced Jim up to the yardarm.

'Thar she blows!' one of the lookouts cried. 'Three points on the lee bow! A hundred and fifty yards!'

Other voices carried the cry down to the captain. Jim looked forward and off to the port side, in the direction the wind was blowing. There he saw the twin jets of steam rising from the rolling sea: the leviathan, a massive silvery shape moving quickly away from them.

'Keep your eye on him!' the captain shouted. 'Mr Pollard! Stand by to lower boats!'

Even though they knew it was coming, the crew looked at one another in disbelief. Only a madman would take a whaleboat out in seas like this. The smallest of these waves could swamp it. Pollard and another crewman struggled to keep the wheel under control. The first mate was a Nantucket man, come from a long line of sailors, but there were some places even he would not follow his captain. As he began speaking, the leviathan disappeared beneath the waves.

'Sir! We'll never catch it!' he protested. 'It's turning into the wind! Even if we launch the boats, we'll never be able to—'

It was as far as he got before Bushnell's fist caught him on the jaw, knocking him back across the deck.

'Twenty lashes for you, Pollard, when I can spare the bloody time!' the captain roared as he took the helm. 'Lower the boats! Let's sink our irons into this demon!'

Then something slammed into the bow of the ship, stopping her dead in her tracks, splitting timbers and hurling men into the sea, their lifelines serving only to break their backs before snapping like threads. All over the deck, men tumbled helplessly against walls and gunwales.

Jim felt the initial jolt through the ropes before the

rigging cracked like a whip, nearly throwing him out into the sky. He barely managed to hold on. The ratlines were still shaking when he heard a loud, cracking sound. There was another shudder through the rigging and he looked down to see the bow plunging underwater, the bowsprit splintering like a matchstick against something beneath the surface.

But that wasn't the sound that Jim heard. The foremast was starting to tilt over. It was cracking at the base and leaning drunkenly to one side, dragging sails and rigging with it. Jim and Zachariah looked at one another and then started to scramble down the lines.

They jumped the last ten feet, just as the mast crashed down on the port side, driving a gash into the gunwale before toppling into the sea. The water caught it and twisted it back against the hull of the ship, pulling more rigging into the water. Jim, sprawled in a tangle of lines, saw a rope snake past him at high speed. Zachariah was on hands and knees, trying to free himself from the mess of ratlines.

'Rope!' Jim yelled.

But it was too late; a loop of rope closed around the boatswain's hand. He tried to snatch it out but the loop jerked tight and tore away three of his fingers. He screamed and threw blood from the stumps as he flailed around. Jim rose and stumbled back, distracted long enough to step into a knot of other lines just as they were being dragged overboard by the weight of the mast. It took him by the ankle, jerked him off his feet and swept him over the side. The icy water stamped the air out of his lungs. The yardarm followed him off the deck, nearly coming down on his head, hitting the water by his shoulder.

It took all of his nerve to suppress the panic as he searched for air. He was caught in a web of ropes, and the more he thrashed the more tangled he became. One of the jib sails had landed next to him and he was being drawn underneath it. That would drown him for sure.

Pulling out his pocketknife, he cut his lifeline, still bound to the fallen mast, and then started sawing through the thicker rope around his ankle. It seemed to take for ever. The blade slipped a couple of times, drawing blood, but he paid it no mind. Finally, with his lungs spasming, the last strands parted and he slipped through the gaps in the swirling ropes, striking out towards the dull light above him.

He barely had time to get a breath before a wave crashed down on him. Jim lost all sense of direction, tumbling in the churning water. It was impossible to tell which way was up. Then he ran into a timber wall. The hull of the ship. He scrabbled up it, jamming the point of his knife in to try and get purchase, following the hull's curve to the surface and heaving in breaths of air.

The *Odin* should have been long gone, leaving him in her wake, but he wasn't going to complain. He screamed for help over and over again. The ship was side-on to the wind now, leaning away from it at a perilous angle, brought almost to a complete halt. Surely they were waiting to rescue their drowning men? The captain must have come to his senses and stopped the chase. But something made Jim turn round. Out there, not far off in the roiling darkness, he saw a metallic grey, serrated dorsal fin rise from the water, approaching the ship at terrifying speed.

The first time the leviathan had struck the ship, it had been a glancing blow. The second time, when the mast fell, it had crippled the vessel. The *Odin* would not stand a third strike. Jim kicked away from the hull and started swimming. He spotted a coffin-sized wooden sea-chest floating in the water ahead of him and made for it. Grabbing on with difficulty to the box with his frozen hands, he turned to look back at the ship.

The monster left a tumultuous white wake trailing behind it as it charged towards the vessel. The dorsal fin must have been nearly forty feet behind the head, for it was still in clear water when the deep bass crunch of the impact carried through the air. The fin kept going, sinking below the surface and disappearing.

As he was carried up onto the crest of a wave, Jim saw air belch from the belly of the ship, saw shattered ribs and protruding beams in the waist of the vessel as the water rushed in to fill the *Odin*'s carcass.

The dorsal fin broke the surface again, coming back towards him. It was slower now, as if calmer, having despatched its enemy. There was no way he could escape it. The sea bulged over the leviathan's back, trailing strands of foam outside of the clear white V of the fin's wake. Jim saw two clusters of pale green lights beneath his feet as its head passed under him. Its eyes. Around them, he spied long spines, like whiskers or feelers.

The creature was at least as long as the *Odin* – probably longer. It was by far the largest engimal he had ever encountered, much bigger than any land behemoth. As the hump of its silver-grey back rose under him, Jim found himself wading, as if walking up a moving beach. Unable to stay on his feet as the water dropped around him, he let the massive back come up under him and carry him and his wooden chest for some distance. The leviathan's skin appeared to be some kind of soft, flexible *metal*, dotted with clumps of barnacles. The remains of harpoons jutted like spines from its hide. The scars of a hundred battles criss-crossed its skin, along with triangular markings of darker grey on the silver, mimicking the broken surface of an unsettled sea. Jim ran his fingers over the netted texture.

The creature started to submerge again. Jim slipped off its back. It was only then, when he had returned to the water, clutching his box again, that he spotted the line of faint circular lights along the leviathan's side. Almost like . . . almost like windows, he thought.

Then it was gone, a last flick of its tail flukes tossing spray into the air. Treading water to face the oncoming waves, Jim had no choice but to let them toss him and drop him while he put his faith in his trusty sea-chest to keep him afloat. Whenever he got the chance, he turned his attention back to his ship.

The Odin was almost on her side, the ragged remnants of her sails dipping in the water. Her crew – what was left of them – were struggling to launch the longboats. By the time they saw the huge wave, it was too late. Like a moving mountain, it rushed towards the stricken ship, curling over and collapsing on her, burying her in water and leaving nothing but scattered debris. It continued on towards Jim, bearing down on him. He hugged the wooden box, closing his eyes as it loomed over him, its heaving wall lifting him, carrying him upwards, a mere speck on its surface, before the top of the watery cliff face broke into foam and fell upon him.

I

THE MISSING DUKE OF LEINSTER

HMS *Scafell* was a ship-of-the-line, carrying seventy-four guns. Her gun deck alone was over one hundred and eighty feet long. Built to be powerful but nimble, she was one of a breed of ships that made up the backbone of the Royal Navy. With elegant lines, sturdy construction, her intimidating firepower and a highly-disciplined crew of more than five hundred men, the *Scafell* represented all the qualities that had enabled Britain's navy to rule the seas for more than two hundred years.

She could have been a leaky gondola for all Jim cared. As long as her crew had water and food aboard and got him out of the sea, he'd kiss their feet for the rest of his life if they wanted. The ship's lookouts spotted the floating field of debris from the *Odin* two days after the storm. Jim's voice was failing him by the time the ship drew near enough to hear him. His arms ached from clutching the sea-chest, his body exhausted, his mind confused by salted, water-dazzled eyes and shimmering hallucinations.

Still, he didn't stop hoarsely calling out until he saw the longboat being lowered and rowed towards him. They handed him a flask of water even as he was hauled into the boat. He drank too much at first, his thirst-shrunken stomach throwing most of it back up.

The day was bright, the sun casting warmth out of a washed-out blue sky, but Jim shivered uncontrollably when he was brought up on the deck of the ship and wrapped in blankets. He was half led, half carried down to the surgeon, who pronounced him 'remarkably healthy, given the circumstances'.

The captain and second lieutenant joined him in the sick bay, sitting on chairs across from him and introducing themselves as Captain James Wyndham and Lieutenant William Dempsey. They were both dressed in their immaculate Royal Navy uniforms; dark blue jackets with epaulettes on the shoulders, worn over white trousers. Their turnout was a stark contrast to the rough and ready clothes worn aboard the whaler. The men were eager to question Jim, but were decent enough to wait until he had drunk his fill of water and eaten two bowls of chicken broth. He was happy to make them wait.

'Best grub I've had in months,' he croaked at last in his Liverpool accent. Sitting back in the bunk, he looked up at the officers. 'Been livin' on salt horse and biscuits and tea with molasses for what seems like for ever. Gets so you don't even mind the weevils or cockroaches in 'em – adds a bit of variety.'

'You were on the *Odin*?' Captain Wyndham asked.

He was a competent-looking man in his fifties, with a pronged moustache and salt-and-pepper hair. His tone was businesslike, but not unkind.

'Aye, sir,' Jim grunted. 'Ship went down with all 'ands but me. Twenty-eight good men.'

'You were lucky it was only a summer storm. In winter in these parts, the cold would kill you minutes after you entered the water.'

'Tell that to me gonads,' Jim sniffed. 'It'll be days before they unshrivel.'

'Mind your tongue, m'lad. We don't stand for foul language on Her Majesty's vessels. Had you been aboard the *Odin* long?'

'Me and a bunch o' lads joined the crew at Boston in April, while the ship was in for repairs,' Jim said. 'Thought they were settin' out for a normal voyage, but Captain Bushnell had plans of his own. Out for revenge for the death of his son, so he was. I'd bet a month's wages even the owners didn't know.'

'So what happened?' Wyndham inquired.

Jim told them everything about the *Odin*'s last day, wondering if they would scoff at his description of the monster. They didn't bat an eyelid. There were more than enough tales doing the rounds about colossal creatures from the depths – including this one off the New England coast.

'We've heard such stories before,' the captain said, nodding. 'The loss of a ship is a tragedy under any circumstances, but to be attacked by this . . . this abomination . . . its existence is an affront to God. Perhaps, someday, Her Majesty's Navy will turn its attentions to destroying the beast.'

Lieutenant Dempsey, a muscular-looking man in his forties or fifties with dark skin almost Mediterranean or even Arabic in complexion, framed by black hair and garnished with a clipped little moustache, nodded but said nothing. Jim noticed the man was studying him closely, as if his story was of only passing interest, to be set aside at the earliest opportunity. Captain Wyndham confirmed Jim's suspicions.

'As it happens, we were in the area, searching for the *Odin*,' the captain told him. 'We have been seconded to the North American Trading Company and have been tasked with finding a gentleman named Nathaniel Wildenstern, the Duke of Leinster. He went missing about three years ago. Our investigations led us to Boston, and we suspect he may have joined the *Odin*'s crew there. There is a reward for anyone who can help find him. Do you know him?'

Jim appeared to think for a moment, but then shrugged and shook his head.

'No, sir. Never 'eard of 'im.'

'He may well be travelling under an assumed name,' the second lieutenant spoke up. 'In his current state, his dress and appearance might not be that of a gentleman. We have a picture of him here. Perhaps you could take a look at it.'

A sepia photograph was laid on the table in front of him. It showed a proud-looking young man with a somewhat long but handsome visage and fair hair cut in a dashing style. Jim regarded the image for some time. It was so unlike his own, his face burnt by the wind and sun, his hair and beard faded and bedraggled. He reached out to touch the picture for a moment, then pushed it back across the table.

'Sorry, no. Doesn't ring any bells. Whaler captains aren't picky, they'll take on anyone who'll work. But he looks a bit posh for a life in whalin' if y'ask me.'

'We didn't,' Wyndham replied as he stood up, quickly followed by Dempsey. 'All right. Given that the ship we were after is now at the bottom of the Atlantic Ocean, it seems that our trail ends in Boston for now. We will return there and set you ashore. You will be provided with some fresh clothes and accommodated as a passenger until we reach port.'

'I'm 'appy to work me way,' Jim insisted.

'This is a ship-of-the-line of Her Majesty's Royal Navy,' the captain informed him. 'Every man here has his place and his duties. Your help is not required. We are three days from Boston, four at the most. Please take this opportunity

15

to convalesce, make sure you are presentable whenever you leave your cabin and try to stay out of the way. Good day, Mr Hawkins.'

The lieutenant nodded again and followed his captain out of the room. But there was something in Dempsey's expression as he cast a look back at Jim before leaving; something like barely suppressed hatred.

Jim was quartered in the clerk's cabin, a small, simple room that still felt like luxury after the cramped quarters on board the whaler. The clerk had been most understanding as he vacated his cabin, regarding Jim's survival as nothing less than a miracle. Jim slept for most of the rest of the day, eventually rising in the evening to pull on the clothes the cabin boy had provided for him.

One look out the porthole told him the fine weather was holding, but there was enough wind to enable the ship to make good time. It was an excellent vessel, so big that he could barely feel the motion of the water beneath his feet. He should have felt safe here, but he didn't. The sooner they got back to port, the better.

The rest had done him good, but his whole body still ached. His face, neck and arms were badly sunburnt, and the gashes in his back from his most recent flogging stung constantly. The edges of the cuts were white and swollen from being immersed for so long in the salt water. Jim left his shirt off, staring at himself in the small rectangular mirror propped on the cabin's tiny desk. He read the worst events in his life, carved there in the scars on his skin. His new injuries would fade in a matter of days. He never had to suffer pain for very long: it was a quality that ran in his family.

'You should keep yourself covered up,' a voice said from behind him.

He turned to see Lieutenant Dempsey standing in the doorway. There was open hostility written on his dark-skinned face and it put Jim on edge. Something familiar in the officer's posture, his looks, bothered Jim, but he couldn't put his finger on it.

'The captain is a very able man,' Dempsey told him, stepping inside and pulling the curtain across the doorway. He spoke softly. 'But he is blinded by his perception of class. We have a detailed description of the scars on your body – the one on your side and the one over your heart are particularly noticeable. And even though we know you've been working in manual labour and as a sailor since you left Africa, the captain still can't imagine a gentleman ending up looking like the tramp he saw when you came aboard.'

Nathaniel Wildenstern glanced down at his own chest and then stared back at the officer. He didn't answer immediately. He had not been recognized in over a year.

'No doubt he'll have a change of heart when he sees how well I scrub up,' he said. 'Or, if he is so sure that the clothes make the man, perhaps I'll be able to persuade him

I'm one of his crew if I slip on some blue and whites.'

'Wyndham's no spark, but he's no fool either,' Dempsey continued. 'If he sees your scars, he'll recognize you. Don't shave off your beard until you leave the ship. And see if you can keep up the Liverpool accent – if that's what it's supposed to be.'

'What's your game, then?' Nate asked. 'Why aren't you telling him?'

Dempsey scowled. Casting his eyes over his shoulder to check the curtain behind him, he moved closer to Nate.

'I have no great love for the Wildenstern family,' he said in a hoarse whisper. 'My wife is dead because of them, and they have all but stolen my son. He lives with them now, and they chose my ship to send in search of you so as to keep me out of their way. I have been back once since my wife died and had to seek permission to see my own son. I'm happy to cause your family any distress I can.'

'Cathal,' Nate said, almost to himself, searching old, unpleasant memories. 'You're Cathal Dempsey's father.'

'Not if the bloody Wildensterns have anything to say about it, I'm not.'

'And yet, if you brought me back, you would see your son again,' Nate said, moving backwards slightly so that he could lean on the desk, where his knife lay beneath his shirt. 'Why don't you want me to be found?'

'Because to Hell with them, that's why!' Dempsey growled, clenching his teeth. 'I'll get my son back my way and make sure the thrice-damned, night-soiled cur who took him pays a heavy price.'

'Now I know where your son gets his charming bloody-mindedness,' Nate observed. 'I seem to remember my young sister learning some delightful swearwords from him.'

'I know why you fled your family, Nathaniel Wildenstern,' the lieutenant went on. 'And I can tell you, they have grown worse in your absence. Ireland is suffering because of their infernal schemes.'

'Really? Doesn't sound like much has changed at all.'

The officer glared at him, and for a moment Nate thought he saw something of himself in the Navy man. The same loss, the same bottomless anger. Dempsey's wife had been a Wildenstern. She had been exiled from the family and imprisoned in a mental institution before she met him. Years later, she had been killed for her Wildenstern blood – the same blood that made Cathal so valuable to the family. Dempsey had good reason to hate them. This would not be a good time for Nate to mention that it was he who had brought the man's son to Wildenstern Hall. His fingers were close to the knife, but it was purely reflex; this man was no threat to him. Not yet, anyway.

'If you had any sense of duty, you would go back and join the struggle against them,' Dempsey said. 'But I suppose any man who has spent the last three years running away from his demons, as you have, can hardly be expected to change his colours.'

'I have no colours left,' Nate retorted. 'And my demons are all dead. Tell your captain who I am if you wish, or don't tell him. It's all the same to me. I'm past caring.'

'I don't think you are,' Dempsey replied as he turned toward the doorway. 'And your family are certainly not done with you. Whether that's a good or bad thing, I'm not sure. All I know is they want you back and I can stop them from having you. That's good enough for me . . . for now.' He stopped for a moment, turning back to look at Nate. 'You'll need money when you get ashore. There's a tavern called the Peggy Sayer, in Charlestown in Boston. Look for a man named Ronan. He'll pay good money for men with fighting skills. I'm sure you haven't forgotten your family traditions – you might as well make use of them.'

With that, he left, drawing the curtain closed behind him. Nate watched the fabric settle and stayed staring at it. He picked up his shirt and pulled it on, buttoning it up over his scars. Pressing his hand to his belly, he felt the slight movement beneath his abdominal muscles, just above his belly button, as if part of his intestine was shifting position.

'It seems they refuse to be forgotten,' he muttered. 'No matter how hard I try.'

II

A REFUGE FOR ESCAPED SLAVES

The *Scafell* reached Boston on the morning of the fourth day. Nate had spent much of that time in troubled sleep, memories and dreams mingling in a sickening stew. He tossed and thrashed, trying to push away images of Tatiana, his beloved sister, and Daisy, whom he missed more than he would ever have believed. And Gerald. Goddamned Gerald. Only sometimes would Nate dream of the son he had left behind in Ireland. He longed for home and burned with shame at the way he had deserted those who needed him most. But he could not go back. The terrible visions that had driven him away to Africa had awakened something in him that he could never bring home. He moaned in his sleep, clawing for unconsciousness, but then he would wake screaming at the memories of his last view of his brother Berto's face.

Disembarking from the Navy vessel, Nate thanked the captain and took his leave, climbing down into the longboat that would take him to shore. Dempsey went with him, but the two men did not speak to each other or to the sailors who rowed them to the dockside. Nate shook hands with them, stepped out of the boat and trotted up the stone steps. His body swayed unnaturally as his sea legs struggled to walk on solid ground for the first time in months. He hurried along the docks, losing himself in the throng of wagons, horses, fish stalls and the foul-mouthed stevedores loading and unloading the ships.

He didn't feel safe until he had put a few piles of crates, barrels and cargo nets between him and the men from the *Scafell*. Boston was a good place to hide. With its deep harbour and thriving business community, it had become a centre for trade in rum, fish, salt and tobacco among other goods. The oil from whale blubber was, of course, another major export.

Nate wondered if he could find another whaler with room for one more able seaman, but he quickly dismissed the idea. The family had dogged him this far and clearly would not give up until he was found. If they were sending whole ships after him, going to sea again would not help. He had to make himself scarce.

Perhaps he should have told the Navy men that Nathaniel Wildenstern had gone down with the *Odin*, but that would have meant admitting he'd known the man.

As the last link to the missing man, Jim Hawkins would have been subject to an uncomfortable amount of attention. Somebody had traced him to the Odin's crew, so that meant someone in Boston could identify him. He needed to get out of the city.

The captain had given him fifteen dollars to tide him over when he went ashore. Not far off the docks, on a street of tall, attractive red-brick buildings, Nate found an eating place where he treated himself to a large breakfast of gammon steak, eggs and pancakes with maple syrup.

At the next table, some Creole blacks were arguing in French about something, ending the argument with a joke and booming laughter. It was strange to sit in an American city and have black people sharing the same space, eating the same food as white folk. Boston had become a refuge for escaped slaves, and with the Civil War between North and South in full swing, slave-catchers from the plantations in the southern states had better things to be doing than searching a hostile city for their quarry.

Nate wondered how many of these people were truly free and how many were fugitives like himself. No, he thought – not like me. I was one of the slave-drivers, not one of the slaves.

He finished his food and left, heading into the city, making sure to take a winding route. Not long after he'd started walking, a small tan and white basset hound came up to him with its tail wagging and he made the mistake of scratching it behind the ears. The dog gave a joyous bark and ran in circles around him. It then proceeded to follow him down the street, delighted with its new best friend. Nate snapped at it a few times in exasperation, but it forgave him for this on the grounds that they were just getting to know each other, and kept trailing him. Nate sighed and walked on, doing his best to ignore the animal.

He walked the day away. His route took him through some of the less salubrious parts of town. A dull morning brightened slowly into a sunnier afternoon, the sun's momentum seeming too much for it as it tumbled down towards evening. Nate took his time, mixing with the growing crowds as he meandered through the muddy streets, past the grog-shops and dancing houses, the oyster cellars, pubs and bawdy-houses. He kept stopping to check behind him, gazing into windows, perusing the wares of various stalls, or simply fixing his bootlaces. Despite his efforts to blend in here, to look at ease, he was constantly alert, his senses heightened. His teeth were pressed together, but his limbs were loose and ready to react at a moment's notice. The hound was never far away. But it was the dog's owner who had Nate's nerves on edge.

Somebody was following him, and he doubted that it was a representative of Her Majesty's Royal Navy. For one thing, they were too good at staying out of sight. And the dog made Nate very easy to spot. It was a clever trick, or would be until he decided to get rid of the dog.

But for the moment he would let it serve its purpose.

The Irish had taken over in Boston much as they invaded everywhere else they settled; moving in with a good-natured work ethic and then breeding like rabbits until they ruled by sheer weight of numbers. Nate heard the accents all around him; mixed in with the Boston drawl, there were traces of Galway, Limerick, Kerry, the sing-song voices bringing on a sudden wave of homesickness. But he also passed signs advertising accommodation with the infamous 'NINA', or 'No Irish Need Apply'.

He walked through Half Moon Place, among shacks and buildings that seemed to be competing with each other to see which could slump in the most ungainly fashion. Street urchins played with stray dogs in the maze of laneways, amused themselves at the expense of passers-by, and picked the occasional pocket. This was one of the oldest parts of town, yet still a mere infant compared to places like Dublin or Cork in the Old Country. Mills and factories had sprung up in the city with the onward charge of the Industrial Revolution, the smoke of the business boom rising from a hundred tall chimneys. Science was beginning to render skilled humans obsolete, and the city had been introduced to the concept of smog.

After hours of what seemed like aimless wandering, Nate arrived in Charlestown. The basset hound was flagging, its short legs struggling to keep up with Nate's long strides. It still wagged its tail whenever it found Nate looking down at it, but while its spirit was willing, its body was weak. It panted at high speed, its unfeasibly long tongue almost dragging on the ground. Nate took in his surroundings, noting the heights of the roofs on the buildings above him. Then he suddenly darted down a narrow alleyway and vaulted over the six-foot-high wall at the end. The dog tried to follow but, finding itself stranded behind the obstacle, gave a long dejected howl and then started barking frantically.

Nate scrambled up a pile of crates and hurried along the top of another wall to the roof of a shed, from where he climbed a drainpipe to the flat roof of a brownstone building overlooking the alley.

Lying down, he crawled up to the wall at the edge of the roof and peered over. Below and to his left, he saw the dog standing with its front paws against the wall, barking its head off. A man in a dark grey hat and coat walked up to it. The dog stopped barking and turned to nuzzle its owner's hand. Nate could not see the man's face under the hat, but he recognized the walk, the posture, immediately. Pulling away from the edge, he rolled onto his back and stared up at the sky.

It really was time to get out of Boston. And to do that he was going to have to make some money, fast. It was probably just as well – he needed to let off some steam.

Nathaniel knew the Peggy Sayer by reputation – everyone who spent any time in Boston knew of it. It was a pit of a place, the kind of tavern that never truly closed, with men staggering drunk from its double doors at all hours to collapse in the street, raucous music jolting through its timbers and the sound of shouts and breaking glass filling its interior.

Evening was falling as Nate walked up to the doors of the pub, glancing in through the slats in its shuttered windows at the commotion inside. Outside, to one side of the door, a young man lay groaning in a pile of rotten turnips. A worn-faced woman in a drab, woollen dress stood over him, her head and shoulders wrapped in a black shawl. She directed a breathless stream of abuse at him in guttural Irish. The man did not respond; though whether he did not understand, or he did not care, it was hard to say.

Inside the Peggy Sayer, the air was saturated with the smell of pipe smoke, beer, whiskey, sweat and stewed meat and pastry. From somewhere wafted the bile stench of vomit. Nate would have been willing to bet that fresh air had not intruded on this place in decades. The crowd was mostly made up of men, with a few martyred wives drowning their sorrows and some cackling strumpets added to the mix. If cleanliness was next to godliness, there were no saints to be found here.

The stools, benches and tables were bare wood, any varnish long worn away. The bar was little better – a rough slab of boards, coated in spills, running the full length of the large room. An array of bottles was displayed on the shelves behind it, along with the obligatory mirrors. Framed prints of famous boxers were gradually turning yellow on the walls all around the room. Nate pushed his way through the throng to the bar. The proprietor, wearing a white apron, was in the middle of cleaning a glass by spitting in it and wiping it with a rag.

'What can I get you?' he asked.

'Ronan,' Nate said to him.

The barman tilted his head towards a door at the back. Nate zig-zagged among the revellers to the door and knocked. It was opened by a bald man with cauliflower ears and no neck.

'I'm looking for Ronan,' Nate told him.

'Who sent you?' the man demanded with a heavy Boston accent.

Nate paused for just a second. He doubted if a lieutenant in the Royal Navy would be held in high regard in these parts. He took a gamble.

'Bushnell, captain of the *Odin.*'

'Hah! Bushnell, is it?' the man barked, his face splitting into a wide grin. 'How is the old goat?'

'Dead,' Nate told him. 'Killed by a sea monster.'

'Had to happen sometime,' the doorman replied with a grunt. 'Down the stairs, along the corridor and through the door. Ronan's down the back, in the tweed jacket. The first bout's just over. You'll want to get your money in fast for the next one.'

Nate passed two more sentries on the way down the corridor. They watched him as he went through, but said nothing. The door at the end of the corridor opened onto a roaring mob of men. There were hardly any women to be seen, but one or two shrill voices were raised among the mass.

This room was smaller than the last, with all the stink of the front of the building mixed with the iron smell of blood. There was no furniture to be seen among the crowd milling round the centre of the floor. Nate squeezed through to the circle of men surrounding the empty space in the middle of the room, where two men were struggling to revive a third. The unconscious man was stripped to the waist, showing an overfed but muscular body covered in red impact marks that would soon become nasty bruises. His face was bloodied and disfigured.

Standing over them, shaking his fists in the air, was a man who stood about six and a half foot tall, with the shoulders of an ox and arms heaving with muscles. A man in a smart tweed suit was holding up the fighter's arm and shouting to the crowd in a hoarse Kerry accent.

'. . . Undefeated for more den four years and dis evening, once again, he hes showed you why! Dee greatest fighter in dee North American states! Gintlemen, I give you Pat "Dee Axe" Healy!'

The mob bellowed their approval and the Axe shook his fists again and roared like a man possessed, loving his victory. Nate waited until the proceedings had died down a little. Another man stepped up and announced the next bout, and in the crowd money began to change hands. Ronan was making for a door at the back of the room. Nate intercepted the man before he reached it.

'My name's Jim Hawkins,' he said. 'I'm looking for a fight. I hear you pay well.'

Ronan regarded him closely for a moment, sizing him up. He saw a young man with work-hardened hands and a face weathered by time at sea. And he saw Nate's eyes, a gaze that lacked . . . something. Hope, perhaps. Some men came here because their lives were empty, or they were consumed with guilt. They came to be punished. These men did not last long in the ring. But some of the most entertaining fighters were those with nothing to lose – and entertainment was Ronan's stock and trade.

'Yur a little on the willowy side for dis business, led,' he said in a grating Kerry brogue. 'What makes yeh think yeh make de cut?'

'Does it matter if I don't?' Nate replied.

'Not to you, perhaps. But my customers come here lookin' for sport – a real prizefight,' Ronan replied, ushering him into the office. 'Brawls are ten-a-penny. I deal in the art of pugilism. Skill, speed, power, nerve, endurance. Can yeh deliver dat, young Hawkins?'

'Put me on with your best man and we'll find out,' Nate said to him.

Ronan laughed, walking across the plush office to sit down behind a teak, green-baize-covered desk.

'My bist man?' he chortled. 'My bist just lift a professional pug half-did. And lucky not to be full-did at dat. Yeh hef to earn the right to fight him. Lit's start you off easy, shall we? I'll put you on wit "Mangle" McDaid. A hard man, but punches like a drunken windmill. He's taken too many tumps to the hid to tink in a straight line. Less money to be made, but sure, yer more likely to be alive at dee end of it. Den we can see if yer up to a serious metch.'

Nate took a few seconds to look around the office, looking for a way to get the most out of this man. He needed a fight with as large a purse as possible. He only had time for one bout before he left Boston for good. Nate didn't give a damn how tough . . .

His eyes fell upon a picture on the wall to his left. It was one of perhaps twenty covering the wall. They were well-framed, some photographs, others engravings or drawings. But that one picture froze Nate to the spot.

'What are these?' he asked.

'Pest champions,' Ronan informed him. 'De best fighters to come tru here.'

'Who's this one here?' Nate asked, unable to help himself. 'Looks like a right yaw-yaw.'

'Hah! One of our "gintleman" pugilists.' The man stood up from his desk and moved closer to the pictures. 'Det's Marcus Wildenstern, of *dee* Wildensterns. Yeh wouldn't credit it, would yeh? A proper toff like him, one of the bist fighters I've ever seen. If y'ask me, he wiz a man who couldn't live life by halves. Worked harrd in business, and den kem down here to play even harrder. Only iver beaten de once.'

'By who?' Nate asked.

'By Pat "Dee Axe" Healy,' Ronan said softly. 'De man you saw outside.'

Nate stared at the picture of his beloved older brother, who had died . . . it seemed so long ago, but could not have been much more than four years. Killed by their cousin, Gerald – by Nate's best friend. What did this mean, that Marcus's face was on the wall here, in this place? Was there anywhere Nate could go to get away from the Wildensterns? Was this why Marcus had come here? To face down life without the protection of money, power, influence or family connections? Nate found himself grinding his teeth.

'Put me on with Healy,' he growled quietly. 'I'll give you a show you'll never forget.'

Ronan looked from the picture to Nate and back again, a frown on his face. A light came on in his eyes.

'I tink you might at det,' he muttered.

III

TOO PRETTY TO SPOIL

Nate was led through the crowd to the centre of the room, where a circle of burly men formed a ring. No ropes or corners here. The sawdust on the floorboards was stained with blood in places, some dried in, faint and brown with age, other splashes still bright and wet and red. He would have to watch his footing; some of that would be slippery.

He was taking a chance in removing his shirt – someone might still recognize his scars. But it was one of the few rules: no shirts, no shoes, no weapons . . . no referee, no judges. Just the crowd, looking for a good fight. The bout could be won only by knockout or submission.

Nate stood in the empty space at the centre of the crowd, waiting for his opponent. All around him, the spectators gave him disparaging looks and spoke poorly of his chances. They knew who he was fighting. Odds were given. Money was passed back and forth.

'God, Ronan, don't put dat fella on!' a woman's voice called out. 'Sure, he's too pretty to spoil!'

The other women in the room laughed, and some of the men too.

Then the Axe strode through the mob, which parted like water around him. He raised his fists in the air, circling the ring, snarling like an animal, working the spectators into a feverish excitement. Nate studied him – his gestures, his movements. Pat 'The Axe' Healy was the worst kind of opponent: muscular enough to be fearsomely powerful, but without the kind of bulk that would slow him down. His hands were like the paws of a bear, but he moved with the savage grace of a big cat. By the looks of his face and body, and the gold teeth in his mouth, he had taken batterings in the past – but not recently. There was a cruel intelligence in his eyes. The Axe was a terribly violent man, but he was no mindless thug. He was everything Nate did not want to fight.

'Ladeez and Gintlemen!' Ronan bellowed, stepping into the ring. 'Ladeez and Gintlemen, we bring you a very special bout tonight. For five years, Pat "Dee Axe" Healy has ruled the ring, since taking the title from the previous holder; de man we discovered wiz none other than Marcus Wildenstern! And what a bettle det was!'

The crowd roared their agreement.

'Well, tonight Healy defends his title once more!' Ronan announced, his blood up, his face going a bright red. 'And baying for his blood is a mighty contender indeed – one who has more reason than most to bury the fearsome Axe!'

Nate kept his eyes on the floor, but felt his heart skip a beat. Could Ronan know? Surely he wouldn't—

'Ladeez and Gintlemen, I give you a man who disappeared three years ago, after his family wiz attecked and many of dem killed outright! After the family chapel wiz destroyed by a *bomb in a coffin*, Ladeez and Gintlemen! Here is the man who chased down the blackguard responsible, beat the tar out of him and *threw him off a cliff*! Now, after three years of wandering the world, he hes returned to claim his birthright, and with it the bare-knuckle title in Boston, Massachusetts!

'Ladeez and Gintlemen, I give you NATHANIEL "THE AVENGER" WILDENSTERN!'

Nate swore under his breath. There was no escaping it now. But that was just fine. Let the cards fall where they may; he simply did not care any more.

Rolling his head around, he shook out his arms and bounced on the balls of his feet. On the other side of the circle, Healy spat on his hands and rubbed them together, a man about to start his work. Then he gobbed on the floor and nodded to Nate. There the pleasantries ended.

They met in the middle of the floor and Healy laid in with a couple of lazy swings. He was feeling Nate out, seeing how he would move. Nate dodged them easily, but was caught on the chin by a jab that seemed little more than a flicker of Healy's left hand. It rocked Nate's head back and he staggered, ducking under a right hook that looked powerful enough to shatter his skull. Healy anticipated the duck, coming in hard with a left uppercut as Nate's head came down. Nate deflected it and came up hard, driving his fist into Healy's throat.

It was a good hit and Healy felt it, coughing as he stumbled back towards the edge of the ring. One advantage to being a shorter opponent was that you could punch up, driving up with your whole body – you had less power when you punched downwards. Nate followed him, fists raised, swivelling at the hips as if preparing for another punch. Healy raised his guard, but Nate whipped his shin out instead, knocking Healy's right leg out to the side. Almost in the same motion, he caught Healy's left knee with a back kick. Then he brought his foot back down and up hard into the big man's groin. Instead of hitting soft testicles, Nate felt a hard, piercing pain in his shin and pulled his leg back. There were spots of blood on his trouser leg. Healy was wearing some kind of groin guard, one lined with sharp studs.

'I've fought too many Chinamen to be caught with those fancy kicks, lad,' Healy chuckled. 'Try something else!'

He laughed – as did some of the crowd – and then he came in fast. Nate evaded the first two hooks, and the uppercut that followed just scraped past his jaw, but as he stepped to the side, he walked right into a punch to his abdomen that drove the air out of his lungs and dropped him to his knees. He narrowly avoided getting a knee in the face, rolling to the side and then again to avoid Healy's stamping foot. He was up on his feet before the Axe could get in another kick, but that right hook came swinging round again, and this time it hit Nate's face like a lump hammer. Nate felt an explosion across his cheek and the crack of bone breaking. He cried out, falling back towards the crowd, breathing blood through his teeth. He couldn't take another hit like that.

They pushed him forward before he was ready and he stumbled.

'Go on, Pat!' one man roared. 'Stick the head on 'im!'

Trying to block out the fire in the flesh of his face, Nate slipped past Healy's jabbing left fist and hit the bigger man in the floating ribs, slamming the heels of his hands in to either side of his opponent's torso. Healy's body was like wood, but Nate got a grunt of pain out of him. And then got another blow to the belly for his troubles. He bent forward and Healy swung a forearm down like an axe. Nate moved at the last instant and the blow fell on his shoulders rather than his neck. It still nearly flattened him, white-hot darts of pain shooting down his spine and through his injured face.

He had no doubt that strike would have broken his

neck. That was the Axe's finishing blow – a killing blow. But Nate had seen Healy's left arm swing back behind him as he brought his right down. The move opened him up on the left side of his body.

Healy went to butt him in the face. Nate jerked back, grabbed his upper arm, spun sharply and flicked his hips up into Healy's hips. The man flew across the ring, landing on the boards on his back. But he was up in a flash, wiping sawdust from his shoulders, not a bother on him.

'Jaysus! Will yeh come on, Healy!' one of the men on the edge of the ring exclaimed. 'He's makin' a holy show of yeh!'

Healy clearly objected to the criticism, turning to ram his fist into the man's nose. The boxing critic dropped like a sack of bricks. His limp body was dragged away into the crowd, his place taken by another eager spectator.

The ancient thing beneath Nate's ribs squirmed, wanting to help. He felt a flush of unnatural power glow in his abdomen. Nate willed the thing into submission, fearful of releasing his hold on it. Besides, this was his fight. His body ached, his face felt as if his whole head had been run over by a train, his left eye was already swelling shut, but this was his fight. Pushing forward, he swung his shin into the side of the Axe's thigh to slow him down. It had hardly any effect. Nate's strength was failing.

Healy lashed out with his foot, aiming for Nate's groin. But he wasn't as quick with his feet as he was with his hands. Nate rode the blow, falling into a backward roll. Let the Axe try his finishing move again, Nate just had to land with his feet right . . . Healy was lunging in at him as Nate came up into a crouch. The back of his neck was exposed for just a second and Healy's forearm came down with the force of a falling tree.

But Nate was ready for it this time. Twisting to Healy's left, inside the arm, he drove his whole body up from the floor, swinging his right elbow from the waist, pushing with his feet – he straightened and rammed the elbow hard up under Healy's chin. The blow lifted Healy off his feet, sending him back in an arc, spitting blood as he landed flat on his back in a spray of sawdust on the wooden floor. Two gold teeth and a single white one clattered to the floor after him.

Nate waited another few seconds to be sure the man was down, then he sank onto his knees. All around him, people whooped and shouted, delighted with the mill, even if most of them had lost money on it. As notes and coins changed hands, Ronan pushed his way through the roused crowd and lifted Nate's right arm.

'Ladeez and Gintlemen, I give yeh the new bare-knuckle champeen of Boston, Massachusetts, efter an epic bettle here in the Peggy Sayer – NATHANIEL "THE AVENGER" WILDENSTERN!'

Many cheered, and there was more than a few wolf whistles. Others, however, were already counting the cost of betting on the favourite. Ronan leaned in close to Nate and whispered in his ear.

'Someting tills me you won't be hanging around, lad. But if yeh fancy it, there's some serious money to be made with a performance like dat. Yiv got flair, boy, and plenty of sand – no doubt about it. Come inside when yer ready, I'll have yer money for yeh. I'm always happy to pay for a good show!'

He patted Nate on the back and walked back through the crowd, graciously accepting the congratulations of the spectators. He paid no more attention to Pat 'The Axe' Healy, who still lay on the floor, an anxious friend slapping him lightly on the face.

Nate put his hand against the misshapen left side of his face and winced, hissing in a breath. The cheekbone was broken. He poked his finger into his mouth and felt a molar come loose, and then the left canine. He spat them out onto the dusty floor. It would take him weeks to grow new ones. His left eye was swollen shut, the vision in his right a little blurred. By the feel of it, he had broken a couple of ribs too – he most probably had internal bleeding, though he had no way of telling how serious it was. His knuckles were raw and bloody, his shin too. His stomach, shoulders and upper back felt as if they had been beaten with an iron bar. Two women strolled past, and one tutted in disappointment:

'Tch. He ain't pretty no more.'

Still Nate did not let the snake-like thing in his abdomen

work its power on him, despite its restless movements. His extraordinary talent for healing would do the job quickly enough – and there was less of a price to pay. He groaned and leaned forward, taking the weight of his body on his hands.

Someone squeezed his shoulder with a strong but friendly grip.

'There are simpler ways to ease your conscience, sir, than picking fights with men the size of steam engines,' a voice said.

Without looking up, Nate replied: 'I don't think I care for your tone, Clancy.'

'My tone is appropriate, sir, if I'm addressing Jim Hawkins, formerly of the *Odin*. However, if I am addressing Nathaniel Wildenstern, Duke of Leinster, rightful Chairman of the North American Trading Company and Patriarch of the Wildenstern clan, I shall temper my words accordingly.'

Smiling sadly round bloodstained teeth, Nate looked up at his old manservant. He squinted through his one open eye.

'That remains to be seen,' he chuckled, coughing. 'So . . . when did you get yourself a dog?'

IV

NEWS FROM HOME

The two men did not talk as Clancy helped his former master walk to Ronan's office to collect his winnings, and then out of the Peggy Sayer. The basset hound was tied up outside and Clancy took its lead with his free hand as he led the Duke of Leinster to a slightly more civilized tavern.

They sat in a pair of overstuffed chairs near the roaring fire in the hearth. There was a whiskey for Clancy on the table between them, a coffee and some hot buttered toast for Nate. The bow-legged hound flopped down by its master's feet. The two men had never done this before, shared a drink as equals. Despite this ghost from his past, Nate savoured the comfort. He cradled his drink and tried to forget his injuries for a few moments. He would not have thought Clancy would be such a welcome sight. Perhaps it was the pain that was making him so vulnerable.

'It's good to see you again, old friend.'

Clancy was not accustomed to such warm words from those he served, and he lowered his eyes and sipped his drink to hide his unease.

'How long have you been looking for me?' Nate enquired.

'Since you left, sir,' his old servant replied. 'From the very day you disappeared. I was charged by some of your family to find you as quickly as possible, and at any cost. We employed the finest detectives: Dupin, Holmes . . . and then the Pinkerton agency over here. The final piece of information was supplied by a Lieutenant William Dempsey, from the ship that rescued you from the sea. He took a handsome price for the information, and has since jumped ship. He will be making his way back to Ireland, hoping to retrieve his son. I wished him luck. But to get back to you, sir – you led us a merry chase.'

'It was not meant to be a chase – I did not intend to be found.'

'My apologies, sir. But it was imperative we found you before others did.'

Nate grunted. He stared into his cup, casting his mind back over the three years he had spent away from his family.

'Tatiana and Daisy, they're alive, aren't they? I thought at first that they had died in the explosion in the church. But I saw a newspaper – one of the society pages – while I was in Johannesburg. They were at a ball or a dance or something.'

'They are alive and well, sir. As is your *son*.'

Nate sniffed and nodded, suppressing the terrible longing that welled inside him. More than anything, he wanted to go back and make things right, go back to Tatty and Daisy and especially to his son. It seemed he was an even more neglectful parent than his own, cold-hearted father. When he was younger, he would have expected better of himself. Not any more. But he was still determined not to return home. The risk of others discovering what he had learned was too great. His coffee smelled good, and as he sipped it he could feel its warmth spread into his bones. For some reason, he was suddenly very sensitive to the draught from the window behind him; he felt a chill on the back of his neck. Clancy leaned forward, locking his eyes on Nate's.

'Sir, that is not all. I gather you've been avoiding high society at every turn, so it could well be that you're not aware of this . . . but . . . your cousin, Gerald, is also still alive.'

Nate felt his stomach lurch, the drink turning sour in his mouth. Sensing a change in the atmosphere, the basset hound raised its sleepy head and looked around. Clancy put his glass down on the table.

'That can't be,' Nate coughed, spilling some of the coffee over his hand. 'He's dead. I *saw* him die. I bloody killed him!'

His voice was a little too loud, and heads turned, but

Nate paid them no mind. He laid his cup down and grabbed Clancy's wrist.

'How can he still be alive, when I threw him off a bloody cliff?'

'How can *you* still be alive, sir,' Clancy asked quietly, 'when he stabbed you in the heart?'

Nate breathed out and absent-mindedly put a hand to his chest, where the scar still marked his skin. The thing inside him twisted and turned, agitated at what it was feeling – what *they* were feeling. Gerald; the man who had been his best friend, who had murdered both of Nate's brothers and tried to kill dozens of their family – Nate could not bear the thought that the cur was still drawing breath. But there was more to this feeling of sick dread than his personal hatred for his cousin.

When Nate had last known him, Gerald had been making headway with his research into intelligent particles. It was an area of study Nate now knew could lead to disaster.

'He is guardian to your son and is consorting with Elizabeth, the child's mother,' Clancy told his master. 'Because you are missing and your *son* is Heir, Gerald has been able to take control of the family, and the Company with it. Your cousin has proved himself to be a ruthlessly efficient opponent to anyone who stands against him. He is effectively the Patriarch, and he is not shy about wielding that power. He has reintroduced the Rules of Ascension.

There have been several murders in the last three years.

'And he has not forgotten about you, sir. He too has sent people out in search of you. Teams of assassins have been hunting you since he seized power in the house.'

'Mmm,' Nate mumbled. 'That would explain those chaps who attacked me in Natal, in Cape Town. Their approach was a bit too professional for a gang of local muggers. Tenacious buggers. Barely escaped with my life.'

'Yes, sir. And they will not have been the only ones hunting you,' Clancy agreed. 'But they are merely a sideline. Your sister-in-law keeps me informed with regular letters. Miss Daisy says the schemes Gerald has set in motion across the country and beyond have created even more enemies. The rebels are talking about revolution . . . I suppose they always talk about revolution, but this time they may well be serious. The government, the Crown, even the Irish people are saying Gerald is insane, sir, but I fear that he is not.'

There were many times when Nate had wished he could have spoken to Daisy, but the feeling had been especially strong recently. He wished he could apologize for leaving her and Tatty alone in that house. To tell her he had stayed away for everyone's sake. That he'd stayed away despite what he felt for her now. But he had decided it would be simpler if he was dead to them – gone for ever.

'What about his research?' he asked in a low voice. 'Is he still working with the engimals, with the intelligent particles?'

'With single-minded devotion,' Clancy replied. 'And on an unprecedented scale. His control of the Company seems steered by his need to learn their secrets.'

Nate lowered his head into his hands and let out a guttural string of curses. Damn Gerald, curse him and the rest of the rotten-souled blackguards who helped to make him what he was. Nate pushed breath out through his teeth. He could never get away from them. No matter how hard he tried, his accursed family always dragged him back in.

'I have kept all of the letters, so that you may read them yourself,' Clancy continued. 'As well as a selection of the Irish newspapers from the last couple of years. I have chartered a ship that will carry us to Cork.'

'You seem very confident that I'll be returning with you,' Nate muttered.

'No, sir,' Clancy said to him. 'I only pray that you do. It is now the sole purpose of my life – and I will spend the rest of that life trying to convince you to rejoin your family.'

'Good God, Clancy!' Nate sighed. 'There's no escaping them, is there? I'd have an easier time shaking off the plague.'

'Perhaps, sir,' Clancy agreed. 'Though I suspect many of your relatives will welcome your return with the same enthusiasm that they would greet that famous disease. Should I take this to mean you will be coming home, sir?'

'I suppose so.' Nate climbed stiffly to his feet, a resigned expression on his face. 'But only if you curb that insolent tone of yours.'

'I can assure you, your Grace, that from this moment on, I will address you with all the respect due to a man of your rank.'

As the manservant stood up from his seat, the basset hound also jumped up, tail wagging furiously, tongue out, big watery eyes looking eagerly from one man to the other, ready for action.

'What's the dog's name?' Nate inquired.

'Duke, sir. He's somewhat selfish, bloody-minded and a trifle irresponsible. But he has a good heart and makes up for his belligerent nature by putting himself in the way of harm for the sake of those he loves.'

'Sounds like a bloody liability if you ask me.'

'Nevertheless, he gets the job done,' Clancy said. 'And I am very fond of the animal.'

'Right, then,' Nate grunted, a new resolve setting on his face as he hobbled for the door. 'Let's go home.'

V

THE ROUND WINDOW

Daisy stared at the plans, studying the dimensions and symbols, her brow furrowed in frustrated confusion.

'But what *is* it?' she demanded.

She and the chief architect were examining the plans of the church that she had commissioned, which was under construction on the Wildenstern estate. It was being built to replace the last family chapel, which had been utterly destroyed by a bomb in a coffin at a funeral. The architect looked uncomfortable for a moment and then shrugged.

'No idea, ma'am,' he said. 'But whatever this feature, this . . . contraption is, your cousin has already had the bulk of it installed. It is taking up more space than we had anticipated, and I have had to compensate. As you can see, the balcony is now deeper, and the nave below it is shorter by several feet. That's at least two fewer rows of pews – so that's about thirty fewer people that can be fitted in. And we can't simply make the chancel at the other end shorter.' He pointed at the platform where the altar and lectern stood. 'It would ruin the entire balance of the building's interior. But Mister Gordon is insistent that his design for the organ and its surrounding structure takes priority over everything else.'

'His lordship has never struck me as a devoutly religious man,' the architect commented. 'But perhaps this obsession with the organ and its surrounds is his way of showing his love for Christ.'

Given that he was the one who blew up the last church, Daisy thought, I would consider that highly unlikely. She was more inclined to suspect it was a means of also destroying this one.

The architect was a dapper, middle-aged man with thinning hair, a neat moustache and a blunt but professional manner. Daisy had found him to be a pleasant and capable man. He moved his finger towards the back of the church, pointing at the outline of the balcony that would overlook the congregation of worshippers.

'This is the organ, but these other structures are a mystery to me. Mister Gordon has had them manufactured and fitted by his own people. We were ordered to simply provide the stone base and supports to his specifications and leave space. You see these here? I presume they are pipes, but they are shaped more like the roots of a tree. What this thing is or what it does is beyond me. I've never seen some of these symbols before, but . . .'

'But what?' Daisy prompted.

He winced, unwilling to put his thoughts into words.

'But . . . well . . . they look like something one might see in a book on *mathaumaturgy*. My son reads such books for titillation and he sometimes leaves them lying around the house. I believe they make use of symbols such as these.'

'That is not as strange as you might think,' Daisy told him. 'Thank you, Arthur. I'll take this to Mister Gordon and discuss it with him in person.'

'Discuss *what* with me in person?' a voice said from behind them.

Standing at the door of the spacious boardroom was a slender man in his twenties. He had a shock of dark hair that was not cut often enough, a pale complexion and a face that was slightly misshapen. Thin pink scars traced irregular patterns on the skin of his face. His eyes were a cold winter's blue and hinted at the arrogance of someone who was confident that he was more intelligent than anyone else he knew. That confidence was well-founded.

But Gerald had changed in the last three years. In fact, most of the changes had been sudden. Daisy suspected that this was down to the fact that he had felt forced to betray the people closest to him. Or it might have been from the trauma of being thrown by his best friend off a four-hundred-foot waterfall onto the submerged rocks below. It was difficult to tell. But the sardonic spark that had always been at the root of his personality had been extinguished, leaving a jaded, obsessive intensity. It made him next to impossible to deal with.

'You've changed the church plans *again*, Gerald,' Daisy said to him. 'We were almost finished, for heaven's sake. What is it all about?'

'It is an experiment,' Gerald replied, as if that explained everything. 'I had to rethink the dimensions of my design. It couldn't be avoided. Walk with me, Daisy. I'd like to talk with you.'

Daisy sighed quietly and excused herself from the architect, catching up with Gerald as he walked out of the room. The boardroom was a large, light, airy room on the tenth floor of the main tower of Wildenstern Hall. Gerald led her to the lavishly appointed elevator and told the uniformed boy working the brass lever to take them to the top floor.

Trapped with him in this enclosed space, Daisy tried to suppress the fear she felt. The tension of living in this house for the last five or six years had aged her. She was not yet thirty, but she felt older, and she was starting to find lines on her strong, attractive face, etching their contours too early. The first few strands of grey had appeared in her thick black hair. Some of the colour even seemed to have gone out of her blue eyes, but that probably had more to do with how she regarded her life now.

While her husband, Berto, had still been alive, she had spent so much time worrying about his safety. But there had been a kind of system of life in the house that she had come to understand. Gerald's actions had changed all that. These days, everyone lived in abject fear of him . . . especially after what he had done to his cousin, Ainsley. And now here she was, going up to the top floor with him.

Shutting her eyes, she told herself over and over again that she was there of her own free will. He had not hypnotized her or taken over her mind or whatever it was he did. Gerald could not make her do anything she didn't want to do. She focused on this with all her will.

'Don't get your knickers in a twist,' Gerald said to her, staring at the ceiling. 'I have no reason to wish you any harm . . . do I?'

'I see your paranoia is in full flower,' she retorted. 'Are you still trying to sleep with your eyes clipped open?'

'That was merely a theory I was testing,' he told her in a petulant voice. 'I am convinced that sleep was originally an evolutionary mistake that accidentally kept animals out of trouble. I see no reason why we shouldn't be able to do away with the habit, given sufficient training.'

'I believe lack of sleep can lead to insanity,' she said, staring into his face.

'You believe all sorts of nonsense,' he sniffed. 'Your church is proof of that. Ah, here we are!'

The boy brought the elevator to a stop and its bell

chimed. The ornate brass doors opened and Gerald stepped out, taking Daisy by the hand. They were on the top floor, most of which was occupied by a massive study where Edgar Wildenstern had once held court. Her father-in-law had been the unopposed ruler of the family for decades, until some even older relatives had murdered him at the dinner table.

'Let's take a stroll outside,' Gerald suggested, as if the idea had just occurred to him.

Daisy thought again of Ainsley, and she tried not to pull back from Gerald's grip. The corridor off the lift was not a welcoming place. It was dimly lit, and she always found the décor disturbing; the walls were hung with gloomy oil paintings of savage Biblical scenes, particularly those of the Old Testament, while the patterns of the carpets and the wallpaper suggested raw flesh opened by sharp edges. She told herself this was all in her imagination. She told herself this any time she came up here.

But she would not allow Gerald to see her fear. He was headed for the stairs that led up to the roof, so she walked in front of him, striding up the steps and opening the door. The wind caught her hair and skirts as she did so, giving her the wild appearance of a banshee. They were thirty storeys up and the gusts were cold and violent. She was not wearing a coat and her green silk dress was heavy in the skirts but thin round the shoulders and waist. The chill wind cut her to the bone.

They walked out onto the section of flat roof that sat between the tiled turrets at the top of the tower. The Wicklow mountains framed the view to the south, the sea was visible to the east, the fields of Kildare out to the west and the city of Dublin to the north.

Daisy was becoming wise to Gerald's ways. Since taking over the family, he had become far more interested in human nature and how to manipulate it. He had studied Edgar Wildenstern's journals, learning how to wield power. She knew that leading her out here into the cold was intended to make her tense up, increase her unease. She shivered and wrapped her arms around herself, turning to face him.

'Make this quick, Gerald. I haven't got time for pneumonia.'

He put his hands into his pockets, drew out a slim silver case and a box of matches and lit one of his favourite French cigarettes, cupping the flame against the wind. Sucking smoke into his lungs, he held the gasper inside his hand and gave her a friendly smile.

'How goes your search for Nate?' he asked.

'Clancy perseveres, but without success – as I suspect you know already,' she snapped.

She had given up trying to keep the search a secret, since Gerald could monitor all the correspondence coming into the house. But she knew he was listening to *how* she answered, not the answer itself. She glared at him for a moment and then lost patience with him.

'Gerald, what the bloody hell are you building in the church? It's not another bomb, is it?'

'Daisy, Daisy, Daisy,' he chided her. 'You have such a suspicious mind. And your language is positively foul at times.'

'Don't patronize me. What are you up to?'

'I have been studying the work of Isambard Kingdom Brunel,' Gerald replied. 'It has been quite enlightening. You probably don't know of him. He is an engineer—'

'Builder of the Great Western Railway in Britain and much of the track in Ireland,' Daisy cut in, rubbing her arms, her hair whipping across her scowling face. 'Yes, I've heard of him. Studied Euclidean geometry before the age of eight. He is the designer of various wondrous bridges and pioneer of propeller-driven iron ships, as well as being largely responsible for laying the latest bloody transatlantic telegraph cable. What about him? What's he got to do with our church?'

'He had a stroke in eighteen fifty-nine,' Gerald said. 'It was only his knowledge of engimals that saved him from paralysis, possibly even death. He has since become a master of engimal reconstruction. Some joke that he is almost half engimal now, he has transplanted so many of their parts into his own body. His theories on engimals are very *mechanical*, but fascinating. Funny . . . Nate took the opposite view – he always thought of them as animals. A zoologist by nature. The truth is that they are neither animal nor machine, but something in between.'

'Gerald . . . it's *freezing* up here. Will you be getting to the point any time soon?'

'The point is this. Brunel used engimal parts in some of his engineering designs with varying degrees of success. But his ideas have opened up a host of new possibilities. I have decided to try something along those lines myself. I shall be making occasional use of the organ in the church, so I chose to have it built to my own specifications.'

Daisy regarded him for as long as she could stand.

'Are you telling me that the church organ is made up of engimal parts? That's barbaric, Gerald.'

'No more than having your chair upholstered with leather,' he replied. 'Or burning a tallow candle, or using a hairbrush with a bone or ivory handle. Even your late father-in-law had his missing hand replaced with an engimal claw. We use animal parts every day, in every part of our lives.'

'But . . . *engimals*, Gerald. Each one is unique. They don't breed – every time you kill one, it cannot be replaced. They're *thousands* of years old! Think of what they've seen! I really thought you believed that of all God's creations they were among the most fascinating, the most precious.'

'God? Are you still making decisions based on that old mythology? That way lies insanity, Daisy. Remember in 'fifty-seven, how those Sepoy soldiers in India were so outraged about the beef grease in their bullet cartridges that they started a bloody mutiny? Because it was against their religion. The British nearly lost control of *India* because of *beef grease*. It is absurd. These kinds of beliefs are religious poppycock that has no place in a rational world. And don't you pretend to be squeamish about such things, Daisy. It doesn't suit you.'

He gestured towards a circular window set into the wall of one of the turrets. It had an unusual steel frame and could not be opened. Daisy glanced towards it, but then averted her eyes.

'Edgar Wildenstern kept his wife trapped in that room for years, did you know that?' Gerald said to her.

'Yes,' she said.

'I've read Edgar's journals. Dear Aunt Miriam defied his will. As punishment, he had her committed to an asylum not long after Tatiana was born. For some reason, he brought Miriam back home after little more than a year, but kept her imprisoned up here. No one knew she was here, but there were times – when the house was quiet and the wind was right – that you could hear distant screams. If she wasn't deranged when he had her committed, she was well and truly insane by the end of her life.'

Gerald turned to Daisy.

'He loved her, you know. And yet he was prepared to do that to her – to maintain control of the family. I admire his strength of will. I know you and Tatiana – perhaps even Cathal – have been making moves against me. Obviously you are more subtle than some of the troglodytes in the house, but I am not fooled. I tolerate Tatiana out of some soft-hearted affection – and because she amuses me. Cathal is valuable to me, and his defiant character is also entertaining. I put up with you because, bizarrely, you have a better head for business than most of the men in the house. But you must be aware that there are costs for interfering with my plans, Daisy. Don't push me too far.'

Looking down at his cigarette, he saw that it had gone out. He flicked it into the wind and it was whisked off into the vast space beyond the roof. Then he turned away and strolled towards the door to the stairs. Daisy stood there, trembling in the cold for a while longer, preferring to walk back downstairs alone.

No matter what happened, she refused to let him see how terrified she was of him.

There was a letter waiting for Daisy on her desk when she returned to her office and her heart lifted when she recognized the handwriting on the envelope. She could tell that the letter had been opened and resealed, but she had grown used to that. Gerald allowed her little privacy.

Daisy did not open it immediately. Her hopes for the future hung on these letters, sent to her at regular intervals by Nate's man, Clancy. Or, at least, the man who had once served Nate so devotedly, and who now searched for him with equal diligence. Ever since Nate's disappearance, Daisy and Tatiana had waited impatiently for each letter from Clancy, hoping each time that it would announce that he had found his master and was bringing him home.

It was unfair to leave Tatty out of this, but after a week of frustration over the church and her ordeal with Gerald on the roof, Daisy wanted this moment to herself. Closing the glass and wood door of her office, she sat down at the desk and laid the envelope in front of her, flattening the already-flat fold of ivory-coloured paper with her fingers. Clancy had lovely handwriting – masculine, but elegant – and he insisted on using a high quality nib, always carrying his own ink.

Daisy took a breath and let it out. It seemed a pity to spoil the glow of anticipation, but she supposed it was best to get the disappointment over with. She broke the wax seal, opened the envelope and drew out the single sheet of paper. The first few lines made her next breath catch in her throat:

My Ladies,

I have reached Boston, where I believe his Grace boarded a whaling ship several months previously. The vessel was set for a three- to four-year voyage depending on its catch. Having spoken to an officer of Her Majesty's Navy, I have learned that the ship, the Odin, *was sunk in stormy seas off the coast of New England, with all hands lost but one. This man was questioned, and claimed to have no knowledge of his Grace, or anyone matching his description.*

> *I have not given up hope that either the reports of his Grace boarding this ship were mistaken, or that he somehow survived unseen. I will endeavour to resolve the matter either way. At this point, however, I must confess that the trail has grown cold.*
>
> *My search continues, my ladies. As ever, I will keep you informed of my progress.*
>
> Yours faithfully,
> Clancy

Typical of the man, he never used his first name. Daisy bit her hand. Glancing towards the door of her office, she rose from her upholstered, walnut swivel chair and crossed the carpeted floor to the door, opening it and peering out into the corridor. There was no one about. She closed the door and clutched the letter to her breast.

'YES!' she cried, jumping a couple of times on the spot.

Composing herself, she waved the letter in front of her face to cool her flushed cheeks and then read it again. There could be no mistake. The report of Nate's possible death had shaken her for a moment, but then there came that line: '*At this point, however, I must confess that the trail has grown cold.*' Before he had left, Clancy had counselled against speaking openly in their correspondence, in case it should be read. Instead, they had agreed a series of sentences to transmit confidential signals. The sentence he had just used was one of these. Put simply, it meant: '*I have found him, and we are coming home.*'

There was no telling how soon they would be here. They could well have come on the same ship as the letter, but Clancy would be too cautious to travel on a scheduled vessel. They would have to employ a great deal of stealth.

Daisy bit her knuckle again, resisting the urge to let out another yell. She could play mind games with Gerald until the cows came home, but as women in the Wildenstern house there was nothing she or Tatty could do about going on the offensive against him. And their trusted cousin, Cathal, had no real power in the family. However, being offensive was Nathaniel's area of expertise. With him, they had a chance of knocking Gerald from his position of power . . . with physical force, if necessary.

And as time had numbed her grief for her murdered husband, Daisy's feelings for Nate had changed too. Their relationship had never been easy, but his disappearance had cut her deeply, making her wonder if her feelings for him had always been more . . . *complicated* than she had imagined.

Dear God, she thought, clutching the letter to her breast, but can I tell Tatty? Her sister-in-law was her best friend and an unshakeable ally, but the girl was something of a flibbertigibbet. Cathal could possibly be told, but Daisy was not entirely sure Tatty could keep a secret of this magnitude. Daisy groaned. How could she *not* tell her? How could she tell Cathal and keep Tatty ignorant of it? Tatty idolized her big brother; when they were together, they were as thick as thieves. But if Gerald found out that Nate was coming back, he would do everything in his power to have him killed. And he had almost limitless resources with which to do it.

'What's got you all up to high doe?' Tatty asked from behind her.

Daisy's heart thumped the front of her ribcage in fright. She turned to find her sister-in-law standing behind her, having entered the office with uncharacteristic silence. A small, bird-like engimal perched on her shoulder.

'Daisy? Are you all right? You look quite piqued.'

'Tatty!' Daisy exclaimed in a slightly shrill voice, hiding the letter behind her back. 'I just came down from the roof – a charming chat with Gerald. That bracing cold air . . . you know.'

'And fearing for your safety, no doubt. I was down the hall in the press office. I thought I heard a cry.'

'I stubbed my toe.'

'God, I hate it when I do that. I kicked the leg of my bed the other day, nearly split my bally pinkie right open. It was jolly sore. Do you want to go for a ride with me? I was thinking of taking the brougham out towards Enniskerry.'

The bird opened its mouth and emitted a passable impression of a horse cantering along a gravel road to a chorus of joyful animals and birds. It looked pleadingly at Daisy, eager as it was to get out of the house. The creature's name was Siren, and it was capable of generating almost any kind of sound, including peculiar, pulse-pounding pieces of music that Daisy was sure had no place in any civilized society. It was certainly unpopular in Wildenstern Hall, due to the near-demonic influence it had on Tatty's taste in music, and the volume at which she liked it to be played. Tatty suspected more than one family member of plotting her pet's untimely demise. Its fist-sized, blue and silver body was made of some kind of almost weightless metal and an even more mysterious feather-like material. The little engimal had a white breast, a copper-coloured beak and bright, intelligent orange eyes. It chirped hopefully at Daisy.

Daisy, in return, regarded her sister-in-law with suspicion. Over the last few years, Tatty had developed an obsession with a local criminal known as the 'Highwayboy'. Some held that he was a Robin Hood figure, stealing from the rich to give to the poor. To most of the gentry, however, he was just another brigand. Tatty took frequent trips along the roads he was known to haunt, in the hope of happening across him. Daisy was unsure if it was in some romantic hope of capturing him, or if Tatty entertained thoughts of actually joining his gang. With Tatty, it could be hard to tell which way her mind was working.

'I'm very busy here, Tatty. Besides, it's a bit late to be setting out for Enniskerry, and it's not a good road to be travelling after dark.'

'It's not fair!' the younger woman protested, flopping down in the armchair Daisy kept near the south-facing window of her corner office. 'You never do anything I want to do.'

While Tatiana gazed out the window, Daisy slipped the letter under the blotter on her desk.

'That's not true at all, Tatty, and you know it. Only yesterday you had us both running like geese round the edge of the pond, trying to catch carp with those nets. One of the gamekeepers could have fished a couple out in an instant, but you insisted we do it ourselves.'

'It was fun! And I wanted to have some for a bowl in my room. Now I can watch them swim around waving their marvellous little tails.'

'That's what the *pond* is for,' Daisy pointed out.

'I can't be lulled to sleep in my bed, looking into the *pond*,' Tatty pointed out back. 'Anyway, if you won't come for the ride, I'm not going to go either. I'll just stay right here and contemplate life. I believe I'm getting awfully good at it. What fascinating subject did Gerald want to discuss? Mathematics? Microscopic biology? His complete moral turpitude?'

Daisy sighed. It was unkind to think it, but sometimes it was like trying to hold a conversation with a springer spaniel.

'No, he wanted to talk about us,' she said in a tired voice. She wished Tatty would be careful of what she said and where she said it, but was reluctant to pass on Gerald's threat. 'He thinks we're interfering again.'

'Well . . . we *are*, aren't we? Only last week we were investigating what had happened to those steam-powered pressing machines – the ones that have gone missing from the factory on the North Wall. They weighed several tons each. I daresay they weren't carried away by pickpockets. We know he's taken them for some reason. He can't go about removing industrial machinery from the family's factories and expect us to turn a blind eye.'

'That's exactly what he expects,' Daisy said. 'Nothing can get in the way of his research.'

'All right, so he's had his quiet word with you,' Tatty chirped. 'What are we going to do?'

Daisy was silent for a moment, picturing in her mind the steel-framed window on that windy rooftop. Then she thought of the letter lying under the blotter on her desk.

'We're going to keep asking questions. But we'll tone it down for a while. Let him think he has us under his heel. We must avoid drawing his attention over the next few weeks. I fear that, as a result of his obsessive quest – whatever that is – Gerald has developed a very short fuse. We must be careful not to light it.'

VI

AN AWKWARD SILENCE

Dinner in Wildenstern Hall had become a tense, fraught affair. Ever since Gerald had taken over as acting Patriarch, there had been unrest among the more ambitious relatives. Three assassination attempts later, that simmering rebellion had settled into a murmur of dissent. Simply put, Gerald had terrified them into submission. The family had been on edge after Gerald had foiled the first two murder attempts. But Ainsley's death had put an end to any further thoughts of disposing of him in the traditional manner.

On the evening of Daisy's rooftop discussion with Gerald, the expansive meal started with the slurping of oysters, followed by soup and breads and then baked fish. The main course was roast beef with a fine variety of vegetables and more bread. Some of the diners indulged in wine, stewing their spirits in silence. These days, those of a junior rank in the family found it was very easy to say the wrong thing, so it was best to say nothing at all. Others, more confident of their position, took advantage of this gathering to make their case to the Patriarch.

Every adult male member of the Wildenstern clan had a position within the North America Trading Company. As Gerald was Chairman, every important business decision had to be run through him. But as Gerald wasn't all that interested, these decisions were often delegated to Daisy – a situation many considered bad form, and a few declared downright intolerable.

And yet, it *was* tolerated, because Gerald said it must be so.

There were over thirty people at the huge table, with Gerald at one end and his mother, Elvira, at the other. She was in a wheelchair, ancient and disabled but still able to out-think younger, more agile minds. Her sense of hearing was failing her, however, and had to be compensated for with a listening horn and a tendency to bellow her way into conversations.

To Gerald's right sat Leopold. Young children were not normally permitted at the main table, but Leopold's mother, Elizabeth, had insisted the four-year-old sit at Gerald's right hand. She fully intended that when the child was old enough, the positions would be reversed and Gerald would sit at the right hand of the true Patriarch. She sat beside her son and helped him with his food.

Daisy sat opposite Leopold, on Gerald's left, and Tatiana was beside her, opposite Elizabeth. Gerald used these four as a kind of buffer between him and the rest of the Wildensterns at dinner. He acknowledged the family's need for firm control, but resented the amount of time he was forced to devote to it.

One of the chief pests was his Uncle Gideon, who was in charge of the Company's enormous fleet of ships. A large, loud oaf of a man, he wore too much gold on his person and hair on his face. He had five sons who hated him as much as he hated them, but who still regularly joined him in his greedy, nefarious schemes.

'Gerald,' Gideon began, with his mouth still full, crumbs of turnip shooting out from his black beard, 'we are having a frightful time with the British Navy. They have got into the habit of stopping our ships on the way out past Gibraltar. They accuse our captains of transporting slaves. Something must be done.'

'Perhaps somebody has told them that you *have* been transporting slaves, Gideon,' Gerald replied. He was only picking at his food; he rarely showed any appetite these days. 'I suggest you stop, before someone finds one of the Company's ships with slaves aboard. We would all hate to see you hanged. It is your operation – I can assure you that you will be the only one to go down with that particular ship.'

Gideon was still considering his response when Elvira

shouted up from the other end of the table. 'And what about the contracts with the East India Company?' she called. 'They want to buy our gold mines in California. It is important we sell the dratted things before those nabobs discover they're empty. This "Gold Rush" has become more akin to a "Gold Trickle". The contracts must be signed as a matter of urgency!'

'Let Daisy handle it.' Gerald waved his hand towards her.

'She can't handle it,' one of the other men said. 'She's a *woman*. She can't sign contracts. She can't represent the family, and if we send her to negotiations no one will take us seriously. You need to seize the reins, Gerald.'

Daisy listened, but did not speak. She was forced to put up with the bigotry in the family because it merely reflected that of the wider world. Having long ago resigned herself to the idea that women of her generation would never achieve equal status to men in business, she had set about finding other ways of achieving her goals.

'What about the bloody Civil War in America?' Oliver demanded. He was Gideon's second eldest son. He was responsible for the estates in Ireland, but fancied himself as a leader and business strategist. 'Silas over there, he says the place is awash with vacant land – what with so many of the menfolk dead and all that. According to him, we should be buying up farms now, while all the widows are still single and desperate. There's a killing to be made, what? Loosen the purse-strings a bit, Gerald, eh? That's what I say!'

'I'll have Daisy look over it,' Gerald muttered, cutting through a piece of beef.

'Daisy can't sign cheques!' Oliver protested.

'And what about the talk of these Irish-American Fenians?' Gideon called out. 'Hardened veterans from that blasted war of theirs, coming back in their thousands to fight the British here? Some are already here, training up the native rabble! They'll cause havoc!'

'This idea of a returning army is a myth for the most part,' Gerald replied, jabbing his meat with his fork. 'I think most men in Ireland are concerned with going in the opposite direction. Certainly, thousands spend their life savings to leave on our ships every year, with little prospect of returning. The Irish-Americans make a lot of noise, but they have their own problems to occupy them.'

'How can we be sure?' someone asked.

'More to the point, should we be charging more for the passage to America?' another voice piped up. 'If it's such a popular route, I mean.'

'We have not resolved the matter of selling our empty gold mines,' Elvira shouted. 'There is still money to be made there, before it all falls flat. This must be completed, before we discuss buying more land from destitute widows or taking the life savings from emigrants.'

'What are we going to do about this blasted Highwayboy?' someone else called up. 'I've been robbed twice by the little rotter, and now we hear the cur's got all the ruddy peasants on his side by throwing them money he steals from *our* pockets!'

'What about all the money we lost on that fool Livingstone's expedition up the Zambezi?' a new voice asked. 'How—'

'Who gives a damn about Africa?' another snapped. 'It's more trouble than it's worth. As far as I'm concerned you can stick that bloody Livingstone up *your* Zambezi and be done with it!'

'We must discuss California!'

The voices rose in volume and number, shouting each other down until no one voice could be heard. As the crescendo of arguments became angrier, Gerald pinched his nose and sighed. Then he started to whistle.

It was a sound that every ear in the room recognized. Even Elvira's. There was a sudden silence as Gerald continued to whistle Brahms's *Lullaby*. It was a sweet, innocent tune and Daisy was amazed at how quickly it had its effect. Voices faltered and fell quiet. Those who had stood up to make their points abruptly sat down. Everyone exchanged anxious looks and then picked up their cutlery and started eating.

Daisy could not be sure if it was the whistling itself that had physically forced them all to shut up, or if it was merely the fear of it that had the effect. Either way, nobody spoke again after Gerald stopped whistling. Apart from the clink of cutlery and the nervous gulps of wine, there was hardly a sound.

Until Leopold started banging his spoon on the table and demanded another tune. His mother gently took the spoon off him and waved to a servant, who nodded briskly and walked out. Seconds later, the man was back, holding a violin. His gentle music accompanied Leopold's eating for the remainder of the meal.

Gerald was first to leave the table. Elizabeth and Leopold went with him. Daisy waited a full minute before following them. She allowed them to reach the elevator and step inside before coming round the last corner. Ringing the bell to summon the other lift, she walked in as the doors opened. The boy controlling the lever looked up at her.

'The laboratory, please,' she said.

Occupying much of the basement space at the foot of the tower, Gerald's laboratory was the only part of Wildenstern Hall that truly reflected his state of mind. Once, this place had been orderly, laid out with careful deliberation. Daisy had often found it an exciting place – with its Bunsen burners, glass vessels, gutta-percha tubes and array of chemicals, the smells of chemistry hung in the air. A place dedicated to intellectual exploration.

Even when he had started experimenting on engimals, Daisy could see the reasoning behind Gerald's cold-blooded dissections. Back then, she had believed that he was not being cruel in any calculating way. He simply would not let sentimentality stand in his way of solving the mystery of their existence. In some ways, it appealed to her own curiosity, even though the sight of those dissected creatures turned her stomach. Once, they had been full of life, only to be reduced to ruined corpses of metal, ceramic and other, unknown materials.

But now, there was very little rational thought to be seen here. The laboratory equipment was unused for the most part, gathering dust, and the glow from the thickly glassed grates up at ground level was dulled by dirt – Gerald would not allow the staff to do any cleaning down here. And yet he spent more and more time out of the house. Whatever he was doing, he wasn't doing it here. Still, the place bore fresh signs that he had been here. There were pieces of paper everywhere, some in piles, some left discarded on the floor. When he couldn't find paper, Gerald had written on tables and walls with a pencil, or even scratched into their surfaces with a nail or a knife. The place was covered with haphazard notes. None of them made any sense.

When she entered the laboratory, Daisy found Leopold running up and down on one of the sturdy worktops, jumping over the equipment there like a horse at a showground. There were times he reminded Daisy so much of his father.

Elizabeth was standing at another table, looking through a pile of the notes. Most of them were covered in mathaumaturgical symbols, like the ones Gerald had scribbled on the plans for the church. This was an arcane mathematical language that some scientists around the world thought was a means of communicating with engimals, and possibly with the very elements of the world itself. Others dismissed it as nonsense, and the false magic of pagans.

There was a frustrated frown on Elizabeth's face and Daisy allowed herself a smile, before quickly hiding it again and clearing her throat. The older woman looked round. At first she seemed annoyed, but then her expression became more neutral and she returned her attention to the page in her hand. The two women lived in a constant state of antagonism, but were too civilized to show it.

'Still trying to figure it out?' Daisy asked.

'It is fascinating . . . staggering work,' Elizabeth said to her, without raising her gaze from the paper.

'You haven't a clue, have you?' Daisy sniffed. 'All this time you've spent with him, working on him with all your charms, and you still can't fathom what he's up to. You must be tearing your hair out. Has there ever been a man before whom you couldn't wind round your finger?'

'It's only a matter of time, my dear.'

'It's been three years,' Daisy snorted. 'But then, I suppose you've never come across anyone like him before, have you? He must seem as if he's from another world. What passed for science in your time, I wonder? Had the Normans conceived of higher mathematics? They probably weren't paying too much attention to what the Hindus or the

Muslims were doing. Too busy trying to conquer them, I expect.'

'This is just another knot to unravel,' Elizabeth said. 'Men bind us into this world *they* have constructed, so that we cannot make a move without their assistance. But I will not stay bound.' She caught her breath, as if she had said too much, and turned to face Daisy. 'My love and admiration for Gerald are real, no matter what you think. He is worthy of me, and I of him. He is strengthening the empire that my darling Leopold will inherit.'

'Is he?' Daisy asked. 'How can you possibly tell?'

'I can see into his heart,' Elizabeth assured her. 'Sometimes we must obey instinct over intellect. I must support him in any way I can. You do not understand his plans, but he shares them with me. You *will* see, one day. Someday, the whole world will understand.'

'Perhaps, but by that time I rather suspect it will be too late to do anything about it.'

'Are you two fighting again?' Gerald's voice interrupted them. He was standing in a doorway that led to the room where a bank of large refrigerators had been installed. Like so many other things, Gerald would tell no one their purpose. 'Honestly, you're like ferrets in a sack, the pair of you. And don't think I'm fooled by the civil tone – I felt the temperature drop when Daisy walked into the room.'

He strolled over to the table where Elizabeth was reading the notes. He had a cigarette in his hand and he blew a few smoke rings in a playful way that Daisy had not seen in some time. Considering his foul mood at dinner, he seemed positively cheerful now.

'I have been concerned with your shortcomings for a while now,' he said to her. 'I think I have been unfair to you. It's high time I did something about it.'

'Shortcomings?' Daisy said in a clipped tone.

'Your gender,' he explained. 'It is a handicap in the world of business – though I know you have worked incredibly hard to overcome it. I commend you for that, but the family is right; there are some things you simply cannot do.'

Daisy drew in a breath, but said nothing. She hated this; no matter what she did, or how many times she proved herself, the world would not allow her to succeed. Despite Gerald's increasingly cold nature, she had thought that he was beginning to respect her abilities.

'You will still handle the day-to-day affairs for now,' he told her, 'but I'm bringing someone in who is better suited to man the helm, so to speak. An individual who can help you manage the business, while keeping the family under control. I think you will find his commanding presence of great benefit.'

'What are you talking about?' Daisy snapped at him, resenting the fact that he had succeeded in sparking her temper. 'It can't be any of the buffoons you silenced at dinner. You're bringing someone in from the outside? Who? What outsider could hope to get to grips with this family?'

'Oh, he's not an outsider,' Gerald said, stubbing his cigarette out on one of the worktops. 'Quite the opposite, in fact. He has a deep knowledge of this family, born of a long acquaintance. An *exceedingly* long acquaintance.'

With that, he turned and walked out of the room, ignoring Daisy's protests to know more. Elizabeth lifted Leopold off the table, set him on the ground and began to lead him out of the room after Gerald. She stopped and turned round to face Daisy, taking the younger woman's hands in hers with a slight, but smug smile on her face.

'You haven't a clue, have you?' she sighed. 'But I'll tell you this about your new superior, my dear. You'll never have come across anyone like him. He'll seem as if he's from another world.'

Then, turning to look down into Leopold's big, curious blue eyes, Elizabeth held out her hand, linking fingers with him. She led her son out the door, leaving Daisy standing among the dusty remnants of the laboratory, wondering what was coming next.

VII

BRAHMS'S LULLABY

Nate woke from a fitful dream of a dead and blackened landscape. He opened his eyes and looked at the plastered brick wall stretching up over his head to the wooden beams above. A sheet of canvas hung over the single window beside the front door. The dawn light was filtering in around its edges. If Nate had been asked to choose a safe place to hide from those hunting him, a formidable British fort on the coast of County Cork would not have been his first choice. And yet here he was, waking up in one of the small terraced houses that backed onto the inner wall of the huge, seaward ramparts of Charles Fort, a massive star-shaped stronghold that overlooked Kinsale Harbour.

This house belonged to a friend of Clancy's and it would be very difficult to trace back to him. The soldier who had provided this safe-house lived here with his wife and two children. It doubled as a storeroom for the barracks, and there was hardly room for the residents, let alone Nate and Clancy as well. But the family had made their secret guests feel as welcome as they could.

Nate sat up and rolled his head around on his neck. No matter how many times the nightmares came, it always felt as stark and as horrifying as the first time. The stiffness in his neck and shoulders told him that his body had been knotted with tension in his sleep. There were times when it came as a surprise to wake up and find the world had survived his night's slumbers.

He had long ago grown accustomed to rising early, and yet there was Clancy, sitting by the stove on a short, three-legged stool, making porridge in a black iron pot. Duke, the basset hound, was curled up beside his master, snoring through his floppy ears.

'Don't you ever sleep?' Nate asked his manservant quietly, as he threw off the threadbare blankets that covered him.

'Everyone else is up and out, sir,' his travelling companion informed him. 'We chose to let you rest. The lady of the house rouses the two children at the same time as their father rises for duty. Life starts early in an army barracks.'

'Mm,' Nate mumbled, pulling on his jacket. Even with the stove going in the small room, there was a damp chill in the air. The occupants would normally have shared this house with two other families, but the army was using it as an extra storeroom, so they had the place to themselves – along with several large crates, whose contents were unknown to them. Nate dragged one of the crates out to sit on. 'So, when do we leave?'

'Not today, sir,' Clancy replied. 'According to Sean, there is a party of dignitaries taking a tour of the fortress. The sentries will be especially diligent and might look twice at a pair of unfamiliar faces. Sean was able to sneak us in, but we will have to wait until the watch is relaxed before he can get us out again.'

'Surely there could have been somewhere else to stay – somewhere that did not involve allowing ourselves to be surrounded by heavily armed miscreants?'

'I should have thought it would make you feel at home, sir. But as I believe I have already explained, all of the more loyal of your relatives in Cork are being watched. The watchers would not think to look here, partly because of all the miscreants to which you allude. The proximity of the British soldiers, whom Gerald can call on to serve him if needs be, is proof that you could not possibly be hiding here.'

Nate grunted, pouring water from a jug into the canvas basin held up on a metal stand. It was a useful piece of military kit, given that it could be folded up and put away when not in use. When quarters were as tight as this, every spare inch counted. Splashing cold water on his face and neck, he rubbed some life into his bleary eyes. He wished he could shave his beard, but every bit of disguise helped.

He took the bowl of porridge Clancy handed to him. It was pretty basic stirabout, but it was warm and filling and gave him comfort. As Nate was eating, Clancy climbed the narrow steps to the room upstairs. There was some moving of boxes and other things, and then he descended again, holding a package wrapped in plain brown paper and bound with string.

'This was hidden here, in anticipation of your return, sir,' the manservant told his master. 'Miss Daisy felt it wise to get it out of Dublin. You will remember that before your departure from the country, you and your brother discovered your father's secret journals?'

'Yes,' Nate said, nodding. 'We weren't the only ones either. I'm sure Gerald had found them before us. The way he played the family against each other certainly stank of Father's methods. Berto and I had them removed from the house and stored in a safety deposit room in a bank in Dublin.'

'Yes, sir,' Clancy acknowledged. 'Unfortunately, Gerald found out where you had hidden them and took them for himself.'

'What? How did he get them off the bank? We do still have some semblance of law in this country, don't we?'

'When they wouldn't accept that he was representing your interests,' Clancy replied, 'Gerald *bought* the bank and fired the managers. No one tried to stop him after that.

When the journals were being transferred back to the house, your sister-in-law was able to remove these three volumes. Of all the records, she thought these would be of greatest interest to you.'

Nate took the package, pulled off the string and unwrapped the paper. The three hardback, leather-bound notebooks had a musty smell. He checked the dates and immediately understood why Daisy had kept them for him. They were for the years 1845, 1846 and 1847. It was during this period that his father, Edgar Wildenstern, had turned on his wife and had her imprisoned – first in an asylum and then in a room at the top of the tower in Wildenstern Hall. Nate took a deep breath and rubbed his hand over the cover of the top book. These journals might tell him the truth about his mother's incarceration.

He opened the first book and found a passage he had read before. It was dated November, 1845:

The peasant unrest grows as the water mould known as 'potato blight' spreads, rotting the vegetables in the ground. Hardly a crop seems untouched. The lowest of humanity have been hit hardest; soon there will be no food for the winter. They know they will starve, and they aim their anger at the landed gentry. Harsh measures will have to be taken to maintain order. This is not the first time in our history that the rabble's food has become infected, and it won't be the last. It will change nothing in the long run.

'The beginning of the Great Famine.' Nate sniffed. 'Father was typically unsympathetic. Interesting that Gerald should be so fascinated with the journals, though. I would have thought that once he'd taken control of the family he wouldn't need any more guidance from this blackguard.'

'He must still *control* the Wildensterns, sir,' Clancy pointed out. 'And judging by Miss Daisy's letters, the family did not give in easily. It took three assassination attempts to convince them that he was committed to the position.'

'Only three in three years?' Nate gave a quizzical frown. He had avoided talking about the family on the voyage over. He had spent most of the time locked in his cabin alone, or walking the deck staring out to sea. Clancy had tried a number of times to engage his attention on the matter, but with no luck. Now, it was clear that the young Duke was ready to listen. 'That's not much of an average. Are they losing their touch, do you think?'

'He was very convincing, sir. The first attempt was made by one of your cousins, Charles. Gerald was in his laboratory late one night when Charles entered quietly, under cover of darkness, armed with a claymore sword. A struggle ensued. When it was over, Charles was dead, his body cut into several pieces. Gerald had the body parts removed from his laboratory, then returned to what he was doing as if nothing had happened.

'As you can imagine, this alone was not enough to shock

your relatives. Three months later, your uncle, Gideon, launched another assault on Gerald. Your cousin had taken to walking in the gardens at night, and Gideon waited until he was far from any cover and then charged him on horseback, armed with a shotgun. He fired both barrels with reasonable accuracy. Gerald was wounded in the shoulder and leg. Gideon made to run him down with the horse, but Gerald avoided the charge and seized the horse's reins. With what can only be described as supernatural strength, he stopped the horse dead in its tracks, flipping the animal onto its side. Gideon was thrown off and broke several bones. Gerald let him live – Gideon himself told the story to everyone.'

'I'm sure he painted a very colourful picture of the event,' Nate commented. 'Not like Gideon to try something like that on his own. The man's a complete poltroon. He's incapable of picking a fight unless the odds are overwhelmingly in his favour.'

'I suspect it was desperation,' Clancy replied. 'Gerald hates him with a passion. Gideon is convinced that it is only a matter of time before he winds up dead anyway. And yet, he still lives.'

'More's the pity.'

'Indeed. But since Ainsley's death, sir, no one has dared to try their luck. That one put the wind up everyone.'

Clancy finished his porridge and put the bowl down.

'Miss Daisy described it in detail in one of her letters.

The family was eating dinner, with Gerald at the top of the table as usual. Ainsley came in through the kitchens, entering the dining room via a side door. Gerald did not seem to notice him until Ainsley was standing by his side with a shotgun pointed at his head. Ainsley drew back the hammers on the weapon, ready to fire. And then Gerald started whistling. Brahms's *Lullaby*, apparently. Ainsley let the weapon drop to his side, holding it loosely in his hands. He appeared to be in some kind of trance.

'Gerald stopped whistling just long enough to tell everyone to go outside to the back garden. He was obeyed immediately – the family obviously knew they were watching some terrible power at work. Gerald did not follow. Instead, he walked towards the elevators and Ainsley walked with him like a lost child, a line of drool dripping from his mouth. Gerald did not even take the weapon off him.

'The family waited out in the cold breezy day in the back garden. They didn't spot the pair at once, but then someone pointed towards the top of the tower. The two figures could just be seen, silhouetted against the sky. They were a few feet apart, neither making any move towards the other.

'And then Ainsley fell. He fell thirty storeys to the ground below. He must have regained his senses in time to realize his fate, for he let out a long shriek as he fell. His body burst across the gravel, and there was a loud bang as the shotgun hit the ground in the mess of his remains. As far as anyone can make out, the only thing Gerald did that entire time was whistle a lullaby. And Ainsley did not let go of the shotgun until he was falling from the roof. Since then, no one has made any further attempt on Gerald's life.'

Nate nodded. Gerald's powers had grown far greater over the years that Nate had been away. And yet, even now, it wasn't Gerald's strange abilities that he feared the most. It was what they could release if Gerald continued to use them.

'We need to leave as soon as possible,' he said to his manservant. 'Your dog will have to stay here, I'm afraid, Clancy. I'd be the first to admit his charms, but we cannot be waylaid by his stunted legs. We have a hard walk ahead of us. We'll need horses at the earliest opportunity. And we need to arm ourselves properly. These pistols we have are not enough.'

'I anticipated that need also, sir,' Clancy said. 'And my friend has already agreed to give Duke a home.' He pulled a leather case from behind one of the crates and unbuckled it. It unfolded out onto the floor, revealing a range of firearms, edged weapons and cudgels held neatly in straps.

Nate gave the contents the once-over and then nodded.

'Good. Oh, and I'll need a decent suit for when we reach Dublin.'

'That might be a bit more difficult, sir. I could have a telegram sent to one of our tailors there. But if your measurements were recognized, and the tailor was of a mind to tell the family . . . it could tip Gerald off that you were coming.'

'That's what I want,' Nate replied, picking up the first of his father's journals. 'I want the cur to know I'm on my way. Let him build up a head of steam for when I get there. Rattle him a bit. I'm the vengeful ghost, Clancy. And I'm coming for him.'

'Very good, sir. We can only hope that his abundance of steam does not improve his whistling, sir.'

Nate opened the notebook at the first page and sat back against the stack of boxes.

'If I know Gerald, he'll have something a little more dramatic lined up for us,' he said. 'It's a pity about Ainsley. I quite liked him. Of all the Gideonettes, he was the least obnoxious. Had a certain sense of honour. But, unless I miss my guess, Gerald is setting the stage for some epic performance. With poor Ainsley, he was just clearing his throat.'

VIII

TYPICALLY UNSYMPATHETIC

It was unsettling for Nate to read his father's words. Edgar Wildenstern wrote as he spoke, his statements made with a sense of inevitability. When Nate's father made any kind of declaration, it was either already a matter of certainty, or soon would be. The closest thing to God that Nate had ever known was the will of his father. To be reading Edgar's words after the old man's death brought back memories of fearful meetings in his father's study, mentally battered by lectures about duty to the family. The stern warnings against disobedience delivered by this terrifying man had been enough to send young Nathaniel to bed with nightmares, the following days spent dreading the next time he would be summoned to an audience with his father.

Even holding this notebook left Nate slightly nervous that it might anger the dead Patriarch. He shook off the absurd feeling and began reading from the start. This was something he had learned to do more thoroughly since leaving home — read. Before, the thought of reading three such densely packed tomes would have filled Nate with dread. Now, he eagerly sought out the mysteries these books held.

The first book was actually the last few months of 1845. It was not long before he reached an entry for December, one that brought to mind the fearsome old man whose shadow had hung for so long over Wildenstern Hall:

As winter bites, the last flares of resistance are burning out. What hunger had begun, the cold is finishing off. The anger of the peasants towards the family is abating as they are faced with more pressing concerns. After a summer of starvation, the destruction of the crop of potatoes continues to cause desolation among the population. Those that cannot grow enough to eat on their farms must agree to do the additional work we set them and take the American grain we pay for that work. They can no longer afford to protest at evictions or what they perceive as unfair terms. This famine will not be like the others that have preceded it. I believe that this shall prove the breaking of the Irish peasant.

Even at their height, the acts of rebellion were sporadic at best. As it happens, exports of calves, most kinds of livestock, and meat such as bacon and ham have actually increased during this famine, though they travel through the country under heavily armed guard. Enraged at the wagonloads of grain and other foodstuffs being taken out of the country, a band of local rabble have recently been engaging in 'clifting' cattle on our estates. Only last month, an entire herd of forty cattle were driven over a cliff to perish on the rocks below. This barbaric practice has cost the family much money over the last few months, as have the fires in our stables and the attacks on our bailiffs. But our strength of will is already bearing fruit. In a country more densely populated than China, any kind of reorganization is difficult. This famine is a great opportunity.

It is a time to bring in new changes to Irish farming. These tiny family farms are inefficient. By moving the tenants off the land and combining these small holdings into larger farms, we can unify production and increase our control over the management of the harvest. I have undertaken to learn as much as I can about the peasants' situation, that I might use it to make Ireland a better, more productive place.

This country is a disgrace. People survive on the potato simply because when one has only a limited amount of land to grow one's own food, the potato is often the only crop to offer nutrition enough to feed a family living on an individual holding. The common people here do not eat bread. Unlike their counterparts in England, not enough wheat or corn can be grown on their small plots to feed the Irish peasant.

The island is too crowded. Half the population lives in one-roomed, windowless mud cabins, their entrances obstructed by piles of manure. Pigs sleep with their owners. The evicted and

*the unemployed put roofs of boards or turf over ditches to sleep
in, or they burrow into banks or live in bog holes. 'Poverty worse
than the Negro in his chains' I have heard it called. Indeed, I
have been to Africa and there was little in that misbegotten
sprawl of a place to equal the disgust I feel when I ride past the
typical dwelling of an Irish peasant. I am ashamed for my
country. These people need to pull themselves up by their boot-
strings. The land they farm could turn out twice what they
produce, if they had the gumption. Modern methods seem
beyond them. Even millstones for grinding grain are rare in the
countryside. Many cannot use a plough!*

*But in the wake of the disease that has destroyed the potato
crop, and the famine it is causing, the peasants' usual slovenly
squalor has given way to scenes of true horror. It is as if the land
is inhabited by limping, staggering, staring figures of the living
dead. I recently asked Warburton to explain to me the effects of
starvation, that I might better understand the pictures of
suffering I see through the windows of my carriage.*

*In his words, a body that is suffering starvation effectively
begins to digest itself. It starts to break down the muscles and
other tissues to keep the most important organs alive. It
succumbs to diseases such as dropsy, beriberi and scurvy, and can
be afflicted by diarrhoea, skin rashes, and fungi among others.
The organs begin to fail, along with the eyesight and other
essential functions. The wasting away of the muscles and the
areas of dried, cracked skin can make moving extremely painful.
Ironically, extreme starvation can lead to throat infections that*

make swallowing agony. The victim becomes lethargic and experiences loss of hope. Death is eventually caused by severe organ damage.

Add to this the outbreaks of diseases such as cholera, tuberculosis, measles and smallpox and you have an entire nation that is in the process of being broken down much as a starving body is. But from that death can come new life, just as one might demolish a city slum in order to build anew. This is a human catastrophe, but I am determined that Ireland will emerge the better for it. And the Wildensterns will be among the first to herald in that new future. I smile as I remember something Gideon said at dinner:

'Frankly, I never liked potatoes anyway!'

But this country is facing desperate times, and desperation makes even the most submissive people dangerous. I have warned Miriam about taking the children beyond the estate without a proper guard. Apart from the risk of catching one of the many types of fever, it would be all too easy for them to be attacked and hurt — or captured and used as leverage against me. Particularly if any of our relatives got involved. The threat is all the more potent now as Miriam's pregnancy progresses. She is almost six months on at this point, with the child due in April. I do not normally concern myself with womanly matters, but I had always believed pregnancy to be a debilitating condition, what with nausea, discomfort and back pain and all that. But it seems to have slowed her down not one whit.

The fact that Miriam also seems to have gone in for

archaeology — showing a particular fancy for exploring the origin of engimals — leads to a net result in that I am burdened with a wife who seems determined to put herself, and our unborn child, in harm's way.

I will never understand this desire to wander the land, digging holes in the ground in order to discover the garbage of past generations. On top of this, she has informed me that where she disturbs the crop of any farm she visits, she is paying the tenant for the inconvenience. It is one thing for her to put herself in danger by gallivanting around without a proper escort. It is quite another for her to dish out good bloody money to our tenants for the pleasure of digging holes in our own land.

When I married Miriam, I thought her a good match: a young new wife whose forward-looking character would complement my plans for a modern Ireland. Instead, I seem to have been lumbered with something of an intellectual ninny with less sense than God gave a gaggle of geese. It is time I reined her in, I think, before she does herself a mischief.

Nate marked the page with a piece of string and closed the book. Whatever his mother had been, an intellectual ninny she was not. Though Nate had never heard mention of her interest in archaeology. But then, he would have been three years old in 1845 and, truth be told, he had not enquired into her interests much after her death. As a child, it did not occur to him, and as an adult it seemed . . . too late.

IX

A TRADITIONAL DEATH TRAP

Daisy carried a small lamp, but did not light it. She was wearing a light dress, a warm cardigan and comfortable shoes. It was three o'clock in the morning. The gas-lamps in the corridors of Wildenstern Hall had been turned down and most of the rooms were completely dark. Daisy was making her way down to the basement where Gerald's laboratory lay. In one hand, she held the little oil lamp. In the other, she carried a broom handle.

At the door to the laboratory, she stopped. All was quiet around her. The huge house emitted little ticks and creaks and groans as its structure settled in the cold of the night, but otherwise she could hear nothing suspicious.

Three days had passed since her conversation with Gerald on the roof of the tower. In that time, she had continued combing through the accounts for their many businesses throughout the country. Over two dozen wagons, as well as numerous horses and men, had been pulled away from their normal work for some purpose she could not uncover. Pieces of machinery and equipment from a score of different factories were also unaccounted for. Many of these businesses were suffering from these losses, struggling to stay up and running.

And then there were the engimals. Many were missing from the Wildensterns' zoological gardens, and Gerald had been buying more in from all over Europe. Engimals, particularly the rarest types, could be hideously expensive, but he didn't seem to care. They were imported – and then they disappeared. None of the relatives seemed to realize that Gerald was driving the North American Trading Company towards bankruptcy. Either they didn't know, or they were too scared to do anything about it.

Keeping three feet back from the door to the laboratory, and a little to one side, Daisy reached out with the broom handle. She tried to push down the handle of the door, but it was hard to get any leverage on the handle while standing so far back.

Daisy had little experience in dealing with booby-traps. Many of the family members lived in such fear of being killed in their sleep that they set lethal devices around the doors and windows of their rooms. The house was riddled with secret passages and hidden rooms, some of which were also death traps. She had no idea if Gerald had rigged this door to kill any intruder, but she had seen devices that used blades, spikes, garrotte-wires, crossbows, firearms of various descriptions, acid and explosives. She hoped that standing three feet back from the door would give her some degree of safety.

'What are you doing?' a loud voice said from behind her.

Daisy gasped and turned round to find Tatiana staring at her. The girl was wearing a frilly white nightdress covered by a pink dressing gown. She was hugging a badly worn doll and Siren, her ever-present bird-like companion, sat perched on her shoulder, close to her ear.

'Is it your mission in life to give me a heart attack?' Daisy hissed.

'More of a hobby,' Tatty retorted. 'Why are you sneaking around trying to open doors with a broom handle?'

Daisy felt annoyed and foolish at the same time. 'Keep your voice down! And what are *you* doing up at three o'clock in the morning?'

'Following my sister-in-law around in the dark. You haven't answered *my* question yet.'

'I was trying to see if I could find Gerald's private accounts books,' Daisy told her. 'They might tell us something about this secret scheme of his. I know he keeps them down here – or at least he once did.'

'I see,' Tatty said. 'And the broom handle?'

'Obviously, I'm trying to avoid any lethal devices that might be set around the door.'

Tatty took the stick off her sister-in-law and laid it on the floor. She held out her hand for Daisy's lamp. Daisy sighed, struck a match and lit the lamp's wick before handing it over. Tatty used the light to look all around the edges of the door. Then she examined the frame. Siren leaned forward with her, as if ready to offer an opinion on the matter at hand. Daisy watched nervously. She knew that Tatty had taken to educating herself in the ways of the family, but this was a serious matter. A person could be killed opening the wrong door in this house.

'Perhaps he doesn't keep anything of value here any more,' Tatty commented. 'There doesn't seem to be any trigger that I can see.'

And with that, before Daisy could stop her, she tried the handle. Nothing happened. The door was locked. Tatty laid her doll on the floor, took a small purse from a pocket in her dressing gown and opened it, taking out two thin pieces of metal. She slid one, and then the other into the keyhole.

'Since when could you pick locks?' Daisy asked in a shocked whisper.

'Since I was about nine,' Tatty replied. 'My nanny taught me.'

The lock clicked open, and Tatty picked up her doll and pushed the door open. Siren let out a frightened squawk and launched itself into the air. Daisy grabbed Tatty by the collar and pulled her to the side an instant before a semi-circular blade flashed down from the ceiling, swinging from a cable-like pendulum. It swept back and forth through the doorway as Tatty clutched her doll to her breast, taking deep breaths. A lock of her blonde hair floated down through the air – the blade had a keen edge. Daisy picked up her broom handle and used it to stop the swinging blade.

'That would have cut your head right down the middle,' she muttered. 'Your nanny should have taught you some caution.' She stepped across the threshold, peering into the darkness and the floor suddenly gave way beneath her. Tatty caught her friend's flailing hand as she fell, but it took all of the girl's strength to stop Daisy from plunging down onto the spikes lining the bottom of the pit fifteen feet below. Putting down the lamp, she and Daisy clasped their hands together and, with Daisy pushing against the wall of the shaft with her feet, Tatty was able to haul her out.

'A ruddy trap door,' Tatty sneered. 'How *traditional*.'

'Good God, you're *strong*, Tatty,' Daisy remarked. 'I wouldn't have thought you capable of holding me up like that. You're a marvel. Perhaps that Wildenstern blood has its uses after all.'

'It's all the training I've been doing,' Tatty told her. 'Though I do worry I'll end up with hands like a boy.'

'You're one of the richest, most fashionable women in Irish society, dear. If the worst came to the worst, you could always start a craze for gloves.'

'That's true, I suppose.'

Thinking this must surely be the end of the death traps,

Daisy picked up the lamp and they jumped across the gap. Siren followed them in, swooping around the room on the lookout for more hazards. The two young women waited on the stone floor on the other side of the trap door for some new surprise. Nothing presented itself.

It was a large room, echoey and chilly at night. Off to one side, they could see the double doors that opened onto a corridor leading to another part of the basement. There, among the massive steel stanchions that formed part of the building's skeleton, Gerald had a bank of hideously expensive refrigerators. In these, he stored some of the subjects of his experiments. He still kept some of his arcane electricity generators there too, though Daisy wasn't sure if he had any use for them now.

They continued on across the cold and dusty laboratory to the door that led to Gerald's study. Daisy looked at Tatty, who shrugged, then she took a deep breath, grasped the door handle, twisted it and then jumped back. The door opened with a squeal, but it was merely the hinges needing oil. Once again, nothing tried to cut, stab, shoot or blast them.

'I daresay he's getting mellow in his old age,' Daisy said. 'That wasn't so hard. I'm half expecting the desk drawers to explode or something like that.'

'I wouldn't put it past him,' Tatty warned her.

As it turned out, it wasn't necessary to open any drawers. The study was about twenty feet square and filled with shelves, filing cabinets and a few glass display cabinets showing small, dissected engimals with their parts labelled. The books that Daisy was looking for were on a walnut bookcase which stood against the wall behind the desk. Taking note of where each one stood, she took a few down and started to examine their contents.

The pair of young women would not be able to reset Gerald's booby-traps, but Daisy didn't want him knowing what the intruders had done there if at all possible. Tatty, who found book-keeping extraordinarily boring, kept watch at the door, hugging her doll. Siren started to play a low spooky tune, but Tatty shushed it – she needed to be able to hear if someone was coming. Siren flew to the other end of the room in a huff.

Daisy did not want to stay too long. She knew Gerald was out of the house, as he so often was at night now, but he could still come back early. Or Elizabeth might decide to come down and root around in his work again. She wasn't too worried about the servants. They knew to mind their own business where family manoeuvers were concerned.

There was no way of telling where Gerald went at night, though Daisy had tried to have people follow him on more than one occasion. Knowing his obsessions, she was sure he had another laboratory somewhere and, judging by the amount of money and resources he was siphoning from the family business, whatever experiments he was carrying out must be taking place on an industrial scale.

Looking around this dark, neglected space, she played with the idea of trying to find out who Gerald planned to bring in to help him control the family. She had already accounted for all of the relatives, and Gerald didn't trust any of them, but she could not conceive of anyone without Wildenstern blood who could handle the task. Whatever their quarrels, the family always closed ranks against outsiders.

For the sake of speed, Daisy only read down the columns labelling each entry in the books. Gerald kept direct control over some of the Company's factories, as well as a few ships in the fleet and a small army of private soldiers. He kept a number of armouries well stocked and maintained too.

'He's pulled machinery from three different factories,' she said quietly to Tatty. 'Steam presses, pumps, engines, steel mills. But there's no mention of where they've been taken. What's he up to?'

Tatty knew she was not required to answer and, for once, actually stayed silent. Daisy kept combing through the ledgers. Then she came to something that didn't fit.

'Tatty? Do you remember when we had that run-in with the Knights of Abraham? And we forced them to hand over the orphanage, because they were using some of the orphans in their experiments?'

'Of course,' Tatty replied. 'You said it was a vile place. We closed it down and arranged for the children to be sent to foster homes. Why do you ask?'

'Well, you and I saw some of them delivered to the foster parents ourselves,' Daisy said. 'But we didn't follow up on all of them personally. We just assumed our instructions would be followed, didn't we? And that if there were any problems, we would be informed.'

'Yes. So?'

'Well, according to this' – Daisy pointed to a recent entry in one of the ledgers – 'we're still paying to feed and clothe nearly a hundred children from that orphanage. And Gerald has added a note to the end of this column: "Have words with Red. Rates of accident and injury are unnecessarily high. Productivity is being affected."' She looked up from the book to gaze at her friend. 'What the dickens does that mean?'

The following afternoon found Tatiana sparring with Cathal, as Daisy spectated. A young man and woman crossing bare blades like this was considered highly improper, but Tatty was on a mission to throw such conventions aside, and Cathal had never cared much about them in the first place. Siren was flying in circles around them, playing a lively waltz, which jarred somewhat with the aggressive antics of the combatants.

Daisy was bouncing Leopold on her knee. Elizabeth entrusted the boy to her like this sometimes and Daisy suspected that this was intended as an insult – Elizabeth treating her as a kind of nanny or governess – but she was happy to spend time with the boy. The two of them got on well, and Daisy felt that someone should teach the lad some morals before he got too old for them to sink in. The only principles he learned from his mother were concerned with scheming, manipulation and betrayal, along with the Old Testament style of religion that his mother felt was appropriate for a future ruler of the world.

Daisy, on the other hand, believed a child needed a more rounded code of ethics if he was to live a good Christian life. And seeing as his wayward father was not here to do the job, Daisy, Tatty and Cathal had taken it upon themselves to ensure that Leopold grew up as reasonable a human being as his breeding would allow.

Daisy had mixed feelings about letting the boy see Tatty and Cathal at their fencing practice, but she couldn't deny it was good fun – and given the nature of the family, there were some skills Leopold needed to start learning early. For the Wildensterns had a unique means of encouraging ambition, cunning and ruthlessness in their family: they permitted the assassination of one male member of the family by another, as a means of improving one's rank in the family. In the Wildensterns, a man could kill his way to the top of the pile. But any such killing had to be carried out according to the family's Rules of Ascension. As long as this was the case, the crime would be covered up, hidden from the authorities. There were eight rules:

Number One: *The Act of Aggression must be committed by the Aggressor himself and not by any agent or servant.*

Number Two: *The Act must only be committed against a man over the age of sixteen who holds a superior rank in the family to the Aggressor.*

Number Three: *The Act must only be committed for the purpose of advancing one's position and not out of spite, or because of insult or offence given, or to satisfy a need for revenge for an insult or injury given to a third party.*

Number Four: *All efforts should be made to avoid the deaths of servants while committing the Act. Good servants are hard to find.*

Number Five: *The Target of the Aggression can use any and all means to defend themselves, and is under an obligation to do so for the good of the family.*

Number Six: *Retribution against the Aggressor can only be carried out after the Act has been committed. Should the Aggressor fail in his attempt, and subsequently escape to remain at large for a full day, only the Target of the Aggression and no other person will be permitted to take Retribution.*

Number Seven: *No Act of Aggression or Retribution must be witnessed or reported by any member of the public. All family matters must be kept confidential.*

Number Eight: *Any bodies resulting from the Act must be given a proper burial in a cemetery, crypt, catacomb or funeral pyre approved by the family.*

Leo clapped his hands as the young man and woman clashed blades, watching with rapt attention as the well-matched opponents glided around the floor.

They were using epees: swords with thin, triangular-sectioned blades that were wielded with small, sharp movements, designed to develop speed and fine accuracy. Tatty had been training with this weapon for longer, and she had a natural grace that suited this style of fencing. But Cathal had the agility of a cat and astonishing reflexes. What he lacked in technique, he made up for in savagery. And, Daisy noticed, the two were learning from each other. Even their fighting styles were becoming very alike.

'You still move like a donkey,' Tatty informed Cathal as she lunged forward, aiming a strike at his chest.

Cathal took a step back and parried her blade. He was breathing heavily behind his mask, but showed no signs of slowing down. With two quick steps, he darted back along the line of her lunge, nearly landing a strike to her stomach. She deflected it and danced sideways.

'And you repeat yourself like a parrot,' he replied, waiting for her to make the next move. 'Pipe down and fight.'

'What's the matter, can't you talk and fight at the same time?' she asked breezily, circling him, waving her sword in the air. It was difficult to see her expression through her mask, but her body language said it all. '*I* can. I can do *lots* of things at the same time.'

'It's true,' Daisy spoke up. 'There was one time, after a

party, that Tatty maintained a lively conversation while throwing up several times in quick succession. She hardly needed to pause for breath. It was something to behold.'

'Daisy!' Tatty exclaimed. 'My God! How could you tell him that?'

'I prefer the time when we spent that week in Brittas Bay,' Cathal said, poking his sword at Tatty and forcing her to put up her guard properly. 'She was bathin' in the sea and started talkin' to a crab as she walked after it along the sand. She followed it into the sea and I kept pace with her. She was still talkin' after her head went underwater. You could even see the bubbles coming out of her mouth.'

'That's not true!' Tatty protested. She jabbed clumsily at Cathal and he sidestepped, tapping his blunt blade against her fingers where they held the sword. Tatty pulled away with a petulant motion and stabbed towards the inside of his thigh. He laughed and jumped away. They started duelling more aggressively, as they so often ended up doing. Daisy pointed at them and whispered in Leo's ear:

'It's funny how people sometimes fight more when they like each other, isn't it, Leo?'

'Can I have a sword?' Leo asked. 'There are lots of people I like. Can we go to the seaside?'

'Perhaps you can have a sword when you're older,' Daisy told him. 'And we'll go to the seaside someday soon, I promise.'

'Can Uncle come?' Leo added, looking up into her face

with an expectant expression. 'Mother said he'll be very busy, but I know she'd like him to go to the seaside with her. She hasn't seen him in so long.'

Daisy regarded him for a few seconds before answering. There were no brothers left alive on either side of Leo's parents.

'I'm sure Uncle can come if he wants,' she answered lightly. 'We often go with others from the family. Do you mean one of your cousins, Leo? Or do you mean Great-Uncle Gideon?'

Leo laughed as if this was the daftest thing he had ever heard.

'No! Uncle Gideon's *silly*, and he has funny hair!' He giggled, as if these were reason enough to rule him out. 'No, I mean *Big* Uncle!' His smile faded slightly and he leaned in closer to Daisy. 'Mother says we love him, but I think he's a bit scary. And he never smiles at me. He has big feet and he walks funny. I don't think he's as big as a house, but he hit his head going through the door once, so he's definitely bigger than a door.'

Before Daisy could find out anything more about this mysterious new uncle, Tatty and Cathal let out simultaneous yelps as she struck the side of his head and he stamped on her toe. Siren saluted the moves with a burst of trumpets, as if to say 'Ta-da!' They had just started bickering again when Gerald walked in. The bird-like engimal swooped down and fluttered onto Tatty's shoulder. Engimals behaved nervously around Gerald now, as if they could sense the cold-blooded, destructive nature of his interest in them.

'Cathal,' he said, 'it's time to get back to work.'

Cathal said nothing for a minute, letting his breathing calm down. He pulled off the mask to reveal a round, freckled face set with a slightly belligerent expression and topped with a damp mop of wavy red hair. Ignoring Gerald, he wiped the sweat off his neck and forehead with a towel provided by one of the footmen standing nearby, and pretended to study the balance of his sword. Gerald watched him patiently – if he felt any irritation at being made to wait, he didn't show it. He treated Cathal differently from anyone else in the family, but it was not always in a good way.

'I'm tired of all your proddin' and your tests and needles,' Cathal said at last. He spoke with a lower-class, Dublin accent. It was a mark of his old life that he had held onto despite Tatty's insistence that he take elocution lessons. 'I'm not one of your engimals, to be cut up and studied.'

'That's a ludicrous statement,' Gerald declared. 'I have never cut you. Even when I use a hypodermic, I rarely draw more than a couple of fluid ounces of your blood – and you have said yourself it has no effect on you. You have also said you are eager to learn about your physiology.'

'I haven't learned anything from you that I couldn't dig out of any half-arsed biology book,' Cathal retorted. 'I could read *Henry Gray's Anatomy of the Human Body* and lose a lot less blood in the process. Most of what you know about engimals and intelligent particles, you keep to yourself. And to be quite blunt, Gerald, I think you're losing your grip on reality. And I don't want to be near you, or your knives, when you finally lose the last of your marbles.'

Everyone else in the room was holding their breath. None of them would have dared to speak to Gerald like that – even Siren had tucked itself in against Tatty's neck. But Cathal stared straight back at Gerald with bare-faced defiance. This confrontation had been building for some time. Cathal had Wildenstern blood, but he was different from the rest of the family. He was almost sixteen, the son of a Wildenstern woman – a woman who had been exiled from the family. As a result, he had grown up beyond their influence. A secret society called the Knights of Abraham had killed her in their efforts to learn the secrets of *aurea sanitas*, the quality in the Wildensterns' blood that gave them almost supernaturally good health. So Cathal, like Gerald, had become interested in the intelligent particles that gave the family their power.

He was also the only other person who had been treated by the same serpentine engimal that had saved Gerald's life. The only other one, that was, except for Nathaniel. This mysterious creature had changed all three of them, and Gerald was determined to learn how. The only raw materials he had to work with were his own blood, and

Cathal's. These limited resources were a constant source of frustration to him.

'I'm sorry we've had our disagreements,' Gerald said in an even voice. He turned towards Leopold. 'Leo, your mother is waiting for you. Come with me and I'll bring you to her.' Then he looked back at Cathal. 'I can see that you're tired. You should take some time to recuperate before joining me downstairs. I'll be waiting.'

He spun on his heel and walked towards the door. Leo slid down off Daisy's lap and hurried after him.

'You'll be waiting down there a shockin' long time,' Cathal called after him. 'I'd have a bed made up if I was you!'

But Gerald was gone. Tatty and Daisy were staring, eyebrows raised, at the young man. He looked back at them, taking in their reaction, and shrugged.

'I'm worried I might have hit you too hard on the head,' Tatty said to him. 'Or is the loss of one's marbles an infectious condition?'

'I'm tired of pussy-footin' around him,' Cathal told her. 'I'm not some put-upon little gutty he can study like a kept animal. And don't think I'm the only one he's got his pins stuck into. This whole place has become like an experiment for him. You're all involved. He's got us wound up so tight you can hear our hair squeak. I reckon it's time to pull out some pins and do some stickin' of our own before we all start snappin', one by one.'

'This isn't the way,' Daisy cautioned him. 'You can't take him head-on like this, Cathal. You're not thinking this through.'

'That's been the problem, Daisy,' he sighed. 'I've been thinkin' this round in circles so much I've got myself convinced there's nowhere to go. I've never been a great one for strategies. And I can't face livin' under his glass for the rest of my life. Enough is enough. If he wants my blood, he'll have to take it all in one go or not at all.'

Daisy and Tatty looked at one another. They could understand how Cathal felt, but they both felt his wilfulness was getting the better of him. Daisy sighed and shook her head at the young man.

'I'd worry that Gerald might think that a reasonable proposition.'

X

ARROGANT, BUT WITH A
SENSE OF STYLE

Gerald was in his laboratory, wiping down a blackboard. He rarely spent time here any more, not since moving the bulk of his research to the new site. But an idea had occurred to him, and he wanted to work out the permutations while they were still fresh in his mind. The tap of the chalk on the board often helped him order his thoughts, enabling him to focus his busy mind on the beautiful simplicity of a mathaumaturgical problem.

So it was with some irritation that he saw Gideon enter the room, his uncle's hands opening and closing in an expression of anxiety. Gerald took a long, slow breath and kept his eyes on the board, watching the numbers and symbols flow from his fingers.

He had been investigating the behaviour of intelligent

particles in human blood and engimals' bodies for years, but he had lately theorized that the mysterious particles might be found in the wider environment as well. If that was the case, he wondered if they might behave like the spores of a fungus when released into the open air, and he had just come up with a means of testing the theory. But first, he had to frame the theory in the right mathaumaturgical terms.

Whenever human beings tried his patience with their petty, irrational claptrap, he would often seek comfort in science.

'Gerald!' Gideon wheezed, making his way between the worktables. 'This is no time for scribbling on blackboards – I have some grave news.'

'Do tell,' Gerald replied in a sullen voice.

'I have received word from one of the tailors we use in Dublin,' Gideon said, in the gruff voice he used to disguise any fear he might be experiencing. 'The man told me of a telegram that arrived this morning. It was an order for a suit – to be made up on the family's account, but to be picked up rather than delivered. The tailor recognized the measurements. He says that though they have changed a little in the intervening years, he is sure the suit is for *Nathaniel*.'

Gideon took a step back, lifted his chin and opened his arms a little wider, as if expecting an explosive response. Gerald regarded him for a few seconds, glanced back at the board and then down at the floor. There was a faint smile on his lips.

'Gerald?' Gideon spluttered. 'Do you hear what I'm telling you? This surely means that Nathaniel is on his way *here*! The tailor knows, of course, that the Duke of Leinster has been missing for years. He rode up here with this news himself. I have sworn him to secrecy, but . . . but . . . what do you make of it? If Nathaniel means to challenge you, he has made a foolish mistake in allowing his arrival to be anticipated in this fashion. He has shown his hand!'

'Not really.' Gerald smirked, rolling the chalk between his fingers. 'The information I have been receiving had led me to believe he was back in Ireland – this merely confirms it. And he can only be back for one reason. He knows that I have my hunters out after him and, in characteristic fashion, he intends to get past all of them and deal out some harsh justice, at least as he sees it. So he has sent us a message to make his intentions clear.'

'A message?' Gideon scowled in confusion. 'He sent the measurements for a suit!'

'It's a nice touch. Arrogant, but with a sense of style. His disappearance is one of the most notorious mysteries in Ireland, connected to the explosion in the church; a mystery that has led to an international search for one of the world's richest men. But anyone else who sees that telegram – it was transmitted from the south coast, I am sure, most probably Cork – anyone else who sees it will not understand that it means that the vanished Duke of Leinster has returned. Nate wants us to know, but not the rest of this gossiping country. Improbable as it might seem, Nate may well have developed some subtlety. He has certainly thrown down the gauntlet. It is like a challenge to a duel, Gideon. He is coming home, and it is up to us to stop him.'

'This is not good, Gerald. He hates this family. If he seizes control – and as Patriarch, it is his right – he will ruin everything. If he takes the reins, he will steer this ship right into the . . . the . . . the . . . eye of the hurricane. He and Roberto, and that interfering wagon, Daisy, nearly brought our house of cards crashing down on our heads like . . . like . . . like a greenhouse. And now the worst of the bunch is coming back. You know what he's like when he's got the bit between his teeth – he'll ride us 'til we shout stop.'

'Gideon, your ability to mangle the English language remains undiminished,' Gerald said with a smile. 'But your judgement of character is as poor as ever. Nate has no interest in taking over the family. He never did. As you said, he hates the lot of us. He ran from his responsibilities last time, and he will no doubt shirk them once more when he has finished what he is coming here to do.'

'And what *is* he coming here to do?' Gideon asked.

'Kill me,' Gerald replied. 'He has to kill me before I kill him, or vice versa – whichever way you want to look at it. It is a deliciously simple situation.'

Cathal was on edge as he walked back to his room. The corridors, normally familiar territory, had taken on a menacing air. He had not noticed before the large number of paintings in the hallways that featured violent scenes. It had felt good to stand up to Gerald, but here in these dark corridors Cathal was beginning to feel less sure of himself.

He stopped at the door to his rooms, but did not touch the handle. First, he checked the single hair that he always left stuck across the jamb of the door. If anybody used this door, it would be broken, but it was not. There could still be someone waiting for him in the room; they just hadn't used this door. Or perhaps someone had been and gone, and somehow replaced the hair?

Shaking his head at his own paranoia, he went to grasp the handle – but then stopped. Instead, he moved down to the next door along the corridor. This room was vacant, but he had a key. He let himself in and found his way through the gloom to the full-length mirror mounted on the wall. He reached up and pressed a catch on the top of the frame. The mirror swung open, revealing a doorway, and he stepped inside. It was an entrance into a secret passage that ran between the walls of his bedroom and this vacant room. Closing the hidden door behind him, he felt around in the darkness, finding the barrel of the revolver. It was rigged to fire at anyone trying to break into his bedroom from this passageway. He detached the tripwire, slipped past it, unlocked the door and opened it. Then he reattached the wire after him, ensuring the booby-trap was armed again.

'You'll be trying to sleep with your eyes open next,' he muttered to himself, shutting the tall oil painting that hid the door.

He sensed the movement to his right before he saw it. Dropping his head down and to the left, he just barely avoided the leather cosh that swung at his skull. It clipped him across the ear, but he was already rolling to the left. His roll took him right into the legs of a second intruder – Cathal drove his heel straight up, hoping to catch the man in the groin, but the man had stepped aside. Cathal rolled again, trying to stay out of their reach until he was out into the open floor of his bedroom.

He should have been expecting the third man. Gerald would not send less than three against him. Rising to his feet on the momentum from his tumble, he lunged straight into the waiting fist of another attacker. It caught him across the left cheek, bursting sparks across his vision. Reeling from the blow, he took a step backwards and someone grabbed his right arm. He slid back further, elbowed the man in the sternum, pulled his hand free, and drove a side-kick into the man he knew would come from his left. The kick connected with a thump and a wheeze.

His eyes were already adjusted to the darkness, and he was able to dodge the next blow from the man in front of him. If they had come expecting the easy seizure of a fifteen-year old boy, they were in for a shock. Cathal ducked to his right, pulling away from the man to his right and sidestepping the man in front of him. One long leap took him onto the bed, another got him to the window. They hurried after him, tripping and stumbling in the unfamiliar room. He reached out to a bookshelf without looking, grabbed a solid teak book-end in the shape of a lion's head, and hurled it at the nearest attacker, hitting him square on the head.

The man went down, and the one behind fell over him. The third one kept coming. Cathal grasped a heavy hard-back off the same shelf, used it to block the cosh that swung at him and grabbed the man's upper arm with his free hand. He rammed the rigid spine of the book into the man's ribs, jabbed it into his throat and then slammed it against the bridge of his nose. The attacker went down like a sack of potatoes.

The last man crept forward more carefully. He reached behind his back and brought forth a short but evil-looking knife.

'Let's get this over with,' Cathal snarled at him.

'Right you are,' the man replied.

Something crashed down on the back of Cathal's head with a force that made his skull feel as if it was splintering. A heavy weight, that might have been his own head, dropped him to his knees and the room rolled around him, getting steadily darker. A sack was pulled over his head and shoulders, he was pushed forward onto the floor and his hands were tied behind his back. He wanted to struggle, he wanted to throw up, but more than anything he wanted to get away from the terrible pain pounding through his head.

There were four of them. He should have expected four. Gerald always played it safe. Cathal's breath was forced out of him as someone sat down heavily on his back.

'Yeh haven't changed, lad,' a voice said in his ear. 'Still all piss an' vinegar. And dey've turned yeh into a proper little pug, with dose quick fists of yers, haven't dey, by Jaysus? But I've got yer measure, young Cathal. I've been some time waitin' for this, so I'll be takin' me time and me pleasure with yeh. Not to worry, dough, I'm not here to kill yeh. But by dee end, you might be wishin' I was.'

Even in his stunned state, Cathal recognized the voice. But the man's presence here made no sense. And there would be no time to reason it out – Cathal felt something soft pressed against the sackcloth covering his face. He smelled ether, and then his head swam down into oblivion.

XI

THE CASE OF THE EMPTY ORPHANAGE

Daisy was glad of Tatty's company on the trip to the orphanage near Crumlin, but she could have done without having to look at her friend's growing collection of newspaper clippings. They left early in the morning, before most of the family was up, for it would take a few hours to reach their destination.

Daisy had always found the wild tales of the young rapparee known as the Highwayboy entertaining – the juvenile criminal had already achieved almost legendary status for his daring exploits – but unlike her sister-in-law, she had few illusions about the criminal class. She did not believe that this fellow 'stole from the rich to give to the poor'. He might throw some token coins to a peasant or two as he passed, but it was far more likely he merely stole from the rich and kept the loot for himself, like every other highway robber.

Still, it made for lively conversation, especially as Tatty talked with the feverish excitement of someone discussing their favourite star of the theatre or music hall:

'. . . And then he gave the lady back her wedding ring, for it was well known that she truly loved her husband. With this act of chivalry, he completed his robbery. He took the rest of his loot, doffed his hat, leaped onto his mighty steed – which reared up in a dramatic salute – and they galloped off into the woods.'

Siren, who sat at its usual perch on her shoulder, accompanied her narration with some appropriately heroic music.

'I love the way you combine chivalry and robbery in the same sentence,' Daisy remarked. 'I'm not sure Mrs Harker and her travelling companions would look at the theft in quite the same way.'

'Oh, go on!' Tatty sighed. 'You have to admit it was a nice touch.'

'I suppose he does have a certain style,' Daisy acknowledged. 'But he still robs people for a living, Tatty. Not exactly what you'd call a Christian gentleman . . . or boy . . . though how he's still a *boy* after being in the business for nearly four years is beyond me.'

'Who says he does it for a living? Perhaps he's rich, and does it for fun?'

'The wealthy don't need to use sabres and firearms to

rob other people,' Daisy told her. 'As Berto used to say, "That's what lawyers are for." Ah, here we are now . . .'

The orphanage was a forbidding granite and brick building set on neglected grounds. Its sagging structure had been propped up with a range of mismatched repairs, resulting in a particularly depressing eyesore on the land-scape near the village of Crumlin. Its rusting iron gates hung from brown-brick pillars that threatened to collapse at any time under the weight of their loads. The dark blue carriage clattered over a mucky drive to the front doors. The driver reined in the four horses as the footman climbed down and opened the carriage door. Tatty, sensing that Daisy wished for silence in their exploration, tied Siren to the seat of the carriage with a leash of thin silver chain, then she and Daisy laced up their bonnets and the footman helped them to step down from the carriage. They walked carefully over the rough, weed-strewn ground to the steps up to the front door.

The door had been forced open some time ago – no doubt someone breaking in to see if there was anything in the deserted building worth robbing. There wasn't. Daisy waved away the footman who offered to help and pushed the door open, stepping inside. The roof of the hallway inside was at the height of the second floor, with wooden stairs winding up at right angles around the space. Dust hung in the air, caught in the shafts of light from the windows. The smell of mildew, decaying plaster and rotting wood assailed their nostrils. Animals had also made their homes here, and brought their odours with them. From off to one side, they heard something scuttle away into hiding.

'I'm sure it was better kept when there were children here,' Tatty said.

'Are you?' Daisy asked. 'I came here before we closed it down. It wasn't much different. Dear God in Heaven, what a horrible place to grow up. But clearly there's no one here now. If the family is paying for the upkeep of nearly a hundred children, they're not being kept here. So where are they?'

'It's a mystery!' Tatty exclaimed, clapping her hands with a smile. 'Like one of those cases investigated by that famous young consulting-detective, Mr Holmes: *The Case of the Empty Orphanage*. I wish Nate was here; he would be intrigued.'

'Yes . . . it is a pity,' Daisy said, thinking of Clancy's letter and trying not to let it show. 'But not to worry; he'll be back some day, Tatty.'

They walked further into the building, taking the flight of stairs to the first floor. Cobwebs wafted in the draughts blowing in through every crack and cranny in the walls. Once again, Daisy felt guilty about hiding Clancy's letter from Tatiana, telling of her brother's return. Tatty had every right to know, after all, and she was tempted to tell her here and now, but Tatty's next remark stopped her in her tracks.

'I was talking to Elizabeth and Leo the other day, and

they were asking if there was any news about Nate. They already knew Clancy was out looking for him. I suppose everyone knows. I said we hadn't heard anything, of course. But it's been a long time since Clancy's last letter, hasn't it? Do you think something's happened?'

Daisy was leading the way along the landing, making for the nearest dormitories, where the children had once slept in rows and rows of narrow bunks, under threadbare blankets.

'He has the whole world to search, Tatty,' she replied. 'I'm sure he'll be in touch when he has something to—'

She let out a yelp as something darted out in front of her, scampering across the landing from one doorway and through another. At first she thought it was an animal, the speed at which it moved, but then she saw it was a child. A girl no older than six or seven, dressed in a ragged cotton dress with tangled brown hair, her legs and feet dirty and bare.

'Don't let her get away!' Daisy called quietly to Tatty.

They moved carefully through the doorway, looking around them. This dormitory had beds for thirty or more children – there had probably been more than one child per bed. Daisy cursed her long, bulky dress as she knelt down, peering under the woodworm-infested bunks, trying to spot the little girl. Tatty was moving further down the room, calling out 'Coo-ee!' in a friendly voice.

Like a frightened cat, the girl flew past Daisy, swerving round her outstretched hands. Daisy spun round, knowing she couldn't catch the little mite before she reached the door. Instead, she threw her weight against the nearest set of bunks, tipping them over. With a creak, the tall rickety wooden bed-frame toppled to the side, knocking over the one next to it, which knocked over the one next to that, which came smashing down against the door, slamming it shut and landing against it in a convenient barricade.

The little girl let out a squeal and changed direction. She ran right for the dirt-smeared window – and it didn't look as if she was going to stop. They were more than twenty feet above the ground outside.

'Oh God, no!' Daisy cried.

The girl jumped straight at the window, but Tatty caught her in mid-air, closing her arms around the child and holding her up as she thrashed and flailed. Her head caught Tatty on the chin a couple of times and she landed a couple of good kicks and elbows, but Tatty had trained against somewhat harder opponents and took it all with good grace.

'I don't want to go!' the girl screamed. 'You can't make me! You can't make me go!'

Daisy held out her hands, smiling and trying to soothe her. 'It's all right! It's all right! We're not going to hurt you! I promise you we're not here to hurt you!'

But the girl seemed inconsolable. Daisy sighed, unsure what to do. Then she grinned and undid the lace on her bonnet. Taking it off, she held it out to the child.

The girl stopped struggling and looked at it with

fascination – she had probably never seen such a fine piece of clothing up close. She was still trembling, her eyes filled with suspicion and fear, but she didn't struggle as Daisy put the bonnet on her head, gently tied it under her chin and pretended to tidy up the trim of lace and silk flowers. It was far too big and looked ridiculous, but the girl seemed to be hypnotized. Daisy took a small mirror from her reticule and showed the girl her reflection.

Tears started streaming from the child's eyes and she sniffed back some snot that was starting to drip from her nose. Then Daisy found she was welling up too. Tatty released her hold and the girl just stood there, crying silently as she took the mirror in her hands.

'You look beautiful,' Daisy said to her. 'But now it doesn't match your dress! That won't do, will it? We'll have to get you a nice dress, and a bonnet that fits, so everyone will see what a beautiful little girl you are. Wouldn't you like that?'

The girl didn't answer, but it was clear the idea appealed to her. Daisy would have been willing to bet that this child had never owned a new dress, of any quality, in her life – let alone a bonnet.

'You can keep that mirror too, if you want.' Daisy felt a twinge of shame as she realized this silver-backed mirror was worth more than all the clothes this child had ever worn put together. 'But we need your help. We need to know what happened to the children who lived here.

Can you tell us that? What's your name? You can tell us your name, can't you?'

'Mary,' the girl said. 'Me name's Mary.'

It was a common name; half the girls in Ireland were named Mary. Daisy moved over to the windowsill, dusting it off before sitting down on it. She motioned to the girl to sit down beside her. Mary did so, one hand playing with the bonnet where it came down either side of her neck, the other gazing at herself in the mirror. Her elbows were tucked tightly into her sides in a defensive posture.

'Tell me about the other children,' Daisy prompted her. 'Where did they all go?'

'Dey go' taken away,' Mary replied in a small, innocent voice. The dirt on her face made her large blue eyes seem enormous. 'Some was taken to homes, I tink. I remember yeh comin' here, Miss. Yeh came an' took Bren an' Maeve an' dat. Yeh said yeh'd be back for the rest of us, an' we was all goin' to some place nicer. Bu' yeh didn't come back.'

'I'm sorry I didn't come back myself,' Daisy said. 'But I sent some people to look after you. Didn't they take care of you?'

The expression on the girl's face as she gazed up at Daisy was one of confused fear. She was slowly shifting back along the windowsill. Tatty was standing relaxed, with her hands behind her back, but Daisy knew she was ready to grab the girl if she went to run again.

'Dah was *you* sent dem?' Mary whimpered. '*You* sent Red?'

'I don't know anyone named Red,' Daisy replied. 'Who is he?'

'He's . . . he's deh fella who . . . who came,' Mary sobbed. 'Bu' . . . bu' we *know* Red. He worked . . . worked for deh fella wha' ran dis place.' She pulled out her sleeve and held out her right arm. 'He gave me dis.'

The grime on her arm was raised in a weal across her arm, just below her elbow. Daisy took the girl's hand and ran her fingers lightly over the scar. It was an old injury, most probably from a bad burn – the kind you might get from having red-hot metal laid across your skin.

'Dear God,' Daisy said under her breath. 'Mary, how did this happen?'

'I spilled deh coal back when I was little, wen I was bringin' it in. Some of it got on Red's shoes. So he go' deh poker from the fire and tol' me dis was wha' happened to clumsy girls.'

Daisy exchanged looks with Tatty. This man would have to be found.

'So, anyway,' Mary continued, pulling her sleeve back down as if the scar was no longer something she ever thought about, 'after you went dat time, he shows up wit' a few wagons and he takes all deh ones wha' are left. On'y I says to meself, I'm not goin' wit' him, not even if he's takin' us to the biggest mansion that ever was. So I hid in deh cellar while dey was loadin' everyone else on. I could see deh lot of 'em tru one of dem little windows. An' one of deh lads – he as'd Red where dey were goin', an' Red says to 'im: "Yer goin' to be well important, boy. Yer goin' to work for deh Wildensterns, an' in a lovely spot in the mountains too". An' den dey drove off.' The girl chewed her lip and gazed at Daisy, as if measuring her up. 'I've been here ever since.'

'And do you know where they went?' Tatty pressed her.

Mary shook her head. Her face hung forward, her eyes directed at the floor. 'Yer deh Wildensterns, aren't yeh?' she asked in a hushed voice. She was trembling again. 'You should know where dey are. Don't be askin' me.'

XII

THE WILL OF GOD, INDEED

Nate sat at the top of the mountain, reading. Despite the late morning sunshine, the wind had a bite to it, tugging at his hair and his coat. Standing on the shoulder of the peak, Clancy was peering down the slope using a telescope. He was looking back at the foot of the Devil's Ladder, the steep gully that led up the last precipitous slope towards the peak of Carrauntoohil. Even without the telescope, Nate could see the tiny figures of several men moving quickly towards the mouth of the gully. But for now, his attention was on the pages of his father's journal.

He recognized the world his father was describing – he had been a young boy during the years of the Great Famine – but it was still strange to read about it. In the years he had been away from home, Nate had been hungry many times, and had learned how hard life could be for those without his family's advantages. Even so, it was hard to comprehend how the blight had turned Ireland's green pastures into an alien landscape. The page he was reading was written in February of 1846:

The land is finally recovering from the rot of winter. It was a disturbing sight, to see the blight take hold, and at such astonishing speed. From the earliest discovery of black spots on the leaves and stems of the first few plants, a field of green crops could rot completely in a matter of days – turning the land black with its decay. The stench was intolerable . . .

Nate stopped reading, the image of a blackened landscape bringing to mind the nightmarish visions he had been suffering for much of the last three years. He felt the thing squirm inside him, visions springing into his mind; flashes of paradise broken up with images of human bodies bursting, dissolving. Blinking the nightmarish sights away, he took a few breaths, quelling the serpentine in his gut, imposing his will on it once more. He continued to read:

Potatoes could be taken out of the ground with the appearance of health, only to turn to a foul-smelling pulp later on. I have seen nothing like it before – it was as if the land itself were cursed. It is fortunate that this disease only affects the potato, and not any of our money crops. Now the air is clearing and the land has lost its unsightly appearance – so long as you are not looking in the direction of the peasants. As spring comes upon us, my plans for modernizing Irish farming are well underway.

Miriam came to me in the drawing room today, as I was reading the morning papers. She was in a state of excitement, her cheeks flushed and her eyes bright, hands clasped in that engaging manner of hers. She started babbling about a find she had made; a bronze artefact she believed to be of great historic significance. It was with profound reluctance that I allowed myself to be led out to the elevator, and down to the basement of the building where she has established a workshop of sorts. All around us, people were handling bits of mucky bronze, pieces of bone, broken engimal parts or fragments of pottery; laying them out on the tables and treating them as if they were the finest pieces of jewellery. I will never comprehend this fascination with a long-dead past.

Having just returned from a trip to Newgrange in County Meath (an old collapsed burial mound the locals call 'Brú na Bóinne'), Miriam was raving about her discoveries, blind to the risks she was taking given that she is past seven months pregnant. She had ignored my demands, and Warburton's medical warnings about the risk to the baby, choosing instead to lead her ever-growing team of misbegotten mudlarks to this treasury of ancient garbage to see what they could dig up. What's more, she had taken young Roberto with her to wallow around in the bogs. The boy is already a trifle odd, and I protested that this was poor preparation for a lad bound for the world of business. But she is wilfully stubborn when she has an idea in her head, and I am loath to resort to physical chastisement to put her in her place, particularly as she is with child. She is such a delicate vessel.

Her great prize was nothing more than a bronze cauldron, blackened by dirt, with a serpent crafted around its rim.

'See here, my darling,' she said to me in a breathless tone that was more fitting for a corset-bound maiden in her first throes of adolescent romance: 'This wondrous artefact is in superb condition, and the serpent is a clue to its owner. The creature on the rim here is swallowing its own tail, to form a circle. This is an old pagan symbol for regeneration, rebirth, or even eternity.'

'It is a splendid pot, Miriam my love, and I am sure you must be very proud,' I replied. 'But only a blasted pagan would consider having a taste for one's own flesh to be a positive quality.'

'Don't be so dismissive, Edgar dear,' she chided me. 'These old systems of beliefs are all part of our development from savagery to civilization. Had you been born in this period, I am sure you would have been a pagan chieftain like Fionn MacCumhaill or Cormac MacArt. But you were born a Christian – in our time – and I thank God for that; for I see this cauldron as a sign, Edgar. A sign from God that He has a purpose for me – and you, my darling, have the earthly power to make His will a reality.'

I know my wife well enough to recognize any early sign of a new obsession, and this one was trumpeting like an elephant. The will of God, indeed.

'And what is this purpose for which God has chosen you, my love?' I asked.

'I believe we have found the legendary Dagda's cauldron,' she said in a near-whisper. 'The Dagda was one of the most powerful of the ancient Irish gods. He had a cauldron that could cure any illness or injury if the sufferer was placed inside. It was said that it could even bring the dead back to life – the kind of power symbolized by the serpent eating its own tail, do you see? But most significant for us was that if you used it to cook a meal, it would feed however many people came to eat from it. There are stories of armies feeding on porridge from a single cauldron. From the descriptions I have read, Edgar my dear, I believe this may be the Dagda's cauldron. He lived near Newgrange. Not that I believe it has magical powers, of course, but I think it could be the cauldron of a great man who inspired the legend. And as such it would be the perfect symbol to drive a great endeavour.'

As I have already said, I could spot her oncoming obsessions at a great distance, and immediately anticipated this one. There could be no doubt about what 'great endeavour' she had in mind, and it was no task for a woman, pregnant or otherwise.

'A charming fairy tale, my love,' I said. 'Though I suspect that anyone suffering a grievous wound would be less than pleased to be plunged into a bottomless pot of porridge. And cooking food in a cauldron used to hold the diseased and the dying could hardly be said to be hygienic.'

'I'm being serious, Edgar,' Miriam said, taking my hands

in hers. 'The poor of this land are starving to death. I cannot describe the horror of what I have seen on my travels. Dying children, Edgar! Decaying bodies! I encountered a man walking along the side of the road carrying the stick-thin body of a dead child, her bulging eyes still open. On the walk into Newgrange, I saw families living like animals in ditches under makeshift roofs. I was told they had been evicted and driven away from their homes, reduced to little more than tortured skeletons by starvation. They looked like walking corpses and I was sure they were not long for this world.' Her face was twisted with grief. 'Edgar, I feel a fool that it has taken me so long to see, but we have so much when others have so little. With . . . with the power you wield, we could do incredible things. And I don't just mean charity — you control the way the land of our estates is worked, and all the food that is taken to the ports. You could set an example to the other landlords. You have the ear of the Lord Lieutenant, even the Prime Minister himself. You could make them understand what is happening.'

I tried to hide my exasperation. Miriam is very intelligent in her own feminine way, but she has little understanding of business or economics. It is a man's world, and it takes a man's mind to grasp how it is all organized. This is why the law does not allow for a woman to own property or run a business — they simply do not have the head for that kind of thing.

'Heytesbury and Peel are well aware of the situation, my love,' I assured her. 'Don't you think they have their own sources of information? Much is being done already. But it is a complicated problem, and these wheels turn slowly. If you interfere with the economics of it all, you risk doing far more damage.

'If you simply hand out money, the rebels could very well use it to buy weapons to fight the British, instead of food, and that could lead to even worse disaster. Nor is it as simple as flooding the country with cheap food – that would cause chaos. Businesses would collapse if nobody had to pay for anything. That is why the politicians make their decisions so carefully, methodically. They may seem to be dawdling, but the matter is well in hand.'

'You can't truly believe in all that laissez faire nonsense,' she said sharply. 'I realize there is no profit in feeding starving people who can't pay for it – and we don't want to upset the market, do we? But you can't just amputate the dying peasants from your workforce as if they were an infected limb, and hope the rest will live on, Edgar. Turning your back is no answer to anything. You put the family business before everything, my darling, I've always understood that. But this is too big; it will affect everything. This is our country, and it is dying.'

'And that will herald a great rebirth, as you say your cauldron symbolizes,' I replied gently. 'This is a traumatic time but, as a nation, we will be the better for it. You must believe that our future is in capable hands, and our leaders know what's best. It will be painful, but we will pull through in the end.'

Miriam gazed up at me for what seemed like an age, and it

was as if she read something inside me. It is one of her virtues that she does not ask anything of me more than once; she does not nag or try to coerce as so many women do. She knows my character, as I know hers. Her face changed, taking on a more placid expression, and she released my hands.

'Of course, dear,' she said. 'You are right, as ever. But you won't object if I use some of the family's resources to engage in some philanthropic projects of my own? Soup kitchens, perhaps, or some involvement with the workhouses?'

'Whatever you feel you can do to ease the plight of the unfortunates,' I told her, resolving to ensure she did not get too firm a grip on the purse-strings. 'I will support you in any way I can.'

'I have no doubt of it, your Grace,' she said. She only addresses me as 'your Grace' when she's absolutely furious with me. 'Now, if you don't mind, I would like to get on with cleaning up this artefact. There are a number of eminent authorities who will wish to see it, and I want it looking its best.'

I took my leave of her, but unless I miss my guess, that won't be the end of the matter. While she may have decided not to involve me, her mind is set upon a course of action. I will have to task Elvira, Eunice and some of the other women with keeping a watchful eye on her. She must not do anything to embarrass the family, or interfere in the workings of the estate. And knowing Miriam, there is every chance she might do either – or both.

Nate could not contain a smirk at the scene between his mother and father. That was the woman he remembered – light-hearted but single-minded. He remembered how his father had often been at a loss when faced with her simple, unyielding logic. Edgar could not intimidate her as he did everyone else. Tatiana had never known her mother, but Nate and his brothers had always suspected that Miriam had never been scared of Edgar because he never showed her the worst in his nature. Despite being an implacable blackguard, he was too afraid of losing her love. So he put up with behaviour from her that he would not tolerate in anyone else. At least, until the very end.

Nate's thoughts strayed to Daisy and Tatiana. Both were every bit as headstrong as his mother, in their own way. Tatiana, at least, had Wildenstern blood in her. And for all her innocence, she had excellent survival instincts. Daisy was another matter. Despite her formidable intelligence, she was weighed down by her peace-loving Christian beliefs. An absolute disability when living among the Wildensterns, most of whom hated her for her refusal to bend to rule or convention. Nate smiled to himself as he recalled some of their arguments.

There were so many memories of her that he savoured: the suppressed defiance in her entrancing eyes; the way strands of her hair would fall across her face, never quite tamed; the way her lips parted when something caught her interest . . . But most of the memories that stuck in his head were composed of some put-down she had cast at him, or one of the many times he had driven her almost to profanity with his high-minded arrogance. And Tatty had always been there, thoroughly amused by the pair of them. It was funny the things one remembered about those one loved most, long after one had been parted from them.

Life would not be easy for either Daisy or Tatty in Wildenstern Hall. They too would be driven to defying Gerald and the rest of the family. Sooner or later, one of them would go too far and would suffer for it. A horrible fate awaited any woman who went against the interests of the family. Once again, Nate found himself wondering what his mother had done to incur his father's wrath. Why had she been sent to the asylum, and then to that terrible cell in the attic of Wildenstern Hall?

'They've almost reached the Devil's Ladder, sir,' Clancy declared, bringing Nate back to the mountaintop with a start.

He realized that a chill had settled into his bones as he sat there on the cold stone. Nate turned to look up at his manservant, who had the telescope up to his eye.

'That's too close for my liking,' Clancy added. 'We should not tarry any longer. And they appear to have a drawbreath. I think there can be no doubt about it now – they are Gerald's men, and they are dogging us every step we take.'

A drawbreath was an engimal, often used – by those

who could afford the expensive creatures – to clean the carpets of manor houses with their wide mouths. But many of them could also track scents better than any bloodhound.

'Not Wildenstern men – probably bounty hunters,' Nate replied, standing up and taking the spyglass in time to see the last man disappear into the mouth of the gully. 'But as long as your man from Limerick comes through, we'll have horses waiting for us when we get down to the other side and our new friends won't. We'll put some distance between us and them.'

'Unless they've anticipated us, and sent a man ahead with their mounts,' Clancy muttered. 'I suspect this is an un-common group of manhunters. They move with purpose. This detour may not have been wise, sir.'

'It gave us a clear sight of them,' Nate pointed out.

'We did not have to come miles out of our way, and climb the highest mountain in Ireland to do that, sir,' Clancy replied. 'Some might say you were looking for another unnecessary challenge.'

'Oh, might they indeed?' Nate remarked, while putting his book away and slinging his pack onto his shoulders. 'Might they not believe that this was all part of my cunning plan, then?'

'They would not know, not being party to this plan to which you refer, sir.'

Nate suppressed a grimace and looked away, feeling a

hint of shame at his behaviour. True, Clancy was a servant, but he was also so much more.

'I'm sorry I'm keeping you in the dark about much of this, Clancy,' he sighed, looking back at his manservant. 'After all we've been through together – all you've done for me – you deserve better than this. But this is a bizarre situation, where knowledge itself is the enemy, even more than Gerald himself. The very nature of his research is the real threat, and the less people know about it, the safer everyone will be. And I'm trying to put all the scattered pieces together, so I can understand my role in all this. You see, it's not just Gerald that we need to be scared of. I'm part of the problem too. I'm sorry that I can't explain why – even to you.'

'There is no need to apologize, sir. If that is your judgement, I trust it completely.'

'Really? I wasn't sure I'd ever given you reason to trust my judgement.'

Clancy had the good sense not to reply. Nate turned away and started walking. One of the things he did not mention was that, having learned the truth about the intelligent particles, he had spent much of the last three years trying to keep their terrible potential from his mind. There were times when he had wondered if it might be better for everyone if he was dead. But learning that Gerald was still alive had put an end to that line of thinking.

So he had resolved to tell Clancy as little as possible,

relying on the man's loyalty, as he had for most of his life.

They set off north-west, down the ridge towards Beenkeragh, the next peak. The weathered layer of grass-covered soil was thin here, the jagged protrusions of stone pushing up like teeth through gums. Instead of climbing up towards the next peak, they turned left, scrambling down a dangerous scree-covered slope towards a pair of round lakes below and to the west of them; Coomloughra Lough and the smaller Lough Eagher. They were both carrying back-packs heavy with supplies and weapons, and Nate had a short-handled shovel lashed to his. The ground was steep and treacherous, and stones slipped from under their boots, threatening to fall away from under them and send the two men tumbling down the rocky slope. Climbing up these mountains was tough, but it was far more dangerous coming down. A badly twisted ankle could leave a person stranded, and there was little shelter against the harsh elements in these mountains.

After a few near-misses, the two men reached the small valley that held the two loughs. The tops of their thighs, the sides of their knees and the muscles of their backs burned from the exertion. Nate strode to the near edge of Lough Eagher, searching for a distinctive boulder he knew would be there. There was a rough 'W' carved into the underside of the rock, confirming he was in the right place.

A glance up the hill showed no sign of the men who were following them, but if they were in good shape, they could not be far from the top now. And Nate had no doubt these men were physically able.

Taking out his compass, he counted out a number of paces due east, taking him uphill again until he came to a patch of green grass that hinted at deeper earth. He shook off his pack, untied the shovel and started to dig.

In the past, Clancy would always have insisted he did any manual labour – and Nate would have agreed – but things had changed. This was a very personal moment, and Nate was no stranger to hard graft now. And he had to remind himself that Clancy was getting old. The manservant had struggled up the last stretch of Carrauntoohil, and he was breathing hard now, leaning forward, his hands on his knees. Nate looked at him with concern, but knew the man's pride would not let him slow the pace, or allow Nate to take some of the weight from his pack.

'Remember when Marcus, Berto and I took a trip here years ago?' Nate reminded him as he dug into the hard, stony Kerry soil. 'It was before Marcus was due to head off to America to take up the reins of the business there. It was the last time all three of us were alone together as . . . well, as friends – before we all took our different paths into manhood, I suppose. Anyway, we felt it was a significant time. Berto had brought this little steel strongbox along – Marcus and I didn't know anything about it, but it turned out to be some of our mother's personal effects. Things she had left with Berto before she died.'

Nate stopped digging for a moment, gazing at the ground.

'She and Berto always had a special bond. He was different from the rest of us — and not just because of his . . . you know, romantic tastes. He was the only one who ever had the nerve — or the bloody-minded stupidity, whichever you want to call it — to defy Father's will. So while we were out walking up on the peak, he produced this box. Mother had not wanted Father to see it and I guess she gave it to Berto after their marriage started to turn sour, though I didn't think of it that way at the time. The point was, Berto wanted us three to bury it out here together — without looking inside — where Father and the rest of the family could never know about it or find it. A kind of ceremony, if you will.'

He prodded around in the fresh wound in the earth until he heard a dull 'thunk'. Cleaning the last bit of soil away, he knelt down and used his fingers to scrape round the edges of a rectangular shape about a foot long and nine inches wide. Getting a hold, he pulled it out of the ground. It was a steel box, wrapped securely in an oilcloth in an attempt to keep it dry. Rust had crept across the surface of the box, but it was still intact.

Clancy was standing next to him now, watching with interest. The key was wrapped in the oilcloth and Nate picked it out and slipped it into the lock. Miraculously, it still worked. There was a click and Nate opened the lid.

Inside was a bundle of letters tied with string, a curled broken piece of metal a few inches long that appeared to be bronze – what might have been a piece from the rim of a large pot or urn – the folded front page and a few inner pages of a yellowing newspaper entitled *The Nation*, and a woman's handkerchief stained brown with old blood. Nate took out the handkerchief and held it up, frowning as he examined it in the dull light of the overcast sky.

There was also a small tarnished silver flask that, when opened, revealed a clear liquid that was obviously not water. Nate sniffed it, frowning, but was unable to identify it. He held it out to Clancy, who held it up to his nose.

'*Poitín*, sir,' the older man said, pronouncing the Irish word 'putcheen'. 'And from a strong batch, if I'm any judge.'

'What the hell was Mother doing with some of that stuff?' Nate muttered.

Poitín was Irish moonshine, an illegal form of alcohol brewed using potatoes and sugar. It was one of the strongest drinks in the world, and if distilled badly it was pure poison, which could leave a person blind, or even dead. It was not an appropriate drink for a lady. Nate put the bottle back in the strongbox, shaking his head in confusion. Carefully folding the stained silk handkerchief into his own linen one, he slipped the small bundle into the inner pocket of his jacket, left the rest in the box and closed the lid, putting it away in his pack. He tied the shovel back on and stretched his limbs, rolling his shoulders before pulling the pack on.

Clancy had his spyglass out again, training it on the ridge above them.

'There they are, sir,' he said. 'And I daresay they've seen us too.'

'Then it's time to move,' Nate replied. 'Let's hope your man is punctual, Clancy. We'll be in sore need of those horses. And there'll be no more detours from here on in. If they like, they can dog us all the way to Wildenstern Hall.'

'I'm sure they look forward to the chase every bit as much as you do, sir.'

XIII

REORGANIZING THE
DRAWING ROOM

Daisy sat at the grand piano in the light of the huge bay window, playing the tune a little too slowly, and thinking about Nate. She had been more honest with herself about her feelings of late. Ever since the death of her husband, she realized she had become increasingly lonely. Her work, and the mystery of Gerald's grand scheme, had helped distract her from that loneliness, but it was always there now, lying beneath her other emotions.

With a start, she realized what she was playing. It was Chopin's *Nocturne in C-sharp minor*. The tune Berto's manservant had heard being played on a violin, shortly before the man discovered his master's decapitated corpse. The tune Gerald had played to hold Berto in place while he killed him. Daisy swore under her breath and pulled her hands back from the keyboard as if she had been burnt.

In a moment of sheer exasperation, she slapped the keys, knocking a jangled bang out of the instrument. The sound of the jarred strings reverberated around the large drawing room. Daisy glared at the piano as if it were the root of all her troubles. She grabbed the book of sheet music that lay on top of the piano and hurled it across the room, the pages flapping like a panicked bird. It struck a tall side-table beside one of the sofas, knocking a vase of flowers to the floor.

Two maids who, by position and posture, had remained invisible just outside the room, moved in to clear up the mess.

'Out!' she snapped at them, pointing at the door as if she were about to send them flying back through it by the sheer force of her thoughts.

In moments, they were gone, cowering outside and holding others back who came to investigate the commotion.

Daisy's fist came down on the keyboard, a clash of ruptured notes, followed by another thump and another. Standing up, she picked up the piano stool and stood foolishly looking at it, unsure of what she was doing. With a gasp of frustration, she put it down again and stared at it. Then, with an almighty shriek of long pent-up emotion, she seized it up again and hurled it through the large window pane with a crash, watching with satisfaction as it bounced and broke on the paving stones outside.

'Is this a new trend in musical performance?' Elvira asked

in her deep nasal voice, rolling up the path in her engimal wheelchair and stopping in front of the unfortunate stool. The old battleaxe's bulbous head turned on its accordion of chins and she aimed her listening horn in Daisy's direction. 'I must confess I am more partial to the old-fashioned mode of *sitting* on one's stool.'

'When one reaches your age and stature,' Daisy replied, making no attempt to regain her civilized composure, 'I imagine that being forced to sit on one's stool for long periods of time is a daily hazard.'

'Perhaps,' Elvira droned on in her overloud voice, 'but neither is it proper to eject one's stool in public, and propel it across the garden.'

'Better out than in, as they say,' Daisy retorted. 'I am of a mind to reorganize the drawing room. I suggest you keep your wandering, oversized seat well clear of the window.'

Elvira grunted and tapped her fingers against the arm of the chair. Daisy watched the obese old harpy roll away. That chair had been designed by Gerald for Berto, using a self-propelling wheelbarrow. Daisy had learned not long after that it was the very same engimal that had held her husband down, commanded by Gerald's music, while Gerald carried out the murder. Gerald had since made a 'gift' of the chair to his mother. Daisy, like most of the family, suspected that the living wheelchair had more to do with impeding her poking nose and her caustic tongue than transporting her bloated backside. It was easier to keep her in her place if one could control the places to which she could go to.

An image of a steel-framed window, looking out of a sealed room in the attic, flashed across Daisy's mind. She was reminded again that there could be a heavy price to pay for any woman who defied the head of the Wildenstern family.

Daisy turned round to find Leo standing right behind her.

'Hello, Daisy!' he said cheerfully, a beam of sheltered innocence lighting up his face. 'What happened to the window? Did you break it? How? Mummy and I were with Big Uncle in the mountains! We saw Mister Gordon's new machines!'

'Did you really? Daisy asked. 'Where was that?'

'In the *mountains*, I said, silly!' Leo said impatiently, rolling his expressive blue eyes. 'Mister Gordon says we're going to—'

'Now, Leopold, what did I say about our day trip?' His mother spoke up, standing at the door of the drawing room.

'You said it was "our little secret",' Leo sighed, as if he felt the time limit had already run out on that particular agreement. 'Can't I even tell Daisy?'

'Not even Daisy, my love. Come away from that broken glass, we don't want you to ruin your good shoes.' Elizabeth glided into the room, looking resplendent in a royal blue dress. She settled gracefully onto one of the sofas and laid her hands upon her lap.

'It's a secret,' Leo said, shrugging apologetically to Daisy and then walking over to the piano.

He glanced shyly at Daisy, and with an exaggerated motion brought his right index finger down on one of the keys with a plink. Daisy smiled and came over, playing the first few notes of a tune that started with his choice of note. He tapped out another note, and she followed it with another snippet of a tune.

'Mister Gordon has a piano in the mountains . . . but with *pipes*,' Leo said softly.

'You mean like a church organ?' Daisy asked.

'Remember what *I said*.' Elizabeth's voice cut across them.

There was a tone in it that sent a chill through Daisy. Leo's face went pale and he swivelled on his heel, trudging away from the piano and sitting down beside his mother on the sofa.

'You know boys and their imaginations,' Elizabeth breathed, her smile not quite reaching her eyes.

Daisy held her gaze for a few seconds, but then another voice behind her made her look round.

'Have you seen Cathal?' Tatty asked, standing on the paving stones outside the window.

'No,' Daisy replied. 'He wasn't at breakfast either.'

'I need him to help me look for Siren,' Tatty told her. 'The little rotter's gone missing again. I swear, it'll go back on its chain for good if it keeps flying off like this. Here, what did you say to Elvira? I just saw her roll past and she . . . What's that phrase Cathal uses? "She had a face on her like a slapped arse".'

The girl's face broke into a wide grin as she said it – a common expression whenever she uttered some verbal bombshell designed to shock.

'Dear God, Tatty, that's no way to speak.'

'But—'

'And I don't *care* if Cathal says it. He's hardly a shining example of etiquette.'

Tatty gave the shattered window an obvious glance and raised her eyebrows at her friend.

'I'm reorganizing,' Daisy explained again. 'Here, I'll help you look for Siren.' A thought occurred to her, and she glanced back at Elizabeth. 'We'd better look for Cathal too. I . . . I wanted to ask him a few questions of . . . of a scientific nature.'

'Gracious, your life is full of questions!' Elizabeth observed. 'Why, you must spend half your life in a state of befuddlement. How bewildering it must be, to be you! Perhaps Cathal suffers from the same malady and he simply wandered off in a fog of his own making, just as Nathaniel did. And speaking of states of confusion, have you begun compiling a briefing for your successor? Don't forget, your new master will be arriving any day now. We wouldn't want you to be unprepared.'

Daisy wondered how many hours a day she spent trying to ignore Elizabeth. Too many, she decided.

'We'll start by looking in the gardens,' she said to Tatty. 'Let me get my coat and hat, and I'll join you.'

'Excellent,' Tatty replied. She looked at the spread of shattered glass and broken wood around her and lifted her face up to Daisy again. 'Will you be using the door, or shall I wait by one of the windows?'

Daisy laughed, and was about to reply when one of the footmen came into the room. One look at his face told Daisy that their hunt for Siren – and Cathal – would have to be postponed.

The dead body of a man lay somewhere amid the muddy ruins of the three tiny houses. The distraught family had been prevented from digging it out until Detective Inspector Urskin, of the Royal Irish Constabulary, had finished examining the scene. So the broken mess that was the ruined clachan of thatched turf cabins was almost unchanged when Daisy arrived. She spotted Urskin, standing in the shadow of the enormous engimal known as Trom. Opening the carriage door as soon as the vehicle came to a halt, she stepped out into the light spray of rain that was falling, and made straight for the inspector. Tatty was close on her heels, neither young woman bothering to mind her shoes in the marsh-like mud surrounding the site of the wreckage. A footman tried to follow them with an umbrella, intending to find a cleaner path for them to take, but Daisy waved him away impatiently.

There was a hostile tension in the air, and the rain failed to dampen that aggression. Women stood in groups, upset and grieving and bitter. Dressed in ragged dresses and scarves, their feet bare of shoes, they cursed the soldiers and police and the hated Wildenstern family. But the men were quieter, standing with hats in hands, their faces stiff with frustration . . . and barely restrained violence. Some of these people would once have lived in the cottages that were now no more than a crushed area of turf, stone and wood. Others were here in support, trying to block the army and the policemen from getting to the cabins. Those soldiers and peelers had now created a cordon around the ruined buildings. But the troops had only been there as crowd control – rumour had it that some of the men had connections with the Fenian rebels and might cause trouble. The people being evicted would be prevented from taking refuge with their neighbours, and anyone who took them in would risk being evicted themselves. That was the policy – landlords could not tolerate any unwanted miscreants hanging around after they had been ejected from their homes.

On most estates, the eviction of tenants who could not pay their rent was carried out by 'crowbar brigades' of bailiffs, forcing the inhabitants out of the house and burning the thatched roof of the building or destroying the cabin itself. The Wildensterns had a more thorough method, one Daisy had been trying for years to bring to an end.

Trom was the type of engimal known as a bull-razer, a creature larger than most of the cottages the tenants lived in. It was a ponderous, dull-witted creature that moved along on rolling tracks, guided by its driver who stood on its back, reins in hand. Trom's jaw jutted out before it like the blade of a giant plough, or the cow-catcher on the front of an American steam locomotive, but much, much bigger. This beast could reduce a peasant cabin to rubble with one unstoppable charge. Daisy had once seen Trom ram a steam train off its tracks. It was both cruel and ridiculous to use a monster such as this against ordinary people's homes.

But Oliver, Gideon's son, was responsible for managing the estates, and he cared little for Daisy's opinions. It was his view that control of the peasant workforce was made all the easier if one could 'instill a bit of lively terror' from time to time.

Oliver now stood leaning against the edge of Trom's jaw, looking wearily at the gold pocket-watch in his left hand and fingering the waxed tips of his black handlebar moustache with his right. A thug-faced bailiff looked desperately out of place, standing behind him holding an umbrella over his employer's head. Inspector Urskin was writing with a pencil in his notebook, having made a careful examination of the scene in his slow methodical manner. He kept his head bent over the notebook to shield it from the rain. He was a thin-featured man dressed in a long grey coat, a plain blue suit and shoes that were normally well cared-for, but today were caked in mud. A well-used bowler hat sat on his head. The policeman had a crumpled face that made him look older than he was, and his thick lip-whisker – not nearly as well groomed as Oliver's – was a shade lighter than his auburn hair. Daisy and Tatty knew him, and felt reassured by his presence. Urskin was a quietly intelligent man, and one who managed to balance a sound ethical sense with the unpleasant practicalities of his job.

Detective inspectors did not normally attend evictions, so Daisy assumed he had come here for another reason and had now taken control of the scene of the incident. He looked up and raised his hat to her when he saw her approaching.

'Good afternoon, your Grace,' he greeted her in his earthy Midlands accent. 'Word travels fast hereabouts, it seems. The accident could only have 'appened half an hour ago. Though, if you don't mind my sayin' it, I am not surprised to see you takin' a personal interest.'

'Good afternoon, Inspector. And *was* it an accident?' Daisy responded.

'Have you any reason to think otherwise?'

'I'm sure I don't know, not having witnessed it. All I have heard so far is that a man has been killed under the feet of one of the family's engimals, while under the direction of my *dear cousin* here.' She tried not to refer to Oliver with too much sarcasm. 'Would you mind very much providing me with the full facts of the case?'

'Oh, for God's sake, woman!' Oliver snapped at her,

barely keeping his voice low enough to prevent the people around them from hearing. 'The bloody fool ran back into the house after the bailiffs had dragged them all out. Trom was almost on top of the shack when the noodle dived inside. There was no helping it, that's what I say. Everyone could see that, eh? And this is no concern of yours anyway. Why don't you go back to your papers and leave the harsh realities of business to the men who can deal with them?'

'And when you start dealing with them, will you let us know?' Tatty inquired, looking very pointedly at the waste ground around them. 'We eagerly await the day when we will see your management skills come into full bloom.'

'These are the facts as I see 'em so far, your Grace,' Urskin said to Daisy, choosing to ignore Oliver's protests. 'Mister Wildenstern here had requested a police presence to provide support for his bailiffs, as he suspected the tenants to be Fenian rebels, or rebel sympathizers. His suspicions were passed on to me in Dublin Castle, and they concurred with some reports I had received from informants in the area. I arrived accompanied by some of my own men, and a detachment of soldiers from the local barracks, whom you see here around us.

'Mister Wildenstern brought a team of bailiffs and this engimal, with a view to removin' the occupants of the houses and demolishin' said houses. They ejected the families with some force.' He glanced over at Oliver. 'A level of force, sir, that bordered on the excessive, in my opinion.'

'I didn't ask it,' Oliver retorted.

'I'm givin' it anyway,' Urskin said in a warning tone. Then he continued his narrative: 'The occupants, havin' been removed, were standing off to one side when the bailiff in control of the engimal set it to smashing down the houses. Whereupon Patrick Ahern – a man in his fifties, with a wife and two children – pulled free of the bailiffs and ran back into the house. It's thought he had some money hidden away in there somewhere and was desperate to get it out before the bull-razer went in.

'But the beast was already up to speed, and Patrick didn't get out in time. He was crushed with the house. The use of engimals such as this in evictions has been questioned for some time, and some legislation may well be in order, but that's not my role here. Patrick ran into the beast's path of his own free will. There'll be an inquest, and I'll make my report. But for now, that's all that can be done.'

'Dear God in Heaven,' Daisy muttered, putting her face in her hands. 'Dear God, that poor man. God help his poor family. We must do everything we can for them.'

'Here now, steady on!' Oliver said. 'Don't go accepting any obligations, Daisy. Fate played a hand here, that's all. We couldn't have seen this coming.'

'You drove that *thing* over their *house*!' Daisy snarled at him, looking up with a savagery that caused Oliver to take a step back. 'A man is *dead* because his family couldn't afford the rent we charge them. And because you deal with such things by swatting a fly with a sledgehammer. You *disgust* me!'

'Actually, they *did* have their rent,' Urskin pointed out. 'But your family wouldn't take it, because of where it came from.'

'What?' Tatty exclaimed.

'What do you mean?' Daisy asked.

'They had the money for the rent when the bailiffs arrived today,' Urskin said again. 'But the tenants normally pay their rent with their labour, not with money, as you well know, your Grace. If they can't make their quota with the crops they grow for their landlord, they get evicted. Most of these people hardly deal in money at all. So Mister Wildenstern here had reason to believe it had been given to them by the criminal known as the Highwayboy. Mister Wildenstern wouldn't accept the money. In fact, he said their taking the money from the Highwayboy was reason enough to evict them.'

'It's not the first bloody time it's happened, either,' Oliver snorted. 'The last few times we've come to evict someone, they've handed over the back rent, happy as you please, after months of not bein' able to pay it. How else would they get their hands on that kind of money, eh? Half of these snirps wouldn't see a coin from one week to the next, let alone a lump of ready money like that. It's obviously robber's loot, that's what I say.'

'That'd be a very generous and considerate robber indeed,' Daisy observed.

'A robber nonetheless,' Oliver sniffed. 'One who is no doubt intent on sowing the seeds of rebellion by pretending to support the peasants. Throw a few coins their way today, lead a mob through the door of Wildenstern Hall tomorrow.' He glared at Urskin. 'And what are you doing about it, eh? Nothing! That's what!'

'He's a slippery customer,' the police inspector admitted. 'I'm not on that case myself – at least, not yet – but the lads'll catch up with him in time.'

'*In time?* Is that your idea of a manhunt?' Oliver barked. 'Well, while you're dilly-dallying, this wretch is causing unrest, and I won't have it, y'hear? I won't have conspirators on our land, and that's the end of it.'

'We'll have to send our whole family packing, so,' Tatty chirped. 'Can I be the one to break the news?'

Daisy was walking over to the Ahern family, with the intention of offering her condolences. The footman dithered between following her with the umbrella, or staying to protect Tatty. One sharp look from Daisy fixed him in his place, and she continued through the rain alone. She was reaching her hand out to the grieving wife when the woman beside her turned and spat in her face.

'You're murderers!' the older woman shouted, her voice already croaking from grief, her eyes and cheeks red with tears. 'Don't tink yer any different from dem over dere, yeh high an' mighty witch! Dey murdered my Paddy – and you wit' your grand airs, you just stand by and watch dem get away with it! Dey destroyed his poor body beneat' the feet of dat monster!' She pushed Daisy aside to aim her spite at the police inspector. 'And dey're going to get away wid it now too! An' you shillin'-takin', peeler hoors will just let it happen. What abou' *justice*, yiz feckers? What about the *law*? But den wha' do deh rich know about such things? Justice don't matter a spent piss to dem.' She pointed at Oliver and Daisy and Tatty. 'Livin' deh life of deh gods, and wipin' yer feet on us poor mortals! Suckin' the blood from our bodies! But yer time will come! Yer time will come, yiz feckin' vampires!'

Daisy stepped back, her hand over her mouth, as the woman broke down crying. The widow's legs gave way and her family had to take her arms to stop her falling to the ground.

'Oh, spare me,' Oliver sighed, rolling his eyes as he waved to his men that they were leaving. 'God, if I have to listen to another minute of this claptrap, I'll take a dive under Trom's feet myself.'

'Would you?' Tatty asked, a hopeful tone in her voice.

'Try and show some respect, Oliver,' Daisy hissed at him, striding back through the mud with tears welling in her eyes. 'The woman has just lost her husband.'

'Dying all the bloody time, aren't they, though?' he grunted with a shrug. 'Gives them something else to moan about. Beats *doing* something to raise themselves up, doesn't it? All mouth and no trousers – that's the problem with the

Irish peasant, and always has been. No matter how riled up they get, let them have a few drinks and a good moan and they'll stick their head right under your heel again.'

He snapped his pocket-watch shut, put it away and stroked his moustache one last time, giving Daisy a self-satisfied smile.

'Your problem, my dear, is that for all your vaunted woman's intuition, you have a very poor understanding of human nature. It is the peasant's nature to suffer their ignominious lives and obey their masters. That is where their happiness lies, and far be it for us – or any Highwayboy – to remove them from it.'

'I wonder, Oliver, if you are just *acting* the swine – I mean, is it merely a piggish air you give off?' Tatty mused. 'Or, if a butcher were to cut you in half, would one find pork running the whole way through?'

Daisy did not hear Oliver's reply. She was already back in the carriage, taking deep breaths to hold in the wave of emotions breaking over her. She would do what she could for the evicted family. But wasn't that the problem she always faced? She would come into contact with one case of the human misery the Wildensterns created, and would try to compensate with what could only be a small gesture, instead of achieving any meaningful change in the overall way the family did business.

They were not afraid of her. That was the problem. Even their fear of Gerald could not be made to extend to her in any useful way. They knew Gerald did not pay enough attention to what they did, and she couldn't make him. Once again, Daisy found herself thinking about Nate and where he might be. There had still been no word, and she realized that she still had not told Tatty that her brother was coming home. She must tell her soon.

Tatty climbed into the carriage, stamping her muddy feet on the steps before coming inside. Urskin leaned in the door before the footman could close it after her.

'An unpleasant business, your Grace,' he said softly to Daisy. 'And if you'll excuse me for sayin' so, the woman there was understandably upset, though you shouldn't have been the target of her words. People around here . . . they do know the difference, ma'am. Your efforts don't go unnoticed.'

'Thank you, Inspector,' she replied. 'I appreciate your saying so. And I'll see to it that a new home is found for the family. But it's not enough, is it?'

'It's a start, ma'am. It's a start. Have a safe journey home, your Grace – Miss Tatiana. We'll tidy up here.'

They said their goodbyes in return and he closed the door. The footman took his perch beside the driver and the carriage set off. As they moved away, Daisy heard one of the policemen ask Urskin about Ahern's body.

'We're all done here, son,' the inspector answered. 'Dig him out. But whatever you do, don't let his missus see what's become of him. It won't be a pretty sight.'

The miserable scene fell away behind the carriage as it

rolled down the rough mucky road. Daisy took out her handkerchief, wiped her eyes and blew her nose. Tatty gazed out the window, looking unsettled, or even angry, rather than upset.

'I wish Nate was here,' she said quietly. 'I wish he'd come back and hit that bloody Oliver right in the nose. Frankly, I'm of a mind to do it myself. Or perhaps Cathal would do it for me. I think if he'd been here, and heard Oliver talking that way, he'd have knocked his bally head off. I don't think it's fair that a man can lose his temper and hit someone, but a woman must maintain her composure at all times. I need a jolly good loss of composure, so I do.'

Daisy nodded, and was about to throw caution to the wind and tell her sister-in-law that Nate was on his way home, when a thought occurred to her.

'Where *is* Cathal?'

'And where's my *bird*?' Tatty added. 'If I find Gerald's taken that for his experiments too, I'll . . . I'll . . . I'll make him wish that Nate had thrown him off a higher bloody cliff.'

XIV

THE UNDERGROUND LAIR

Cathal sat on the bench in the dark, tiny room, listening to the sounds of heavy machinery nearby. The walls of the room were solid rock – not built of blocks, but actually cut out of stone. He must be underground, possibly in one of the oldest, deepest parts of Wildenstern Hall – the old disused dungeons under the South Wing, perhaps. The walls were damp in places, and there were more damp patches on the bare floor. The door was made of slabs of oak or some other hardwood, reinforced with bands of iron. It was very securely locked.

The throbbing in the back of Cathal's head had started to subside, allowing him to think a little easier. He was gagging for a drink of water. So far, his newly-recovered ability to think had not improved his situation in any way. His hands were bound behind his back. He hadn't seen anybody since he'd woken up, and the only light came from the gaps around the door. It was impossible to tell how long he had been here, or even how much time had passed since he had woken up.

The feeling was returning to his left arm. He had woken to find himself lying on his left side. Because of the way his wrists were tied, his arm had gone completely numb and now the feeling crept back into it with the tingling of pins and needles. The ropes which bound his wrists had been expertly knotted. He could not undo them. He had no means of picking the lock or forcing open the door, and had no way through the solid stone walls.

The noise he could hear from the other side of the door was obviously some distance away, but there was no mistaking the rhythmic rumble, hiss and clank of large steam engines driving pistons and presses. They seemed to beat in time with the pounding in his bruised head. These industrial sounds did not belong in the foundations of Wildenstern Hall.

Well, he wasn't dead, at least – that was something. Cathal rubbed the inside of his right elbow against his side, feeling a familiar itch in his arm. Gerald had taken some blood again. Chewing the inside of his lip, he recalled the last voice he had heard before he was knocked unconscious – the voice of a cold-blooded murderer named Red. There was a man he had hoped never to meet again. Casting his mind back to when he had first run into that hard case, he remembered being hunted through Dublin after the death of his mother.

Red and his partner, Bourne, had been working for a secret society known as the Knights of Abraham. One of the key members of this society had tasked them with finding Wildenstern women who had been exiled from the family. The two criminals led a team of men who captured and drugged these women – and then drained all the blood from their bodies. The miraculous blood of the Wildensterns had been used to help cure the rich members of the society of a variety of disabilities and illnesses. Unfortunately, the process was quite fatal for the blood donors. The perpetrators had eventually been tracked down by Nate, Gerald and Daisy. Bourne and his boss had been killed, but Red had escaped.

It appeared he had found new employment, with Mr Gerald Gordon. Gerald had learned a great deal about the intelligent particles from the Knights of Abraham. Cathal shifted uneasily on the bench, wondering if his former mentor was adopting some of their techniques. Was he done fooling around with small samples? Did he intend to take all of Cathal's blood in one go? Cathal tried the ropes again, with no more success than last time. He cursed, looking around the room in the dim light to see if there were any sharp edges he could use.

A key turned in the lock and the door opened. Cathal came to his feet, but then swayed unsteadily as a wave of dizziness came over him. Someone with an oil lamp looked in. Cathal had to squint against the light, temporarily blinded by its brightness, but he caught a glimpse of a revolver held in the man's other hand.

'Deh boss wants to see yeh,' Red's voice growled, his hand rubbing the bridge of his nose. 'Yer goin' to walk ahead of me down deh passage. You try any more of yer fancy moves, or look at me funny, or do anytin' I don't loike, and I'll put a bleedin' bullet through yer kneecap, y'understand? I only 'ave to keep you alive. Boss said nothin' abou' keepin' yeh whole.'

Cathal walked towards the door. Red gave him plenty of room and kept the gun trained on him. The cove had a new scar. It was a weal – most likely caused by a blade – that started over his right eye and traced a line diagonally across his nose to his left cheek. Cathal was careful not to stare at it – or smile at the sight of it.

Captor and captive walked up the passage like that, the way lit by lamps hung every six or seven yards from the wooden joists supporting the ceiling. The dull glow between them allowed his eyes to adjust, and Cathal was sure now that this was not Wildenstern Hall. It was more like a mine, though what type he could not tell. They continued up the tunnel for three or four more minutes. As they walked, another sound reached Cathal's ears – the delicate strains of violin music. As they grew stronger, they had a disturbing effect on Cathal. They relaxed him. He knew he should not be relaxed in this situation.

'Right, then left,' Red grunted, and Cathal followed the directions.

The music became clearer as they followed the branches to a wider chamber. Cathal did not know much about music, and could not identify the piece, but it was a classical tune with an Irish lilt to it. The chamber was about forty or fifty feet square, with massive wooden columns reinforcing the middle of the roof. The walls, ceiling and floor were still stone, but this room was furnished as if in a house. There were rugs on the floor, bookcases against the walls; even some framed paintings and drawings hung from the stone surfaces. Two armchairs, a sofa and a stove sat on one side of the room, while a large desk, some filing cabinets, a plans chest and a couple of worktables took up the rest of the space. The most bizarre feature of the chamber, apart from the fact that it was obviously underground, was the small church organ standing against the wall at the far end of the room.

Gerald sat upright in one of the armchairs, playing his violin – though Cathal wasn't sure that word could actually be applied to this particular instrument. The sounds it emitted were more or less what one would have expected, and it was the same essential shape, but there all similarity ended. For it was clear that Gerald had made this instrument himself, and had used the body of an engimal to do it.

The creature's head formed the scroll. Four pegs for the strings had been inserted into its skull. Its long neck served as the fingerboard, its backbone widening slightly as it joined the body. The curling sound-holes looked like they might once have been gills, or mouths. Four strings of engimal gut were stretched from the creature's skull, along its vertebrae, to the scaly hump near its tailpiece.

Cathal felt a shiver run though him at the sight of the thing. Despite the sweet, soothing music that Gerald was playing upon it, the thought of how it had been made turned Cathal's stomach. Gerald obviously had no such misgivings. The warm expression on his face as he played was marred by the slightly misshapen bones beneath the flesh, and the scars that threaded across its surface, but he seemed to be relishing the experience.

'Cathal,' he said, pausing for a moment, and looking up with that tired smile of his. 'Welcome to my underground lair.'

'What the bloody hell is going on?' Cathal demanded.

But he was not feeling as aggressive, as fearful as he should have. In fact, he felt quite at ease as Red untied his hands and ushered him into the other armchair. Gerald continued his playing once more and Cathal sat down, closing his eyes to listen.

'In a way, I'm glad I had to bring you here,' Gerald said in a very reasonable, affable voice as he stroked the bow across the strings. 'Red and his men are a competent bunch, but are not given to theoretical thought. Elizabeth is an intelligent woman, but her modes of thought are old-fashioned, and ill-suited to understanding what I'm about. Simply put, Cathal, I have nobody to talk to about my work, secret as it is. I would involve Daisy, if I did not think her small-minded religious beliefs would drive her to constant interference. And Tatty, of course, is a feckless ninny. It is at times like this that I quite miss Nate. But our friendship is long over and his destruction is entirely necessary.

'So that leaves you as the only other possible partner for informed conversation. And as you can double as a valuable resource into the bargain – I naturally refer to your blood – I consider your arrival quite timely.'

'Mm,' was all Cathal could manage. The words were clear to him, but he paid them little attention. The music was like a warm pool of water that he could float in – a gentle sunshine dappled across his face. And then it stopped abruptly and he tried to splay his hands and legs out as if he were falling. 'Uh! What? What . . . ?'

He was still sitting in the armchair, but there were steel shackles around his wrists and ankles. Glaring at Gerald and then up at Red, who stood over him swinging a bunch of keys, Cathal gritted his teeth and pulled uselessly at the chains.

'You know, you talk an awful lot o' shite,' he growled. 'Have yeh got so borin' that yeh have to chain people down to listen to yeh now, or wha'?'

Gerald put down the bizarre violin and stood up, his smile gone.

'I'm sorry this is necessary. There's no possibility of you escaping from this place. Only Red and I can operate the means of entrance. The chains are merely to dissuade you from doing anything rash. You are here for the duration, Cathal. The sooner you acknowledge that, the sooner we can establish a proper working relationship once again.' He came over to Cathal and took his left hand. Squeezing it gently, he leaned in closer to the young man's face. 'We are in one of the mines owned by the Company. It's a honeycomb of tunnels beneath the mountain of Camaderry. The rock above and around us is rich in lead, zinc and silver – but I have closed the mines for my own purpose—'

Cathal lunged forward, trying to ram his forehead into the bridge of Gerald's nose. But Gerald had been waiting for the attack. His grip on Cathal's hand tightened with inhuman strength, so hard and so fast that the pain pulled the young man up short. Cathal cried out as his thumb dislocated. The vice-like, crushing pressure on his hand continued and Cathal yelled in pain as he felt the bones of his hand begin to crack. Then Gerald released him and shoved him back into the seat. He gazed down without hostility at the younger man, who was clutching his hand, tears of pain in his eyes.

'Again, a demonstration to dissuade you from doing

anything rash. You're quite like Nate in that respect – you act before you think. But I am a living example of the full potential a human being can achieve, Cathal. Don't think that you can win in a physical confrontation. You are trapped here. We can make it intellectually stimulating, or we can make it unpleasant. It's up to you.'

He took Cathal's hand again, holding the dislocated thumb with the right and the back of the hand with his left. Cathal hissed breath out through his teeth as Gerald pulled the joint back into line. A clicking sound could be clearly heard as the bones of the knuckle joint popped across one another and found their place again. Gerald let go and Cathal felt the tingling in his joints that told him his accelerated healing process was already beginning. The hand should be fully recovered within a few hours. But the pain wasn't going away just yet.

Red was standing off to one side, rubbing the scar over his nose, a smirk on his face. Cathal remembered the threat the man had snarled in his ear, back in his bedroom, before knocking him out: '*I've been a few years waitin' for this, so I'll be takin' me time and me pleasure with yeh. Not to worry, dough, I'm not here to kill yeh. But by dee end, you might be wishin' I was.*'

When they had last known each other, Cathal had hurt and humiliated Red on two separate occasions, but he wouldn't have thought that enough for such vindictiveness. And it was a long time to bear a grudge, even for an

Irishman. He wondered if Gerald knew about Red's intentions.

Cathal grimaced and flexed the fingers stiffly. His wrists turned in their heavy steel bands, testing the weight of the shackles. His face was drained of colour and the usual defiance was missing from his eyes.

'What are you doing down here, Gerald?' he asked hoarsely. 'And Daisy says you're building something in the new church too, but nobody can tell what it is. What's so secret you have to hide it from the family? God knows, there are more than enough secrets in that house – one more isn't going to make any difference.'

Gerald paced away for a few steps and then back again, an expression of hopeful excitement lighting up his face. Finally, he had someone who might comprehend the scale of his achievements.

'What I'm doing is for the good of mankind,' he declared. 'The family wouldn't understand. There's hardly a man among them who is capable of thinking beyond their petty greed. They would only get in my way, or misuse my discoveries to try and make short-sighted gains in money or power. I am focused on an altogether bigger picture. Come with me, Cathal. Let me show you.'

Gerald gestured to Red, who took Cathal's elbow in order to pull him to his feet. Cathal shook his hand off, rising out of the chair.

'Touch me again, yeh stinkin' crawler, and I'll shove

me *foot* so far up yer *arse*, I'll kick yer *teeth* out.'

Red laughed and jerked his head in Gerald's direction. Cathal glowered at him, but then hobbled after Gerald, the shackles on his feet keeping his steps frustratingly short. All three left the chamber and made their way along another stone passageway braced with stout timbers.

They passed a warmly lit room and Cathal was able to glance in, catching sight of a wall of leather-bound books, all alike, and an armchair drawn up beside an oil lamp which stood on a rough wooden table. A massive figure sat in the chair, which was positioned to the left side of the door. The seat barely contained him, his legs stretched out to the front, his ape-like arms jutting over the sides, hanging from shoulders that were at least as wide as the armchair itself.

Dressed in shirt, trousers and good shoes, the huge man with whitening hair was reading one of the books in the light of the lamp. He held the book in his left hand. His other arm ended not with a hand, but with a kind of claw. It was not unlike a crab's, except that it appeared to be made of metal or ceramic, like an engimal's. The giant held it to his brow, obscuring his face, as if deeply moved by what he read. Cathal stopped to try and get a better look, but Red pressed him on.

'God, yer fierce nosey. Be a good dog, dere boy. Don't be pokin' yer snout in where it's not wanted.'

'Go an' shite!'

Gerald chose to ignore the friendly banter going on behind him. He slowed down to let Cathal catch up, and told Red to go on ahead. Once the man was far enough ahead to be out of earshot, Gerald began speaking as a schoolmaster might to a favoured student with whom he was sharing an afternoon stroll. The clinking of Cathal's chains echoed along the stone corridor, spoiling the image somewhat.

'I don't need to explain to you that it is the intelligent particles in our blood that give us our *aurea sanitas*, our . . . physical advantages. And that engimals are at least partially formed by the same particles. It is what allows them to heal; an ability in these machines that has confounded humans for hundreds of years. The particles may well explain how these machines can be alive at all, if we can learn enough about them.

'I have studied mathaumaturgy for years, the mathematical language – once thought a kind of magic – that can be used to communicate with engimals. I tried showing some of the most intelligent engimals symbols and projected flashing lights into their eyes, even had them listen to a telegraph key in an attempt to convey messages. I have had some success, but it is incredibly slow and crude. You can say things like, "Sit down", "Are you thirsty?", or "Follow me". Each message could take an hour or more to complete. The process was intolerable. If there was once a means of using this language to control engimals, I am sure it had to involve a machine that could translate this code, something that could convey instructions far faster than this ham-fisted method.

'And then I discovered that one could transmit one's intentions through music. Once I realized it, it made perfect sense. Music is basically a kind of mathematics, given fluid, graceful substance in the form of sound. I learned that if you focused your thoughts while playing a musical instrument, you could pass instructions on to an engimal.'

Cathal didn't say anything. He had seen engimals perform complicated series of tasks while Gerald stood nearby, playing his violin – his old, *normal* one – or sometimes just whistling. And he also knew that Gerald had gone much further. Cathal's mind was distracted from the monologue for a moment as he noticed the noise of industrial machinery he had heard earlier was getting much louder now.

'But if one can do this to *engimals*,' Gerald continued, 'and if this form of command is acting upon the intelligent particles in the bodies of those creatures, then surely you could take command of the same particles if they were flowing in someone's *blood*?'

He came to a sudden halt and turned to face Cathal, an intense look on his features.

'And as you have experienced for yourself, I was right. So far, my ability extends as far as controlling the movements, sometimes even the emotions, of anyone with *aurea sanitas.* That includes myself, of course. I have consciously increased my strength, speed, reflexes, my powers of healing and so on. My mind has far more control over my body than any normal human, and my body is reinforced like no other. Even your gifts are faint in comparison.

'Imagine, if you will, a few well-chosen, rational people with my abilities,' Gerald said with a hint of wonder in his voice. 'Placed in influential positions, we could end wars, enforce the law, cure disease. We could raise mankind up from the gutter of ignorance, superstition, greed and brutality in which it currently languishes. We could finally have a world ruled according to level-headed reason, rather than emotional or instinctive urges. It would require harsh measures in the beginning, as I have had to demonstrate, but in the end everyone could share in the benefits of control over the intelligent particles.'

There was a rectangle of brighter light ahead; the end of the tunnel. The sounds of machinery clanked, clattered, gushed, thudded and hissed in the space beyond.

'Yeh mean, "the world would be a better place if only everyone would live the way I told 'em"?' Cathal snorted. 'Where have we heard that one before? Oh, yeah . . . from *every dictator in history*. Face it, Gerald, yer gibberin' like a baboon. Yeh want to use yer head to make the world a better place? Top yerself and donate your brain to science. There's *real* doctors who'd love to know what's goin' on in there.'

'Now, you see, *that's* the kind of repartee I've been missing,' Gerald laughed as they reached the end of the tunnel. He had to raise his voice to be heard over the noise now. 'You haven't quite got Daisy's talent for the cutting remark, but, by Jove, there's spirit in that blunt delivery of yours. You were always one for the well-targeted insult.'

Cathal emerged with his captor into a cavern, and his repartee failed him. The sight before them left him speechless.

'I forgot to mention!' Gerald shouted over the racket. 'My research has moved to a new level! After some recent discoveries into the nature of intelligent particles, I realized that merely attempting to control human behaviour betrayed a certain lack of ambition. As a result, I require the particles in bulk supply! It took me some time to perfect the system, but I think I've cracked it. Welcome to the Engimal Works!'

Cathal stared at the macabre scene before him, the noise almost overwhelming his senses. But only one question forced its way through his battered consciousness, and he turned and yelled it at Gerald:

'Why are you using children?'

XV

UNINTENDED CONSEQUENCES

Cathal stood at the pipe organ in Gerald's room in the underground lair, still in his shackles. Gerald was droning on and on about his experiments, but Cathal could not bring himself to pay him any attention. He was too badly shaken by all the things he had witnessed – in particular the demented scenes in what Gerald referred to as the 'Engimal Works'. Cathal closed his eyes, tapping keys on the organ's keyboard one at a time, listening intently, as if the sounds might give him some insight into the workings of Gerald's mind. An organ like this normally relied on air pumped in-to it to work, but Cathal could see no trace of a pump. Probably because no pump was needed.

Like Gerald's violin, this instrument had been made largely from engimal parts. Having seen the slaughterhouse where these parts were harvested, and the children who worked there as slaves, Cathal had finally become convinced that Gerald was either truly evil or irretrievably insane.

Gerald was sitting in one of the armchairs, holding his violin. He was not playing it, but rather stroking its strings with his fingers, as if it were a pet, while he outlined his dreams of healing the human race. The engimal's dead body did not respond to his affectionate caresses. He was just launching into another outlandish theory on human-engimal relations when the roar of some animal echoed down the passageway leading to the Engimal Works. Gerald sat up abruptly, placing the instrument on the table beside him. Cathal looked up, but otherwise did not move. The sound came again, and this time Cathal thought he heard words in the bellow, though the noise sounded more likely to have come from the lungs of a buffalo than a human. In a moment of amused hope, Cathal wondered if one of the larger engimals had got loose from its pen and was wreaking havoc among its keepers.

There came the irregular beat of numerous running feet, along with urgent, panicked shouts. The door to the passageway was closed over, and as the footfalls came closer one heavy pounding pair could be made out, leading the rest. Cathal and Gerald heard the panting breath of a large animal, then there was another incoherent bellow and the door was smashed open, some terrible force tearing it from its hinges and sending it clattering across the floor.

The man who squeezed through the doorway was

almost seven feet tall, and nearly a yard across at the shoulders. His large head was hung with a rectangular jaw that jutted out almost as far as his wide, flattened nose. Heavy brows hung low over deep-set blue eyes and his thick, wild hair was pale blond turning to white. The giant was trembling like a beast in shock, his eyes wide and crazed. Sweeping his gaze around the room, he exhaled a tortured, rasping breath and lumbered straight for Gerald, his massive arms outstretched. The fingers of his normal left hand were curled, grasping like a bear's paw. Where his right hand should have been, a crab-like claw jutted out instead, opening jagged, grasping pincers.

'Cathal, help me!' Gerald had time to cry before that bear-like hand clamped around his throat and the engimal claw swung back as if to knock his head from his shoulders.

Drawing a slow breath in through his nose, Cathal folded his arms as best he could with his shackles, watching as Gerald was lifted out of his seat by the neck.

'Cathal!' Gerald cried again, then his voice was choked into silence.

Cathal decided to wait and think this through, wondering if this new development was likely to help his situation or make it worse. While he pondered, six of Gerald's men piled into the room and threw themselves onto the giant's back and shoulders. The massive man smashed one over the side of the head with his right forearm, then seized another by the ankle and swung him away across the room. The other four managed to drag him back, distracting him enough for Gerald to break his grip. Gerald delivered a sound punch to the giant's jaw, hard enough to turn his head, but then the huge man grabbed him by the face and hurled him flailing against the bank of filing cabinets.

A boulder-like fist splintered another man's ribs and tumbled him into a crumpled heap on the ground. The giant was about to break the next man's neck on the edge of one of the worktables when Cathal finally decided things were getting out of hand. He bunched himself up and dived against the back of the giant's knees. The man toppled backwards and Cathal rolled out from underneath him, whipping the chain of his shackles across the brute's face. He seized Gerald's violin, intent on smashing it over the giant's head.

'Stop!' Gerald shouted, leaping over to get an arm around the maniac's neck. 'Cathal, no!'

His headlock cut off the blood to the giant's brain, and the brute's eyes went glassy, but he managed to get up into a kneeling position. The three men still able to move scrambled over and grabbed hold of his arms. Gerald gritted his teeth, keeping the lock on, and Cathal raised the violin again.

The giant's eyes rolled up into his head and he started shaking uncontrollably. This was not an effect of the head-lock. Gerald released him, but the shaking continued. Foam seeped from between the brute's tightly clenched teeth.

'He's having convulsions!' Gerald barked. 'Get him over to the organ, quickly!'

It took all five of them to carry the violently jerking body over to the pipe organ, and as Gerald pulled a metal cable from the base of the organ, Cathal and the others clung on, trying to control each of the giant's limbs as if they were thrashing snakes. The end of the cable was fitted with a threaded nut, and Gerald ordered them to flip the giant onto his front. Under the hair covering the back of his neck, Cathal was intrigued to see about an inch of the threaded end of a bolt protruding from the base of the man's skull. Gerald hurriedly screwed the cable onto the bolt, then lunged over to the organ's keyboards and began playing a soft, soothing tune.

The giant's fits grew weaker, subsiding to a twitching that eventually settled into stillness as the music continued to play. Cathal stayed where he was, on his knees by the giant's engimal claw.

'You can leave now,' Gerald told his men. 'He is subdued.'

The three men rose and staggered eagerly away. Helping their injured colleagues to their feet, they left the room, casting fearful glances back at the slumbering form on the floor. When they were gone, Cathal let his head hang, catching his breath before he spoke.

'What in the name of Holy Jaysus was that all about?' he demanded.

'He was dead for a long time, and I brought him back to life,' Gerald said in an offhand way as he wound down the tune. 'But it was not achieved without cost.'

Cathal regarded the still body, and then looked around the room at the destruction it had caused.

'Well,' he said, snorting, 'if you were going to bring someone back from the dead, I'm glad you picked the biggest, meanest, maddest bloody gouger you could find. Perhaps you should've started with some recently dead bank clerk or somethin'. Or a poet, maybe. Somebody who was a bit less of a bleedin' berserker.'

Gerald chuckled, and turned away from the organ to gaze down at the giant's face. His expression could almost have been one of regret.

'I can assure you, when this man is thinking clearly, he is far more dangerous. Most of us are.' Gerald knelt down and unscrewed the cable from the back of the huge man's neck. 'Part of the reanimation process involved injecting new intelligent particles into his brain. For some reason, these new particles are in conflict with those already present in his body – he had high concentrations of his own before I started. I have been unable to resolve this conflict. Every few days his body rejects the particles in his brain and I have to inject new ones – as I have just done. Obviously, I left it too long this time, distracted as I was by other matters. The way things stand, our over-sized friend here is unable to live more than three or four days without this process.

I have no idea why that is. It is incredibly frustrating.'

'Heavens, Gerald!' Cathal exclaimed. 'You mean you're foolin' about with a science beyond our understanding, and it's havin' *unintended consequences*? Well then, usin' mindlessly violent barbarians for your experiments is the only rational course of action. What's next? Rabid bleedin' tigers? Armoured polar bears, maybe?'

'A mindlessly violent barbarian?' Gerald said softly, shaking his head. 'Yes, I think we can do better than that.'

He clicked his fingers near the giant's head.

'Come on, wake up,' he muttered. The giant's eyelids flickered and began to open. 'Come on. That's it.'

A deep, rumbling moan issued from the unconscious man's lips, turning into a growl. Cathal stood up, his hands clutching the chain of his shackles, wishing he was capable of more than hobbling with his ankle chain. The giant let out another growl, opened his eyes and slowly sat up, pulling himself back to lean against the wall. Gerald crouched down in front of him, snapping his fingers again.

'Do you know who I am? Do you know where you are?'

The giant's engimal hand moved with startling speed, but with graceful control, catching Gerald's fingers in its firm grasp.

'Get your confounded fingers out of my face,' he said in a grinding voice that sounded old, malevolent. 'Yes, I know you. You're the blackguard who has raised me from the grave to help you counter the conniving schemes of that pit of vipers we call a family. And I am here, in this dungeon of a place, while you engage in your arcane and fiendish experiments upon me, in the hope of sustaining my life long enough for me to throw some reins on our relatives.'

The giant's head rotated, his gaze falling on Cathal for the first time.

'*You*, I do *not* know – but then it seems much has changed in my absence. And not for the better, I might add.' His attention turned back to Gerald. 'You must put an end to these convulsions. Their effects cloud my mind, and they leave me suffering terrible furies, which I struggle to control. My thoughts are still somewhat addled, even now. If I am to be capable of tackling the complexities of the finances of the North American Trading Company, and disentangle the machinations of some of our more ambitious kin, I will need my wits about me, Gerald. These violent rages must be brought to an end. I cannot – I *will* not – tolerate such a vulnerability.'

'That is unfortunate,' Gerald replied as Cathal watched this exchange in baffled surprise. 'Because much as I would love to allow you to make a more thorough recovery, the time has come, I think, for you to meet the family.'

'Jaysus,' Cathal sniffed, gazing round again at the wrecked room. 'Good luck with that.'

Daisy sat in an armchair in her office, high in the tower of Wildenstern Hall. She was reading Clancy's letter again. It was the only source of comfort she had as she sat there, in the early hours of the morning, fretting over Cathal's disappearance.

She read the coded message again:

'*At this point, however, I must confess that the trail has grown cold.*'

Nate was coming, she told herself. Even having Clancy back would be a great support. Now that Cathal was gone, she only had Tatty, and Tatty . . . well, she just wasn't very *grown-up*. Daisy was oppressed by an enormous weight of responsibility, one she felt she couldn't share with her sister-in-law. On top of everything else, there was the matter of the vanished children to contend with, and the tenant crushed to death in his house. And now Cathal was missing too. He had not been seen all day. Daisy had instructed the staff to inform her as soon as he returned, and even left a note in his rooms, but now it was nearly four o'clock in the morning and she feared the worst: Gerald's men had taken him.

Gerald won't kill him, she told herself. He needs Cathal for his research. He likes Cathal. But he had loved Marcus and Berto and Nate too. He had murdered Marcus and Berto in cold blood – and had done his level best to do the same to Nate. The man was capable of anything.

He knows I would stop working for him if he killed Cathal, she thought. He needs me to run the business. Doesn't he? But isn't he bringing in someone new? Some relative none of us know? Even so, he needs me, if only to help with the change of management. And if he kills Cathal, he loses my cooperation. That's worth something, isn't it?

But he still has Leo, she thought, her heart sinking. He has Nate's child. He knows I couldn't turn my back on that. Oh, dear God, please don't let him take Cathal from us too!

Daisy put her fingers to her cheek and found her face wet with tears. Her breath caught and she let out a sob. More followed, and soon she was crying with her face down on the desk, like a little girl. She was loath to show any weakness to the other inhabitants of the house, but no one would hear her at this time in the morning. She had sent her maid to bed, and there were only offices on this floor. So much emotion rose like a wave up through her that she felt dizzy, struggling to breathe through her sobs. She was so sick and tired of this horrible place, full of inhuman people.

When she and Tatty had climbed into their carriage with that girl, Mary, Daisy had considered taking the little mite back to Wildenstern Hall and adopting her. Ever since Berto's death, Daisy had felt his loss all the more every time she saw a young child – more than anything else, she wanted children of her own. But they had, instead, arranged to find a good home for Mary through an orphanage of which Daisy was both a patron and one of its directors. Wildenstern Hall was no place to raise a child.

Clutching the top of the desk and pressing her forehead

against the blotter that lay on its surface, Daisy cried for her dead husband and the children they would never have. She cried until she was hoarse and her throat was sore, sobbing for her beloved missing cousin, for Leo's endangered soul. She raged through her tears at Gerald's murderous betrayals. Feeling as overwhelmed as a helpless child lost among hostile strangers, she wanted someone to help her carry all this, to love her and support her and stand up for her and fight for her. For the first time ever, Daisy admitted to herself, allowed herself the selfish thought, that she desperately, desperately wanted Nate to come back – for *her*.

Eventually, her breathing calmed down and her eyes were red and raw, emptied of tears. Her throat had a ragged, jagged feel and she took a drink from a cold cup of tea she had poured hours earlier. She dabbed her cheeks with her handkerchief, then went into the bathroom attached to her office – an indulgence she had allowed herself, since every other person working on this floor was a man. Splashing cold water on her face, and a little on the back of her neck, she dried her skin and looked at herself in the mirror, straightening her hair. Her make-up was long gone, but she would leave off replacing it for now. Her lilac silk embroidered dress, with its fringe and tassel trim, was a little crumpled, but she had been wearing it for nearly twenty-four hours, so that was to be expected. It would do for a little while longer. Blinking her tired eyes, she let out a long, steady breath as she stared hard at herself.

'All right now, Daisy,' she muttered in a firm voice. 'That's quite enough of that.'

Walking back out into the office, she picked up the book that lay on her desk. It was entitled *Mechanical Biology: An Illustrated Study of the Anatomy of Engimals*. The author was the engineer Gerald admired so much: Isambard Kingdom Brunel. She drew her watch from a small pocket in the folds of her dress. It was half-past four. Many of the servants would be rising now, but none of the family.

'No point going to sleep,' she said aloud, as much to hear how her own voice sounded as any other reason. 'Right then, Gerald. Parts from dead engimals, indeed? Let's see what you've been up to in my church.'

She went to open the door out to the corridor, when she noticed a folded piece of paper lying on the floor. It had obviously been pushed under the door. Opening the door quickly, she peered out. But there was nobody in the corridor. Unfolding the piece of paper, she found four words written in a scrawled handwriting – either the work of someone who was nearly illiterate, or someone who was deliberately trying to disguise their handwriting.

The mines in Glendalough

Daisy chewed her lip. The family did own mines in Glendalough. She had been looking into selling them, after

Gerald had ordered them to be shut down and sealed off. Examining the paper and the handwriting, she sniffed the note and held it up to the light, but could learn no more about it. Did she have a secret ally in the house? She would have to take a ride out to Glendalough as soon as she could. It was a beautiful part of the country – more than enough of an excuse for a visit. Though she wouldn't put it past one of the family to try and lead her out into the mountains for more malevolent reasons. Placing the note in a drawer in her desk, she tucked her book under her arm and left the office.

She didn't see a sign of anyone who might have left the note as she walked through the hallways. The house was chilly and dark as she made her way through it, but the servants were already in evidence, lighting the gas-lamps, preparing breakfast for the staff and clothes for the family members. Shirts and trousers were being pressed, collars and cuffs starched, dresses hung up, make-up and accessories set out, shoes polished. The cleaning had already started too – a small army of maids and footmen dusting, polishing, shining; everything from the silver cutlery to glass in the cupboard doors of the trophy cabinets. For every surface, its own specific treatment, for every item, its proper place. Drawbreaths wandered the rooms and hallways, sucking dirt from the carpets. Spin-feathers hovered around the corners of ceilings, eating cobwebs.

As Daisy found her way outside, the sun's watery light

was starting to soak across the grey sky. She saw the gardeners were leading the lawn-cutters from their pens – the creatures' spinning metal jaws whirred as they prepared to mow the grass. Some of the grooms were already walking horses. In the nearest paddock, she saw Hennessy, the head groom, out riding a grey mare, and waved to him. He tipped his flat cap in salute. On the lane running level with the nearside of the paddock, a man was pushing a barrel of water in a wheelbarrow out to the engimal stables. Kept in a separate building to the horses, the velocycles could be heard growling and chugging, eager for some exercise.

Striding through the gardens, she avoided the road leading out the gate and went across the grass to the fence that ran along the edge of the trees. Her feet were already wet in their shoes from the morning dew as she climbed through the narrow gap with the stile in the fence – no easy task in the dress she was wearing. But from there, it was only a few yards to a path that led her into the family's graveyard. Beyond the cemetery, off down the slope to her left, near the base of the hill, were the train tracks on which the Wildensterns ran their private train. Through the graveyard to the right, the path led to the church, hidden behind the copse of yew trees.

Work on the building was almost complete. The roof was already tiled; they would be taking down the scaffolding once the last of the carved stonework was in place. Stone angels hid the ends of the gutters, the water running between their wings and out of their mouths. The stained-glass windows had been fitted, as had the oak doors. Daisy was not a fan of ostentatious places of worship – for her, God could as easily be found in the humblest turf cabin as any majestic cathedral. But she was proud of the church she had helped build. Its footprint was in the shape of a cross, its pews able to seat a hundred people – though it would be restricted to members of the family and their friends most of the time. This exclusivity, insisted on by Elvira and other women in the family, made Daisy sick, but she was confident that she could wear them down over time, and allow greater access to people living around the estate. She envisioned a day when Protestants and Catholics might even sit in the same church. They were all Christians, after all.

Taking the key from her reticule, she let herself in through the front door and took a lantern from the hook inside the door. She lit it with a match and walked through the inner door, under the balcony where the organ stood and into the nave, the central hall of the church where the congregation would sit. Wandering back and forth across the floor, she savoured the craftsmanship, enjoying her time alone with the place.

The warm light from the lamp picked out the marble pillars that ran down either side, just in from the marble-lined walls, creating aisles either side of where the pews would be. The pillars stretched up to arches that helped support the stone beams of the pitched roof. The floor was paved in a diamond pattern of black, white and peach mosaic. The markings for the aisle in the centre were incorporated into the design. For an absurd moment, Daisy felt as if she were a bride who had, in a surreal nightmare, shown up at her wedding to find the church empty and shrouded in the darkness of storm-clouds. But she did not feel uncomfortable in this building. She had helped design it, had watched it grow, built by honest, hardworking men who enjoyed their work and took pride in it. She would not allow Gerald or the Wildensterns to spoil this place.

The building was still cold, with a clammy feel to it, but that would change over time as it was heated regularly and life began to pass through it. Daisy walked as far as the chancel, the platform on which the altar stood. She turned to look up at the pipe organ on the balcony. The morning light was starting to break in through the stained-glass windows on the left-hand side, sending sprayed fragments of colour across the space. Still the organ was in shadow, light glinting off the lines of columns formed by its brass-coloured alloy pipes and the intricately carved façade that loomed over the keyboards. The casing, like much of the church's woodwork, was oak. The organist's chair was a swivel seat which was bolted to the floor, a feature she thought a trifle odd. There were four keyboards, or manuals, climbing like steps, with the rows of handles for the stops – which controlled the air flow – on either side.

Gerald had told her once that large pipe organs such as this were considered the most complicated man-made devices in the world. He used the word 'considered' because he maintained engimals were man-made, and the simplest engimal was far more complex than anything designed in modern times.

Most organs needed a *calcant*, someone to constantly work the bellows to provide wind for the organ as it was played. Some instruments were now being developed which had their wind provided by steam engine. This organ was entirely different. Gerald would not explain how, but the instrument provided its own air pressure. The architect who had built the church was still confounded as to how this air pressure was achieved. But Daisy had seen some of the engimals Gerald worked with: creatures that could lift enormous weights, turn wheels at amazing speed . . . or blow hot air continuously for hours.

She had noticed before that the organ was never completely silent. There was a bass hum, just at the edge of her hearing, which could be heard in any part of the church, but was most audible while standing on the balcony. It had a gentle swell to it, almost as if the thing was breathing.

Biting her lip, she stared up at the massive, ornate instrument. She walked back towards the door, out into the entrance hall and up the stairs to the balcony. Crossing over to the organ, she ran her fingers over one of the ivory keys of the lowest manual. Somewhere inside this thing lay the parts of dead engimals. But what was it all for? The organ was solidly built, and the door on the right side that led into its innards was securely locked. Only Gerald had a key.

It had occurred to her long ago, of course, that Gerald used music to control the will of other human beings. And if he could walk his cousin off a rooftop just by whistling a lullaby, God only knew what he could achieve with an instrument of this power and complexity. But even a pipe organ of this size could not be heard far beyond the confines of the church. She had heard Gerald testing it. And no member of the Wildenstern family in their right mind would come anywhere near this building if they knew Gerald was within reach of this organ.

The main structure of the building had been built along the same lines as the original church, which had stood for more than three hundred years before Gerald had destroyed it. Most of the granite came from the original stones recovered from the ruins. But Daisy had added some modern features and extra colour. There was under-floor heating, based on a more efficient version of that used by the Romans. The interior was lined with sections of red and yellow sandstone, and tapestries would soon be hung, all to give the whole place a warmer, less austere feel than one found in so many churches. There were gas-lamps to bolster the light of the candles, but only to be used if necessary, for the staining and lead-work on the glass in the windows had been produced by the best craftsmen in Ireland. Daisy wanted this to be a warm, welcoming and beautiful place.

I won't let him ruin this, she promised herself. Whatever he intends to use this organ for, I swear that — on Sunday mornings, at least — it will be nothing but a maker of beautiful music. He can sit here all night long during the week, playing for the owls and the bats and the rats if that's what pleases him, but this is a house of God, and people must be able to come and worship in peace.

Daisy examined the lock on the organ door, wishing she had Tatty's lock-picking skills. Thinking of Tatty made her think of Cathal and she clenched her teeth, a hard flatness coming into her eyes.

'To hell with it,' she said in a voice that sounded louder than she intended in the empty church.

Setting the oil lamp and her engimal biology book on the floor, she strode to the far side of the balcony where the builders kept some of their tools. She searched through the line of wooden shafts leaning against the wall until she found a sledgehammer. Its weight surprised her, and she grunted as she lifted it free from the other tools and carried it back to the door. She hefted it in both hands, trying to figure out how best to swing the heavy steel head against the small door. The door opened inwards, so she settled on simply using the hammer as a battering ram.

Spreading her feet apart to give her a strong stance, she held the sledgehammer in a horizontal position and swung the head against the door, striking it just beside the door-handle. It wasn't a particularly powerful blow, though she heard the crack of wood. The door did not give. She swung again, but had stepped back too far and the second blow almost ran out of power before it hit the door, causing nothing more than a loud knock. Damn it all, this bloody thing was heavy – and with all the weight at one end, it was hard to keep hold of.

She let out a very unladylike growl. Stepping closer to the door, her left foot forward, she swung the hammer right back and drove it as hard as she could into the wooden panel. The solid lump of steel smashed the door open and her grip slipped, letting the hammer-head fly forward through the doorway. She caught the end of the handle with her left hand just as the hammer was falling to the floor. Something flashed down from the ceiling inside the organ, almost invisible as it swept past. Daisy felt something brush the fingertips of her leading hand and flinched back.

The sledgehammer fell, its hardwood handle clattering to the floor, cut cleanly into five pieces of equal length. Daisy felt something wet drip from her left hand and then a pain began to bloom in the fingertips. Holding them up in the dim light, she gasped as she saw the ends of her index and middle fingers had been cut off – over a half an inch of flesh sliced diagonally from each finger, revealing the tips of the bones. Blood poured from them like a pair of dribbling hoses. She cried out, more in shock than pain, for the cuts had been so clean and so quick that her nerves had not fully registered the damage.

A short sob escaped her lips as she hurriedly pulled out her handkerchief and bound up her fingers. The pain was growing steadily – had it become worse after she had *seen* the wounds? Tears welled in her eyes, but she sniffed and clammed up any further cries. She had come here to do something and she meant to see it through. But she felt so stupid; *of course* Gerald would have his precious bloody creation booby-trapped against anyone wishing to poke around inside it. She should have known. It was only pure blind luck and her clumsiness in letting the sledgehammer slip from her grasp that had saved her life. Those had not been blades which cut through the stout ash handle of the hammer – more like wires on some kind of frame, so thin as to be almost invisible. They had sliced through that wood as if it were cheese, and would have done the same to her body. She knew of no wire that strong, and reasoned that it must have been some strands of material pulled from the body of an engimal.

Daisy squeezed the handkerchief tightly round her sharply throbbing fingertips, trying to staunch the bleeding as she peered through the dark doorway, careful not to lean her head too far forward. The scene inside was as disturbing, as surreal, as any nightmare she had ever experienced. She could see now why Gerald had taken up so much of this end of the church. The organ wasn't just sitting on the balcony; it was built into the wall, and its innards disappeared downwards into the floor and upwards into the ceiling. Apart from the pipes one would expect to see, there were engimals built into the complex workings of the organ. And at least some of them were still alive.

She could make out the heads, snake-like necks and shoulders of four drawbreaths on one side, connected by tubes to a line of pipes, presumably contributing to the flow of air. Embedded in an iron framework set into the middle of the floor was what appeared to be a velocycle. The wheel suspended from its back legs had been stripped of its rubbery outer layer and was now being used to run a drivebelt, to power some other part of the machine. The front wheel had been pulled off entirely, the creature's front legs amputated. Its head hung limply over its streamlined chest, but Daisy could see faint plumes of steam from its nostrils. It was alive, but this creature would never race across the Wicklow hills again.

In the cluttered void inside the organ, she saw other creatures, living and dead. There was a spider-fly the size of a hatbox, with wire wound round its legs – part of the booby-trap, perhaps, the rotating legs acting like a high-speed spool. There was also a frog-like creature about the same size, whose wide mouth could spew hot air at high pressures, built into the pipe system like the drawbreaths. Much of the metal and ceramic and other materials used in the construction seemed to have come from the bodies of engimals. Those accordion-shaped valves, which appeared to be made of paper, were in fact constructed with the pliable, wafer-thin forms of leaf-lights.

She was concerned that she might find Siren, Tatty's engimal bird here. It would be just like Gerald to trap the thing in an organ, but there was no sight of the creature.

Daisy's handkerchief was now soaked in blood and she felt sick to her stomach, though she did not know if it was from the sight of the blood, or the loss of so much of it, or the horrific spectacle in front of her or the combination of all of them. She wanted to throw up, but would not allow herself the indulgence of doing it in the church. There could be no doubt about it; Gerald was utterly insane.

'Pardon me, yer Grace?' A man's voice made her start, interrupting her thoughts.

She turned, realizing there was now enough dawn light on the balcony to make the oil lamp on the floor redundant. Hennessy, the head groom, was standing at the top of the stairs. The gentle, nimble-looking middle-aged man had once been involved in a relationship with Daisy's husband – a love affair that had deeply hurt and humiliated her. But their shared love for Berto had given them a bond after his death, and now the man was one of the few members of staff she trusted completely.

'Yes, Hennessy?'

'Pardon mae fer enterruptin', yer Grace, but Mister Gerald has requested yer company in the drawin' rum, ma'am,' he drawled respectfully in his Donegal accent. 'He said et was emperative that everyone come at thar earliest convenience.'

Which was a servant's politest way of saying that Gerald was demanding their presence immediately – or sooner if possible.

Hennessy was diffidently waiting for her reply when he spotted her blood-soaked handkerchief. With an exclamation of alarm, he quickly came forward, pulling his own handkerchief from his pocket. Despite the dirty nature of his profession, it was spotlessly clean and, leaving hers wrapped round her fingers, he tied his coarse square of linen firmly over it.

'Yeh need to hawv a doctor see to this, yer Grace, and quickly. Et'll need stitchin' at the very least. And yev lost quate a bet of blood. Yeh need to get into the hise and lie yerself dine with yer feet raised, lest yeh come over faint. Yeh don't want to make this worse by havin' a fall.'

His movements were gentle and assured, from a lifetime of dealing with injuries associated with keeping and riding horses. She noticed he did not seek her consent before engaging in this forbidden level of contact between a servant and his mistress. He was appalled that she had suffered such an ugly wound, and acted without thinking to help her. Only after he had finished did he realize he had overstepped his bounds, but she smiled at him and held out her uninjured hand to clasp his.

'Thank you, Hennessy,' she said softly. 'You always take such good care of me.'

'In a place like this, ma'am,' he replied awkwardly, his eyes trained on the floor, 'someone has to.'

XVI

AS BRUTAL AND AS DAMAGING AS
ONE WOULD EXPECT

Hardly any of the family rose this early in the morning. It was barely half-past five and Gerald's summons were met with much indignant protest – but they were obeyed nevertheless. There were not enough seats for the nearly forty members of the family present in the house, so more chairs were brought in. Even so, not everyone sat down; outrage is better expressed from a standing position.

Daisy had her decapitated fingers cleaned and dressed properly before turning up, and she was still one of the first there. She was careful to hide the hand from Gerald's sight.

He sat in an armchair, saying nothing as they all filed in. His chair was next to the door which led to the smoking room. The door was closed, and there was something about his posture which stated it would be staying that way until he said otherwise. Elizabeth sat in a chair next to him, looking stately in a beautiful deep purple dress, with her black hair gathered up at the back, tresses hanging down the sides to frame her pale-skinned face. She was holding Gerald's hand in a rather formal, possessive fashion, as a queen might hold her king's to demonstrate her authority. Leo was not there, so she was able to direct the full force of her superior air over the room of relatives.

Gerald was less regal, his blue suit rumpled as if he, like Daisy, had been up all night, and his silver silk cravat was worn a little too loose. He waited until everyone was present, and then interrupted the hubbub of sniping comments by clearing his throat. The Wildensterns fell immediately silent.

'Thank you for coming,' he began, ignoring his mother's snort of derision from the front row. 'I have an announcement to make, and I wanted to make it before you were all drawn away by your day's business. As you know, I have struggled to give the Company the time and attention it requires. Daisy has done her best to compensate, but has been hampered by the unfortunate restrictions of her gender. With this in mind, I have taken the liberty of finding someone to take over some of those responsibilities – an eminently capable man who will answer to me, and me alone.'

'And who is this man, pray tell?' Elvira asked in an imperious tone. 'And how can someone none of us know presume to have any authority in this family's business?'

Gerald gave his mother a faint, polite smile; the warmest expression he could muster for her these days.

'But you *do* know him, Mother, although the two of you have never spoken. Most of you have seen him before, and you all know his sister very well indeed.'

With this, he glanced at Elizabeth, who favoured him with her most gracious smile. There was a chorus of confused grunts and puzzled exclamations. Gerald stood up and stepped over to the door of the smoking room. He opened it with his right hand and stood back, gesturing to the crowd with his left.

'Ladies and gentlemen, I give you . . . Brutus Wildenstern!'

There were gasps of shock and disbelief. Those who had seen Brutus before were aghast at the sight of him now; those who hadn't found it hard to believe that this was the man Gerald claimed him to be.

The man's massive frame filled the doorway. From the styled mane of white-blond hair framing his jutting brow and wide jaw, down the tailored suit to the expensive, made-to-measure shoes on his over-sized feet, Brutus had been groomed to appear as much like a gentleman as possible. Quite a feat, given his rather primitive roots.

Daisy thought he looked remarkably well for a man who had been murdered by religious fanatics, lain buried for six hundred years, only to be resurrected and promptly killed once more by a fall from a window high up on Wildenstern

Hall. She had been sure that Gerald had destroyed the body once and for all, but clearly the temptation to tinker had been too strong. Brutus's resurrection had not been completely successful; his right hand had been amputated not long after the mummified bodies of himself and his brother and sisters had been discovered. Gerald had replaced the hand with a crab-like engimal claw – a claw that had once occupied the same position at the end of Edgar Wildenstern's right arm.

'In any other house,' Daisy muttered to herself, 'this would all be highly improbable.'

Somehow, through the strange science of intelligent particles, Gerald had succeeded in bringing this medieval barbarian back to life once more. Elizabeth looked beside herself with joy – and smug satisfaction. She had been the last of her brood, her elder brother and younger sister having died in a violent power struggle years before. No doubt she saw Brutus's new position as another way to increase her own authority.

But Daisy could not understand how a man who had grown up in a time when America had not even been *discovered* by Europeans could hope to understand the continent where the family made most of its money. How could he hope to grasp even the basics of all the modern business practices necessary for running the North American Trading Company? Especially since, by all accounts – including some from Elizabeth herself – Brutus was more at home swinging an axe on a battlefield than dealing with international economics. Aside from all that, could his brain even work properly after all the punishment it had taken?

'It is good to be back among my family,' a deep, cavernous voice croaked, cutting across her thoughts. Brutus was standing in front of the fireplace, hand and claw clasped behind him. There was a searching look on his face, as if he was struggling to gather his thoughts. 'As you can imagine, my . . . recovery has been a long and trying one. Since regaining consciousness, I have spent my extended convalescence learning all I can about this modern world, and that education shall continue as I take the reins of this mighty enterprise. I have no illusions regarding the scale of my new responsibilities, and I have no doubt that you will all grace me with your various areas of expertise, to assist me in my task.'

He paused, and there was a change in his features that stopped anyone from speaking up before he could continue. It was an expression that was easily recognized in that house – the look of a man who was accustomed to power, and would be ruthless in wielding it.

'Let me conclude by assuring you that I am fully cognizant of the nature of this family's business, of the Rules of Ascension and all that they entail. As I hail from a time when such rules *did not exist*, I shall do my very best to adhere to them. Should any of you attempt to undermine my authority, or defy it by putting those rules into practice, I promise you that my response will be as brutal and as damaging as one would expect from the "barbarian" you all believe me to be.

'So, in the spirit of cooperation, I appeal to your good-will and family loyalty to aid me in any way you can during this transition. We will have time for a more social discussion this evening at dinner, but for now I must immerse myself in my new duties. Thank you for your attention.'

'Golly,' Tatty said from behind Daisy. 'That's certainly throwing the cat among the pigeons.'

Daisy looked back at her sister-in-law and nodded a greeting, but then turned to watch Gerald, Elizabeth and Brutus walking out of the room. As Brutus passed the two young women, he stopped and turned to Daisy. Gerald and Elizabeth hovered, waiting for him.

'Daisy. Gerald tells me that your help in clerical matters has been most useful,' he rumbled slowly, like an idling steam engine. 'You will join me in my office after breakfast, to begin familiarizing me with the details of your activities. You have shown considerable talent as a clerk, and I will have need of that ability in the future. But your interference in business decisions and your "investigations" into Gerald's activities will end today. Your usefulness does not excuse the overstepping of your bounds, my dear.

'We will start our discussion this morning with local

matters; the running of the estates, our transport networks, and I also wish to look into your attempts to sell the mines in Glendalough. I will see you at nine o'clock, in my office.'

'Will you?' she replied in short, bitten words. Her talent as a *clerk*, indeed. The bloody nerve of him! 'And where *is* your office, exactly?'

'On the top floor,' Gerald informed her. 'Edgar's old rooms.'

Daisy levelled a hostile gaze at him. By setting up Brutus in the Patriarch's old abode, Gerald was making a clear statement; Brutus now held the seat of power in the family. Would Gerald be able to maintain control over him if that was the case? Did he even want to? She was seething at the effortless way in which he had swept her from her position, suddenly treating her as if she were some lowly secretary whose only purpose was answering this Neanderthal's demands.

'I believe I know where that is,' Daisy said to Brutus. 'Nine o'clock, then. I will see you there.'

Brutus nodded to her and continued on towards the door, Elizabeth tucking her arm under his. Gerald was about to follow them when his eyes fell on her bandaged fingers, which in her distracted state she had neglected to hide behind her back. They were bound together in the dressing, the tips thickly padded, but blood had already stained the linen once more.

'You've hurt yourself,' he murmured.

Tatty gave a little gasp as she too noticed the injury for the first time.

'Why do you assume I did this to myself?' Daisy snapped back.

'That's not a minor wound, if I'm any judge,' Gerald said evenly, ignoring her question. 'Come down to my laboratory before breakfast, and I'll have a look at it.'

'Never mind my *fingers*, Gerald. I'm not about to let you touch me, let alone make me a guinea pig for your unnatural science. Where's Cathal? What have you done with him? Is he even *alive*?'

Gerald lifted his head to look into her face, a placatory expression in his eyes. She could see now that he still needed her. He did not want to drive her to the point where she felt she had nothing to lose, fearing she might go off and do something reckless and damaging. She showed him the fingers, keeping her voice low so that only Tatty, and none of the other relatives could hear.

'I took a look inside your insane pipe organ, Gerald!' she hissed. 'It nearly cost me my life, but I've seen what you're doing to those engimals. What the hell's it all for? And *where's Cathal*?'

'He's alive and well, at least for now,' he muttered. 'And he'll stay that way if he causes me no more trouble.'

'And how long, exactly, do you expect Cathal to remain obedient?' Tatty demanded. 'Given that he is quite the most contrary creature on the face of the Earth?'

'Come down to the laboratory and let me have a look at your fingers,' Gerald said again to Daisy. 'They could become infected if they are not treated properly. There's no need to be suspicious, I'm only being rational. I need you in full health, Daisy. Brutus needs your help.'

She glared back at him, but the selfish part of her knew Gerald could probably do more to repair her fingers than anyone else in the country. If they became infected, they might have to be amputated. The nerve damage was already affecting her ability to move them properly and she was concerned the disability might be permanent. She was also still vain enough to worry about how disfigured her hand would be.

'I'll come down after I've met with Brutus,' she told him. 'I need some time to gather the relevant papers together.'

He nodded and walked out. Tatty wanted to ask about the damaged hand, and chat about everything else that was going on, but Daisy excused herself and started out into the corridor. It could take all day to outline the workings of the estates and the transport network – all year, if Brutus turned out to be in any way simple-minded, which was a distinct possibility.

He had asked about the mines in Glendalough too, which surprised her, as Gerald had closed them down the previous year with no explanation. He had fired most of the miners and moved the rest, and most of the equipment, off to other sites. It was one of the many times that he had moved workers or resources from one job to another without consulting her, or giving any reason. But the surveyors said there were still rich seams of ore under Camaderry, and since they were sitting there unused, she had set about selling off the mines to make up for some of the money and property Gerald was draining from the Company.

Daisy came to a sudden halt in the corridor, clutching her brow with her uninjured hand.

'Aaaaah . . . oh, you idiot!' she exclaimed.

She had forgotten the note that had been slipped under her door: *The mines in Glendalough.* Of course! Hadn't Leo told her about his trip out to the mountains to see 'Big Uncle' and Gerald's new machines? God, sometimes she felt like a dimwit. She started hurrying towards the elevators as fast as dignity and her skirts would allow. Ringing the bell to summon the mechanical lift, she bounced restlessly on her feet as it descended. The lift took far too long to reach the fifteenth floor, where her office was located. She emerged from the lift, told the boy to wait there for her, ran to her office, unlocked it and rushed inside, taking a large ring of keys from her desk drawer. From there, she took the elevator down to the tenth floor, where the property office was located. None of the staff had shown up for work yet – the office did not open until eight o'clock.

She did not know how long she would be allowed to keep these keys, which could unlock every door on the business floors of Wildenstern Hall. She had to make good use of them now.

Turning a corner in the corridor, she discovered Tatty crouching down at the door of Oliver's office. She was picking the lock. With a gasp, she looked up and saw Daisy. Then she let out a shaky breath.

'Good Lord, you gave me a fright,' she said. 'Thought you might be Oliver.'

'What in God's name are you doing?'

'Poking around,' Tatty replied, as if this were a perfectly satisfactory reply.

'For what? You know Oliver hasn't stolen Siren. Gerald has spirited the thing away to his hidden lair.'

'Of course I know that,' Tatty replied tartly. 'I'm looking for whatever I can find. What are *you* doing here so early in the morning?'

'I'll explain later. Do you want to join me, or would you prefer to carry on with what you're doing?'

Tatty thought about it.

'I can come back and look tomorrow,' she reasoned, and rose to her feet to follow Daisy.

Inside the property office, which occupied nearly half a floor of the building, most of the wall space was taken up with wooden filing cabinets. The family owned a lot of property. Daisy traced her fingers over the labels on the cabinets until she found the one she wanted. Unlocking it, she yanked open the drawer, rifled through the files and pulled one out, holding it up for Tatty to see. She flipped open the cover to make sure she had everything she needed, and took a deep breath.

'Time to start burning some bridges. God forgive me for this sin,' she sighed. She slammed the drawer shut. 'Because Gerald won't.'

XVII

GUNSMOKE IN LIMERICK

It was early evening as Nate and Clancy rode north along the last stretch of road towards the city of Limerick. Nate had driven the horses on at a punishing pace, and the beasts had slowed to a steady walk now, lathered with sweat, their breathing heavy as the buildings rose up on the dimming skyline, shrouded in a thin cloak of smog. They were fine animals, the best that could be had at short notice, but they had reached their limits.

Clancy was showing his exhaustion too. They had covered nearly a hundred miles in two days, much of it on tracks and rough roads, and the aging man had not spent much of his life in the saddle. Even Nate was showing the strain; there had been few opportunities to ride during his travels as he had spent much of his time as a labourer. The lack of practice was telling on him. Their pursuers had been lost from sight for much of the journey, but that afternoon they had appeared again on horseback and were gradually closing the gap.

Nate pushed his glasses up onto the bridge of his nose. As he sweated, the spectacles with their green-tinted lenses kept slipping down his nose every time he dropped his head. He had hoped that these, along with his beard and the cap pulled low over his brow, would prevent people from seeing his face. Even here, miles from anyone who should know him, there was always a chance that someone might recognize him from all the pictures that had appeared in the papers.

With their weary heads hung down, Nate and Clancy did not notice the shape in the sky at first. The round black object passed overhead, flying at a height of about sixty or seventy feet, following the road towards Limerick. The two men looked up in time to see the spider-fly well enough to make out its legs spinning almost silently around the base of its circular body like a propeller. Nate squinted up into the green-tinted sky, letting out a tired sigh.

'Now that's just damned unfair,' he muttered.

They were under no illusions as to what that sight meant. Spider-flies were extremely rare, very valuable, and sightings could not be a common occurrence in the poverty-stricken south-west. Their pursuers were even better resourced than Nate had feared. Unable to catch up with their quarries, the bounty hunters had used the flying engimal to leapfrog them, sending the creature ahead with news of their impending arrival. Somebody in Limerick would soon receive the message and would no doubt set about preparing a welcome.

'Damned unfair,' Nate said again.

Clancy did not reply. His eyes were fixed on the smoggy skyline, as if trying to gauge where the threat might show itself. They were due to meet a man on George's Street in the centre of the city, where they would hand over the horses and find lodgings for the night. But it was still a few miles into town. There was nothing for it but to keep their appointment. Both men checked the weapons they wore as they rode, and reached into their packs to supplement them. Two pistols instead of one, plus a small four-shot pepperbox revolver each, tucked into the boot, a knife slid into the belt.

This route did not show Limerick's best aspect. The railway line to Cork ran alongside the road, and beyond it, off to their left, they could see a large factory and, further west, the forbidding walls of a military barracks. On their way in along the road, the usual scattering of farm labourer's cabins gave way, as they approached town, to larger, squarer brick and stone houses. The uneven mud road became more level and urban, turning away from the railway line but leading them through an area of goods yards and warehouses. The sounds of steam engines could be heard, a train's whistle and the hard metallic sounds of men at work in the trainyard. The acrid taint of smoke hung in the air and blurred distant buildings with its haze. Soon, the road was starting to look more like a street, lined with some houses on either side, and then a school.

Clancy's face lifted a little as they made their way further and further into his home town. He had been taken from this place when he was still a young boy, and raised in Wildenstern Hall to be one of the loyal and multi-skilled personal servants to that family – it had been over a decade since he'd passed through here. Most of his family was dead or had emigrated. He wouldn't recognize the younger ones now. But there was still a part of his heart that recognized this place as home.

Nate realized that he and his loyal manservant had far more in common than they once did. Not for the first time, he wondered why Clancy had never married or had children of his own. Perhaps life with the Wildensterns had put him off the idea. Having children left you exposed – made you vulnerable. They could be used against you. Unless you were Edgar Wildenstern, and you didn't give a damn about them. Or you were *his* son Nathaniel, and you simply deserted them by running to the far side of the world.

'We're just passing the county gaol, sir,' Clancy said. 'You can see it there next to the lunatic asylum over on your right-hand side. Not too far at all now, sir.'

Nate nodded, but his nerves were on edge. He pushed

his glasses up onto the bridge of his nose and started whistling to himself. It was getting dark now, and there weren't many streetlamps in this area. There was another barracks further up the road, and all these high walls and fences, coupled with the network of narrow streets ahead, looked like dangerous ground to him. Holding the reins with one hand, he kept the other under his jacket, resting on the butt of one of his Colt 44 revolvers. There were children playing on the road nearby, grimy little bare-footed scuts in short trousers and ill-fitting caps, shouting raucously and chasing each other round. From an open doorway off to one side, he heard someone playing a harmonica. There was a group of women in shabby dresses with shawls over their shoulders, exchanging gossip on one side of the street. An older couple walked down towards them on the opposite side.

Nate and Clancy surveyed the rooftops, checking windows and corners. Surely, they thought, no one would make a move this close to a British Army barracks? Unless the army itself was involved. Gerald could certainly wield that kind of influence. After all, hadn't he sent a ship of the British Navy to find Nate in America? If the army were involved, they would be visible on the streets, but Nate's instincts, honed from years of living in Wildenstern Hall, had the hairs on the back of his neck standing on end. He tried to relax the tension tightening up his body, but he could almost hear his heart thumping against his lungs.

Four men strode out from an alleyway, walking at right angles to Nate and Clancy's path some twenty yards ahead. They were led by a middle-aged cove with squinting eyes and a wide, Slavic-looking face ridged with wrinkles. Dressed in a long tan-coloured duster coat and a wide-brimmed fur-felt American cowboy hat, he looked damned odd on that Limerick street. He was playing a mournful tune on a harmonica he held to his mouth with cupped hands.

The four men came to a halt so that they were evenly spaced across the roadway, blocking the way. The man took the mouth organ away from his face and gave a grim smile, then slipped it into his pocket. The two riders reined in their horses, waiting for what came next.

Nate looked to his right and saw that Clancy had taken off his hat and was using it to cover the pistol he had drawn from its shoulder holster. The men in front of them were all armed – Nate could tell by the shapes under their jackets – but had not drawn their weapons. He kept his hand on the butt of the '44, but did not pull it out yet. He glanced behind him, and saw that three more men had stepped out onto the street about thirty yards back. All seven men looked like proper hard cases.

The women standing on the side of the road were frantically calling the children in off the street. Some of the little brats were reluctant to go, but their mothers' shrieks broke their will and brought them running. Shouts of alarm went up and onlookers sought cover wherever they could find it. Nate and Clancy still did not move. Off in the distance, the whistle of a train blew again.

'Do I have the pleasure of addressing Nathaniel Wildenstern?' the cowboy asked, speaking with a mid-western American accent.

'That's *his Grace, the Duke of Leinster* to you,' Clancy growled. 'As well you know it, or you wouldn't ask. What do you mean by blocking our path?'

'His Grace is wannet for murder, both here and back Stateside,' the American replied. 'Me an' ma boys are here to bring him in.'

'You've been had, you Yankee idiot,' Clancy told him. 'He's committed no murder. It's his family who want him – and they've got you running round as their errand boys. What authority do you have here to—'

'Let's not bother with the formalities,' Nate interrupted him, loud enough for the men behind to hear. He pulled off his glasses and lifted the peak of his cap so they could get a look at his face, and so that he could get a better view of the roofs around him. 'Clearly, we are none of us concerned with keeping up appearances. Move aside, or do what you've come to do – but either way, stop wasting my bloody time.'

All four men in front whipped their jackets back and drew pistols. The one furthest to the right was spun on the spot, dropping his weapon as Clancy's first shot took him in the shoulder. Nate drew both his Colts, turned sideways on the horse, arms raised, one to the front, one to the rear. He fired two shots from each gun. The shots to the front missed, but sent two men diving to the ground, while one of the shots to the rear hit a man in the stomach. A bullet buzzed past his ear and another came close enough to pluck at his saddlebag. Nate steered the horse round with his knees, intent on pointing it towards the alleyway, hoping to get clear of the street. He swivelled his body again, firing another pair of shots behind, then bringing both guns round to the front, loosing two more shots into the men there and hitting one more in the chest. A third was lying dead in the mud, one of Clancy's rounds buried in his head.

Clancy had turned to charge his horse back at the men behind them. Three gunshots in quick succession struck his horse and killed it outright, the animal toppling forwards and to the side. Clancy couldn't get his feet out of the stirrups in time, and he let out a cry as he went down with it, his left leg trapped beneath it. Nate had one shot left in each pistol. There was one attacker still standing in front of them, another two behind, and he could see another man on the gabled roof of a shed on one side of the alleyway, aiming down at the street with a rifle.

Nate was caught in the open.

Pulling his feet from the stirrups, he was about to slide out of the saddle and put the horse between himself and two of the men, when a rope whipped down out of nowhere, looping over his head. Before he could react, a noose jerked tight around his neck. Dropping the revolver in his left hand, he got his fingers in under the rope just as it constricted his breathing, but he was wrenched off the horse's back. He hit the ground hard, the impact badly jolting his left shoulder and ribs and knocking the last of his breath out of him. The noose closed with crushing pressure around his throat as he was dragged across the road.

Looking up, he saw the rope extending up into the sky, attached to the base of the spider-fly they had seen earlier. The thing had obviously been trained to hunt. Nate scrabbled with his legs, trying to dig his heels in and hold himself still, but he couldn't get a grip. Even with his left hand trying to pull the rope away from his throat, the pressure in his head was almost unbearable and his vision was blurring. Spider-flies were quick and maneuverable, but they weren't powerful. It couldn't lift him off the ground. Dragging him along like this was probably taking all its strength. He had one shot left in his remaining pistol. One shot.

Taking a bead on the small dark shape in the sky, he pulled the trigger. He missed. Bloody hell. *Bloody hell!* He was starting to black out. The gun fell from his limp fingers. A bullet smacked off the ground beside him, and then another hit the wall near his head as he was dragged into the alleyway. Someone was still shooting at him. There was a cart with a broken wheel in the alley and he jammed his foot into the spokes, pulling the engimal up short. Now the pressure around his neck was unbearable, but Nate was able to brace himself, grab the rope over his head and pull hard on it, relieving the pressure. He struggled to get the noose off his neck. Two men were running down the alley towards him. The spider-fly jerked on the rope, nearly pulling it out of his hand. Nate was choking now, barely conscious. He didn't have the strength to fight the creature . . .

The snake-like thing inside him writhed and shivered, making him feel sick, but then his head cleared and the strength came back into his arms. Reefing the rope down, he looped the slack around one of the broken spokes of the wheel. The release in tension let him work the noose loose and pull it over his head. The spider-fly was desperately trying to get away, but was now tied to the broken cart. Nate couldn't take the chance of it attacking him again. He drew the pepperbox revolver tucked into his boot and fired two shots at the creature. They hit it dead centre and it let out a horrible screech, wobbling in the air and then crashing down onto the slates of the roof over Nate's head and tumbling into the alleyway. It lay on the ground, twitching weakly and making a metallic gurgling sound.

Nate felt something like a white-hot poker plunge through his left shoulder and he was knocked to the ground again. On the roof above him, the man with the rifle was lining up for a final shot. Nate put a bullet through his neck with the pepperbox and the man fell flailing from the roof.

His body hit with a bone-breaking thud and he lay still beside the crippled spider-fly.

A foot stamped on Nate's gun-hand, making him cry out. The foot kicked his gun away across the alley and then jammed its boot-heel into the bullet-wound in his shoulder. Nate screamed out, and in a moment of weakness he opened himself up to the thing inside him. Just the slightest release of his hold over it – just the tiniest loosening of the mental grip that held it in check. In seconds, it soaked up the pain, surging power through him. He grabbed the booted foot with his right hand and slammed the heel of his left hand in just below the man's knee. The man let out a cry of pain as his kneecap dislodged and he fell, but his other foot caught Nate across the head. Nate recovered quickly, rising up on his knees to go for a ground-hold . . . and then the twin barrels of a sawn-off shotgun levelled at his face. The man with the ridged face and the squinting eyes stared up at him.

'There's better money for you alive,' he rasped, his face pale with pain. 'But I'm willin' to forego the bonus for the sake of convenience. Git yourself face down on that there ground, your *Grace*, or I let you have both barrels.'

Nate took a deep breath, staring intensely at the American. He was in a fighting rage now, liable to try for that gun for the sheer hell of it. But a shotgun blast at this range would destroy most of his head. And with the spread of shot from that short barrel, the man didn't have to be very accurate to score a hit. Nate breathed out slowly and backed away, keeping his eyes on his enemy.

'Face down. I won't tell you again. I don't need your head. There are other parts can be used to identify you if needs be.'

Nate lay face down on the ground. He wondered where Clancy was – the fact that he was not here did not bode well, and Nate didn't want to think about why Clancy wasn't here. The billowing rush of emotion and energy that was flowing out of the engimal coiled in his gut was threatening to overwhelm him. He should never have loosened his control over it. He felt a panic-inducing fear that had nothing to do with the shotgun pointed at his head. The creature was trying to seize another chance to turn the tables on him – to take over his mind again. He couldn't let that happen. Better that he die in a shotgun blast than let that happen.

Then the cocking of hammers on pistols and rifles clacked from either end of the alley.

'Drop the gun, Harmonica,' a familiar voice called out, though it was not Clancy's. 'Wildenstern's going to be walking out of here and you're going to let him. There's no need for you to die to make it happen – but there's no real reason for you to live either.'

There were men at both ends of the alley, all with weapons aimed at Nate and his attacker. The American hesitated, a low snarl escaping his lips. One of the other men came forward, a dark-skinned man with black hair and a black beard. He looked more Mediterranean or Arabic than Irish. Perhaps one of those black Irish from the west, who had Spanish blood in their veins. In the drab middle-class clothes and with the new beard and his longer hair, Nate might not have recognized the man if not for his voice. Lieutenant William Dempsey, formerly of the British Navy. Cathal Dempsey's father.

'There are soldiers on their way down the street,' he said to the American, who was putting on a defiant air, his gun still levelled at Nate's head. 'Somebody must have told them to turn a blind eye, but you've caused a right commotion with your little Wild West show, Harmonica, so even they couldn't ignore it. Somehow, I don't think you want to run into them any more than we do.'

That was enough for the American. He picked himself up, grabbed his hat off the ground where it had fallen, and limped on his injured knee to the end of the alley. He disappeared from sight round the corner, and then Dempsey and another man helped Nate to his feet. Nate had his eyes closed and was taking deep breaths, his mind entirely focused on subduing the will of the serpentine engimal coiled within his gut. Slowly, ever so slowly, it settled down and Nate felt his head begin to clear.

'Come on, you,' Dempsey muttered. 'We've a train to catch.'

XVIII

TO IMPOSE ONE'S WILL

Daisy sat on a stool in Gerald's old laboratory, holding her breath as he unwound the bandage that held the dressing in place on her injured fingers. She let out a tiny gasp as she saw them again. The engimal wire had cut in a clean diagonal line across her index and middle fingers, slicing through the flesh to the tip of the bone. The wounds had already started to bleed again as the dressing came off.

'Have you any sensation in the fingers?' Gerald asked.

'Pain,' she replied shortly. 'And it's getting steadily worse.'

'That's better than nothing at all, believe me,' he said. 'You won't be playing the piano again for a while, but I think I can clean the wounds up a bit. Beyond that, you have a choice.'

He gazed at her with a disturbing intensity, as if

231

weighing her up. But his manner was gentle and he handled her injury with a professional tenderness.

'You have been living among us long enough to know we have extraordinary powers of healing. You have no doubt about this, do you?'

'No,' she said quietly. 'Why do you ask that?'

'Because with the tips of your fingers in this state,' he said, 'I can do one of two things. I can trim back the ends of the bones and sew flaps of skin across the tops of the fingers. The wounds will seal up, but you will be left disfigured. Your fingers will never look normal or work properly again. And there will still be a risk of infection, and the subsequent need for amputation, if the wounds do not heal properly.'

'I see. And the alternative?'

'I can inject you with some of my blood,' Gerald told her. 'I leave the wounds open, dress them, and let the intelligent particles in the blood do their work. You would have a chance of regaining the full use of your hand, and possibly even regrowing the ends of your fingers. You know enough about us – about me – to know that this is no idle boast.'

Daisy looked away. She believed that these intelligent particles in the Wildenstern blood could do everything Gerald claimed. She had seen the evidence. The question was whether his strange science would work on *her* body, and if so, what other effects it might have. A memory of a man falling to his death from the roof of Wildenstern Hall flashed into her mind – a man who had walked up there because he had listened to a lullaby.

Gerald gestured to her to hold the hand up above her heart to slow the bleeding. The pain in her fingers felt like a mixture of sharpness and pressure, as if someone was crushing the missing ends in a vice with needles in its jaws, and she could still feel it at the end of her fingers. The fingers were stiff and useless and ugly. Something caught in her throat as she said:

'Do it. Give me your blood.'

It was done with little ceremony. Gerald took a clean syringe, found a vein in his arm, inserted the needle and drew out enough to fill half of the syringe. He drew the needle out. Once it was removed, his arm did not bleed any further. He changed the needle on the syringe.

'I've heard that people have different kinds of blood, and that they cannot be mixed,' she said in a faltering voice. 'That to give someone the wrong blood can be fatal.'

'There is truth to that,' he said. 'But this is not *normal* blood. You will remember how I used some from Elizabeth's brother to save Clancy's life years ago. He was at death's door with a crossbow bolt through his chest, and he made a full recovery. The trick is in the mind.'

'I don't understand.'

Gerald rolled up her sleeve a little to keep it out of his way, then found a vein on the back of her injured hand and rubbed it with some alcohol. He inserted the needle and slowly pressed the plunger on the syringe, injecting the contents into her bloodstream.

'For centuries, the Wildensterns have believed in their innate healing ability. They often associated it with gold, for they found that if they applied gold to an injury, it healed faster. You know how this family loves its gold. The same was true, to a lesser extent, with other precious metals. You will no doubt have noticed how much gold Gideon and his wife and sons wear. They think it lengthens their lives and gives them better health – and then they eat like pigs and indulge like fools in all manner of damaging habits.

'I discovered some time ago that the healing effects of gold are nothing but an ignorant superstition.' Gerald did up the dressing on her fingers and tied it off with just the right degree of tightness. 'What matters is the intelligent particles and the link we create between them and our conscious minds. They respond to our intentions – our thoughts. To a point, they obey *orders*. The particles can float there, thinly scattered through our systems, asleep for all intents and purposes. They have to be willed into action. The gold worked because the Wildensterns of the past – and others with *aurea sanitas* – believed it would work. They, in essence, *commanded* their bodies to heal, even though they didn't know how it worked. Their belief in the gold was a crude, but effective link.

'Now you must do the same. You now have *aurea sanitas*

in your blood. This is not a superstition, or some kind of witchcraft, or even some hereditary gift. You do not need gold or any other mystical material. You have intelligent particles in your body – you must focus your will on healing your fingers, and they *will* heal. Do you understand now?'

Daisy hesitated, and then nodded. Gerald took her un-injured hand and squeezed it. She felt great strength in his grip, but he did not use it. His gaze had the hypnotic grip of a snake's; the pupils of his eyes looked huge.

'You have to believe what I'm telling you, Daisy,' he insisted. 'There must be no doubt in your mind. Whatever your opinions of me, you know I am in earnest about how science will change all of our lives. If there is anything that gives my life meaning, it is that. You have to believe that you can impose your will on these particles and command them to heal your body.'

'I believe,' she said. 'I do, I believe what you tell me, Gerald. I may despise you to the core and think you are on a path that could lead to your own death and the deaths of all those around you, but I believe you know more about these things than anyone else alive.' She clasped her bandaged fingers tenderly in her undamaged hand. 'It's the small matter of what, in your merciless reasoning – or your raving insanity, whichever prevails – you will ultimately do with that knowledge that chills my blood.'

'Try to enjoy that sweet mystery, as I enjoy the challenge

of keeping you in the dark,' Gerald said with a smile as he checked her dressing one more time. 'The answer eludes you for now but, given time, I'll sure you'll put your finger on it.'

The only way Cathal had to judge time during the day was by the shift changes of the guards, and by the meal times. Otherwise, there was just the work. The other children were all much younger than him, the oldest aged around thirteen. They had all been here for some time, though nobody was quite sure how long – weeks, certainly, probably months. Time became blurred here in the noise of the machines, the grey haze of dust from the massively heavy rollers, the smell of torn, ground metal and crushed ceramic. The children's senses had become dulled, as had their minds. It was what happened, Cathal guessed, when you worked in a slaughterhouse. The mind closed down to protect itself.

But it wasn't cattle or pigs that were being killed and dis-membered here; instead, the carcasses of engimals passed across Cathal's workbench. The smaller ones were handed to Cathal by the boy beside him. The larger ones were lifted from one bench to the next by a crane that could reach almost across the ballroom-sized cavern. There were thirty children, some working in teams of three or four, others sat or standing alone at a bench. Each bench was assigned a role – a part to be removed from each engimal carcass. Cathal had been tasked with removing the creatures' brains.

The children did not do the slaughtering. There was a team of three men who took care of that, working in a smaller chamber off to one side of the cavern. Killing an engimal without causing it enormous damage was not all that easy. They came in so many shapes and sizes that there was no single clean method that worked for all of them. Some could be dispatched with a hammer, others could be shot, but some had to be beheaded or worse. Every now and then, a creature was brought forth which had the executioners standing around looking at it and scratching their heads.

Gerald's orders were explicit. Each engimal had to be killed with as little damage as possible. Then the engimal's body was passed across the benches, dismantled piece by piece. The parts would be separated and categorized, and Gerald would examine each bit to see what could be used and what could be discarded. Every now and then, there would be some engimal that he insisted on dissecting while it was still alive, but he did these on his own. There were others that he kept alive while he took them apart and rebuilt them for his own purposes.

Some of the engimal parts could be reshaped to perform new functions, and this was done in the furnace, or using one of the steam presses. Anything that could not be used was emptied into the grinder, with its three sets of massive iron rollers. Anything that went in one end of the grinder came out as powder or liquid at the other end. A near-constant cloud of dust rose out of its workings. This was the noisiest, most overwhelming part of this macabre factory.

Cathal was still new enough to the Engimal Works to feel thoroughly sick every time he thought about what they were doing. He supposed that this was how meat ended up on his dinner table every night, rendered from the corpses of animals; but distasteful as this was, he could accept that human beings would always eat meat, and it had to be got somehow. Farm animals lived a protected life and bore their young before being slaughtered. He could not accept what was being done to these engimals.

Engimals did not breed. There was a finite number of them, and that number was dwindling over time. Cathal did not believe, as some did, that each one was a unique and immortal creation of God. Charles Darwin's (and Gerald's) theory was the creatures had been created thousands of years ago, by some unknown civilization. There were no new engimals being born, or being made. Each one that died meant a permanent loss to the world. This was why they were so valuable.

Each engimal was a beautiful, strange, unique mystery – and Gerald was slaughtering them on an industrial scale. Cathal could only guess at what kind of money it must be costing. According to some of the older children, thousands of engimals had passed through the works. Cathal had heard once that there were estimated to be just a few million on the entire planet, and most of those were in captivity. How many did Gerald intend to destroy?

One of these creatures had saved Cathal's life, years ago. An old woman had come to him when he was dying of tuberculosis and laid a serpentine on his chest. The snake-like engimal had injected something into him . . . and then sang to him. Cathal had not merely recovered; he had become healthier than before – stronger, more agile. Gerald later told him that it had injected a high concentration of the intelligent particles into his bloodstream and the song had been some form of instruction to them. Nathaniel had taken the creature before he left, but Cathal suspected that Gerald had a piece of the thing hidden somewhere. Gerald was convinced that something about that serpentine could unlock untold secrets, if only someone could find a way to communicate with it.

Cathal stared at the self-propelling wheelbarrow that sat on his workbench. It was hard to tell where the brain was in some of these creatures. The wheelbarrow was roughly cube-shaped, but with rounded corners. Unlike ordinary wheelbarrows, it had a lid and four wheels. The two large wheels on the front and the smaller wheels that steered at the back had already been removed. The eyes were on the corners at the front, just under the slightly domed lid, but as Cathal had learned, the brain was not always to be found near the eyes – unlike most of Mother Nature's creations. He had decided to obey Gerald's commands for now – at least for as long as it took him to figure this place out and how to escape from it, and hopefully bring all these poor urchins with him.

He jammed a chisel into a seam between the edge of the barrow and the front and hammered it in, trying to prise out the front panel and see what was behind it. Whoever had built these things, they had built them well. They were devilishly difficult to take apart.

Probably because they're not *meant* to be, Cathal thought miserably.

'Sometimes dere's a wire coming out of deh back of dee eye,' a boy's voice said. 'If yeh take out dee eye and follow deh wire, it can lead yeh to deh brain.'

The boy's name was Pip, or at least that was what everyone called him, and he was standing at the bench beside Cathal. Pip was responsible for removing the eyes from the bodies. He was a worn-out, thin-looking boy with pale skin and shadows under his own large blue eyes. He had a nervous, twitchy energy and a smile that kept coming and going, as if there was a happy thought in his head, but he only got a view of it from time to time.

'Thanks,' Cathal replied. 'Here, Pip; you were workin' on the brains when I got here, weren't you?'

'Yes sir, Mister Dempsey. Mister Gordon says I've got a bit of a knack. But since you got here, tings've been changin'. I hears you're a sort of a doctor like him, so's there's no point me doin' brains while you're here.'

'I'm not a doctor,' Cathal said, rubbing his hand through his ginger hair and over his tired face. 'And you don't have to call me Mister Dempsey. I'm not a whole lot older than you. How old *are* you?'

'Dunno.' Pip shrugged. 'Eleven? Twelve, maybe? I was only in dee orphanage a few years before Mister Gordon moved us here. And dey didn't know what age I was when I got dere. Now we're here, and we don't even know when it's day or night. We could be here years for all we know.'

'Pip, has anyone tried to get out o' here?' Cathal asked, lowering his voice.

''Course, Mister Dempsey,' Pip replied, turning his eyes away, suddenly intent on his own work again. 'First ting a bunch of us did when we got here and saw what we was to do. Queg and me an' a few others made a break for it, but dere was no gettin' past Moby.'

Cathal had heard this name mentioned before, but still didn't know who Moby was.

'Who's Moby? One of the guards?'

'No.' Pip shook his head, surprised at Cathal's ignorance. 'Moby's deh door to deh mine.'

'The door has a *name*?'

'Dat's wha' Red and Mister Gordon call it. It's not your normal hang-on-a-frame door. Didn't you not see it comin' in?'

'No, I was unconscious.'

241

'Well, it's like, I dunno . . . like a big mout' fillin' up deh tunnel and dere's dese pipes or snakey tings attached to it, but we don't know what dey do. Queg says he reckons it's a bit from some huge sea engimal. Like deh jaws of it or sometin' like dat. Anyway, we couldn't get tru when we made a break for it, and Queg caught the sharp end. Red said 'e was goin' to make an example of 'im and broke Queg's arm over his knee, jus' like dat. Mister Gordon wasn't happy about dat – it meant Queg couldn't work so good.'

Cathal looked over at Red, who stood watching the children on the far side of the room. Apart from the slaughterers, there were never less than six armed guards in the cavern at any time. Red supervised them and he didn't take chances. Nor did he tolerate any slacking off. Any child caught working too slowly was threatened or punished with a beating. The orphans lived in a constant state of fear. Time and again, Cathal had wondered why Gerald was using children for this work.

Pip had spotted one of the guards looking over at them, and concentrated on his work again. The dream-catcher on his bench was a battered specimen. Shaped like a large dark metallic blue spider, it was missing three of its foot-long legs. Several of its dead clustered eyes were milky yellow and blind, instead of the usual turquoise. Cathal recognized it as one of the creatures that had come from the Wildensterns' zoological gardens. These things could put humans into a trance-like state; they triggered visions in the person's mind and somehow fed on the brain activity that these visions caused. It was normally a pleasurable sensation for the dreamer, and people had been known to become addicted to them. But Cathal remembered that this one had been damaged, and could only induce nightmares.

Cathal wondered if it could ever have contrived the nightmarish scene around him. Pip grunted as he pulled out a cluster of the dream-catcher's eyes, cut the cord attached to the back of them with a pair of pliers, and set them aside. Cathal looked at the expressions of the other children around him. They were numbed, insensitive. The fear of the guards and the brutality of the work had deadened their emotions.

'Pip,' Cathal called over in a low voice. 'How do Gerald and Red get Moby to open up?'

Pip glanced anxiously up at the nearest guard, to see if they were being observed. With the noise of the machines, there was no real danger of being heard.

'Red's got a ting like a whistle – only it doesn't make any noise when he blows it. Makes no sense, but dat's what they use to get out. I don't tink Gerald needs it to pass through, but for deh rest of us, dere's no gettin' past Moby widout dat whistle.'

Red was speaking to one of the guards; he pointed over at Cathal. Pip pressed his lips tightly together and stared hard at his work. The guard, a heavy-set brute with a head of stubble and a knobbly face, made his way over to Cathal, and then past him to Pip.

'Come on, you,' the man said. 'Your turn to be bled.'

Pip nodded and started putting his tools back in the wooden box on one end of the bench. The man didn't wait, confident that the young boy would obey without question. Cathal had been wondering about this too – the samples of blood that Gerald was routinely taking from the children. Cathal had yet to hear an explanation, and the children simply accepted it as just another part of their ordeal. As he was walking past Cathal, Pip paused and acted as if he was picking something out of the sole of his bare foot. He tipped his head in Red's direction.

'Watch out for dat fella, Mister Dempsey, he's got it in fer you. He'll make you pay for dat scar.'

'What do you mean?' Cathal asked, frowning, but careful not to look up at the boy.

'Deh scar on his mug,' Pip muttered, meaning the weal that cut diagonally across Red's face. 'He's fierce upset abou' you ruining his "good looks".'

'You've got it wrong, Pip. I didn't give him that scar.'

'Aw no, *of course* not.' Pip stopped and looked back at him with a sly expression. 'Sorry, I mean everybody knows . . . sure, wasn't it the *Highwayboy* who gave him dat mark?'

And with that, he turned away and hurried off towards Gerald's laboratory.

XIX

'DO NOT WASTE YOUR TEARS'

The bullet wound in Nate's shoulder ached horribly, and it itched so badly he wanted to dig his fingers into it, but even scratching it would risk re-opening the wound. The itching was a familiar sensation, one that told him the wound would be nothing more than a scar in a few days. Clancy had not been so lucky. One shot had taken him in the side and another through his arm. His left leg had been broken in the fall from the horse. Gerald had once treated the manservant with an injection of Wildenstern blood for a near-fatal injury, and his ability to heal was much improved, but it was not on a level with Nate's. He could have little active part to play from now on.

Nate listened to the click-clack of the train's wheels beneath him, soothed by the sound and the speed with which they were travelling towards Dublin on the Great

Southern and Western line from Limerick. Clancy was lying on the seat across from him, shifting painfully in an exhausted sleep, his arm in a sling and his leg bandaged with splints. Lying on his back, the old man snored like water draining out of an enormous sink. Nate smiled and looked out the window at the darkness beginning to fall over the flat, open landscape of fields and hedges flowing past. Travelling by train was a risk, as it made them easier to find, but now they were not alone.

Dempsey had returned to Ireland after jumping ship in Boston. He had joined up with the Irish Republican Brotherhood in the south of the country, having arranged with Clancy to meet up in Limerick. The Fenian rebels had welcomed Dempsey with open arms – a British-trained military man was a valuable ally in their struggle. And though his hatred was more for the Wildensterns than for the British, the rebels were willing to overlook this character defect in return for the training he could provide.

Nate had mixed feelings about trusting these men – they were a wayward, motley bunch, but Dempsey had chosen a competent gang and seemed to have imposed a military discipline. And Nate had faith in the man's vendetta against the family, if not in the man himself.

Having just finished looking through the box of his mother's effects, Nate was dismayed to find they provided few answers, although there was one connection he had not expected. Some of the letters were addressed to a man named Eamon Duffy. Nate knew a man of that name; he was one of the leading figures in the Irish nationalist movement. A Fenian rebel like the men Dempsey had joined, Duffy was a highly resourceful and formidable character.

But these letters were all dated between February and March, 1846, the period Nate was reading about in his father's journals, nearly twenty years ago – when Duffy would have been a young man in his twenties or early thirties. Could it really have been the same man? At first, Nate wondered if he would discover evidence of an affair – Duffy was not the kind of man his mother would normally have come into contact with. But these were not love-letters; they were civil but businesslike and discussed the plight of the poor, the shortage of food in different areas, the price of seed and grain. Hardly the kind of thing one might expect in a secret romantic correspondence.

The section of the newspaper was from a publication entitled *The Nation*, which Clancy had told him was a nationalist paper from the forties. There was an article in it about the Wildensterns' humanitarian campaign to combat the famine, providing American grain to feed the starving, and the seeds of turnips, carrots and other winter vegetables to replace the seed crops lost to the blight. Other land-owners were urged to follow the Duke of Leinster's example. Nate had a quizzical expression on his face as he read this, for there had been nothing in his father's journals about any humanitarian campaign, and he would have been surprised to find it.

He was still puzzled by the silver flask of *poitín*. It was not his mother's type of drink.

At the bottom of the box was a letter addressed to his father, and Nate read this with a dull pain in his chest. It was dated April of the same year – the month Tatiana was born. There was a hint of a smile as he thought of his sister, but then a pang of regret that he had missed the birth of his own son. He had missed his son's whole life so far. Given the terrible potential Nate carried, perhaps it would be best if he stayed out of it altogether.

The letter was unfinished, and Nate wondered why his mother had not completed it or, if it was not to be sent, why she had kept it. But this was a letter that had been written to a lover and Nate found it uncomfortable to read it now:

My dearest Edgar,

I write this with a heavy heart, but with the hope that we might still recapture the love and devotion that, I am certain, we still feel for one another. I don't know if I will ever find it within myself to forgive you for what you did that night two weeks ago. I have always known that you were raised in an environment that brutalized you and encouraged the most predatory and ruthless instincts within you, and I have spent my entire married life struggling to come to terms with the conflicting sides of your character – the implacable leader of men that is your public face, and the tender, loyal and loving husband that so few people see.

I long ago chose not to involve myself in the family's business, and I have suffered terrible trials of conscience as I have watched this family grind the common people under its heel. I have tried to tell myself that I am just a woman, and that my first duty is to my husband and to my family and nothing should dilute that loyalty in any way, especially with the birth of our beautiful new daughter.

But looking into Tatiana's sweet, innocent face, I find myself desperately ashamed, and determined that she will not grow up in a home full of brutes and scoundrels. I can no longer condone your callousness, and your lack of action, as the people of our country endure the torturous drawn-out death that is starvation. My beloved Edgar, I once promised my heart to you, and it will ever be yours, but the murderous violence I witnessed that night made me realize that part of you, at least, is the monster people believe you to be. And I wonder if my heart is lost for ever to the evil greed that passes down to each man in your family. I write this now, before I leave, in the hope that I might still return, and

And there it stopped, incomplete. Nate gazed at it for some time, pondering its contents. It was a strange thing to think anyone would describe his father as 'tender, loyal and loving', but he could vaguely remember his mother and father speaking in tones they did not use with anyone else.

And everyone in the family had said that Edgar Wildenstern did truly love his wife.

Nate looked at the date again, took out his father's journal, and flicked through the pages, trying to find something that might explain what event had finally driven his mother to such desperation that she was willing to leave her husband. She might have turned a blind eye to the family's business methods for the sake of her marriage, but she must have been aware of some of the tyranny with which the estates were ruled, and certainly knew about the Rules of Ascension and all that they entailed. For all her apparent principles, she must have been either naïve or wilfully obtuse to be ignorant of the family's ways. So what had finally turned her head?

It did not take him long to find it. The entry was dated the 26th of March 1846, not long before her letter would have been written:

As I feared, my dear Miriam has been taken in by the worst kind of balderdash being spread about by the rabble-rousers who hope to use the present difficulties to sow seeds of dissent among the peasants. I had for some time noticed that she was engaged in a project that was not producing broken pots, brown bones or useless engimal parts. Concerned that she might be becoming involved in matters that were beyond her female capacities, I placed her under the surveillance of some of my investigators. They followed her whenever she left the house, recorded any meetings she had and examined the contents of any letters sent to her. It is just as well that I took such precautions, for my men discovered a thoroughly unwholesome association forming with a young Catholic named Eamon Duffy.

Nate frowned. Here was another reference to this man – the man to whom his mother had written a number of letters. Could he be the same Eamon Duffy who would become a prominent figure among the Fenian rebels? Not someone Nate would have imagined being associated with his mother. Nate read on:

The report on Duffy's background raised my suspicions, and an article in today's edition of a nationalist rag confirmed them. Duffy fancies himself as an entrepreneur, but his business is the illegal distilling from potatoes of that poisonous concoction the peasants refer to as poitín. Somehow, I cannot imagine that business to be thriving in a country where all the potatoes are rotting in the ground. So it comes as no surprise that he has wheedled his way into my wife's bottomless well of goodwill, in the pretence of wanting to provide food to the starving peasants.

Today, it was announced in that rag known as The Nation *that 'the Wildensterns are making efforts to feed the starving masses'. This was news to me. I have sanctioned no such campaign, and the manner in which it has apparently been executed is painfully naïve, worthy of my darling's most romantic notions. The peasants do not know how to cook the* tough American grain – and waste much of it in the process. Their complete reliance on the potato over generations means they have lost the knowledge of how to bake bread. Few peasants in this country would possess a millstone to grind the grain, or an oven to bake it.

Planting the new seeds my Miriam has thoughtfully provided will not produce vegetables until October, and these other vegetables will require more land than the potato needs to feed the same number. Land that the Popish rabble do not have. Miriam curses them with false hope through her charitable efforts, instead of letting their desperation spur them into solving their own bloody problems.

All this as the birth of our newest child draws near. It is no way for a woman to behave.

I pressed my investigators into an examination of my wife's personal effects, and they discovered that she has recently disposed of a great number of highly valuable items – paintings, antiques, jewellery, etc – in her possession. How she got them out of the house without being seen confounds my men, though the fact that she is a woman may have given them a foolishly low opinion of her powers of deceit. And being a woman, she could not have sent the valuables to auction herself – I would have to have been consulted. I suspect that Duffy may have taken them to the auctioneers, posing as a reputable businessman, and owner of the items, and sold them 'on her behalf'. Whatever corn or seeds he might have bought with them, I have no doubt that the bulk of the money made *from the transactions will have found its way into his pockets.*

My men learned from a telegram sent to Miriam that she was to meet Duffy tonight, and when the time came for the rendezvous, I used the secret passageways to follow her to the basement, and to the workshop where she carries out all of her archaeological work. Looking at the crates which were packed with her finds, I quickly realized how she had smuggled her valuable possessions out of the house. The large room was dark, and I entered unnoticed through the false support column situated against one of the walls.

Duffy was there. A square-framed man with a hard face and dark brown hair, he was dressed in the work-clothes worn by all the men who do the manual work on her digs. These men come and go through the servants' ways and she no doubt has him listed on the books as one of her helpers. It seemed that she had no shame, and was quite willing to meet with this blackguard alone. I felt a terrible rage rise within me. My wife – almost nine months pregnant with my child – and her criminal consort, the two of them deep in conversation, standing over that bronze cauldron of which she is so proud – the one with the serpent around the rim. It seemed to me an appropriately devious and treacherous symbol of her activities. I moved out of the shadows, approaching silently as the pair conspired together.

They were discussing some new way to transfer the worth of my family's assets into the pockets of the poor when they found me standing over them. Miriam let out a gasp, but Duffy was struck with fear, staggering backwards against the cauldron. I *cannot say that I acted with any rational sense, finding myself staring into the face of the man who had deceived and used my wife and stolen from her and now was set to do more and who knew what else. I was like a wounded beast, blinded by fury. Of all the deaths I have caused, his gave me the least pause for thought. I seized his neck with the engimal claw that is my right hand, crushing his throat. Miriam screamed my name, but I paid her no mind. The spring-loaded sheath strapped to my left wrist shot the dagger out of my sleeve and into my left hand. I drove the blade over and over again into his belly as he thrashed and screamed. Miriam tried to stop me and I shoved her away – the only time I have ever shown her violence.*

When I had finished stabbing, Duffy's abdomen was a torn and bloody mess, his innards starting to slop like giant worms through his clutching hands. But I knew he would still take some time to die, and it would be an agonizing death. Miriam was crouching down against the cauldron, wailing so hard she could not take a breath. I tossed the cur backwards into the old cauldron, where he coughed and groaned as the blood pooled around him. I spat on him and then turned to her, as she pointlessly tried to use her handkerchief to cover his wounds.

'There he is, my darling, the man who would use you as if you were any silly old trollop with more money than sense. And he has learned what it is to cross the Wildensterns. Do not waste your tears on this jack-gagger, my dear. If it is God's will that you be taken in by him, then you should pray for his salvation, and your prayers will surely be answered. Or perhaps your

Dagda's cauldron will cure his injuries and bring him back to life. Either way, I will leave you here with him, as you seem to enjoy his company so much. When you decide to start behaving in a manner befitting my wife, you may show your face upstairs again, where I will be waiting. I will send down some men in a while, to empty that chamber-pot of yours.'

I left her with those words, and did not look back. Her sobs, and the tortured cries of the dying man, followed me up the stairs. Neither sound gave me great satisfaction.

XX

'PREPARE TO REPEL BOARDERS'

'Wildenstern.' A voice broke into Nate's thoughts. 'Rouse yourself, man! The dogs are at our heels!'

Nate blinked and looked up Dempsey.

'What is it?'

'Come and see for yourself.'

Nate marked his page with a piece of string before closing the journal and rising to his feet in a stiff motion. His body was feeling the strain of the days of travel, as well as the aftermath of the recent gunfight. A bolt of pain shot through his shoulder and he grunted, shrugging it away. He moved down the aisle of their second-class carriage, following Dempsey towards the rear of the train. They went through two doors to the next carriage, striding between the rows of wooden seats in the third-class carriage – one had to travel second-class to get cushioned seats. Nate noticed people were peering out the left-side windows at the scene thrown into silhouette by the setting sun. Nate stopped to see what they were looking at, but Dempsey gripped his arm and kept him moving.

Dempsey had told him about Harmonica, the American bounty hunter who was dogging them. His real name was Thomas Radigan, a former US marshal of Polish and Irish descent. The man was famous in his homeland for his determination and resourcefulness. He had turned in his badge and become a bounty hunter after the law had failed to catch his brother's murderer. Ever since, he had devoted himself to the manhunting profession with fanatical resolve, tracking down any criminal with a substantial price on their head. Once he took on a job and set himself on the trail of a quarry, he never failed to finish the job. Now it would be a matter of professional pride with him that he make up for the fouled-up ambush in Limerick. He had earned his nickname by playing the harmonica to condemned prisoners he had caught, as they walked to the gallows. Dempsey had assured Nate that they hadn't seen the last of this human bloodhound.

The train was composed of a steam locomotive pulling a tender – carrying the coal and water – along with six passenger carriages and a guard's van at the rear. The door to the guard's van was unlocked, and three of Dempsey's men were already inside. The uniformed guard was sitting in high dudgeon on a bench alongside some large sacks of mail, where he had obviously been instructed to sit down and shut up. He scowled at Nate and Dempsey as they stepped out the door at the back of the railway car and onto the wide footplate, buffeted by the wind and swaying slightly with the motion of the train.

'I expected to cross paths with him again,' Dempsey growled, scratching his jaw through his beard. 'But I never saw this coming.'

Holding onto one of the roof supports, Nate stared out at the dusk-lit landscape, and at the six velocycles racing across the fields, weaving past trees and leaping hedges and fences in pursuit of the train. Each engimal carried a rider, and the man in front wore a fur-felt cowboy hat and duster coat.

The creatures snarled and screeched, relishing the thrill of the chase. Their wheels left scars in the soft earth where they swerved or jumped or accelerated, spraying soil and tearing through undergrowth. Harmonica took his hat from his head and whooped as he waved it forward, urging his posse onwards after the train. They were closing the gap quickly – the steam locomotive was the fastest form of travel in the Victorian age, but only if you left engimals out of the equation. There wasn't much that could outrun a velocycle.

'It gives a whole new meaning to "catching the train", doesn't it?' Nate observed. 'No expense has been spared, apparently. Those are Wildenstern beasts, I'd know them anywhere. There can't be more than eight or nine of the creatures in the whole of Ireland. So what do we do now?'

'Prepare to repel boarders,' Dempsey replied, leaning on the door and nodding to his men. 'Tell the others to make sure they don't get ahead of us. Shoot the blackguards out of the saddle if you have to. I don't think Harmonica's enough of a lunatic to try and derail the train, but he might try and block its path. And we don't know if they've got more men on the way to catch up with us. I wouldn't put it past him to have more of them to meet us when we stop at Roscrea. If I have to, I'll put a gun to the driver's head and push on through every bloody station between here and Dublin.'

The three headed back up the train to spread out along its length and pass on instructions to the rest of their crew. Dempsey drew a revolver and turned towards the back of the carriage.

'Two of them have gone ahead,' Nate said, pointing at the pair of riders careering over a field to reach the front of the train on the right-hand side. 'And the cowboy is going up the left. You'd want to mind they don't get to the driver before your men do. The last thing you want to have to do is lay siege to the engine.'

'We have it covered,' Dempsey retorted.

In the short time he had known the sailor, Nate had yet to hear the man speak to him in any kind of friendly tone. It seemed Nate could never be forgiven for being a member of the family who had stolen Dempsey's son.

Gunshots rang out, and Nate ducked down behind the low wall at the end of the footplate, but he knew that the thin sheet of iron might not stop a rifle round, or even that of a powerful handgun like the '44 he pulled from his jacket. Two of the riders were making a play for the end of the train. Bullets smacked into the walls and chassis of the train, some ricocheting off at dangerous angles. Dempsey stepped inside the back door and smashed the window. Nate darted in behind him and the sailor used the door as cover, taking careful aim through the broken window at the two riders speeding up alongside the train.

Nate used the butt of his gun to punch through a side window and fired two shots at the nearest rider. His first missed, but the second struck the engimal in the flank. It shrieked and flinched, its rear wheel slipping sideways, nearly throwing its rider. But then regained its balance and, enraged, it rushed forward even faster. But in doing so, it came closer to the guard's van. Nate took a bead on the man on its back and put a shot through his leg. The man tumbled backwards off the velocycle, somersaulting to a halt in the middle of the field. The engimal kept hurtling on alongside, oblivious to the fate of its rider.

Dempsey had injured the other engimal, and it had limped to a standstill, watching the train speed away. There was one left, coming directly up the tracks behind them, the engimal balancing perfectly on one of the rails and using its smooth surface to race ever faster forward. The man on its back was an expert marksman. Whenever Dempsey tried to take a shot, the rider put a bullet through the door with unnerving accuracy.

Dempsey's gun jammed and he ducked back behind the wall, pointing the barrel away from him as he tried to eject the troublesome cartridge. Nate grabbed one of the sacks of mail piled up beside the guard, who now cowered in one corner of the van. Carrying the heavy sack to the door, Nate peeked out and saw the third rider was only a few yards from the rear of the train, his velocycle's wheels still lined up perfectly on the rail. That peek nearly cost Nate his life – a bullet split the doorframe where his head had been only an instant before.

'One of Harmonica's trick-shooters,' Dempsey rasped. 'Can probably shoot like that while standing on his head and whistling *Dixie*. He can keep our heads down until he's on board, but we'll take him when he sets foot on the train.'

'I don't think he means to,' Nate replied, hauling the sack up behind him and wincing at a twinge in his injured shoulder. 'When I looked out, he had a stick of dynamite in his other hand. He's just going to blow up the whole bloody van.'

Dempsey's burst of foul language was drowned out by the sound of three more rounds passing through the wall. Nate kicked the door open and, staying clear of the doorway, he hurled the sack of mail off the back of the train.

There was a thud, a crash, a scream and a thumping clatter as the engimal ran headlong into the weighty sack and flipped over, tumbling over its rider and bouncing along the tracks behind the train. A moment later, there came the loud punch of an explosion as the fuse on the stick of dynamite dutifully did its job.

'First time I've sent a letter in years,' Nate remarked, glancing out through the doorway. 'And to think Daisy claimed I never understood the value of writing.'

Dempsey was already ignoring him, turning to look out the side of the train.

'I can't see any of the rest, can you?'

Nate studied the landscape beyond the side windows, but could not see any of the other riders. One of the Fenians, a spry, middle-aged navvy dressed in a velveteen jacket and a mismatching flat cap, came through the door from the next carriage.

'Thir on the roof,' he said in a toothy Limerick accent. 'Two of thim, at least. Mebby three.'

Nate met Dempsey's eyes and nodded.

'Let's take the fight to them,' Nate said. 'I'll climb up at this end, you go through and try to come up ahead of them. We'll throw the bloody coves right off the train.'

Dempsey jerked his chin out in agreement.

'Jaysus, thet sounds awful dengerous,' the older man objected.

'I'm on for it,' Dempsey sniffed. 'Can't be harder than standing on a deck in a storm.'

Nate went out the back door to the ladder leading up to the roof. He was starting up it when the Limerick man peered out at the passing farmland, and then looked at his watch.

'Wait, wait!' the older man called. 'Wait just a minute.'

Nate hesitated as the man held up his hand and looked out. A harsh scraping sound carried back from the front of the train. It grew in volume, a dragging, clattering noise that caught the screams of two men up in its commotion as it swept past on the roof above. Nate, Dempsey and the Limerick man caught sight of a tree passing away behind them, its branches overhanging the track. One bounty hunter was sent flailing off the roof and onto the rails, coming to a rest in a battered heap. Another was caught in the branches of the tree, looking utterly stunned.

'Thet'll be the Scrapin' Tree,' the Limerick man said. 'Any reg'lar pessenger on this train knows it. Always gives yeh a fright hearin' it drag across the roof like thet, if yer not riddy fer it.'

Nate and Dempsey watched the Scraping Tree whisk away into the distance and they shared a smile.

'Excellent,' Dempsey said. 'All right, Sean, you stay and keep watch here. We'll go forward and make sure we've got clear of all of them.'

Nate followed him as he went out the door, walking past

the terrified train guard who had buried himself in mail sacks and now spouted a stream of verbal abuse at them as they passed him.

There was uproar on the train. Women were screaming, men were shouting, children were crying. Half the passengers on the train were crouching down under the windows, their arms over their heads. The other half were on their feet, in an attempt to see what was going on. Dempsey and Nate pushed through the throng of bodies, trying to find the Fenians scattered along the train's length. Dempsey stopped to question each one, checking to see if any of the bounty hunters had got on board. Clancy was leaning up against his window, pistol in hand, but his face was pale and there was a rattle in his breathing. Nate knelt down next to him and urged him to lie back down. His manservant was having none of it, so Nate gave up with a smile and a shake of his head and went on after Dempsey.

The sailor stepped out of the front door of the second car on his way to the leading carriage – the only first-class one. The butt of a sawn-off shotgun cracked against the side of his head and he slumped down onto the footplate, the top half of his body hanging dangerously over the gap between the buffers and the coupling joint holding the two carriages together. Another few inches and he would pitch over into the gap and fall under the wheels. Harmonica swung through the door. He was missing his cowboy hat, but his long, tan-coloured coat flowed out behind him like a cloak and the barrel of his gun was already levelled at the point where Nate's chest should have been.

Nate was crouching low to the floor, his head down. As the American came through, Nate lunged forward, driving his shoulder into the man's midriff and carrying him back out the door. Harmonica tripped over Dempsey's limp form and smashed through the door into the leading carriage. He was getting to his feet when Nate followed him through, knocked the shotgun to one side and slammed the heel of his hand into Harmonica's solar plexus, just below the arc in the ribcage. The blow took the wind out of Harmonica's lungs and knocked him back along the aisle between some shelves of luggage. Nate jumped after him, but Harmonica caught him with a front kick that shoved him right back over on top of Dempsey. Nate nearly tipped the unconscious man into the gap between the carriages, and only just grabbed his belt in time, hauling him back onto the narrow footplate. Harmonica brought his gun up and Nate kicked it aside again, throwing himself forward once more to prevent Harmonica getting a bead on him.

His left hand gripped Harmonica's right, forcing the gun away as his right hand blocked the forearm strike the American aimed at his jaw. With the wound in his left shoulder aching with pain, Nate butted the man in the face and slammed his right elbow into the man's chest a couple of times. He rammed the hand holding the gun against the luggage rack, trying to break the American's grip. Harmonica got his left fist round Nate's guard and caught him with a powerful hook across the side of the head. Nate's vision swam, and the jolt allowed Harmonica to bring the shotgun up towards the other side of his head, firing off one of the barrels. The shot missed, but the deafening detonation burst Nate's eardrum and the muzzle-flash burnt the side of his head, making him scream. He fell backwards, but Harmonica grabbed hold of his jacket in his left hand, trying to level the gun at Nate's head again and empty the second barrel at him.

With his head pounding and a terrible whining, screeching pain in his left ear, Nate struggled to stay conscious. He brought his knee up between Harmonica's legs, folding the man over, and with his right hand whacked the American's head off the edge of the luggage rack. Harmonica fell back, but his reflexes were lightning-fast. The barrel of the gun came up, his finger tightened on the second trigger . . . Nate seized a stout leather suitcase and jerked it from the luggage rack just as Harmonica fired his shot. The suitcase took the force of the blast, the front of it bursting open like an impact crater. The clothes tightly packed inside it were reduced to rags, but they absorbed the shot and it was only the power of the blow that caused Nate to stagger backwards. He recovered himself as Harmonica swore and pulled a revolver from his belt.

Nate threw the remains of the suitcase at him, then

grabbed a travelling trunk off the rack and hurled that with all his strength. The bottom edge of the trunk fell on Harmonica's shins and one of them broke with an audible crack. The American cried out in pain and frustration, twisting as if trying to escape the pain. Nate drew his own revolver and cocked it, aiming it at Harmonica's head. Harmonica stopped moving, glaring up at Nate as he tried to suppress the agony that wanted to show itself on his face.

'Go on then,' he snarled. 'Get on with it.'

Nate glanced past the wounded man, holding his left hand up to his bleeding left ear, feeling the singed hair, and the blistered skin that seemed almost numb compared to the roaring pain in his eardrum. He hadn't even noticed that this carriage was half full of passengers. A dozen faces stared at him in fascinated terror around the doorframes of the first-class compartments. Shrugging his aching shoulder, his face screwed up in pain, he swallowed and found his throat was desperately dry.

The train's chuffing was slowing down, indicating that it was approaching the station at Roscrea. Soon there would be more people around, perhaps even more of Harmonica's men.

Every instinct in him was telling Nate that he had to finish the American here and now, or face having to deal with him again later. Some enemies would just keep coming back at you. Showing them mercy simply gave them another chance to kill you. Nate dropped the barrel slightly, raised it again, squeezed the trigger almost to the point where the hammer dropped . . . and then stopped himself, shook his head and sighed as he eased his finger off the trigger. He looked at the horrified faces of the people along the aisle behind Harmonica. This was what happened when the lives of the Wildensterns spilled out into the normal world. It was this kind of stupid, unconstrained violence Nate had sworn to bring to an end years ago, along with Daisy and his brother, Berto. But it never seemed to end.

'You lose your hat?' he asked the American, speaking in a voice that was just a little bit too loud – he couldn't hear himself properly over the whining in his burst ear.

Harmonica scowled, coughing as he clutched his broken right leg.

'Fell off when I jumped onto the train.'

'Kind of makes you stand out over here. We don't go in for them in Ireland.'

'It's my lucky hat.'

'Should've kept hold of it.'

Harmonica snorted and looked away, his ridged face crumpled like old leather.

'It's the man you're working for who's the murderer,' Nate told the American. 'And he'll do a lot more killing unless I get home and put a stop to it. Now I know your reputation, Radigan. You were a lawman once, right? Well, this is one of those situations where the law can't help. The

man I'm up against is too powerful for the law to touch –
especially in this country. You understand that kind of man,
don't you? Right. Then you'll know how he uses people
like you. And you *have been used*, Radigan. To him, you and
your men are just a bunch of guns for hire. You've been had.
I'm guilty of a lot of things – most of them committed
against the people who loved me and relied on me – but
I'm no criminal. Now, I'm going to let you off at the next
station. If you like – and you're able to pick up the men
we've left scattered across the landscape – you can come
back at me further up the line and we can do all this again.

'So it's up to you: if you want to get yourself killed – and
maybe even some other, completely innocent folk along
with you – by working for the most dangerous criminal in
this country, by all means keep up your little quest. Or you
could take your Wild West extravaganza and just piss off
back to America and hunt some real outlaws. God knows
you've enough of them over there without having to come
here looking to import them. Anyway, you can mull over it
all after you drag your sorry backside off the train.'

Harmonica took a breath and hauled himself up into a
standing position, using a doorframe for support. His right
shin was fractured, but the bone had not penetrated the
skin. Leaning his weight on his other leg, he hissed through
this teeth and regarded Nate with a piercing look.

'Consider it mulled,' he rasped. 'I know things about
people, Mister Wildenstern. And you *have killed* – but you're

no killer. Not the pure-bred kind anyways. This job always had a stink to it an' now I know why. I won't apologize to you, 'cos it's likely you're no more free of guilt than I am, but I'm sorry about the injuries to your manservant, as he was just doin' his job. And I'm sorry that these people were put in peril for the sake of some lies and some dirty money.'

He picked up his truncated shotgun and slid it into the large pocket of his duster coat. Taking out a wallet, he removed a few pound notes and tucked them into the remains of the suitcase he had destroyed. More than enough to pay for the loss of its contents.

'That's for the damage that I caused to that person's property. I'll pay for any damage to the train too. As for you, Mister Wildenstern, well . . . I don't believe in no God no more, but if it's your fate to confront this man you speak of, then I wish you on your way to it and whatever comes of it. We all have our journeys to take.'

The train was pulling into the small station now. The last of the sun's light was fading from the station and there weren't many people standing waiting on the gloomy, lamp-lit platform. Harmonica looked out from the illuminated interior of the carriage, through the window nearest him, seeing more of himself reflected on the glass than he could of the faces beyond it.

'And may justice prevail,' he added. 'In whatever form it takes. Though I must admit that's another kind of faith that I've lost along the way.'

'It was a faith I never had,' Nate said.

'Then that, Mister Wildenstern,' Harmonica said, 'speaks of a very sad life indeed. I can only hope you find yourself a happier one, once you've done what you have to do.'

He limped past Nate, each painful step cutting his breath short. Then he twisted the handle and opened the door out onto the platform as the train came to a halt.

'Take a word of advice from a man who knows,' he said, turning to Nate after he had stepped down off the train. He took his harmonica from his pocket and rolled it between finger and thumb like a cigar. 'Don't go givin' up your life to take revenge. And don't let it turn you into the very thing you hate most. Some trains just ain't worth catchin'. Goodbye, Mister Wildenstern.'

He put the harmonica to his lips and started to play a melancholy tune as he walked away. Nate raised his hand in farewell, and watched the tired, hurt cowboy limp off down the platform in the last red glow of the setting sun.

XXI

A LOAD OF BULLOLOGY

Cathal's hands were covered in little cuts and scrapes. The strange metals and ceramics that formed the bulk of an engimal's body could form some very sharp edges when cut or broken. Handling them could be hazardous. Needless to say, the children were not issued with gloves to protect their hands. Gerald claimed that gloves would merely make them clumsy, and result in more serious injuries.

'Yeh still haven't told me why yer usin' children,' Cathal said, gazing down at the chains that bound his ankles together.

His hands were free, but his feet were still shackled. He was standing in Gerald's study in the mine complex. As he watched, Gerald was attempting to impose his will on Tatty's pet, Siren, by playing to it with his macabre engimal violin. Somehow, the bird was resisting – or at least, it wasn't doing what he was commanding it to do. Siren was trapped in a birdcage sitting on Gerald's desk, next to a pile of papers. Cathal watched the exchange with interest. Tatiana must be apoplectic with rage at the theft of her pet – and she would know who was responsible. Cathal had sparred with her enough times to know that she had a violent temper. He could only imagine the language that came out of her when she discovered the theft.

Every now and then, the little blue and silver bird would open its beak as if in pain, or shake its head, or become agitated. But Gerald was obviously hoping for something more. Cathal was beginning to understand the significance of the music. At first he had thought that Gerald was using specific notes – hidden in the music – to have an effect on the engimals he played to. But now he began to see that the music itself was creating some kind of connection. Gerald believed engimals had a mathematical language too complicated for humans to understand. Perhaps the music was a way of simplifying it.

It would explain why Gerald and Red used a whistle to open the door of the mine if, as Pip claimed, the door was made out of the mouth of an engimal. Pip had said the whistle made no noise, but Cathal guessed the sound it made had a very high pitch, so that only certain animals or engimals could hear it. He had seen their like before and Gerald had experimented with them a couple of years ago, in his attempts to communicate with engimals back in

Wildenstern Hall. This unorthodox key was why Cathal was here now, even though his work in the slaughterhouse had left him sick and exhausted and desperate for sleep. He needed to find one of those whistles. He needed to steal one if he could.

'What did you say?' Gerald asked.

The violin had stopped playing. Cathal blinked, roused from his musings.

'Yeh still haven't told me why you're usin' children to dissect the engimals,' he repeated. 'It's a barbaric enough practice without destroyin' the innocence of the young into the bargain.'

'Ah, my little flock of lambs. I think you'll find that the children of the poor are robbed of their innocence much earlier in life than those raised in a more sheltered environment,' Gerald replied. 'And I must have children for the work, because it requires small, nimble fingers and open minds. They must learn as they work, and quickly. The dismantling of each engimal offers different challenges, unique fixings and joints, undiscovered materials. An adult mind is closed by nature, and inflexible. I need minds that still have the capacity to adapt to new modes of thought.

'There is the hope too that some of these youngsters – like you – might go on to develop a greater understanding of this new science. I give no priority to class or social rank in my vision of the future. Success should be measured on merit, rather than one's family or property. It is the only rational course.'

'Still, it's convenient that these are penniless orphans – a fact that made their abduction a lot easier, I'm sure.' Cathal sniffed, letting his eyes wander around the room, searching the tops of the worktables, the plans chest and Gerald's desk. 'Why do yeh take their blood? They don't have *aurea sanitas*, do they?'

'Ah! Now that is the key to my entire process,' Gerald declared, placing the outlandish violin down on the desk so that he could gesture with his hands – adopting the position of the lecturer once more. 'You see, my early research suffered from two misconceptions:

'Firstly; that intelligent particles were only found in the blood of a few powerful families. These families have per-petuated this mistaken belief for generations. In fact, I believe there are low concentrations of the particles present in the blood of just about every human being. Obviously, proving this beyond a doubt is a practical impossibility, but one can theorize. And I can at least prove the so-called *aurea sanitas* families are not nearly as exclusive as they think. Apart from the scientific significance of this, I would take great pleasure in kicking the pedestal out from under their inbred feet.

'Secondly; I believed that intelligent particles could only *survive* in the medium of blood, and could only affect changes *within that medium*. In short, that these particles, like antibodies – or indeed, parasitic viruses or bacteria – could only take action through the body of their host. I believed that our microscopic allies could not exist independently of us – that they needed to act *through* us to have any effect on the outside world. But I was wrong. Very wrong.'

Cathal lifted his head at that, distracted from his search.

'What? Yer sayin' that these things can move around outside our bodies?' He frowned. He was struggling to grasp what Gerald was telling him. 'So . . . what . . . you . . . you can catch them. Like a *disease*?'

'I'm saying much more than that.' Gerald smiled. He walked across the chamber and sat down at the church organ that had been installed in the far wall. He started softly pressing keys, randomly at first but then building slowly into a quiet tune. 'I'm saying that it may be possible to perform the kinds of feats that would appear as magic to the untrained eye. I'm not just talking about curing disease or healing supposedly fatal wounds. Even when my skills were relatively undeveloped, I succeeded in bringing the long-dead back to life.

'Think of the legends passed down to us from ancient times. There are the hints of the possibilities in those old stories. Blades that can cut through any material; a medium that can show you events on the far side of the world; vehicles that can carry a person faster than the speed of sound; even the ability to change the shape of an object at will.'

The music rose swaying from the instrument, Gerald's fingers still coaxing the notes out softly. Cathal noticed that Siren was hopping restlessly on its perch in the cage. It seemed to be growing increasingly nervous. Could it sense something that Cathal could not?

'Imagine being able to reshape your body to perform different tasks,' Gerald went on. 'Do you remember the legends you heard as a child – of famous warriors who transformed into demonic giants in battle? Gods who could harness the very elements; taking control of the air, the sea, the earth. Imagine being able to *fly*, Cathal. It might all be possible, if we can only learn to communicate our instructions clearly and specifically enough for the particles to understand.'

'I don't believe it,' Cathal said. 'It's a load of bullology if y'ask me. I know what you're capable of, Gerald. There's no denyin' yev got power – a type I'm only beginning to understand. And I've seen what intelligent particles can do. I've had it done to me. But what yer talkin' about . . . that's . . . that's just the stuff of fairy tales.'

Siren was flapping frantically in its cage now, desperate to escape. It was screeching so loudly it was hurting Cathal's ears.

'Music and blood!' Gerald shouted above the noise. 'These are the keys. Siren here has an extraordinary range of sounds. Its size and mobility would make it an excellent instrument for commanding the particles, but I would still have to find a way to "play" the creature as I would an organ or a violin. That is a problem, particularly as the little beast is almost as wilful as its former owner. It is not enough that I talk *to* it. I must talk *through* it to the intelligent particles. For the kind of control I need to exercise over them, I need a complex instrument to convey my intentions. This little songbird would be an excellent instrument. But the engimals with the greatest range of sounds, Cathal, are the *leviathans*. Like whales, they are capable of sophisticated language, and can transmit signals through miles of ocean waters. If I could control a leviathan, I could command the very fabric of the Earth itself.'

Cathal desperately wanted to think Gerald's ideas the products of insanity, but he had seen enough to know that at least some of what Gerald claimed was true. He realized that it wasn't just his own life at stake here, and the lives of the children kept captive in this dungeon factory. If Gerald succeeded, he would be the most powerful man on Earth. Possibly the most powerful that had ever existed. And if he was willing to work children to death in this engimal slaughterhouse, what would he do if he could unleash this kind of power upon the world? He had to be stopped, no matter what it took. And to do that, Cathal had to escape as soon as possible.

The organ music was rising in volume and tempo. Siren squawked in panic, thrashing around its cage. Cathal covered his ears. There was something about the music that seemed to be changing the air pressure in the room.

'What are you doing?' he gasped.

Then a breeze started to blow through the room. Papers got caught up in it, pens and other instruments rolled across the worktables, the framed pictures flapped against the walls. It wasn't a draught from any of the doors. They were all closed. The wind centred on the birdcage sitting on the desk. The cage began to wobble and turn on the desktop, rocking and spinning like a coin dropped on the floor. Then it was whipped off the desktop and thrown across the room. Siren screeched in pain and fear. Gerald stopped playing, and the wind died almost instantly. Cathal stared in amazement and then, forced to take short steps by his shackles, he hobbled over to the cage and picked it up, making soothing sounds to Siren. The engimal was trembling and cawing quietly.

As Cathal carried the cage back to the desk, stepping over the papers and other objects scattered all over the stone floor, he spotted something lying on the ground under the desk. It was a bone-white whistle, about three inches long. Glancing towards the end of the room, he saw he was still in Gerald's eyeline. There was no way of reaching down for the whistle without Gerald noticing. He leaned back against the desk and waited for his chance.

'It will appear as magic to those who don't understand it,' Gerald said in a low voice, laying his hands flat on the keys and staring down at them. 'And most of the people in the world fall into that category. The intelligent particles are present all around us – in the air, like the spores of the dry rot fungus, or carried through moisture, like the spores of the dreaded potato blight. And like a spore, they can inhabit certain kinds of matter and can use their host to reproduce.

'But they are formed of tiny combinations of atoms, smaller even than a microscopic fungal spore. They are almost undetectable. Each one somehow has the capacity to communicate with those around it – think of that, Cathal! One can only marvel at the science that could have created such things! And they can act as a swarm by exercising some kind of force on one another. The only way I have been able to gather them into concentrations thick enough to view under a microscope is in the medium of human blood – they seem drawn to inhabiting it. A behaviour instilled in them by their creators, no doubt. But this difficulty in studying them directly is most frustrating – I am hampered by the limits of today's science.

'The engimals are laced with these particles. The creatures were made using the particles both as tools and building materials. Destroying the engimals, crushing their body parts in the grinders, fills the air of this cave with the particles. But mankind does not possess any material capable of capturing them easily. As swarms, they are like the most pervasive gas, but they are little larger than the molecules that form most materials. Each one is so small they can pass through any fabric – even leather or some types of rubber. I have had difficulty containing them even in glass or steel. But in this cave, the children breathe them in, and ingest them into their bodies. The particles can also enter their blood through the many little wounds the children pick up in their work. They invade our bodies like a disease, but a disease that strengthens us, rather than attacking our systems. And I, in turn, mine the children's blood for the particles, just as the miners of this mountain would have sought out rich veins of silver.

'I have been experimenting with the materials with which the engimals themselves are made, and have had some success in containing the particles. Once I learned to gather and store them, I began to exercise the kind of control over them that I have over my own body. But what I want is to be able to control them *wherever they occur—*'

Red burst into the room, his revolver raised. Cathal stood up straight, stepping away from the desk.

'What was all dat noise?' he barked. 'Is this fella givin' yeh any trouble, Mister Gordon?'

'It was nothing, Red,' Gerald replied, lifting his hand as if trying to fend off a bad smell. 'Cathal and I were having a civilized conversation and I merely carried out an overly dramatic demonstration to prove a point. There is nothing to concern you here.'

Red did not look satisfied; he came closer to Cathal, eyeing him with a hostile expression. The scar over his nose ran like a slash of white skin across his flushed face. Cathal wondered how much the hard man knew about what was going on in this mine. If he was being kept in the dark, these strange goings-on were likely to make him suspicious, even fearful. And it was easy to get a rise out of a fearful man.

'That's right, Red,' Cathal chuckled. 'It's best to keep yer *nose* out of the business of gentlemen. A professional toad-eater like you doesn't want to get *marked* as bein' an eavesdropper. Might threaten yer prospects for employment. And yeh should know that a servant isn't supposed to show their face – *especially* a face like *yours* – unless they're summoned.'

'You shut yer mout', or I'll shut it for yeh, yeh little scut!' Red hissed, casting a wary eye in Gerald's direction.

Gerald watched the exchange, but made no move to interrupt.

'Don't let the shackles fool yeh,' Cathal replied, tilting his head towards Gerald. 'I'm of more use to him than you are. Thugs like you are ten a penny. Yer easily replaced. Makin' a move against me would be like cuttin' off your nose to spite yer face ... but then it looks like you tried that already.'

Red's fist caught him hard across the jaw, knocking Cathal backwards. He fell against the desk, the edge of it hitting him in the upper back. He grunted, sliding down it as Red went to swing a kick at his face, but Gerald stopped the attack with a word:

'Enough.'

Red stepped back, obeying like a well-trained dog. He slid the pistol into the holster on his belt and let his hands dangle down by his side. But there was still an animal ferocity in his face. Cathal read the message in his expression: this wasn't over – not by a long way.

Cathal rolled his head on his neck and worked his jaw, wincing at the pain in the hinge on the right side. Red had a lean, wiry build, but he could punch like a heavyweight. Placing his hands down on the floor behind him, Cathal waited a moment, as if recovering his senses. His left hand closed around the whistle under the desk and, bracing his elbows on the desktop behind him, he slipped it into his pocket as he got shakily to his feet.

'Someday, Cathal,' Gerald remarked, 'you're going to have to stop sticking your fingers up at the world and start playing your part. I would not expect you to be like that flock of sheep out in the cave, but bloody-minded defiance will only get you so far in life. Reason will always win out over emotion and instinct.'

'Up the yard with yeh, Gerald,' Cathal retorted.

Gerald gestured to Red to take the captive out, but Cathal hung back.

'I have one question,' he said. 'Why are you tellin' me all this stuff? I would've thought you'd want to keep it all secret.'

'And who are *you* going to tell?' Gerald smirked, waving his hand around at the solid stone that surrounded them.

'Besides, I haven't told you the half of it . . . and I shan't. But it's ego, I suppose. I want someone to appreciate what I've achieved. What's more, I miss our conversations, and the stimulation they provided. As for what you might do with that knowledge, well . . . there's only so much . . .'

He did not finish the sentence, as if thinking the better of it. But Cathal took his meaning. There was only so much someone of his inferior intelligence could do with this knowledge. While Gerald treated him as a student, the man's belief in his own genius had inflated enormously. He almost regarded Cathal more as a pet. And a master did not fear the plans his dog might lay. Cathal fingered the whistle in his pocket.

'You know, bein' more intelligent than everyone else doesn't mean you're always right,' he grunted.

'No,' Gerald replied. 'But it does make you right more often. That's good enough for me. Try to get some sleep. I'll see you tomorrow.'

Will you? Cathal wondered.

XXII

A DYING LANDSCAPE

Nate moaned in his sleep, twitching and shifting about under the blankets, as if trying to avoid looking at something. But the nightmare was all around him. It was inside him. He was unaware of Clancy lying in the next bed across from him, watching with concerned eyes; or Dempsey, in the top bunk, hissing through his teeth because he couldn't sleep with the young man thrashing on the bunk below.

All Nate could see, right out to the horizon, was a dying landscape. Rain fell from the brooding, bruised clouds overhead. The twilight was not a natural one, coming as it did at midday. The land was cast in shadow, and it was changing before Nate's eyes. Plants were being eaten away, dissolving into pulp. The trunks of trees cracked and shattered in explosions of dust, as if abruptly, catastrophically riddled with dry rot. The leaves liquefied. The wood turned to charcoal, the charcoal to ash, the ash to dust. Then the dust was stewed into mud by the unrelenting rain.

Nate saw beautiful, majestic buildings, grown up from the very soil and rock and trees of the landscape; he saw them crumble and topple in on themselves, their forms disintegrating to join the churning soup that had once been a civilization. They left no trace of their structures behind. The decay claimed the animals too. Nate saw a sabre-tooth tiger, someone's prized pet, wade frantically through the seething mud. He watched the mighty cat burst, its skin vaporizing, the remains of its flesh and skeleton claimed by the mud. A herd of mammoth, escaped from their handlers, stampeded across a nearby river. Some were dragged under. Others made it to the other side, only to stumble in this new swamp, their hair falling out in massive clumps, their legs seeming to grow shorter as they were eaten away, the beasts faltering and falling. One made it to a low hill, where the mud was only ankle-deep on the huge beast. It reared, raising its front legs, trunk whipping around its enormous tusks. Thin, snake-like tendrils erupted from all over its body, like worms being born from a corpse. The mammoth reared once more, trying to escape something that was inside its own body.

Before its feet could touch ground again, its balding flesh exploded outwards in a cloud of blood and gas and smoke, its very cells breaking down into their basic elements. Its skeleton fell apart, collapsing into the mud and disappearing.

Nate gasped at the sight, though he had seen it before. He had witnessed this scene a hundred times before, but each time it seemed to get worse.

He was trying not to look at the people. There were still a few left. Those who could exercise the greatest control over their own bodies. They sought the high ground, trying to shelter from the rain under rocky outcrops or any trees that were still left standing. But even these people were consumed in the end. Their skin unwound in strings, twisting off their bodies and dissolving or vaporizing. Sometimes Nate thought he could see the things that were destroying them, where the concentrations were so high that they appeared almost as clouds of gas, or swarms of tiny insects.

Only the engimals escaped. Alerted by their instincts and given some limited protection by their inorganic forms, they fled from their masters, and from the scene of the devastation, before they too could be absorbed into the primordial mass.

Nate covered his face. He could never keep his hands over his eyes for long, however. He had to keep watching. But this time, when he looked again, he saw Daisy, Tatty and Leo standing just a few feet from him. A cold horror settled over him. He had never seen this before.

'What are you doing here?' he whimpered hoarsely. 'This can't be! Why are you here?'

Without a word, Daisy turned away from him, looking to the others, anguish carved into her face. Leo screamed as his flesh began to unravel. Tatty crouched down by him, but her body too was beginning to come apart. Daisy shrieked at Nate, begging him to help. She threw her arms around Tatty and Leo, as if trying to hold their bodies together, to save them . . . but their forms collapsed against her, spraying her skin and clothes as they became nothing more than decay and dust and stains. Then she cracked and crumbled and a gust of wind whirled her face away as if it were dry ash, swiftly pulling the remains of her body along with it.

Nate felt his own skin begin to burn, felt his muscles tear and his bones crack. He looked down as his body began its own horrible self-destruction. His skin slewed off, his face cracked and peeled. He went blind, but the sensations lasted a few moments longer . . .

And then he awoke with a high-pitched shriek. His sheet and blanket were drenched in sweat. His body was cold and clammy, trembling violently. He was lying on his front, his hands clutching at the stones in the wall at his head, as if trying to stop himself from falling.

That had been the worst nightmare yet. He breathed in deep, gasping lungfuls of air. The serpentine in his belly, normally eager to comfort him, had his insides knotted up in a terrible cramp. His groaning turned into a low growl as he focused his will on it, forcing it to release its hold on him.

'Jesus Christ, Wildenstern!' Dempsey snapped at him from the top bunk. 'What in the name of God is going on inside your rotted head? If you can't sleep like a normal human being, take your night-time contortions somewhere else and let the rest of us get some goddamned rest!'

Nate felt too tired to reply. The side of his head was throbbing, his eardrum still healing from the fight with Harmonica that evening. He touched his fingers to the healing burns on the side of his head, and singed hair came away on his hand. The injury had affected his balance as well, which was not helped by the bewildered state in which he had woken up. He felt weak, exhausted, hopelessly mortal. This running battle had taken so much out of him, and he hadn't even made it home yet. Gerald was going to win – Nate was sure of it.

But even as the thought entered his head, Nate pushed it away from him. There was no choice to be made, nothing to think about. Gerald had to die, whatever the cost. Nothing else mattered. Nate smiled bitterly at his renewed conviction, fervently wishing he'd killed his cousin properly the first time.

Sitting up, he placed his feet flat on the floor until he felt confident that his head was clear enough for him to walk. Dressed in just his underclothes, he threw the blanket about his shoulders, took his father's journal from his pack, and walked to the door and opened the latch. The building was an old stone-walled stable that had been recently been converted to house as many as twenty men. It was a Fenian safe-house, part of a farm set into some woods near the village of Blessington.

They had disembarked from the train at Sallins in Kildare the previous evening, and taken a wagon across country to Blessington, arriving early in the morning. Nate had only managed to get a few hours of troubled sleep, and now here he was awake again. He felt exhausted and miserable.

The air was cold outside and a light drizzle was falling. The chill made his ear hurt even more, the breeze feeling like it was blowing right into the centre of his head. Shivering slightly, he took a lantern that hung from a nail beside the door. Lighting the lantern with a match, he strode barefoot across the yard, shielding the notebook under his blanket. He came to another stable – one that still housed horses. He slipped inside, set the lamp on the floor and settled himself into a pile of straw in a corner near the door.

There were still a couple of hours before dawn. Nate rubbed his hands together, trying to loosen them up and warm them against the cold, and then opened the journal and began reading. There was little of interest over the next few pages. After finding Eamon Duffy and Miriam together in the basement, Edgar hardly mentioned his wife again for some time. There were occasional words about his newborn daughter, but these were the disinterested remarks made by a distant father who had probably hoped for another son, rather than a new addition to 'the frivolous sex'. Nate read on impatiently, skipping past comments on economics, politics, social unrest and the usual family scandal. He only wanted to know about his mother, but there wasn't another mention of her over the following few weeks.

He finally found what he was looking for, dated the 14th of June:

I have discovered that Eamon Duffy is still alive. My informants tell me that he boarded a ship in Kingstown last week, bound for Canada. How he could have survived the injuries I inflicted upon him is beyond me. There was no doubt in my mind that his wounds were fatal. Is it possible that he is some exiled relative of one of the families with aurea sanitas? Even so, his recovery is remarkable. And by all accounts, he walked aboard the ship unaided. My investigator assures me that the witness is certain of what he saw, and yet I am loath to believe it. In any case, if he is alive, he has learned his lesson and has wisely fled the country. Many of the ships carrying such emigrants have become known as 'coffin ships' because of their lack of seaworthiness, and the high death rate aboard from malnutrition, exposure and disease. With any luck, Mr Duffy will oblige us with his demise.

I have finally settled on a resolution regarding Miriam's betrayal. I had thus far been merciful, even compassionate, in my handling of the affair, but that could not continue. Under my instructions, Warburton has kept her sedated since I discovered, and pre-empted, her intention to abscond with our infant daughter. She has been confined to her room, but has been allowed to see the baby from time to time, though she is hardly conscious on these occasions. But word of her indiscretions has somehow got out to the family – as it so often does – and they are insisting she be 'retired', as our little female-taming process has become known.

At first I would not hear of it, but I must, above all, consider my position. Already, I can hear the rumbling of dissent among some of my more ambitious kin. It has been some years since I have had to put down an Act of Aggression, and I have no wish to kill any more brothers or cousins unless it is absolutely necessary. But I suspect that trouble is brewing. If I am seen to be inconsistent in the imposing of my authority, my discipline, it will be viewed as a weakness. Any sign of weakness invites attack. And if they cannot hurt me directly, they will do it through Miriam. The more compassion I show her, the more certain the jackals are to use her against me. This cannot be permitted.

And so it is with a heavy heart that I have agreed to retire her. To demonstrate the breaking of her will, I had her precious 'Dagda's cauldron' thrown into the furnace. Miriam had been brought to watch, but she turned and walked back upstairs. While gazing at it glowing and disintegrating in the fires, I noticed the snake that had encircled its rim – the one swallowing its own tail – was gone. The moulding of the serpent had been torn or cut off the edge of the bronze cauldron. It was an irritation to see her still trying to defy me in any *way she could, but what could one expect from such a stubborn chit?*

Nate lifted his head, frowning, feeling the movement of the serpentine in his gut. Could that be where this thing had come from? This thing inside him could manipulate intelligent particles – perhaps even make new ones – he knew that. Its uncanny abilities had saved his life – and Cathal's and Gerald's. Had it once been welded onto the rim of that cauldron? If so, it might explain how Duffy had survived Edgar's attack. Perhaps the Dagda's cauldron could perform some of the miracles his mother claimed after all. Nate's mother must have discovered the serpentine was actually an engimal and secreted the creature away, perhaps even sending it to Edgar's sister who lived in exile. It was she who had used it years later, to save Cathal from tuberculosis. Nate shook his head and read on:

Yesterday, Dr Herbert Angstrom was contacted and we arrived at the asylum this morning to carry out her incarceration. It helped that she was so befuddled by laudanum that she appeared only a shadow of her normal character. Her limp body was strapped into a wheelchair, and her once-beautiful face, with its gaunt, grey pallor, was devoid of expression. Her eyes, half-closed, were rolled up under her lids, showing only the whites. A dribble of saliva dripped from one corner of her mouth, which a footman respectfully wiped away at regular intervals.

In a final moment of tenderness towards my love, I took her hand and kissed it. There was no response; I do not think she was even aware of my presence. It was just as well for, as she was wheeled away into the cold damp dungeon that is Philip Richards House, I felt the last of my humanity was wheeled away with her. I have thought little, in the past, of all the women who have lived out the last years of their lives in that place, but I felt a cold breath on the back of my neck as I saw them close the heavy, locked door on my beloved.

We will announce next week that she died of a severe bout of influenza. It will be a majestic funeral – one befitting her passionate and generous character. Part of me hopes that her real funeral, which will necessarily be a secret and hidden affair, will not be too long coming. Truly, this asylum is a horror of human misery. As I turned round to leave, Dr Angstrom asked if I would require the 'procedure' to be performed. Still a relatively young man, he has profited well from his research, and this macabre service that he provides. With so many noble families' skeletons in his closet, I foresee that he could become a very powerful man indeed. He certainly has that ambition, if I'm any judge. Staring up at the curving brown brick walls with their narrow, prison-like windows, I shook my head at his question. At the very least, I thought, let us leave her with her sanity.

But you didn't even leave her that, did you? Nate thought as he read this last passage. He felt sick to his stomach as his father's words confirmed what had happened to his mother. Edgar had obviously felt some pang of conscience. Just over a year later, he had brought his wife back home. Not to live among the family, but to be imprisoned again, in a fortified room in the attic, above Edgar's rooms. On some nights, when the hallways were quiet and the wind blew across the top of Wildenstern Hall, Nate remembered how he and his siblings could hear the barely audible sounds of screams from the attic.

In her final days, Miriam Wildenstern had gone completely and utterly out of her mind.

Sitting in that dark, cold stable with the horses looking curiously at him, Nate put his head between his knees and cried for his mother.

XXIII

SOME FIERCE DANGEROUS EVENTS

Hennessy, the old head groom – and her husband's former lover – was the only person Daisy could trust to take her to the secret meeting. But even with the reins in his expert hands, the carriage ride from the Wildenstern estate to Dublin seemed to take for ever. She could have used the family's train, whose private tracks joined the Great Southern and Western Railway, to carry the train into Kingsbridge Station in Dublin – a much faster journey than the one she was taking. But it was an obscenely decadent way for just two people to travel to the city, and there was something calming about taking the slower route by carriage. Daisy needed as many calming influences as she could muster. And this way, she was spared from having to converse with any of the boorish relatives who might have been tempted to come along for the train ride.

Starting early in the morning, before most of the family was up, she and Hennessy travelled through the villages of Woodtown and Ballyboden, towards Rathfarnham and on through Rathgar and Rathmines, then into the city itself. Passing through some of the rougher areas, she spotted words scrawled on walls in chalk or even paint: 'Long live the Highwayboy!'

Through her windows, Daisy saw the lowest, most wretched hovels built of turf and mud and straw squatting out among the fields. Closer to town, there was less of that, though it could be argued that the poor in the tall, over-crowded, filthy tenement buildings had it even worse than their rural counterparts. Many of these buildings were owned by the Wildensterns, and Daisy knew full well that the few taps in those hellholes gave out contaminated water, and the gutters on the streets in some areas ran with human sewage. Diseases such as tuberculosis, diptheria, whooping cough, scarlatina, smallpox, typhoid and cholera were rife. Dublin had the highest rate of death by disease of any city in Europe. Its death rate was on a par with Calcutta in India. With horrible overcrowding, epidemics were common. Whole families might live in a single room of these buildings . . . and, of course, the Irish were famous for their large families.

Daisy had started a scheme to improve sanitation in the Wildenstern properties and keep the buildings themselves better maintained. She had been shocked to discover that some structures were on the verge of collapsing after years of neglect and cost-cutting. But she was struggling to find the money for these projects now, with Gerald siphoning off huge sums for his private research. The Wildenstern family had massive resources, but like an enormous ship it took a lot just to keep the company moving. If it lost momentum, it could easily end up on the rocks. With all the short-sighted greed of the family's more stupid members, and with Gerald's complete lack of concern as he bled the business dry, rot was setting into the North American Trading Company and its Irish assets. The Wildensterns were in increasing danger of going broke.

It was a fact that had not gone unnoticed by Brutus. The medieval ogre was not the complete ignoramus that Daisy had expected. On the contrary, the meetings she had had with him concerning the business had convinced her that the ancient Wildenstern was a man of keen intellect. Gerald had clearly coached him well, and Daisy was also convinced that Brutus's contemporary education had included a thorough reading of Edgar Wildenstern's journals. She had managed to read a few herself, before Gerald had 'confiscated' them. There was a definite pattern of thought that she recognized in Brutus – a ruthless clarity and an uncompromising belief in discipline. Perhaps he could indeed enforce his rule over the family, just as Edgar had. Soon, it might not matter to Daisy. The plans she was laying had the potential to change everything. But so much rested on the hope that Nathaniel – who must surely be close by now – could somehow draw Gerald's attention away long enough to put those plans into action.

Hennessy drove the carriage to Leinster House, the family's Dublin residence, a large mansion on spacious grounds in Merrion Square. For most of the day, Daisy played the part of a rich socialite, meeting some ladies for coffee and cream scones in the lobby of the Gresham Hotel on Sackville Street before heading off for a spot of shopping in some of the city's most fashionable boutiques. Hennessy followed a few steps behind, carrying a growing pile of boxes and packages.

She returned to the townhouse late in the afternoon and retired to her rooms, telling her maids that she wished to rest and did not want to be disturbed. It took her less than fifteen minutes to change into some unremarkable, positively drab clothes, including a bonnet and veil to hide her face. She left her bedroom through a secret door concealed behind a painting and followed a hidden passage to the servants' entrance to the mansion, where Hennessy was waiting for her, also dressed in ordinary street clothes. They walked with Daisy's arm through Hennessy's, as if they were father and daughter, making their way down Nassau Street, past Trinity College.

Walking along the wide avenue that was Dame Street, they steered off into the narrow cobbled streets of Temple Bar, an area near the river that had started down the slow path to decay. Daisy looked casually around, then turned abruptly past a young boy leaning against the wall. She stepped through an anonymous-looking doorway and descended some stairs. Hennessy, believing he should have gone ahead to ensure the way was clear for his mistress, hurried after her down the narrow staircase.

The pub that they found themselves in was dark, smoky and almost empty. The tables were long, rough, unfinished wood with benches either side and stools at either end. The bar appeared to serve stout or whiskey and little else. There was a myriad other peculiar and unpleasant smells present in the air, and Daisy did her level best to avoid trying to identify them. Women were not normally permitted in such a place, and she thought it was just as well. They might be overcome with the urge to open some windows and call for a mop and a bucket of soapy water.

Apart from the tables, benches, stools and the odd chair, there was little in the way of features in the room. But hints of nationalism could be seen around if one looked closely. A small print of Daniel O'Connell hung on the wall to one side of the bar. A rather romantic and poorly rendered painting of the pirate queen, Grace O'Malley, hung near the door. Daisy cast her eyes over the image of the woman aboard a ship at full sail, as she had done on earlier visits. She felt a certain kinship with the unconventional warrior woman.

There were only five men in the room; three were

sitting at one table under one of the low windows that ran along the outer wall at street level, the other two sitting at the table nearest the door. All five men stood up as Daisy and Hennessy walked in.

'Good afternoon, your Grace,' one of the three said, tilting his head in way of a bow. 'Delighted you could join us. Can we offer you anything to drink?'

'Good afternoon, Mister Duffy. A cup of tea would be lovely,' she replied, confident that if Eamon Duffy provided her with a cup of tea, its quality would be more than adequate, no matter what the surroundings.

She took off her bonnet and veil and gave him a smile, holding her right hand out as he always insisted she should. He took her hand and kissed her knuckles in an old-fashioned, chivalrous gesture. She suspected he harboured feelings for her, but he was too discreet to let them get in the way of their business.

'You have been injured,' he observed with concern, glancing down at the bandaged fingers on her left hand.

'Trifling wounds,' she said in a light voice. 'Pay them no mind. It was a silly thing – I caught my fingers in a door.'

Duffy was a square-shouldered man with greying hair framing a face that had a hard look about it, but inspired trust. He had a no-nonsense manner and the self-assurance of a man who had built his business from the ground up. He was also a leading figure in the nationalist movement – the Fenian rebels who caused the British so much trouble.

Nate had worked with him years before to help keep the peace on the Wildenstern estates, and now Daisy had taken over the role. But neither of them were looking to avoid trouble this time.

'We were worried you might not be able to make it,' he said to her as he ushered her over to the head of the table under the window and provided her with the best chair the place had to offer. 'Your cousin's "secret police" have eyes and ears all over the city. My people tell me his surveillance of you is growing more constant, your Grace. Especially now that there is word that Nathaniel Wildenstern is coming home.'

Daisy caught her breath, feeling her pulse quicken, but tried to hide her excitement under a mild expression of interest. The warm flush in her cheeks told her she was failing miserably.

'And is that word reliable?'

'I can go one better than rumour, ma'am,' he said with a smile. 'I received a coded telegram this morning. He is in Wicklow as we speak, and hopes to be in Dublin by tomorrow. If all goes to plan, we'll be able to meet up with him and Cathal Dempsey's father tomorrow evening. But where we go from there will depend on you, your Grace. We've investigated a whole host of your family's businesses, but with no luck. Tons of machinery, hundreds of engimals and an orphanage full of children, and we can't find any of 'em.'

'I suggest you try the mines in Glendalough,' Daisy said to him, pulling out a leather folder from beneath her brown shawl and laying it on the table. 'And don't be fooled if they look closed off.'

'That makes sense,' one of the other men at the table, a blond fellow with a muscular build and intense eyes under jutting brows, commented to Duffy. 'The evictions in the valley – sure, wasn't the place emptied out last year? And remember the talk back then of a sea monster brought up to the docks durin' the night last Christmas? Some say it was carved up in a warehouse on the quays and the pieces carried on wagons into the mountains. A leviathan, they said. Even in pieces, it'd be hard to hide. But turf everyone out of their homes so you have a whole valley and some deep mines to lose it in – transport it in at night and you're laughin'.'

'Under other circumstances, Pádraig, I'd be givin' short shrift to such fairy tales,' Duffy grunted. 'But with Gerald Gordon, anything's possible.'

He opened the folder and examined the contents, his thick fingers flicking through the documents. Daisy noticed some words scratched into the wood of the tabletop. The table was constructed of rough, unfinished wooden planks nailed lengthways atop a long, simple frame. In her world it was hard to imagine such an object being considered 'furniture'. The words, dug into the wood in rough square letters just as a schoolchild might mark their desk, were in

Irish: '*Rapparee Go Breath*'. 'The Rapparee Forever.' The mysterious Highwayboy was starting to be seen as a nationalist figure, someone the people could rally behind. Whatever about being a celebrated rogue, the boy delinquent would be hard pressed to survive once the British saw him in this new light.

Duffy glanced at Pádraig, and then his eyes lifted up to meet Daisy's.

'It's all here. And *signed* too, I see. I won't ask how you managed *that*, your Grace.'

'No, don't,' she replied. She drew in a deep shuddering breath and let it out slowly. She found she was trembling slightly, and clasped her hands together to keep them still. 'So . . . we move ahead as planned?'

'There's nothing for it now,' he replied, closing the folder and holding it up. 'You've set us on the path, your Grace. With the stroke of a pen, you've given us the break we need, stopped the Wildensterns from using their influence in the police against us . . . and placed yourself firmly in the sights of Gerald Gordon's unholy wrath. It is a cunning plan, and I commend your courage, your Grace. And I hope you're prepared.'

The expression on his face was one of stern compassion. He knew enough about the family to know the price of a Wildenstern woman's defiance. His hand pressed against his belly, as if he had felt a twinge from an old wound.

'I am,' she said firmly, as the image of the steel-framed

window in a turret on the roof of Wildenstern Hall passed through her mind. She repeated more quietly, 'I am.'

A boy came running down the stairs – the boy who had been keeping watch at the door.

'Someone's coming!' he cried. 'I think it's Mister Gordon!'

'Christ! What's he doing, coming down this way?' Duffy snarled, turning to Daisy in alarm. 'He must have followed you! If he sees you here with us . . .'

'In here, your Grace.' Pádraig gestured towards a store-room behind the bar. He grabbed her bonnet and the leather folder and pushed them into her hands. 'Come on, Hennessy! Quickly!'

Daisy and Hennessy hurried behind the bar and into the tiny dark room. Pádraig had only just closed the door behind them when a man came down the steps into the pub. There was a slatted window in the door, and Daisy was able to peer through and get a limited view of the room. It was Gerald. His coming here could not have been a coincidence. Did he know she was still here? Daisy found she was holding her breath and forced herself to exhale and breathe normally. But silently. With the storeroom in darkness, he should not be able to see her through the narrow slats. Even so, she should stay away from the window. But she couldn't.

'Mister Gordon,' Duffy greeted the new visitor. 'We wouldn't have expected a gentleman of your stature to grace us with his presence in an establishment such as this. To what do we owe the honour?'

'Eamon Duffy,' Gerald said, taking off his top hat and laying it on the table, then throwing his navy blue cloak over the back of the chair on which Daisy had just been sitting. 'I wouldn't have expected to find you in such a pigsty. A man of your considerable means can surely find more comfortable surroundings to entertain his charming friends.'

With one hand, Gerald gestured to the other four Fenians, who were too obviously on their guard. Gerald sat down in the chair at the head of Duffy's table. Duffy was seated to his left, with another fellow to his right. The pair of men by the door stayed where they were. Pádraig pretended to polish the bar for a moment – as if that might in any way improve its appearance – before crossing over to sit down at the other end of the table to Gerald.

'I was told I might find you here,' Gerald went on, tilting his head towards Duffy in a leisurely manner as he took his silver case from his pocket, opened it and slipped a French cigarette between his lips. Duffy struck a match and lit the gasper for him. Gerald nodded his thanks. 'Thought I'd drop in for a chinwag. You seem so intent on keeping abreast with my activities, I thought it only right that we should meet and catch up in person.'

'My only interest in your activities, Mister Gordon,' Duffy said, 'lies in their effects on ordinary working people. At the moment, I am particularly interested in an orphanage full of children who have disappeared while

under the patronage of your family. We know you have no
qualms in using children in your factories. We were
wondering if perhaps you had found them gainful
employment and had neglected to tell anyone.'

'You appear to know more about the matter than I,'
Gerald replied, dangling the cigarette casually from his
fingers. 'I haven't the foggiest, frankly. Children, to me, are
merely adults who are not yet ripened; small, dense, difficult
to prepare and quite lacking in any kind of taste. The ones
you seek are setting a good example, as far as I'm
concerned. Children should be neither seen nor heard until
they have reached a sufficient level of maturity and usefulness. Now, as to the whereabouts of my cousin, the
Duchess, you might be able to enlighten me better.'

'I'm sure I don't know what you mean.'

'Did you know that she has a unique *scent*, the Duchess?'
Gerald inhaled through his nose, holding the cigarette away
from his face as he did so. 'She uses a particular skin cream
imported from Paris, and sometimes she wears *L'Air du
Temps* . . . but not today.'

His gaze dropped down to the top of the table, and Daisy
thought he might have seen the words written there, for his
fingers brushed its surface. He lifted his head to meet
Duffy's cold stare.

'You're up to something, the pair of you. I have to say
I'm intrigued. I've had you investigated, of course, and from
what I've learned of you, Duffy, you are a resolute man.

A man with a cause. That's a type of enemy I do not underestimate. Understand, however, that I have a cause of my own. One of immense importance to the wider world. I am a mere cog in a great machine. Now, I'm sure any threat I made regarding your safety or that of your men would have little effect. But take care that you don't involve any Wildenstern women in your schemes, Duffy. I think you know even better than I how that can turn out.'

Duffy's face was set in a tense mask that hid a sudden fury, but he did not move from where he was. Pádraig jumped to his feet at the other end of the table, a knife appearing in his right hand.

'What kind of cur are you, to be threatening a woman?' he rasped. 'I don't care who you are, or who your family is, I'll—'

Sticking his cigarette between his lips, Gerald gave a crude grin and struck the edge of the table with the heel of his hand. The force of the blow snapped nails and splintered wood as the plank drove forward into Pádraig's groin. As Pádraig howled and fell to the floor with his hands between his legs, Gerald seized the loose plank and hurled it across the room like a javelin, catching one of the Fenians on the head. The plank dropped to the floor with a clatter, the man following close behind. The rebel at the table beside Gerald pulled a gun, but Gerald swept his arm in a lock up behind his back and slammed his face down on the tabletop. The arm-lock that Gerald maintained with one hand kept the man securely pinned there. The second man near the door drew a revolver. In a blur of motion, Gerald's free hand whipped to his body and then out, and the remaining Fenian found the sleeve of his gun-hand pinned to the doorframe by a throwing knife.

'Enough!' Duffy snapped, his jaw set in a look of impatience. 'Enough. This is a stupid waste of time.'

'I agree,' Gerald replied, releasing the arm-lock and plucking the cigarette from his mouth. 'You are amateurs playing a professional's game, Duffy. You play it at your own cost. But take care that others don't end up paying that price for you. Do not involve the Duchess in your meddling, you tired old bog-trotter. It'll end badly for both of you.'

And with that, he took up his hat and cloak and departed, leaving the rebels to pick themselves up. When they were sure he was gone, Duffy went back to the storeroom and let Daisy out.

'So it begins,' he remarked to her. 'You'd best go out the back way, your Grace, in case he's still waiting nearby, although I don't think he means to harm you directly. There's no tellin' what he'll do once we put your plan into action, though. You've unleashed a dangerous one there, ma'am, and no mistake. What's that famous quote everyone uses at times like this? "Cry havoc; and let slip the dogs of war!" A fitting line, I'd say.'

'It's from *Julius Caesar*,' Daisy said. 'Are you a fan of Shakespeare?'

'No, ma'am,' he said as he walked her to another door on the far side of the room, with Hennessy following a couple of strides behind them.

'Too much old-fashioned language?'

'Too much violence,' he replied with a grim smile. 'I've seen enough in my life, and I've had my fill. There's something immoral about portraying it for the sake of entertainment. I prefer a spot of poetry myself.'

Stopping at the door, he took her hand and kissed it once more.

'Take care, your Grace. You've set some fierce dangerous events in motion.'

'Call me Daisy, Eamon.'

'Take care, Daisy,' he said, bowing his head. 'God be with you.'

'And with you,' she answered.

He put his hand to his belly again.

'I've been blessed with one miracle in my life. It would be too much to expect any more Divine intervention. But maybe, with a bit of luck, we'll come through.'

Daisy said goodbye, and she and Hennessy made their way up a flight of stairs, through a house joined onto the back of the pub and out a door onto another of Temple Bar's narrow cobbled lanes. It had grown dark, and Dublin's smog was congealing, forming a soupy gas that obscured everything in its gritty fumes. Daisy walked away towards Dame Street with Hennessy close behind her.

As she disappeared into the smog, Gerald stepped out of the shadow of a doorway and straightened the cloak draped over his shoulders. His eyes gazed out from under the rim of his top hat, his face illuminated momentarily as he struck a match and lit a fresh cigarette. He blew out some smoke and turned in the other direction, his heels clicking against the cobbles as he made his way in the direction of the river. Everything was shrouded in blurry fug, and for his own amusement Gerald whistled while he walked. And as he did, the smog parted before him as if it were curtains that could be drawn aside. Then the dirty fog closed around him and thickened behind him, and in moments he had disappeared.

XXIV

MOBY

Cathal stood at his worktable, pulling the brain out of a wheel-wolf. Each of the creature's four stumpy legs ended in a chubby wheel with a heavily ridged, flexible covering. The legs themselves were short but powerfully sprung, the shoulders and flanks broad, with the narrow back bowed as if to take a saddle, which many of these creatures did. They were not as fast as velocycles, but were easier to ride and kept their footing better over very rough ground.

With a pair of heavy pliers, Cathal detached the brain from its bonds in the elongated skull. The brain itself was the size of a small marble, joined to the inside of the skull with engimal-gut, those strands of filament that were as thin as fishing line but as strong as steel wire. With a heavy breath, he wrote a description of the creature on a label and tied it to the brain, before placing it in a box beside others that he had removed that day. Gerald insisted that all of the engimals' vital organs be labelled – a service only a few of the children could provide, as most of them could neither read nor write.

Lying in bed the previous night, Cathal had studied the whistle he had stolen from Gerald's study. It appeared to be made of a hard, creamy white material, which could possibly be whalebone or one of the many types of ceramic which formed parts of the engimals' bodies. He had been afraid to blow into it in case it should alert Gerald or the guards. There was no telling if it was the right type of whistle, or if it worked or not, or if it would have the desired effect even if it did work. That was a lot of 'ifs'. But there was nothing for it – they might not get another chance at this. And Gerald seemed to be getting very close to achieving his goal of gaining control over the intelligent particles.

If he could do even half of what he claimed, he would be virtually unstoppable.

Cathal wished they could have made their move last night, but there had been no time to organize the children. And besides, they didn't know where all the guards were at night. At night, the children were penned up in some small chambers off the main cave, and none of them knew where the guards slept or how many stood watch. None of them had fully explored all the tunnels in this part of the mine. Besides, there were other advantages in waiting until the morning.

The noise of the machinery in the slaughterhouse made communication between the children difficult, but also made it hard for the guards to overhear them talking. Cathal looked up from his worktable to see Pip mouthing words to him. He moved around his table so that he could hear his friend.

'Queg's given us deh wave,' the boy said. 'We're on.'

Cathal nodded, and went to raise his hand. Pip reached over and stopped him.

'Are yeh sure yeh can do dis, Cathal? I mean, we *believe* in yeh an' dat – we'd follow the Highwayboy to the gates of Hell, but we don't want to see yeh gettin' killed fer us. Dis *is* gonna work, innit?'

Cathal was about to answer, but instead just held up his hand.

'Only one way to find out,' he replied. 'We've got the whistle – and Gerald's gone out somewhere, so at least we don't have to deal with him. And I don't see Red either. We need to use this thing before Gerald discovers it's missing.'

Cowen, the nearest of the guards, came over. He was the brute with the face like a bag of potatoes, all swollen-looking and knobbly. He had a stubbled scalp and fists which were each the size of a child's head. Cathal guessed the thug must have been nearly twice his weight, and Cathal's head only just reached his shoulder.

'I need to relieve meself,' he told the man.

Cowen lifted his chin to his mate, who stood nearby. They were under orders not to let Cathal leave the main cave without being escorted by at least two of them. Cowen held a wooden club in his hand, and used it to nudge Cathal towards the tunnel leading to the cesspit.

'I know the way,' Cathal reminded him. 'You don't have to push.'

With his feet shackled, he could only move with small steps – the chain between the shackles was little more than a foot long. The other man – a burly, wheezy oaf named McCoughlan – followed them as they made their way towards the tunnel. The stench from the mouth of the tunnel was eye-watering, but it got worse the further in you went. McCoughlan stopped at the entrance, gesturing to Cowen to go ahead.

'You're in charge on this trip,' he said in his short-of-breath manner. 'You can take it the rest of the way.'

Cowen scowled and swore quietly, but then prodded Cathal with the baton again. Cathal hobbled forward into the stink.

Since the children could not be allowed outside, and Gerald would not allow buckets for their doings in the main cave, a crude but effective toilet had been constructed. A wide board had been laid over a borehole in the floor of the chamber at the end of the tunnel. The children did their business into the borehole by squatting over a smaller, circular hole in the board. The borehole dropped down into an underground stream which, in theory, would carry away the waste matter. This system did not work perfectly, however – partly due to the low light and the wobbly board, and partly because of the hazardous protrusions sticking out of the walls of the borehole itself.

The hole was large enough for a child to climb down, but not a grown man. This obvious avenue of escape had been blocked off by embedding steel spikes into the walls of the borehole about five feet down. Unfortunately, the spikes impeded a bit of *everything* that was dropped into the hole.

Cathal coughed into the crook of his elbow, trying not to breathe through his nose. His sinuses were already burning and he had to blink his eyes to clear the tears. The chamber had a high ceiling and was roughly twenty feet across, but the only ventilation came from the tunnel.

'Get on with it,' Cowen grumbled.

With a quick glance behind him, Cathal jumped right over the plank of wood, turned, got his toe under the plank and flipped it up into Cowen's shins. The guard snarled, more annoyed than hurt by the move. Cathal staggered back as the man bounded across the borehole, baton raised to put this whippersnapper in his place.

He had been warned about the young Wildenstern, but he had not paid enough attention to the warnings. Cathal easily dodged the blow, darting to the man's right. With his feet together, he leaped towards the wall of the chamber, got his feet up onto the stone surface and launched himself back off the wall, diving right over Cowen's head. The chain stretched taut between his ankles and caught across the big man's throat, hooking under his jaw. Cathal's momentum wrenched the thug off his feet and Cathal absorbed the force of the fall by rolling forwards as he hit the ground, hurling Cowen past him. The bigger man somersaulted over and landed hard on his front, gagging on an injured throat. He made a noise like a strangled bear and shook his head as he started to get to his feet. The club had dropped from his grasp, but he went instead for the pistol in his waistband.

'McCacchlish!' he croaked, his call for help reduced to a cough. 'McCacch . . . McCoughlan!'

As he got up on his knees, he raised his head to keep his eyes on Cathal. But Cathal was gone. A clink of chain behind him caused him to turn his head . . . and then Cathal, still lying on his back, shoved Cowen's arse as hard as he could with both feet. Cowen went head-first into the borehole, his shoulders jamming in the narrow well. His head was well clear of the spikes below, but he was caught with his arms down by his sides. The gun fell from his waistband, hit his chin on the way down, bounced off a couple of the spikes, and then tumbled into the stream twenty-five feet below. Cathal swore as he watched it fall, but managed to catch the man's bunch of keys as they fell from his pocket.

He unlocked his shackles, tossed them aside and stood up.

'You all right there, Cowen?' he asked. 'How's the air down there?'

'I'm gonna cut yer liver out for this, yeh little guttie!'

'You'll have to catch me first,' Cathal snapped back. 'And after a spell in there, I'd say I'll smell yeh comin'!'

Lifting his foot, he stamped down on Cowen's ample backside, wedging him in even further. Cowen screamed blue murder. Cathal heard footsteps hurrying down the tunnel.

'Cowen?' McCoughlan called. 'What's goin' on down dere?'

Cathal picked up Cowen's wooden club and ducked down to the side, tucking himself in against the wall by the entrance, out of sight of the tunnel. McCoughlan trotted down the tunnel and saw Cowen's legs sticking up out of the borehole.

'Jaysus!' he exclaimed. 'Here, boyo, is that you?'

Despite the stupidity of the question, McCoughlan kept his head and hung back from the chamber. His own club, the stout handle of a hatchet, was held at the ready. It was a habit of his to whack the backs of the young workers' legs with it when they weren't meeting his high standards of productivity, but he was equally enthusiastic about cracking skulls, given the chance. Cathal swung out, his hand whipping forward, and Cowen's heavy bunch of keys struck McCoughlan squarely in the face. The man cried out and clutched his face, swiping wildly with his club. Cathal rolled in under the swinging club to slam the heel of his shoe into McCoughlan's groin. McCoughlan squealed and folded in half, putting his head in easy reach of his opponent. Cathal whacked his own club into the side of the man's head with stunning force. McCoughlan collapsed to the floor, moaning dizzily.

Cathal grabbed his discarded shackles. They had been a tight fit on his ankles. He rolled the burly guard over onto his front and pinned his arms behind him. The shackles fit the man's wrists nicely. Cathal pulled the pistol from the holster on his belt, stood up and ran quietly up the tunnel.

Stopping at the mouth of the tunnel, looking out at the main cave, he saw Queg standing at a worktable nearby. A dark-skinned, tattooed, sturdy little gurrier with a shaved head, Queg was watching for the signal. Cathal slapped the wall twice, and Queg nodded. It was time for Gerald's flock of sheep to turn on its dogs.

A guard with a grizzly mop of hair and beard was standing nearby, shouting at one of the girls who had dropped her box of engimal parts on the floor. Another guard was staring over, distracted by the commotion. That one did not see the attack coming until it was too late – four boys jumped him, one hitting him over the head with a wooden bucket. The blow was enough to stun him so they could drag him to the ground. His wrists and ankles were swiftly bound with rope and engimal-gut.

A third guard saw what happened and pulled his

revolver, shouting in alarm. His shouts were not heard over the noise of the machinery. Queg ran in front of him, yelling something and pointing off towards where Cathal was standing. A girl crawled up against the backs of the man's legs. The guard looked over at Cathal, and then Queg shoved the man as hard as he could. The guard toppled backwards over the girl and was set upon by five children. A shot went off and Queg lurched back and staggered to the side. He struggled to stay on his feet as a red stain spread through his shirt from the hole in his chest.

Everyone heard the gunshot. The bearded guard who had been about to beat the girl for dropping the engimal parts looked up, searching for the source of the sound. But the one who had fired the shot was out of sight on the ground. Letting go of the girl's arm, the grizzly guard stepped out between the worktables, his hand going to his belt to draw his own firearm. A mallet hit him across the shin, swung by a boy hiding under one of the tables. The man cried out and fell back against the table, lifting his leg to clutch it to him. More hands grabbed his other foot and pulled it out from under him. His gun was snatched from his belt and a gang of child workers quickly subdued him.

Keys were found. Shackles were unlocked. A shiver of fear and excitement spread through the wide space.

There were six guards – five had been taken care of. The sixth was coming out of the smaller cave where the slaughtering was carried out. A ferret-faced man with a bushy moustache, he froze as he found Cathal pressing the barrel of a revolver against the side of his head. Cathal put a finger to his lips and six children piled on top of the guard, flattening him against the floor. Cathal strode down the tunnel, pistol raised. The stout door was standing open. There were only two slaughterers here, and he found them on the verge of killing a bright-eye. There were two other tables and the room was filled with racks of various weapons, tools and means of slaughter. Another tunnel led to the pens where other engimals waited. The floor was littered with shards of engimal carapace, shreds of skin and lengths of engimal gut. The bright-eye, with its long, multi-hinged neck, turned its large illuminated eye towards Cathal with a pleading look. It was strapped to the heavy table. One man was holding a cleaver over its neck while the other struggled to hold its head still. They stopped what they were doing as they noticed the young man with the gun standing in the doorway, mild surprise written on their faces.

Cathal hesitated for a moment. He had forgotten about Siren. Tatty's singing engimal was up in Gerald's study, a long way down a tunnel in the wrong direction. There wasn't time now to go and get it before they made their break. Pip appeared behind him.

'Queg's dead,' the boy said quietly, his voice choked with a suppressed sob. 'Shot through the heart.'

Cathal nodded, but did not take his eyes or his aim from

the two men. He had known there might be casualties. It could not weaken their resolve now.

'Tell the others to release the bright-eye and strap these two to the tables instead,' he told the younger boy. 'But there's no time to waste. Bring the bright-eye with us. Then unlock the pens and let the other engimals out. I doubt they kill with the same pleasure or merciless efficiency as humans, but these gentlemen can help us find out.'

Three minutes later, Cathal and the children hurried out of the slaughter-room with the sounds of engimals bounding to freedom behind them. They knew closing the door would only slow them down – there were plenty of engimals that could open doors, or knock them down. But it would herd them together for a few moments and give the slaughterers time for some much-needed reflection.

'Right,' Cathal muttered, pulling the whistle out through the tear in the lining of his waistband, where he had hidden it. He clutched it in his fist. 'Let's get the flock out o' here.'

Soon, they were running up the sloping tunnel towards the entrance to the mine, with Cathal urging them on as fast as they could go. The tunnel was low, and about seven feet across. Rails ran along the floor – the carts that ran along them were still sometimes used to bring in some of the larger engimals, or the heavier parts of those too large to fit through the entrance. Wooden beams supported the stone walls and ceiling, spaced regularly along the tunnel's length. The only light came from the lanterns a few of the children carried, and the bright-eye that skittered along on spindly legs by Cathal's feet like a faithful dog. Its eye shone a circle of light on the ground in front of them, and Cathal stumbled to a halt as its glow picked out something ahead – a shape in the darkness that he could not make out at first. The bright-eye backed up and tucked itself behind his legs, cowering there with its head peering around to keep its light on the strange sight.

'That's it,' Pip whispered. 'That's Moby.'

The other children had stopped further back in the tunnel. Cathal could feel their fear, blending with his own, the atmosphere in the tunnel raising goosebumps on his skin. Moving forward one careful step at a time, he examined this bizarre, grotesque door.

Cathal stared in wonder at the mouth of the tunnel . . . for that was exactly what it was – a mouth. It was a concave shape: a deep dome, or cone, that formed into a square to seal off the tunnel entirely with flesh that had somehow been welded to the walls – flesh that appeared to be some kind of graphite-coloured, rubbery metal. Cathal reached out to touch it where it joined the wall and it felt as rough as sandpaper, but warm. The cone, which must have protruded further up the end of the tunnel, was divided equally by three lines which met in the centre. This creature had three jaws that closed together to seal the cone-shaped snout. He had the unshakeable feeling that they were somehow trapped inside the belly of this leviathan.

How had Gerald caught this beast? How could he have kept it alive as he brought it up here and taken it apart? How could he have hidden such a feat from the outside world?

'Why didn't he save himself all the bother and use *a normal bloody door*?' Cathal sighed.

He could hear the sound of shifting feet behind him. The children were growing increasingly disturbed by the sight. And they knew the guards would be recovering back in the cave. Or Gerald or Red might show up at any moment. With the tension in his chest stifling the breath in his lungs, Cathal put the whistle to his lips and blew a long note.

The mouth opened immediately, with a low groaning noise and a slight creaking, and a three-pointed star of day-light blinded them, the creature's maw stretching into an imperfect circle, revealing the square entrance of the tunnel about twenty yards further up.

'Come on!' Cathal called to the others. 'We're getting out of here!'

The rails stopped where the creature's flesh joined the floor, and he felt the strange substance give like soft earth under his feet. Each one of its three V-shaped lips was as thick as a rolled-up rug and as hard as bone. Cathal had to step across the bottom one to go through. Pip went to follow him, but caught Cathal's arm as he came alongside.

'Mister Dempsey, wait! Sometin's wrong. Dere was

another set of doors – normal ones, at deh top dere. Why would dey be open?'

Even as he said it, Cathal heard the violin music and knew they were lost. He grabbed Pip's wrist as the boy started to back away. Gerald stepped into the square of light at the end of the tunnel, silhouetted by the glow as he played that engimal violin of his. Gerald didn't come in towards them, but Cathal could feel the music take him in its grip. Behind him, the children's minds surrendered without a whimper, their bodies turning obediently and setting off back down the tunnel. Pip moved to go with them, but Cathal held on to him, teeth clenched as he struggled to control himself.

'No,' he growled, an involuntary animal noise rising from his throat. 'No. I'm not givin' in to you again.'

It felt as if there were iron filings in his blood, and some massive magnet was acting upon them, dragging his body backwards into the mouth of the leviathan. Turning his head, he saw Red stride through the retreating ranks of the children. He had a white whistle in his hand. He had been back there the whole time. But why hadn't he tried to stop them? Had Gerald been waiting for this all along? Cathal let out another snarl as he was forced to let go of Pip and cover his ears. But that did not make any difference. Gerald was not playing to *him*, but to the *things inside him*. Cathal watched Pip back away and step slowly into the creature's jaws. Cathal seized the boy's wrist again with his right hand, even as his own body fought to betray him.

'No!' he cried. 'No, no, no, no, no, no, no, no, no!'

This is my body, he told himself. Gerald said we could impose our will on these things. I have no music, I can't speak that language, but this is *my* body. He can't take it away from me!

The thought seemed to help, and Cathal turned to glare at Gerald, his whole body feeling as if it were filled with red-hot pins and needles, all surging in waves towards the darkness of the tunnel. But he was starting to slow those surges, his mind slowly picking out each little spark of pain and extinguishing it. This is my body, he repeated to himself over and over again. I can control this thing inside me.

He felt Gerald's focus change. The children were back under the control of the guards now and as Gerald directed all of his energy towards Cathal, the pain and the overwhelming urge to turn back rose again. Pip screamed, flailing at Cathal's iron grip, begging to be released. Cathal shook his head, trying to will away the pain. Gerald's hold over him was weakening. It was not a clash of intelligence, but of will, and Cathal did not bend before Gerald's.

From out of nowhere behind him, a snake-like cable the thickness of a man's thigh whipped forward, coiling around his torso. Another two wrapped around his legs, and a fourth bound his left arm to his body. His right hand still held tight onto Pip's wrist. These things were some kind of tentacle, part of the leviathan. More stretched out on either side of him, blocking off any hope of escape. The ones that held him squeezed him mercilessly, forcing the breath out of him, crushing his flesh and putting unbearable pressure on his bones.

Something snapped in Cathal's head, and he felt a sickening change deep within his torso. He gasped as his bones began to lengthen and change shape. His muscles writhed under his skin, pulling taut like cords and swelling, rippling, squirming like the tentacles that held him. An immense strength filled him and his left arm twisted free, wrapping around the girth of the tentacle in return. With a wrenching turn, he felt the tentacle's flesh split as it folded against itself. He tore the end of the tentacle off so that it dangled by a few strands of engimal-gut and some kind of oily gum.

Another tentacle seized his left arm, nearly yanking it from its socket, but Cathal was growing now, his body swelling, his face distorted. His skull felt as if it would explode, his spine as if it were about to snap, but instead, he grew in powerful, misshapen spurts. The tentacles struggled to hold him. But he was losing his reason too – his mind was fogged with an all-consuming rage, a desire for violence, an aching need to tear his enemies limb from limb.

Pip shrieked in abject terror, thrashing and kicking out, desperately trying to escape from this monster.

Cathal could still hear Gerald's playing, but it just

enraged him further. Releasing Pip, he grabbed the tentacle circling his waist and heaved on it, pivoting his body and ripping the tendril from its roots. He hurled the thing at Gerald, knocking the older man to the ground. Turning his eyes on Red, he saw the panicked cove raise the whistle to his lips, intent on closing the leviathan's mouth. Pip was scrambling across the giant creature's lower jaw as Red blew on the whistle.

Cathal's right arm shot out and shoved Pip through the gap between the three jaws just as the mouth slammed closed with a frightening suddenness. The boy escaped a crushing death by mere inches . . . but Cathal's forearm was smashed to pulp. For the first few seconds, he couldn't even scream, paralyzed by the pain and the horror of it. Like the leviathan's tentacle, his arm was still attached by strands of muscle and sinew. Cathal's mouth opened, and his shriek filled the tunnel as Gerald lunged forward and clamped a hand to the back of his neck, fingers and thumb digging into pressure points. Moments later, Cathal blacked out.

XXV

'SENTENCE HAS BEEN PASSED'

When Elizabeth came to Daisy's office and invited the younger woman to join herself and Brutus outside, Daisy had felt inclined to tell the hag where to insert her invitation. This urge to resort to coarse language had been growing in strength recently, and she saw it as just another symptom of the stress of her situation. But she was in no doubt that the summons had actually come from Brutus, and Daisy was curious to see why Elizabeth had been sent, rather than a servant. Apart from her assertion that it was she who was extending the invitation, the imperious woman did not even seem put out that she had been dispatched by her brother as a mere messenger.

The day was overcast and cold, with a brisk, fresh breeze blowing across the lawns. Daisy put on her bonnet and pulled a white woollen shawl over the shoulders of her

cream and ivory patterned dress before setting out.
Elizabeth wore a heavy silk dress of different greens, and as
they walked along the path towards the woods, Daisy half
wondered if the woman had changed her attire to blend
with the environment. Elizabeth had not told her where
they were going once they got outside, and Daisy decided
she couldn't be bothered asking. Until they reached their
destination, she would try and enjoy the walk in the clear
morning air.

She could hear the family's private train from here.
Beyond the graveyard, at the bottom of the hill, the idling
steam engine wheezed as it waited for whichever illustrious
family member was using it today. Daisy had noted that the
train would make an excellent means of escape in the days
to come, if it should become necessary. But she had dismissed the idea when she reasoned that the rest of the
family would already have included it in any exit strategy,
should the need to leave urgently arise. Over the tops of the
trees, the scattering traces of its exhaust smoke floated
towards the sky.

The path took the two women into the woods, its fine
gravel surface dappled with green and blue shadows cast by
the trees as the sun burnt through the clouds, making way
for patches of blue sky. There was still no warmth in the day,
and it was cooler in the shadows. This path led to the
church, and for a silly moment, Daisy wondered if Brutus
had decided to stop wasting family money building a

church. Then she reminded herself that the building was almost finished and, more importantly, that Gerald had an investment in its construction. Could that be it, then? Had Gerald let her build the thing, only to commandeer it completely now that it was finished? She wouldn't put it past him.

But Elizabeth steered them away from the church, turning into the grandest part of the cemetery instead. Here lay the graves of the most important branches of the family. Monuments of different-hued marble competed with each other in their outlandish glory. Statues of angels vied with soldiers and lions and dragons and other majestic or mythical beasts. Scattered among their shadows, like the undergrowth beneath this forest of petrified figures, were simpler gravestones, still elegant, their graves well-tended.

The mausoleum where the Patriarchs were interred was a large marble building decorated with inlaid patterns of exotic stones and engravings picked out in gold leaf. Six white columns framed its entrance, supporting a shallow gabled roof that caused it to resemble a Greek temple – an effect that was entirely deliberate, she was sure. They walked past this vainglorious crypt to the graves beyond. The headstones here were not as grand as most of the others, though Daisy considered many of them quite beautiful. The yew trees around them gave the place a sheltered feel, and the gusts of wind were not as strong here. Daisy would often have said that she found graveyards to be eminently peaceful places.

That peaceful atmosphere was marred somewhat by the sight of three men on their knees in the gravel covering one of the graves. Their hands were tied behind their backs. Each one had his head pinned to the marble kerb that ran around the edge of the grave. Their heads were held in place by the black iron rail that ran around the top the kerb, though Daisy could not see how they could possibly have pushed their heads under the rail – it barely had space beneath it for their necks. Oliver was one of the men; the other two were lesser cousins, of the gang who let themselves be ruled by Oliver's domineering manner in the hope that he would share his power in the future, after he had seized it from Gerald. Now, their faces all shared the same expression of abject terror.

Brutus stood over them, his right hand – the engimal claw – tucked behind his back, the other holding a smoking cigar. Interestingly, he did not look ruffled in any way. And yet Daisy would have bet good money that their predicament was his doing. Seeing how he stood now, the men could have been wreaths of flowers, for all the attention he paid them.

The bar across their necks did not seem to be allowing them to breathe properly. Oliver had gone a deep red, though there might have been some embarrassment involved, mingled in with the fear. She noticed their faces, hands and clothes showed signs of having recently been in a fight. An assortment of guns and knives lay on the grass around Brutus's feet.

'Thank you for joining us,' he rumbled to Daisy. 'I have asked you here this morning to help me make a decision.'

'If it's about your choice of grave decoration,' she replied, 'I would have opted for lilies. But each to their own.'

Elizabeth gave a condescending laugh and clapped her hands. Brutus glanced down at the three men and huffed to himself, before taking a long drag on his cigar.

'Very droll,' he commented, blowing out smoke. 'But this is a matter of utmost seriousness. These three men have committed an Act of Aggression against me. As you can see, they have failed. Elizabeth was with me, but we cannot be sure they meant her harm. Under the Rules of Ascension, I have the right to carry out retribution against these whelps for their attack. Reason dictates that I do so – I have no wish to leave them in any condition which would allow them to attempt another assault at some point in the future.'

'Clearly, you are a most reasonable man,' Daisy said.

'I found something on Oliver here that adds a new dimension to this decision-making process,' Brutus went on, ignoring her sarcasm. He put the cigar in his mouth and used his left hand to take a folded piece of paper from his jacket pocket. Handing it to Daisy, he added: 'It is a drawing, a piece of a floor plan. Perhaps you recognize the location described hereon.'

One glance at the sheet confirmed that she did. The drawing was of her suite of rooms in Wildenstern Hall. Not just the walls, doors and windows, but also the main pieces of furniture, the secret doors, the tunnels they led to and the booby-traps that protected them. She had only started allowing booby-traps to be set around her rooms for the last two years, and had thought she could trust the small number of servants who installed them. There was only one reason that Oliver would be carrying this drawing. Her stomach felt as if it was carrying a small heavy stone – it was not the first time her life had been threatened, but her eyes were drawn to the small rectangle marked 'Bed'. They had marked the very place where she slept.

'You were next,' Brutus told her. 'Whether it was to be murder or kidnapping one cannot tell from this alone, though I wager I could find out quickly enough. The fact remains, they intended to act against you. That is most certainly against the Rules of Ascension. It is written that no woman can be the target of any Act of Aggression. So the choice is yours.'

'I'm sorry, what choice?' Daisy asked.

'Their fate,' Brutus said simply, taking another drag on his cigar and gazing down at her with hard eyes.

'It would be wise to bleed them for information first, Daisy,' Elizabeth offered helpfully. 'We can be sure that there are other conspirators. They must be sought out. But once they have provided enough answers, the end itself can be quite abrupt. There is no need to extend their suffering if you do not wish to. I know what a soft heart you have. Brutus defeated them without using a single weapon. He can certainly dispatch them in a similarly Spartan fashion. He's tremendously powerful, you know. One stamp on the head would do it for each of them.'

'Now . . . now . . . now look here, Daisy!' Oliver protested, his face as red as a tomato, his voice made thin by his constricted breathing. His head was pressed down on its side, and he could not turn it properly to look up at her. 'We've had our differences, by Jove, but . . . but . . . but there's no need to resort to any petty thoughts of revenge, is there, what? The floor plan was merely research! My wife quite fancied your rooms and thought you might be . . . be . . . be . . . be persuaded to move. I didn't want to cause you any trouble, so I had the drawing done up by one of the servants to convince her that your rooms were . . . were no great shakes and that ours were quite adequate. It's all a misunderstanding, don't you see? A harmless muddle, that's what I say. All right, so we attacked Brutus here, there's no denying that, but that's one of those little eccentricities of our family, and here we three are now, all trussed up like prize pigs and we can all have a good laugh about it, eh? Ha, ha, ha! Eh? Ha, ha!'

The other two men did their best to show the jollity

they shared with their leader. They were a right jocular bunch altogether. Daisy stared down at them. The marble beneath Oliver's mouth was spattered with spit.

'I wouldn't have done anything to you,' he tried again. 'I wouldn't hurt a woman, apart from my wife . . . I wouldn't even hurt my wife, by the Lord Harry! I think women are good . . . good and fine and gentle creatures – especially gentle! And you are such a good Christian, Daisy. Everyone says it of you. What a sweet, blessed, Christian thing she is, people say!' His voice was breaking now, and there were tears welling in his eyes, running down his nose and over his cheek to the cold white marble on which his face was pressed. 'Help me, please, Daisy. Please, please God . . . please for the love of God, don't let him kill me. Please . . .'

He broke off, his body wracked by sobs. Daisy despised him now more than she ever had. Brutus had no right to put her in this position and she hated the ogre too for that. She did not want to be involved, but if she left their fate to be decided by Brutus and Elizabeth, she had no doubt what it would be. And if she chose to let them live, there was every chance they might still be a threat to her. Mercy was a weakness in the house of Wildenstern, not a virtue.

Who were they to force her to make this decision? Only God had the right to decide who lived and who died. For anyone else to make such a decision was a sin.

'You watch,' Elizabeth said to Brutus. 'She'll say something priceless, like, "Only God can decide who lives and who dies."'

Daisy turned away from them. They were trying to make her into one of their kind.

'Damn you – damn all of you!' she breathed through her teeth.

'What is their fate to be?' Brutus's cavernous voice pressed her. 'Either you make a choice, or I shall.'

'Exile, then,' Daisy replied without any more hesitation. 'They leave Ireland, and stay away from any Wildenstern interests anywhere in the world.'

Elizabeth rolled her eyes and sighed.

'Exile is only workable if they are forced to obey the sentence – as you well know,' Brutus grunted. 'What if they refuse to go, or try to involve themselves in our business in some other place?'

Daisy closed her eyes. He was right; the Wildensterns were like rabid dogs in pursuit of their ambitions – Oliver certainly would not sit out the rest of his life quietly. He would devote every waking hour to getting back into the family. Daisy had never had to deal with this side of the business before. When Berto had taken over as Patriarch, it was Nate who had handled all of the discipline and security for his brother. After Gerald had seized power, he had been more than able to control the family on his own, leaving her to deal with the day-to-day running of the business. As a businesswoman, she was used to making harsh decisions, even ones that could deprive people of their livelihoods, for the greater good.

But passing sentence on a person's life had no place in business. Not in any normal business.

'Death,' she said, resisting the urge to clear her throat. There could be no weakness, no doubt in her voice. 'If they come back to Ireland, or if they involve themselves in our family's matters, they are to be killed.'

'Then exile it is,' Brutus declared. He glared down at the three men pinned to the kerb of the grave. 'You will gather what you need to travel and leave today. Oliver, you are married, so your wife and children may leave with you, or they may choose to stay. You must be off the estate before sunset today. You will leave the country before sunset tomorrow, or you will be hunted down. Sentence has been passed.'

With that, Brutus reached down and gripped the black wrought-iron bar in both hands – one human, one engimal – and by main force, bent it upwards, freeing the necks of the three men. They crawled backwards, pulling their heads out from under the bar, groaning and rolling their necks to stretch out their bruised throats. Brutus made no offer to untie their hands, so they rose awkwardly to their feet and stood there in the grave, waiting. Oliver eyed Daisy with a resentful, defeated expression. If he felt any gratitude to her for sparing his life, he did not show it.

Elizabeth did not look pleased.

'They should at least be questioned,' she urged her brother. 'Surely you are not letting them off so lightly? You do intend to interrogate them before they are released? Brutus?'

'The decision has been made,' Brutus said. 'Sentence has been passed.'

Elizabeth made an exasperated sound and lifted her hands in a gesture of dismissal. Daisy could see the frustration in the older woman's eyes. She was not happy, but it was not her place to question her brother's actions. At least, not with others present.

Men emerged from hiding all around the small strange group – concealed behind the monuments and crypts. Daisy felt an icy fear run through her, afraid that these were more of Oliver's conspirators. Or was this part of some complicated trap to have her condemn one of the family and pay the price for her betrayal, as so many women had? She recognized the men as some of the Wildensterns' enforcers, the hard men who were party to some of the family's more illicit dealings.

'I summoned them before I called for you,' Elizabeth told her. 'They are here merely for security, now that Brutus has subdued the aggressors.'

Six of the men came forward, nodding in respect to Daisy, and took Brutus's three attackers by the arms. Oliver and his lackeys were led away like common criminals. Their departure would be ensured; they would be watched until they had boarded their ship and sailed over the horizon.

Daisy wanted to be sick, but she maintained her composure in front of Brutus and Elizabeth, who stood watching her, as if waiting for her to show the chink in her armoured reserve. She turned her face from them, and noticed for the first time who occupied the grave that had formed the centre of this drama.

It was the grave of Miriam Wildenstern. The marble kerb with its bent black rail framed a gravel rectangle. Above it stood a white marble headstone carved into the base of a tall Celtic cross. Daisy had been surprised by the symbol when she first saw it – it was a strange choice for a Protestant woman – and by the fact that she had not been interred with her husband. She had later learned that the Patriarchs were often interred alone, their wives commonly placed in the graves nearby. Though Miriam had been a committed Christian, she had delighted in gathering old Celtic myths and legends, even inviting traditional storytellers to the house to entertain her and her guests. The Celtic cross had been Berto's idea and Edgar had, in a rare act of generosity, agreed.

Daisy wondered what Brutus had been doing out here in the first place – the only people he would have known in this modern world, apart from Elizabeth, were his dead brother and sister. His brother's body had never been found, and his sister was buried on the far side of the graveyard. Perhaps he had decided on the scene for this meeting after defeating the three men. Perhaps he thought she needed a reminder of what could fall a rebellious woman in Wildenstern Hall.

'It will get easier, my dear,' Elizabeth's voice said from behind her. 'These are the kinds of decisions one must take when one holds the reins of power. Gerald has passed those reins to Brutus for the moment, and Brutus decided that you needed to momentarily feel the pull of the horses, in order to better understand the responsibilities of the driver.'

Then it's just as well that I'm going to be jumping out of the coach, Daisy thought. It only remains to be seen if I survive the landing.

XXVI

THE STUFF OF LEGEND

Cathal woke on a narrow bed to a woolly, befuddled reality. He was aware of a distant but profound throb of pain in his arm. It took nearly a minute for him to remember what had happened to it, and then he was sure that the injury could not have been as serious as he remembered, for he could still feel the *shape* of his right hand through the pain. He could almost open and close it, he could flex the fingers.

Then he raised his head and saw that his right arm ended in a bandaged stump a few inches below the elbow. His head sank back onto the pillow and he started to cry. He lifted his head again, hoping that it might not be as bad as he thought. It was. He took a bit longer to study it this time. Part of him, the part with a passion for science, and particularly anatomy, was fascinated by the macabre sight.

His hand was completely gone, and Gerald had clearly trimmed the bone, cleaned and sewn up the stump. The hinge joint of the elbow was intact, and enough of the radius and ulna bones – and their sheath of muscle, sinew and ligament – remained below to make the use of a prosthetic easier.

His breath came in short gasps, his chest shook with growing sobs. It was bizarre to find that the pain in his arm was still *hand-shaped*. If he closed his eyes, he would have sworn his hand was still attached. This was a phenomenon known as ghost pain, and was common in amputees. That was a label that applied to him now – he was an amputee. He thought of Tatty, and wished she were here to say something inane and funny. He needed her to hold him and tell him she would still love him, hook and all. His thoughts were slow and cumbersome and he realized that Gerald must have drugged him to ease the pain. God only knew what it would be like once this laudanum-induced haze cleared.

He clumsily raised his arm up in front of his face, and the stump appeared even more horrifying as he looked at the empty space where his hand should have been. A whimper slipped from his lips. He estimated that he had lost nearly twelve inches from the length of his arm. Hah! he thought to himself, letting out a hysterical giggle. I've lost a foot from my arm!

'It should not have happened, and I'm sorry,' Gerald said to him.

Cathal turned his head to see the older man sitting in a chair by his bedside. The room was somewhere in the mine, and, judging by the furnishings, was Gerald's bedroom. Cathal's vision swam as he moved his head and the room spun. He should have hated Gerald but he didn't. His emotions too had been numbed by the laudanum.

'Bas'ard,' he managed to say, and the effort it took convinced him that it would have to do for the moment.

'Red was terrified of what was happening to you,' Gerald explained. 'He closed the leviathan's mouth out of fear. That was not part of the plan.'

There was a plan, Cathal mused, tipping his head back to stare blearily at the ceiling.

'Pip?' he asked.

'Safe,' Gerald replied. 'You saved his life. Though he was petrified of you too. It was quite a sight to behold, your transformation. The injury seemed to interrupt it, but you were on the verge of becoming . . . something else, Cathal!' Gerald's face lit up as he recalled the wondrous event. 'In Irish mythology, such a thing is referred to as a "warp spasm", I believe. An uncontrollable lust for battle, according to legend, experienced by only the greatest warriors. It was clearly an instinctive reaction on your part, but it must have been triggered by the conflict of your will against mine – you could feel that too, I'm sure.'

Looking past this man he despised so much, Cathal saw a glass tank on a sideboard near the bed. Inside were two snake-like engimals. In fact, they were two parts of the one engimal, whose name was Apple. Here was a portion of the creature that had saved him from tuberculosis nearly four years ago. Could they . . . ?

'Their power is exhausted,' Gerald told him. 'Whatever ability they had was used in repairing my body. After Nate left the country, they became next to useless. There is perhaps one more purpose they can serve, should the opportunity arise . . . But the key part of the serpentine, Apple's *core*, if you like, ha ha—!'

Cathal gave him a profoundly sour look.

'Sorry.' Gerald gently patted his maimed arm. 'Anyway . . . the piece that can perform such miracles on the human body is with Nate. I'm not sure even that wondrous creature could replace your hand. I have made an extensive study of these sections, and have come to the conclusion that they are of no more use to me. If Nate doesn't show up with Apple's third section soon, I'm going to have to dissect them.'

Cathal wondered if there was a chance that Gerald might be shutting up any time soon.

'You know, it might not seem it at the moment,' Gerald went on, dashing Cathal's hopes, 'but this injury of yours is a superb opportunity to learn more about the possibilities of reconstructing the human body. When you changed, I could have sworn you *grew* – you *added mass* to your body. I can't work out how this is possible. But if it is, Cathal . . .

if it is, there might be the hope that we could re-grow your hand. Perhaps the intelligent particles can trigger some kind of chemical reaction in our cells, and then feed them as they grow at this tremendous rate . . .'

I wonder if I could make my body explode like a bomb, thought Cathal. If he mentions 'intelligent particles' one more time, I think I could manage it.

'If they *are* like seeds or spores, as I suspect,' Gerald chattered, 'they could contain some kind of store of energy, along with instinctive instructions for how to build cellular structures. With a large enough reservoir of energy, they could form their own structures without causing those of their host to rot. Imagine it as a fungal parasite or a bacteria that, instead of destroying your flesh, *rebuilt* it with materials that *it* provided! The possibilities, Cathal . . .'

Cathal was becoming convinced that his drug-induced haze was wearing off. The pain in his arm was becoming unbearable, and his mind was actually trying to make sense of Gerald's blatherings. Then Gerald's monologue was cut mercifully short by the appearance of Elizabeth, who pushed open the door to the room.

'What have you done to him?' she exclaimed, her noble face a mask of thinly veiled consternation.

Gerald frowned and glanced down at Cathal.

'It wasn't me – it was an accident,' he began. 'The escape attempt took place as expected and—'

'Not *him*, you conniving weasel!' she snapped, dismissing

Cathal with a wave of her hand. 'Brutus! What have you done to *Brutus*?'

'You mean, apart from bringing him back to life?' Gerald asked. 'Elizabeth, Cathal and I have reached a pivotal break-through in my research. Can't this wait?'

'Whah 'ave you done to Brutus?' Cathal demanded, his voice slurred, thumping his left hand on the bed.

Gerald regarded him with a frustrated expression and stood up to face Elizabeth.

'What seems to be the problem?'

'The problem is that Brutus is not behaving like Brutus!' she replied sharply. 'Only this morning, we were attacked by Oliver and two of his toadies . . . and he let them live! Then he binds them and discovers a paper on them revealing that they were to target Daisy next. My brother has me fetch that scheme-weaving trollop and bring her to him, so that *she* can decide the fate of *our* attackers! It is an outrage!'

Cathal listened with interest, trying to block out the pain that burned up his arm.

'I'm at something of a loss,' Gerald admitted. 'Again, what is the problem?'

Elizabeth strode up to him, her contorted face only a foot away from his. She was as tall as he was, and despite her womanly curves, there was no denying the strength in her frame. Most men would have taken a step backwards. Gerald remained perfectly composed.

'My brother was born for the battlefield!' she snarled. 'He had four loves in his life: violence, women, drink and food – violence being his clear favourite. Hugo was the eldest of us; he was a thinker and a leader. But Brutus was a giant – a beautiful, primal beast! He did not *plan*, he did not *ponder* or *reflect*. He did not show mercy to his enemies, and if that question should ever arise he absolutely, most definitely did not seek *the opinion of a woman* in the matter!'

'Then perhaps my ministrations have enabled him to evolve beyond the beast that you remember so fondly,' Gerald responded. 'This is a science you cannot hope to understand. You are intelligent, Elizabeth, but you lack a curiosity about anything in the world that does not contribute to your power games. I did not need a warrior to control the Wildensterns, I needed a general. That is what Brutus has become.

'If you are disappointed that he has not turned out to be the dim-witted oaf for whom you hold such affection, I apologize. If, on the other hand, you are disappointed because you hoped to be able to manipulate him, then that is your hard luck. I'm certain you played him like a puppet when you knew him before, but now Brutus answers to me, and only to me. Your brother is much improved, in my opinion, but those improvements have come at a price. Without me, he is never more than a few days from death's door. You should remember that, Elizabeth. I can assure you that Brutus can never forget it.'

Elizabeth had murder in her eyes, but her fear of Gerald and her need for him were too great for her to allow her rage full rein. She stood up straighter and took a deep breath, composing herself.

'He is kind to Leopold, at least,' she admitted. 'I'll grant you that. The old Brutus had no time for children. And his manners have much improved. It is . . . it is just disturbing for me to see these changes in him. His memories of our old life too are extremely vague. He is reluctant to discuss them. I blame those journals you made him read. He really does not have the capacity to absorb all of that information. I think it has confused him . . . and that combined with the trauma of his death . . .'

'It's natural that he should find his old life difficult to recall,' Gerald said gently. 'I warned you of that. He was dead for centuries, and his recovery was much longer and harder than yours, his injuries much more grievous. You cannot expect him to be the same man, Elizabeth.'

Gerald took her by the hand and led her to the door.

'Go back to your son,' he told her. 'I will be home very late tonight. I have to run an errand in town.'

She was barely out the door when Gerald closed it behind her and strode over to sit down at Cathal's side again.

'Where were we?' he asked. 'Ah, yes – seeds that rebuild flesh—'

'You knew we were going to escape?' Cathal interrupted him, his words clearer now.

'I knew you were going to *attempt* an escape,' Gerald corrected him. 'Did you really think I didn't see you taking the whistle from under the desk? Honestly, Cathal; your baiting of Red was hardly subtle, and your sleight of hand is not what you think it is. Once I saw that, I knew an escape was imminent and informed Red. We didn't tell the other guards; their acting skills could not be counted upon. I stood ready at the entrance with my fiddle. I was confident that Moby would pose an interesting challenge, and that – given your strong ethical foundations – you would put up a rousing fight for the freedom of the children. I wanted to see what would happen to you in the heat of such a vital struggle. I planned to wind it all up once I had made my observations.

'As I said, the loss of your arm was an unfortunate accident. Red has had it in for you since you got here – he's convinced you're the Highwayboy, the one who robbed him out in the hills last year, and gave him that scar. But I believe this was a genuine act of panic on his part. You aren't the rapparee, are you? Red claims he knew you by the way you spoke and the way you fought. Anyway, it doesn't matter now. He has already been suitably chastised and you will have no more problems from him, if you behave.'

'You let us try and escape,' Cathal mumbled. 'Queg's dead, isn't he? A young boy was shot to death, Gerald.

So ... what? The whole thing was just some kind of experiment?'

'Cathal, Cathal,' Gerald sighed patiently, showing tolerance for a slow student. He shrugged. 'That's why you're all here.'

XXVII

RUN OR FIGHT, KILL OR BE KILLED

Dusk was settling over the mountains as Nate trudged up towards Fraughan Rock Glen, a narrow valley that climbed up between two grassy cliffs. He had been walking for most of the last two days, wandering across the Wicklow Mountains in his search. The bullet wound in his shoulder had almost healed, though his ear still throbbed a bit and his legs ached from climbing up and down hills. He had spent the previous night in a fitful sleep, wrapped in a blanket in the roofless ruins of a stone cabin that had been abandoned years ago, perhaps as far back as the Famine. Cottages like it still littered the landscape after this isolated area had been emptied of people. The boughs of a larch had spread over the ruins, offering some additional shelter, but the cold had still seeped into his stiff muscles and Nate had suffered the nightmares again.

Just as, twenty years before, millions of starving people had seen their crops, their food, rot into foul-smelling pulp, so Nate was forced to watch an entire civilization suffer the same fate night after night. He wondered if he would ever be free of these haunting images. More than three years ago, the squirming creature inside him had drawn him away from his home with the dreams it had planted in his mind, taking him halfway around the world to show him the remains of that civilization . . . and evidence of the holocaust that had destroyed it. At first he had believed it wanted him to reclaim the science that had created the intelligent particles, but he soon realized the truth. The visions it . . . *she* showed him were a warning. A warning that it could all happen again. It made him hate the serpentine coiled in his gut. He despised her for choosing him.

Feeling weak and exhausted as he did now, Nate was oppressed by the weight of the knowledge he possessed, made miserable by it. Right at this moment, he felt utterly overwhelmed by the thought of facing his cousin. He was convinced that if he tried to fight Gerald, he would lose . . . and pay a horrible price for his failure.

He had spent all of that day around Glenmalure Valley, but with no luck. It would be dark before long, and the small bulls-eye lantern he carried was almost out of fuel. The flat-topped hulk of Lugnaquilla Mountain was out of sight off to his right, hidden by the side of the valley. He strode through a clump of heather and—

In a small explosion of foliage, feathers and frantic movement, a pheasant burst from its hiding place at his feet, making a break for the sky. It happened in an instant, faster than a human eye could track. Nate found himself gripping the bird by the neck, on the verge of killing it, his sense of reason reacting slower than his reflexes. The panicked bird squawked hoarsely and struggled to free itself. Nate gritted his teeth, overcoming the powerful, angry urge to break the creature's neck. The scare it had given him had awoken his base instincts: run or fight, kill or be killed. He let the bird go and watched it flap away into the air. This would be his only advantage when facing Gerald – and the greatest danger. All too often, Nate allowed his instincts to rule his actions. Something Gerald would never do. Nate shook his head and sighed.

The stream flowing past him on the left gurgled and gushed invitingly. Beyond this point, the trees thinned out and the ground would be more open, the cutting wind stronger as he neared the top of the ridge. Pulling the pack from his shoulders, he knelt down to drink the cool clear water, giving blessed relief to his parched throat. He sat back on a rock and looked down the glen at Glenmalure Valley below. The landscape was already dark against the dimming sky. Soon it would be hard to see – the sky was overcast so there would be no moon or starlight. A shroud of dejection wrapped itself around him. He had been sure he would find it here. It was where he had first encountered the creature.

Duffy, Dempsey and their men were to meet him in Dublin, but he had something to do here first. On reflection, he should have brought a horse, but the beast did not like horses, and horses most definitely did not like the beast. Dublin was a long way from here, and he would need some kind of transport to get back. There was an inn at the other end of Glenmalure where he might buy a horse – he had the money – but even that was a long walk away. He wasn't even close to the road.

Opening his jacket, he reached inside and pulled out his mother's letter. The one she had written to his father. The one she had not finished before he imprisoned her in the asylum. There was one piece of it that he kept turning over and over in his mind as he walked. He read the lines again:

> *I have always known that you were raised in an environment that brutalized you and encouraged the most predatory and ruthless instincts within you, and I have spent my entire married life struggling to come to terms with the conflicting sides of your character – the implacable leader of men that is your public face, and the tender, loyal and loving husband that so few people see.*

Nate kept thinking of his own son and how he had deserted him – how he had deserted all of the people he had loved. And then, after having his eyes opened in South

Africa and seeing how the intelligent particles had destroyed a civilization, he had been forced to face the violence in his own nature and the consequences of allowing it to overwhelm him.

He had once believed that he was more like his mother than his father, even though he had not known her long. His years spent defending Berto while his brother, as Patriarch, had tried to reform the family, had shown Nate a side of his own character he had found disturbing. Reading his mother's words again, he wondered how she could ever have considered Edgar Wildenstern loving or tender. Nate put his hand up to his ear. The air was cooler and instead of hurting him, it helped ease the throbbing in the side of his head. He thought back to the fight on the train, the gunfight in Limerick, the bare-knuckle match in the Peggy Sayer in Boston and all the other conflicts in which he had been involved. He would not have thought himself a man of violence, and yet his life was filled with it. Was this circumstance, that it was forced upon him, or did he actually seek it out? Could he have lived his life by the standards he demanded of himself, and avoided these conflicts? He was not like Daisy, he knew; with her iron principles, her disciplined mind. She had always refused to sink to the family's levels. The same could not be said for Nate.

In truth, he was more like his father than he wanted to admit. He knew little enough about Edgar's early life.

Perhaps the only real difference between them was that while Edgar had chosen to immerse himself in the family and control it, Nate had fought to get out of the family. He had tried to change his circumstances.

And yet here he was, about to return again. The rightful Wildenstern Patriarch was coming home. And he knew that when he walked through those gates once more, violence would be inevitable.

As if to underscore this thought, Nate heard a low, rumbling growl. He turned to look over at the trees that butted up against the sloping cliff to his right. There was the faintest rustle of something heavy in the undergrowth under the shadows of those trees. Nate tucked the letter back into his pocket and stood up. Two lights gleamed out at him, one slightly duller than the other. A low, bulky shape crept forward out of the tree line. Its front wheel was nearly a foot wide, it was about four foot tall at the shoulders and nearly three across. The horns that acted as handlebars arched up, curving back from the sides of its head, a shadowy shape behind those glowing eyes. The crunch of heather being crushed beneath its wheels could be heard as it came closer, its size and shape difficult to make out behind the light. Its snarl was like a grindstone chewing on gravel. It drew closer still, steam exhaling from its nostrils. It raised the volume of its engine to a roar . . . and lunged forward.

Nate stood his ground as the thing rushed towards him.

It covered the thirty yards between them in an instant, missing him by inches as it charged past, skidding into a turn as it jumped the stream, sending rocks flying from its spinning back wheel. It stopped there, head and shoulders low as if ready to pounce, growling and trembling as it locked Nate with its intense stare.

He knew its powerful, sleek form as well as he knew his own face. Formed of silver metal and black ceramic, with markings of red and gold, its horse-sized body stretched between two pairs of muscular legs holding wide wheels which could withstand high speeds and all manner of terrain. It had haunted this area for centuries, before Nate had caught it and become its master. He had not tamed it – this thing would never be tame – but it had once accepted him and trusted him.

When it turned its head slightly to the side, he noted the ragged scar across the left side of its face. The eye on that side was duller too. Nate winced. He had given the beast that scar. They had not parted on good terms.

'Hello, Flash, you old cur,' he whispered. 'I need you back.'

The growling velocycle, the Beast of Glenmalure, slinked forward and rubbed its head against his chest and he wrapped his arms around its neck.

'I'm headed home, old friend,' Nate said. 'I'm going to need all the help I can get.'

★   ★   ★

Nate whooped with the thrill of the speed, clinging to Flash's back without a saddle as they tore down the road that ran along the valley. Clouds of dust billowed out behind them, the road ahead picked out by the beams of Flash's piercing eyes. They leaped off humps in the road, Flash's engine letting out deep-throated roars that terrified the occupants of the few scattered cottages along the road. It had been some time since they'd heard the beast so close to their homes.

Flash swept into a left turn and raced up a hill flanked by forested slopes on either side, on the road that would bring them to Laragh, and the main road through the mountains to Dublin. It was a wonderful, twisting turning route up into the hills and Nate relished the thrill of maneuvering Flash at high speed along the narrow road. They swung round a tight corner, Flash's rear wheel digging into the clay as it bounded forward—

The back of Nate's head hit the hard surface of the road even as he was abruptly aware of a sharp pressure on his shoulders and throat. He couldn't breathe. The world tilted sickeningly around him. He was lying on his back on the road and his neck felt as if it had been cracked like a whip, his throat as if it had been struck by a burning strap of leather. There was a line of pain across his chest and shoulders. Putting a hand to his head, he groaned, struggling to regain his addled senses. If this was another of Gerald's ambushes, he was in serious trouble. His pistol had fallen from his belt. The one in his boot was within reach, but he was too stunned to coordinate his hand and leg together to pull it out.

He noticed the rope suspended horizontally above and behind his head. It was stretched across the road at chest height. That was what had knocked him off Flash's back. Any further theorizing was pushed aside as a revolver was pointed at his face.

'Stand and deliver, your money or your life!' a voice barked at him.

Nate squinted up at the dark, trying to focus his blurred vision on the masked figure who held the gun.

'I didn't think highwaymen said that kind of thing outside of cheap novels,' he remarked.

'You're rich enough to ride an engimal,' the figure sneered, 'but stupid enough to come through my domain at this time of night? A perfect victim. Your money, you dog, or I'll–'

The robber's threat was cut off in mid-breath as Flash hit him from behind and flattened him against the road, one big wheel pressing down on the miscreant's back. The man, who appeared shorter than average, cried out in a rather high-pitched voice. Pinned there by the mighty velocycle, he squealed in frustration. His pistol was just out of reach, so he went to pull another one from his belt, but Flash gave a low rumble of its engine and the robber went quite still.

Nate sat up and sighed, rubbing his neck and the back of his head.

'Jesus, perhaps this stuff does seek me out,' he muttered.

Standing up, he wobbled for a moment, waited until he had found his balance, and walked over to his attacker. A black tri-cornered hat lay on the ground near the man's head – though he seemed more a boy than a man. He wore a black headscarf covering his hair. Nate picked up the old-fashioned hat and stared at it in bemusement.

'Who are you supposed to be, Dick bloody Turpin?' he asked. 'What century do you think you're in?'

The robber lifted his head and looked up. He tried to twist around to face Nate, but Flash gave a grunt and he went still again.

'Nate?' he said in a girlish voice. 'Nate? Is that you?'

Nate knelt down and pulled the headscarf off the boy, to reveal that he was not a boy at all.

'Tatty?'

'Nate? Oh my God! Nate!'

He pushed Flash off her and lifted her onto her feet. She was dressed in a man's clothes, her tunic, trousers, belt, riding boots and cloak all coloured black. Apart from the distinctive hat, she looked every part the scoundrel. Her arms were around him in an instant and she hugged him as if he was the only thing holding her to the earth. He hugged her back, squeezing her into him. They didn't say anything at first – she just heaved great sobs as she pressed her face into his chest, and he tucked his chin over her shoulder, stroking her blonde hair. His aching chest and back reminded him of his fall and he lifted his head to look into her face.

'I have to say, I was hoping for a less violent welcome home from *you*. What are you doing out here alone at night?' he asked, falling back into his big brother role because he was unsure what else to say. 'Have the Wildensterns sunk so low they're resorting to highway robbery? Or are you out to try and catch this infamous Highwayboy?'

She pulled her head back and wiped her eyes, her eyes adopting a hardened look that took him by surprise.

'Oh, Nate,' she said with a smirk. 'I *am* the Highwayboy. I've been robbing people for years.'

He opened his mouth to say something, but then shut it again.

'I give the money to the poor, of course,' she said. 'Well, most of it, anyway. I treat myself to the odd dress or piece of jewellery from time to time. But most of it goes to help people who are too sick to work, or can't pay their rent on our estates. I break into Oliver's office and get their names from his files – find the ones who are the worst off. I like to think of myself as a redistributor of wealth . . . or a thieving philanthropist, whichever you prefer. My God, I can't believe you're back! And you've got Flash back too! Oh, this is wonderful! And . . .' She wrinkled her nose and sniffed his clothes '. . . And what is that charming *smell* you've brought with you? Good heavens, when did you last *wash*? Still . . . even so, this is the best thing that could have happened!' She thumped him in the chest – it was a surprisingly sound thump and he coughed a little. She laughed, and then her expression suddenly changed to one of petulant outrage: 'But here now . . . why didn't you send word you were coming?'

'Clancy sent a coded message to Daisy months ago,' he replied. 'She definitely received it – she's been in contact with Duffy and Cathal's father since we landed in Cork. You mean she didn't tell you?'

'No,' Tatty snapped, turning away to walk a few steps along the road. She stamped her foot a couple of times. 'The deceitful little witch. I'll pull her ruddy hair out by the roots.' Putting her face in her hands, her shoulders shuddered as she took some deep breaths. 'Oh, Nate, it's been so awful! You've no idea what we've been through . . . what . . . what it's like to live in that house now. It's much worse than before. Gerald is a cold-blooded monster who toys with our lives . . . he's drained the family's money and he's carrying out some bizarre experiments on engimals and now he's taken *Cathal* away somewhere and I *can't bear* to think what he might be doing with him. And he's brought that bloody Brutus back from the grave, and now that *ogre* is running things in the house and in the company and he's as bad as any of the others—'

'Brutus is *alive*?'

'. . . And he's treating Daisy like a secretary and she's . . . she's fit to go out of her mind with all the conniving that's going on; she's doing her best but they're too much for her, you know? She's trying to set up some plan to bring Gerald down, but he's so bloody devious, I think she's just going to get herself into even more trouble!'

Her shoulders and body slumped and Nate came over to hold her again.

'And I'm so glad you're here,' she whimpered. 'Daisy and I . . . we just need someone else to be strong for us, just for a little while. But it's got so bad . . . and Gerald's so damned . . . so damned powerful and clever. I don't know if there's anything you can do either.'

'I'm so sorry I left,' Nate said to her, taking her face in his hands. 'But it had to be done. And now I'm back, and we're going to stop Gerald. Whatever it takes, we have to stop him. We were always stronger when we were together. But you have no idea how dangerous he could become. Listen to me now, Tatty. I have to go on to Dublin, but I'm coming home soon. And Gerald knows it. He's been trying to stop me all along the way, and when I walk into that house, all hell is going to break loose. You have to be ready. I'm not going to ask you to run from it, or hide away. I know you better than that. But you must be prepared for the worst, do you understand?'

Tatty nodded and he hugged her again. He closed his

eyes and wished he didn't have to let her go. Finally, he was within reach of home; not the bricks and mortar and marble of Wildenstern Hall, but those precious few people who really mattered to him. His thoughts went to Daisy. She was only a day's horse-ride away now. Much less at Flash's speed. But he wasn't doing this alone. Like Tatty, he needed to be prepared for what was coming.

'Oh, I know where Gerald's secret lair is,' she said, as if just remembering.

'He has a secret lair?'

She nodded, brushing some loose hair back off her face.

'He's too difficult to follow, but once I'd learned who his lackeys were, I was able to follow them. Some of them are a thick as a bag of hammers – I suppose that type asks less questions. Anyway, he's carrying out his experiments in this mine in Glendalough. I slipped Daisy a note, so she knows too.'

'So she doesn't know you're the Highwayboy?'

Tatty shook her head. 'No. I . . . I . . . I just never got round to telling her. At first I thought she wouldn't approve, and then . . . well, I suppose I just enjoyed being this mysterious figure.'

'How intrepid of you. Some things don't change, I see,' he chuckled. Pushing her back at arms' length, he said, 'I can't delay much longer. We only have a few minutes. Tell me about my son.'

XXVIII

TAILORING ABOVE AND BEYOND
THE CALL OF DUTY

It was not long before dawn, and the streets of south Dublin were empty and quiet. In less than an hour, the bugler in Portobello Barracks nearby would blow reveille to wake the soldiers, the drivers of the horse-drawn omnibuses would set about harnessing their animals and the lamp-lighters would be doing their rounds on the streets, walking along with their ladders, extinguishing the streetlights. But the gas-lamps still burned, diffused in the mist that rose from the canal, and through their pools of light a slight-figured, bent old man with a turkey neck and long thin hands walked along a narrow street leading to the Grand Canal.

Rudolf Bloom was one of the finest tailors in Dublin. More than ten years before, he had arrived from Hungary and built his business up from scratch. He had kept his relatively modest home in the small Jewish community on the South Circular Road, but his business premises were in the wealthy, predominantly Protestant, area of Rathmines. He was on his way there along the dark streets, much earlier than normal, having been summoned by a man who had once been one of his most important customers.

Once. The man was something of a mystery now. It was all highly irregular. Some time ago, Bloom had been sent a telegram by a man named Clancy – one of the Wildensterns' most trusted servants. The message instructed him to make a suit to precise measurements and charge it to the Wildenstern account. A man's measurements were like a portrait to Bloom, and he immediately recognized the dimensions as being almost identical to those of the missing Duke of Leinster, Nathaniel Wildenstern – Clancy's former master. This had immediately posed a moral quandary for Bloom. The telegram had been confidential, but the man's disappearance had caused much pain to the Duke's family. Should he inform them or not?

Bloom was no fool. He was aware of the Wildensterns' formidable reputation. They were the most influential family in the country, one of the most influential in the world. And the new head of that family, Gerald Gordon, had shown himself to be a distracted, rather capricious type with little sense of duty or social responsibility – unlike the Duke's sister-in-law, who handled the family's accounts and was a paragon of respectability and style.

But Mister Gordon scared Bloom. He had made it clear in his press releases that Nathaniel Wildenstern must be found at all costs. If Bloom had knowledge of his where- abouts and kept them from Gordon, and Gordon found out, it could be the ruin of the old master tailor. And Bloom had a beloved wife who suffered from crippling arthritis, and a good-for-nothing fool of a son who dreamed of life as a writer in Paris but could not even get anyone to read the great tome of a book he had written. Bloom could not afford to lose the Wildensterns' business. After receiving the telegram, he had made the long and inconvenient journey to Wildenstern Hall to inform the family personally about his anonymous customer.

And now Nathaniel Wildenstern was coming to be fitted for his suit, before dawn, and in secret. Only Bloom himself was permitted to serve him. Nobody else was to be trusted. It was all highly irregular, but Bloom prided him- self on good service.

He was walking along the Grand Canal, his fragile body still able to maintain a brisk pace, when he was suddenly aware of someone behind him. A hand took his arm, and before he could protest he was turned bodily around and a finger held up in front of his face to silence him. The man before him was Nathaniel Wildenstern. He was older, his face a little more lined and weathered, overshadowed by a peaked cap and con- cealed behind a blond beard, but unmistakable to Bloom nonetheless. The mysterious Duke of Leinster himself.

'I'm sorry for the inconvenience, Mister Bloom,' Nate said. He led the old tailor across the road to the door of a small terraced house that opened to admit them. 'But I'll have to ask you not to enter your building today. It may not be safe.'

As they walked through the door, Bloom found himself facing down the business ends of three revolvers and two rifles.

'Good God!' he exclaimed, his spectacles nearly falling from his gaunt face as his expression changed to one of abject shock.

'Easy, lads, easy.' Nate motioned at the five Fenians to lower their weapons. 'Mister Bloom is an innocent bystander in all of this.'

Nate led the tailor into a tiny, modestly furnished living room, sat him down in the most comfortable chair and seated himself in the chair opposite, leaning earnestly forward to address the old man.

'Now,' he said, 'I have reason to believe that should you and I enter your business premises, there is a strong chance that an attempt would be made on my life, and that your life would be put in grave danger as a result. The man who has his sights on me is rather ruthless and will not shy away from innocent casualties if it means getting the job done. Once again, I apologize for involving you in this, Mister Bloom.

'However, I still mean to collect my suit – which I assume you have ready?'

Bloom nodded, badly shaken by what he was hearing.

'Excellent.' Nate smiled. 'One can always count on Rudolf Bloom for satisfactory service. So here is what I'd like to do. I will go on my own to your shop and pick up the suit myself. I will need your keys and instructions on where to find the suit–'

'But I will need to fit it, your Grace!' Bloom pleaded. 'It may require adjustment!'

The idea that a customer might leave his shop with an ill-fitting suit was almost as alarming to Bloom as the thought of a customer being assassinated while collecting it.

'I will have to make do,' Nate replied. 'You can rest assured that any hint of a poor fit will be down to my haste in taking it away, rather than any lack of quality in your work, and I will make a point of mentioning it when I am in company. And you will, of course, be suitably compensated for tailoring above and beyond the call of duty. Now, I'm afraid time is pressing. May I have your keys, Mister Bloom?'

When Nate came out into the hallway, leaving Bloom in a state of mild consternation, he found Duffy and Dempsey waiting for him.

'This is foolishness, Wildenstern,' Dempsey grumbled, his dark face and beard adding to his glowering look in the dim light. 'Gordon knows you're coming to the shop. Why give him an ideal opportunity to kill you before you even get home?'

'I have to concur with Mister Dempsey, your Grace.' Duffy nodded. 'This seems a needless risk.'

'It's nothing of the kind, gentlemen,' Nate told them. 'Gerald has equipped himself with knowledge that gives him extraordinary advantages over us. He has unmeasured control over engimals, and any number of them to use against us. If you see him pick up a musical instrument of any kind, or even purse his lips to whistle, you can kiss your free will goodbye. I promise you, gentlemen, you have never faced an opponent like him. And these are only the abilities I know of. He is trying to master an ancient science, a potentially catastrophic one. I need to see what level his research has reached, and I need to see it before I walk into Wildenstern Hall, an environment over which he has absolute control.

'Now, if you don't mind, I'd like to go and pick up my suit.'

The smog was not as thick in the area that morning as it was in other parts of the city, but it still had the effect of softening the edges of the buildings along Lower Rathmines Road and giving them a grainy appearance. Nate had left Flash in the back yard of the little house on the canal, so as not to attract attention. After a short walk, he came within sight of a three-storey terrace of buildings facing out onto the street. One of the shop fronts that occupied the ground floor of the terrace was adorned with the sign 'Bloom & Son'. Nate did not approach it immediately. Standing at the corner of a building fifty yards back, he studied the scene before him. After watching for a few minutes, he turned and went down a side street and found the lane that ran down the back of the terrace. Again, he watched and waited, his heart punching against his ribs, before continuing down the narrow laneway with its high walls. One key on Bloom's key ring let him in through the gate into the small back yard, another opened the door to the basement at the bottom of a short flight of steps. This was where deliveries were normally taken. He slipped into the building and closed the door behind him, but left it unlocked.

Another set of stairs brought him back up to the ground floor, but after a quick peek into the shop area, he went upstairs to the fitting rooms and the workshop. Without lighting any lamps, he checked those areas quickly and then climbed up again to the storerooms and office on the next floor. Only when he was satisfied there was no one else in the building did he make his way back down to the fitting room at the front of the first floor, where his suit had been left lying out waiting to be fitted.

It would have been in character for Gerald to choose Nate's most vulnerable moment to strike, so Nate was not about to undress in order to try on the suit. Keeping a wary eye on the doors and windows, he held the jacket and trousers up in front of the mirror to check the size, then the shirt, and bundled them carefully and wrapped them in some brown paper, tied with string.

Still nothing happened.

He looked around at the shelves and rolls of fabrics in different colours and patterns, the wood and leather tailor's dummy standing in one corner, the pairs of scissors and neatly coiled measuring tapes lying on a table beside it. Nate exhaled, pushing all the air out of his lungs and then inhaled slowly. What should he do now? He had been so *sure*. On another table in the corner, there lay two more coiled measuring tapes, lying amidst some scraps of patterned materials. One of them moved. Nate's stomach tightened and he stopped breathing. He felt the serpentine move in his gut, felt his hairs stand on end and his body tremble with adrenaline.

First one, then the other measuring tape uncoiled and slid down onto the floor. In the poor light, he had made a foolish mistake; these were not tapes, they were engimals. His eyes narrowed, unsure if he could believe what he was seeing. In fact, they were not a complete engimal, but two parts of a larger, extraordinary creature named Apple. They were identical, each one a little over three feet long, formed of white ceramic, their bodies segmented with so many tiny hinges that they were able to flex into tight angles and spirals. They had a single silvery eye each. Unlike a snake, they were triangular in cross-section. And Nate knew why.

Each one was one third of the original creature. And the final piece was deep within his own torso.

As they wound across the floor towards him, a cry emitted from Nate's throat, though it was not his voice that made it. He felt a knotting pain in his abdomen that rose up into his chest and blocked his throat. He gagged, falling onto his knees. Collapsing forward onto his hands, he retched once, twice, and then a length of white snaking ceramic emerged from his mouth, slightly stained with blood and bile. His lungs were spasming from being unable to breathe. It wriggled, causing him to flinch in pain. He retched again, and then, knowing the damned thing wasn't about to give up until it was free, he grabbed it with one hand and eased it inch by desperate inch from his constricted throat.

Coughing and hauling in air, he spat a few drops of blood, threw the serpentine at its fellow worms and fell forward onto his hands again, head hanging between his shoulders as he caught his breath, groaning. He raised his head to see the three strands of engimal entwining, winding together like three strands of a rope. In moments Apple, the serpentine, was complete again and she weaved across the floor in front of him, making a contented mewling sound, not unlike a cat.

'Well, I hope you're happy,' he snorted at it. 'That bloody hurt.'

Apple was whole and free again, and he was not entirely

sure how he felt about that, after the years she had spent inside his body, influencing his thoughts. But he was already on his guard again. Gerald had been here and left those things for him. Why? It made no sense. With her power over intelligent particles, Apple would be worth so much to Gerald, and whoever possessed her would benefit from her miraculous powers of healing. Why would he allow Nate to put her back together, knowing what kind of advantage Apple gave him?

Because he had no intention of letting him keep her.

Apple let out a weak, troubled cry. Then she shrieked again, high-pitched and loud enough to hurt Nate's ears. Smoke rose from her open mouth, from her eyes, and from the joints that spiralled along her body where her three parts had reunited. Nate looked on helplessly as she began to thrash around, wriggling in agony as something ate away at her insides. In wild motions, she whipped around the floor, smacking against the floorboards, screeching like banshee. And then she lay, shivering, twitching and then falling deathly still. He did not touch the limp body, just staring at it as he remained on his hands and knees, trying to grasp what this meant.

Gerald had rigged the other two segments, poisoned them somehow, in order to destroy Apple. The message could not be clearer. He meant to put an end to Nate, no matter what it took. Even a treasure such as this serpentine was expendable in order to achieve this goal. Nate felt a trembling in his hands. At first he thought it was his own body that was doing it, and then he realized he was feeling it through the floorboards. It was getting steadily stronger. Of course, the entire street must have heard Apple's dying screams. What better signal for an ambush could you ask for? There came the sound of a deep, rumbling engine.

'Trom,' he muttered, just as that rumbling rose to a thunderous bellow.

Snatching up Apple's body, he wound it up and pushed it into his pocket. Then he grabbed the package containing his suit, and darted out the door. The building shook around him as the bull-razer struck. He heard the sound of masonry being demolished beneath him, felt the floor lift under his feet and saw cracks snake up the walls. The room behind the fitting room, at the back of the building, was a small storeroom. He shoved the door open, crossed the length of the room in a split second and hurled himself feet-first through the lower half of the window. The white wooden sash in the middle of the window grazed his head, and then he was falling in a shower of broken glass and wood.

He landed clumsily on the tiled roof of an outhouse, thinking it was going to hold for a moment, but then the tiles gave way under him and he fell through, dropping another seven feet to knock a sink off a wall with his back-side and shove one foot down the bowl of a toilet. Still holding onto his suit, he let out a string of curses as he clutched his buttocks, yanked his soaking foot out of the toilet and kicked open the flimsy door. Lunging out, he sprinted across the back yard as the enormous bulk of Trom came piling through the building, its massive plough-shaped jaw bursting up from the basement through the back wall. The bull-razer crashed out into the yard and Nate vaulted over the back wall seconds before the wall was crushed beneath the engimal's rolling feet. Behind it, the remains of Rudolf Bloom's building collapsed in on themselves, all three floors effectively demolished in one unstoppable charge.

In the cloud of dust and debris, the slow-witted engimal did not see Nate racing down the laneway. But it was built for destroying structures – the crushing of people was largely incidental, and it was convinced it had completed the task its master had set for it. As Nate ran further from the noise of the demolition, he heard strains of music. Coming out into the side street, he slowed down, making his way more carefully onto the street where Bloom's shop front had once been.

The dust cloud mingled with the smog to form a shroud of thick fog on the street. Lights were coming on in the houses up and down the road and cries of alarm and anger could be heard. But beyond them, Nate heard the strains of a violin, and recognized Gerald in the strokes of the bow. Keeping in close to the wall of a house, he watched Trom reverse back onto the street and begin making its way home. A bugle was sounding in Portobello Barracks, only a few hundred yards away, and Nate knew the British cavalry would be coming, but it would be too little, too late.

Everyone knew who owned Trom. He wondered if Gerald's control over it was sufficient to see the ponderous beast back to Wildenstern Hall without it being steered directly, but he doubted it. Gerald would take a velocycle back to the estate, and the army would waylay the bull-razer if they could. They had behemoth engimals of their own, if they could be mustered in time – though no one of them was an equal to Trom. The Wildensterns would be blamed for this outrage, and their money and influence would not save them from the disgrace it would bring. Gerald clearly did not care. He was not fool enough to anger the Royal Irish Constabulary or the British authorities . . . unless he had no choice. Or he was powerful and arrogant enough to brush off any punishment they might try to inflict upon him.

'But you're still using music,' Nate muttered under his breath. 'Then maybe there is still hope. You haven't figured it all out yet, old friend. Maybe I can even stop you before you do.'

Tucking the packaged suit under his arm, he started walking quickly away from the scene of the disaster. The army had soon spread out through the streets, forming a cordon around the site of the destruction, stopping people and questioning them. Cavalry gave helpless chase to a bull-razer that paid them little mind. Nate took a wide route through Ranelagh and then back along the canal, where a group of soldiers waved him on past the end of Rathmines Road, allowing him to walk on to the small house where the Fenians awaited him.

'What the blazes happened out there?' Dempsey demanded as he ushered Nate in the door. 'It's as if you've started your own little apocalypse!'

'Not yet,' Nate replied. 'But give me time. And I'm afraid the family will have to buy Mister Bloom a new building. Where's Duffy?'

'Gone to gather the rest of the men, and pick up the documents your sister-in-law gave him. He means to be ready to walk into Dublin Castle as soon as she sends word that everything is in position.'

Nate had been informed of Daisy's plan, which would apparently be triggered by his arrival at Wildenstern Hall. He had agreed to play his part, not because he was convinced it would work, but because it was better than anything he had come up with. He smiled as he considered how prepared these veteran fighters were to follow a plan laid down by a woman – one who had no experience of military strategy except that which she had learned from her malignant relatives. At that moment, he felt immensely proud of Daisy. In rare instances of hope for his future, he had wondered if they might both survive this, and whether they could salvage some kind of life together if they did.

Whether she would have any feelings for him, after all she had endured.

But he never let those embers grow into anything brighter. He could not allow himself the luxury of dreams for the future. Ever since Clancy had found him, Nate had resolved to confine all plans of his future to the death of Gerald Gordon. For the sake of his son, and all those he loved, that was the only future he dared hope for.

'Time to get scrubbed up, I think,' he said, looking into a mirror on the wall and brushing his hand through his beard. 'I'll need to look my best when I show up at the old manor.'

'I don't hold with the idea that a good suit makes a man any less of a vagabond,' Dempsey remarked with a sniff. 'I doubt your family will be fooled. Still, I'm sure they'll welcome you no matter what. There's no place like home, as they say.'

Nate stared at his reflection in the looking glass, blinking older, tired eyes.

'Well, there's certainly no place like mine.'

XXIX

HOME SWEET HOME

The gothic, towering, menacing shape of Wildenstern Hall had changed little in the time he had been away. As he rode through the tall wrought-iron gates hung from marble pillars, Nate looked up the gravel driveway to the towering building that loomed above the rest of the manor house and the sight caused him to take a deep, shaky breath. Established in Norman times, Wildenstern Hall had been partly ruined, rebuilt, enlarged and refurbished many times. The tower that now formed the main part of the house was thirty storeys high. Steel girders, anchored deep in the stone core of the mountain, formed the bones which supported the flesh of brick, wood and stone. There was no other building like it in the country – and very few like it in the world. Steam turbines powered its mechanical lifts and it was plumbed up to the very top floor and lit by gas-lamps.

Gothic turrets jutted from its roof into the sky and gutters emptied the rainwater they caught out of the mouths of gargoyles. Any eye looking over the structure would find itself caught by the high arches, flying buttresses and the sculpted terracotta panelling that formed a skin around it.

But these were merely the features that were visible to the casual observer – someone not familiar with the building and its inhabitants. Nate viewed the place from a very different perspective. In his mind's eye, he pictured the layout of the complex structure, mapping out its more idiosyncratic features from memory, such as the armouries, the small weapons caches, the alarmed doorways, the secret passages and the dozens of lethal booby-traps. He had grown up here, playing in the maze of passageways, learning to survive this place in much the same way that other children learned to play schoolyard games.

Gerald would have made changes over the last few years too, as would some of the other family members. Nate tried to imagine the most likely places where new traps might have been set. When it came to creating a killing ground, Gerald could boast a particularly deadly combination of qualities: his profound knowledge of the human body and how to damage it; and a vivid imagination. From the moment Nate entered that building, he could face mortal danger from any direction.

And that was before he even counted possible attacks by enterprising family members.

Flash's engine had a brooding quality as the engimal rolled up the driveway. Word had already spread and people were emerging from the front door of the house to greet the long-lost Duke of Leinster. A small crowd had gathered as Nate drew up near the steps. The expressions on his relative's faces ranged from joy, through suspicion, to un-bridled hostility or fear. Elvira had barged her wheelchair through to the front of the gathering, and was clearly examining him for any sign of neglect in his deportment. The wide smile on Gideon's heavily bearded face could not hide his uneasiness. His wife, Eunice, narrowed her beady eyes in dull-minded calculation as she tried to ascertain how this would affect the ranking of her husband and sons. There was no sign of Oliver, but his remaining brothers, the Gideonettes, were there, scowling through their own various arrangements of facial hair. Nate took note of some of the other cousins, trying to judge which of them could be counted as allies, and which should be labelled as enemies. There were precious few allies.

There was also no sign of Elizabeth or his son. Perhaps it was best not to think about Leopold altogether for now.

Despite the overcast sky, the afternoon light had a slightly dazzling quality that he found hard on his eyes. He dismounted and pulled off his leather helmet, goggles and riding coat, which he handed to a waiting servant. He was clean-shaven, having bathed and had his hair cut before donning his new suit. Even so, the changes in him were obvious. Tatty was first to greet him, rushing forward and throwing her arms around him and burying her face in his new suit. Daisy came forward then. Looking over Tatty's shoulder, she waited her turn, and when it appeared as if Tatty meant to hold on for the rest of the day, looked over her friend's shoulder at Nate. She opened her mouth, closed it, opened it again, and closed it again, completely at a loss as to what to say. Nate could understand, feeling a warm rush of emotion welling up inside him, threatening to choke him and blind him with tears. They stared at each other for a long time as Tatty cried and the rest of the relatives, in a show of good social grace, began to applaud his return.

'You're late,' Daisy managed at last, barely heard over the noise.

'I took the scenic route,' he replied, finding it difficult to get the words out.

'You are absolutely *never* going away again,' Tatty mumbled from his chest.

Nate did not reply. His eyes were on the thin figure that appeared at the top of the steps. Gerald had a cigarette in his left hand and his right tucked into the pocket of his jacket. Struggling to maintain his composure, Nate suppressed a shudder, though whether it arose out of hate or fear he didn't know. It would take every ounce of self-control he had to keep his hands from Gerald's throat. This was not the time or the place for their confrontation. Gerald, in turn, regarded Nate with the kind of contemplative air he might have adopted while looking at one of his test tubes, and drew a long drag of smoke.

'Hello, Nate,' he said. 'Still struggling with your daddy issues?'

'Always,' Nate answered. 'You still pulling the legs off engimals?'

'Only for the good of humanity,' came the reply.

Taking Tatty's right arm in his left, Nate offered her his handkerchief to wipe her face and then began greeting the other relatives as if they were a real family, shaking Gideon's hand and giving Elvira the obligatory kiss on the cheek. Nodding to a few of the servants he would have known well, he walked to the marble steps with the rest of them following behind, and started climbing. Daisy took his right hand and gave it a tight squeeze as she walked alongside him too. He noticed that two of her fingers on that hand were bandaged. As they came to the top of the steps, they found themselves face to face with Gerald. There they all waited, with Gerald standing in their way. Nate looked past him and saw a giant in a tailored suit standing in the hall-way. Brutus, Elizabeth's brother.

Nate brought his gaze back to Gerald's face.

'It's over,' he said to his cousin.

'On the contrary, old chum. Things are just kicking off.'

With a chilly smile, Gerald stood aside and ushered Nate into the house. A house he'd had years to prepare in anticipation of Nate's return. In that moment, even without Brutus standing in the middle of the hallway, Nate would happily have traded this place for the storm-struck, heaving deck of a sinking ship. As his fear threatened to smother him, he leaned closer to his cousin, his voice low so that only those closest could hear.

'I know where the intelligent particles came from,' he said. 'But I'm never going to tell you.'

Gerald's face went a shade paler, but there was no other reaction. Nate stepped past him and went on into the house, a lady on each arm.

'Brutus!' he exclaimed, standing before the huge man. Brutus gazed down at him without expression. 'I believe you're running things at the moment. When's dinner? I'm famished!'

The next hour was spent in the living room, with celebratory drinks all round and a long line of strained chit-chat, which threatened to sap Nate of the will to live before Gerald could even get started on him. Gerald kept his distance, watching the proceedings but hardly taking part. Brutus stood back too, though his expression was harder to fathom – a wariness perhaps, the look of a man who was careful to do nothing in case he might do the wrong thing. Or perhaps it was something more to do with the fact that he would occasionally glance across at Gerald, as if the latter was holding him in check.

Nate told interesting and amusing stories of his travels, as if he had merely been away on some whimsical adventure. The others listened and related their own tales of their doings while he had been away. It was all very courteous and civilized, and when Nate felt that he could not bear any more he excused himself and made his way out to the mechanical lifts.

He took the elevator right to the top floor. Even as he stepped out into the corridor that led to what had once been his father's study, he felt a nervous tremor run through him. His experiences in this part of the house had never been pleasant. Following the corridor until he came to a flight of stairs, he climbed them to the door that let out onto the roof. The wind tried to pull the door out of his hand as he opened it, and he had to close it firmly behind him.

The area of flat roof was overlooked on all sides by tiled gothic turrets, plated in terracotta. In one of these turrets, a round window looked in on a room that connected to the attic. The room where his mother had been imprisoned for years had long been bricked up — it had been one of the last commands Berto had given as Patriarch before he died — but it was still possible to see into it through the round steel-framed window up here. Nate peered into the shadowy place, a heavy weight in the pit of his stomach. Rain was falling in widely spaced drops, lazily, like the light opening notes of a tune that would soon build up to a great crescendo. Walking across to the parapet, he leaned on the wings of a gargoyle and looked over in time to see Gerald on the back of a velocycle, riding away from the rear of the building on the road that led to the church. At the same time, he heard someone come through the door behind him, and knew it was Daisy.

'At a guess, I'd say he's building some kind of complex musical instrument,' he said to her, without turning round.

Daisy came up beside him, standing close enough to put her hand on his where it lay on the stone parapet.

'It's the organ in the new church,' she told him. 'He built it using the bodies of engimals.'

Nate nodded to himself. Gerald was taking what he knew and meant to apply it on a much, much larger scale.

'Then there's still time to stop him.' Nate turned and sat on the low parapet, watching the wind blow strands of Daisy's dark hair across her face. He wanted to take that face in his hands and press his lips against hers. He wanted time with her, and a life with her, one where they were not perpetually at risk and where they could talk about normal, everyday things. But he was not to have it. Looking Daisy in the eyes, he said, 'There are two things you need to achieve to gain control over intelligent particles. You need a clear understanding of what they are, and the acceptance that it is possible to communicate with them on an instinctive, subconscious level.

'Imagine if you had never seen anyone swim, but you were faced with learning it yourself, on your own. You have to consciously work out the strokes that will move you through the water, but you must also accept, deep down, that the human body can float.

'Gerald has achieved the first of these, and he could be on the verge of the second. If he masters this control, he will have the power of a god. Believe me when I say that I am not exaggerating.'

Daisy looked down at her bandaged fingers. She untied the bandage and unwound it, exposing the once-injured fingers. The tips had almost completely grown back, leaving only a slightly flattened shape on the side of each that was still tender to the touch.

'I believe you,' she said, standing against him to seek warmth from the wind.

He put his arm around her, pressing his cheek to the side of her head. For the first time in years, Daisy felt some of the weight lift from her. Finally, there was someone to help carry it.

'I have to tell you a story,' Nate said softly. 'You're going to find it hard to believe. I wouldn't have believed it myself, except that I was made to *experience* it. In a way, I still *am* experiencing it.

'When the serpentine entered my body and saved my life after the last fight with Gerald, she started showing me visions of the people who created the particles. It took me a long time to understand what I was seeing, and . . . well, let me start where this all started. And bear with me, it is a . . . a perfectly bizarre tale.'

He stopped and took a breath, staring out across the mountainous landscape, watching the heavy, saturated clouds scud overhead. Even among the mountains, there were the hedges and fences that marked out farmland. The gleaming twin lines of railway tracks coursed through the trees at the bottom of the hill. Smoke rose from the chimneys of cabins in the distance. In any direction he looked, the mark of mankind could be seen on the land.

'Centuries from now, the human race has reached a point in its science where they are capable of things we could only dream of. But something happens: a cataclysm that wipes out most of humankind. The ones who are left begin rebuilding. Their world is little more than a barren rock, and despite their great advances these people still need to grow food to eat. In its weakened state, their civilization is vulnerable, and when a terrible blight begins destroying their crops they realize that they are going to starve. This fungus is resistant to everything they try, and whenever they attempt to eliminate it, they destroy their food too. Because of a simple fungus, the last members of the human race are going to starve to death.

'Their lives are governed by . . . I can only describe them as *thinking machines* – far more sophisticated than even the smartest engimal. Among their other scientific advances, they have developed the ability to travel through time itself. Now they mean to go back and eradicate the fungus entirely, while it is still a primitive organism, before it can even evolve into the indestructible strain that is attacking their crops. But this travelling through time involves incredible hazards in itself. It was the misuse of this science that rendered the Earth uninhabitable in the first place.

'The machines see no other choice, however. So they resolve to go back so far that any humans who witness this intervention will have no means of understanding it, or making a record of it for future generations. They go back to the Stone Age, over ten thousand years in our past. But the machines don't send humans back in time. They send the intelligent particles. These particles are not capable of thought themselves, but one type can take over the brain of a human being. These ones are designed to use the human brain to create more particles, different kinds, and control them. They take over a tribe of early humans, who then begin thinking in far more advanced terms. They can create particles to perform whatever function they wish.

'In the beginning, these hybrid humans are clear about their purpose, their mission. The first particles they make can seek out the particular fungus that will evolve into the blight that is threatening their future. They can take to the air and dissolve this fungus – and its spores – wherever it is to be found. And these new humans don't stop there. They start gathering seeds, plants and even soil, increasing the scale of their operation, to send supplies forward into the future, to help rebuild the human world. They build engimals, first to help them in their tasks, and then for the sheer fun of it.

'But as they discover a passion for living, they become corrupted by temptation. You see, a machine cannot comprehend how to exist as a human, any more than a human can fathom what it means to be a machine.

'The particles are *designed* to bond with humans of the future – humans who have mastered their emotions, and who are ruled by a purely rational machine government. But these particles have bonded with the minds of *primitive* humans capable of the most extreme emotions. Without the thinking machines to control their urges, this beautiful, fertile world is intoxicating to them, and before long they have begun neglecting their work and are living lives of wild abandon, full of passion and excitement, with intelligent particles to serve all of their needs. And why wouldn't they? They are living in paradise – a world untainted by cities or farming or industrial revolution.'

Nate smelled Daisy's hair, feeling how wet it was becoming in the light rain. Neither of them wanted to move. He could not see her face, but he could feel her body language, and how bewildered she felt about this story he was telling her. And who could blame her? Except for the evidence all around them that this science had existed. Did exist. He gave a bitter smile and went on:

'Then two men fall in love with the same woman. They argue and then fight, and one man is beaten to the ground. In the future world, no human has engaged in violence in hundreds of years. The thinking machines have underestimated the sheer power of emotions such as hate, fear and fury. In a moment of unhinged rage, the beaten man uses the intelligent particles to kill his opponent. The horror of that death shocks him, causes him to lose control of the violence he has unleashed. The particles destroy all of the people standing nearby, including the woman he loves. Faced with the atrocity he has just committed, the man goes clean out of his mind. The strength of his emotion over-whelms the particles, the ferocity surging through them just as an earthquake can trigger a tidal wave. Anything that can rot simply disintegrates in the surge, absorbed into the swamp of feeding particles. The only engimals that survive are those that are made from metal or other inorganic materials, or can move fast enough to escape.'

Nate ran his fingers through Daisy's hair, pulling her closer to him. He felt cold now, and vulnerable, the exhaustion of the last few weeks draining the energy from his body.

'The visions the serpentine showed me led me to a place right on the southern tip of South Africa. I met an archaeologist there, near the Klasies River. He showed me a section of the riverbank where the water has cut deep into the ground, where you can see all of the rock and stone that has been laid over the last fifty thousand years. Like looking at the rings in a tree to judge its age, you can read the age of the ground itself in the layers. In the layers they think are about fifteen thousand years old, there is a dark grey, almost black, line that runs through the ground. The archaeologist told me that this layer of ash and rot can be found in the ground for hundreds of miles in every direction. They can only guess at the disastrous event that left this mark in the earth, but they believe it was something no human could have survived. This new civilization came from the future, and was here for a few short years. They were capable of miracles, but the only traces they left were the engimals, and the stain of their annihilation tattooed in the ground.'

Nate pulled away from Daisy and looked at her. They were both wet through now, and the sky had grown darker, clouds bulging with pent-up rain. The air had a smell of the sea, and they could see gulls over the hills to the north-east. A storm was coming.

'I just wanted you to know what we were up against,' he said lightly.

'I think I was better off merely being scared of Gerald's mutant organ,' she snorted, her gaze taking in the storm-clouds as she shivered. The rain was growing steadily heavier. 'I'm not entirely sure I'm ready to deal with the apocalypse.'

'One thing at a time,' Nate told her. 'Let's see if we can survive dinner first. Then we can start putting this plan of yours into action.'

'Then Duffy did tell you?' she muttered. 'He should reach Dublin Castle soon. There's no going back now.'

'What made you so sure I'd be any use, even if I did

come back?' he asked her. 'You've never had a high opinion of my usefulness in the past.'

'It's all about *how* one uses you, my dear Nathaniel,' Daisy replied sweetly. 'Even the most delicate of operations can sometimes benefit from the forceful application of a blunt instrument.'

'Charming—' he began, but was cut off as she pulled his head down and pressed her lips against his.

He folded her into his arms, kissing her passionately as they both resolved to make this moment linger as long as possible. In what might be the last few hours of their lives, they would at least have this one desperate, hungry kiss in the drenching beat of the rain.

As they parted, smiling slightly, shyly, Nate put his hand to her face, brushing a damp strand of hair from her cheek.

'I should probably tell you, I ran into Tatty out in the hills last night, on my way to meet Duffy. She was most put out that you hadn't told her I was on my way home.'

'I suppose she would be . . . Hang on,' Daisy frowned. 'What do you mean? What was she doing out in the hills last night?'

'So you definitely didn't know? Our little Tatiana is the Highwayboy.'

There was a long pause.

'What?'

XXX

MONSTROUS GOINGS-ON

Eamon Duffy and William Dempsey walked through the tall gates of Dublin Castle, the centre of British power in Ireland. Both had reason to feel nervous. Duffy was known to the Royal Irish Constabulary as a Fenian, though they could never find proof of it, and the Crimes Special Branch – the RIC branch that specialized in collecting intelligence on rebels – was housed within these walls. Dempsey was a deserter from the Royal Navy; if caught, he faced a severe sentence.

Like Wildenstern Hall, Dublin Castle had developed over centuries, starting out as a medieval castle that grew and changed with the city that surrounded it, evolving into a modern administration headquarters that also hosted great balls and parties and was home to a police office and armoury. The two visitors were led across the cobbled

Upper Yard of the castle by a balding constable with a tough, belligerent face. Instead of taking them to the police office, he ushered them in through the door of one of the more modern, red brick buildings and downstairs to the basement level. This was where the Crimes Special Branch was based. Duffy and Dempsey had even more cause to be nervous now. They had heard enough stories of the interrogations carried out in the castle.

Halfway along a dimly lit corridor, they were shown into an office whose walls were hidden behind shelves of record books and rows of filing cabinets. Any bare patch of wall was covered with maps of the country. Two clerks sat at desks here, but the constable led the two men through to a glass-panelled door, with the words 'Detective Inspector John Urskin'.

The constable knocked on the door and entered when a voice answered from inside. Detective Inspector John Urskin was sitting behind a tidy desk in an office that was only slightly less crammed than the one they had just passed through. He dismissed the constable and stood up, a neutral expression on his thin, wrinkled features that hid his puzzlement well. He leaned over the desk to shake the hand of each man in turn.

'Mister Eamon Duffy,' he said, sitting back down in his wood and leather swivel chair and gesturing them to seats on the other side of the desk. 'You're not a man I'd have expected to see down here . . . of his own free will. I must confess to feeling some bewilderment when I received your message.'

The two men removed their hats and sat down.

'I'm sure I don't know what you mean, Inspector,' Duffy replied. 'I'm just a simple businessman who has come to you on a matter of great urgency. It has come to my attention that a large group of rebels has made their headquarters in the mines in Glendalough. With the numbers they have gathered there, I can only imagine that they mean to engage in some malevolent assault against the state.'

'The Glendalough mines? That's Wildenstern land, isn't it? And why on earth would you bring me information of that sort?' Urskin asked. 'Rival mob are they, these rebels?'

'I resent the implication, Inspector,' Duffy said, unruffled by the policeman's manner. 'The reason I've come to you – apart from an expression of public spirit – is that I have recently bought that land and the mines that lie beneath it.' He produced a document from the leather case he was holding on his lap. Pushing the document across the desk, he continued, 'I had intended to put them back into operation when I discovered this nest of vipers barricaded inside. Perhaps the Wildensterns tolerate this kind of thing, but I do not. And I have reason to believe that they have children trapped down there, that they are working them as slaves.'

Urskin stared into Duffy's eyes for what seemed like a very long time. He picked up the sheets of paper and studied them. Sure enough, they were the deeds to the mines and the land around them – complete with the sheet with Gerald Gordon's signature on it, authorizing the sale to Duffy.

'Child slaves, you say?' he asked quietly.

'I believe so, yes.'

'If this were *Wildenstern* land,' Urskin said, thinking aloud, 'not that I would accuse the *noble* Wildensterns of being involved in illegal activity, but if it *were* their land, my boss would have to run this past the Lord Lieutenant himself before committing to any action. He is on friendly terms with the family – they are distantly related to the Queen, I believe. He would be sure to consult with the Wildensterns directly, and have it out with them at the highest level.'

'And they might exercise their influence to see that you would never send your men in against the blackguards in those mines,' Duffy finished for him. 'Restrained by your superiors, you would be unable to proceed. But as you can see, *I* own this property.'

'And so . . . there is no need for the Wildensterns to be informed of any operation the RIC might choose to carry out,' Urskin mused.

'No need whatsoever.'

'That is, if this document is indeed *genuine*.' Urskin held up the papers, emphasizing his words for effect. 'If, for instance, the signature was a *forgery*, and the land still belonged to the Wildensterns, I would be putting my career on the line.'

'I can assure you that it is genuine,' Duffy told him. 'And even – completely hypothetically, of course – if it is *not* genuine, the abhorrent nature of what you will find in those mines will be enough to persuade the Lord Lieutenant, or any of your superiors, that no matter how powerful the Wildensterns might be, a police raid was the only sane action.'

'But the Wildensterns' power has no bearing here,' Urskin repeated. 'Because it is no longer their land.'

'Precisely. And the monstrous goings-on in those mines would be enough to convict the most powerful figure, no matter who they might be. Child slaves, Detective Inspector. Probably murders too. But don't worry yourself with matters of ownership – it is definitely *not* their property.'

Urskin put the sheets of paper down on the desk and tapped them with the fingertips of his right hand, before pushing them back to Duffy. He worked his jaw for a few moments as the other two men watched the resolve set in his eyes. Then he stood up and pulled his long grey coat and bowler hat from a coat-stand near his desk.

'McClane!' he shouted, taking a very modern-looking, short-barrelled Webley revolver from a drawer in his desk and stuffing it into his coat pocket. The constable with the belligerent face appeared at the door. Urskin waved him into the room impatiently. 'Send a telegram to the county headquarters in Wicklow town and let them know we're on our way. Tell them to be ready to move as soon as we arrive. I'll give them a proper briefing once I'm there. I'm going across the yard to the general's office. We'll need whatever troops the army has stationed at the barracks in Laragh, and might have to have more on alert in the neighbouring districts. And we'll need at least one behemoth too, if I'm any judge of the Wil— the *rebels*. We still haven't managed to pen in that bloody bull-razer that ran amok in Rathmines. Well? What are you waiting for man? Hop to it!'

'Yes, sir!' McClane nodded and strode out again.

'If you don't mind, I'll send my man here with you,' Duffy said, indicating Dempsey. 'He can take care of himself, and I'd like a representative on hand when you go in.'

Urskin looked Dempsey up and down. 'Ex-military?' he guessed.

'Very,' Dempsey grunted.

'You're not coming yourself?' Urskin put the question to Duffy as he headed for the door.

'Unfortunately, I have other business to attend to.'

'Something more important than this?' Urskin stopped in his tracks, spinning to glare at Duffy. 'And what might that be, exactly?'

'I'm not at liberty to say, Detective Inspector. But suffice to say that, if we are living in interesting times, this is setting out to be a positively fascinating day. Good luck in your endeavours, sir.'

'I'd wish you luck in yours, *sir*, but that's likely to mean trouble for someone else. Mind how you go, Mister Duffy.'

With that, he rushed out, with Dempsey hurrying to keep up. Duffy watched them leave.

'I'll do that, Inspector. And may God go with both of us.'

Duffy was led out by one of the clerks, who saw him to the gate. Visitors could not be allowed to wander around Dublin Castle willy-nilly. Especially visitors like Eamon Duffy. Standing outside the gate, he took a pipe from one pocket and a pouch of tobacco. It took longer than usual to fill the pipe and light it, because of his trembling hands.

XXXI

A CROSSFIRE OF OBSERVATION

The matter of who was to sit at the head of the table at dinner was resolved by Brutus, much to Nate's surprise. He had not expected Gerald to relinquish that position to his deputy, despite Brutus's obvious claim to seniority. Elvira took her position at the other end, leaving Nate and Gerald sitting across from each other, either side of Edgar.

Elizabeth sat next to Gerald, with Leopold on her other side. Daisy sat next to Nate, with Tatty beside her. Gerald hardly took his eyes off Nate as they waited for the first course to be brought in. Nate watched Leopold, though his eyes strayed to Brutus sometimes, and the engimal claw that had been used to replace the giant's missing right hand. Elizabeth watched Gerald watching Nate. Leopold made a canoe for his tin soldier out of a bread roll, and watched for any sign of the approaching food. Daisy and Tatty exchanged the occasional disgruntled glance, but otherwise watched Gerald and Nate. Brutus's gaze bored straight through this crossfire of observation, his stare travelling down the table to Elvira, though whether she was the focus of his attention or not it was difficult to say, the table being long enough to comfortably seat twenty-four people. This dinner had promised to be such a dramatic affair that all the available relatives had gathered in the dining room, requiring another table to be laid.

Everyone was on edge. It was often at pivotal moments like this in the family's existence that upheavals occurred; conflict, changes of allegiance and betrayal. They waited for cues from the two young men sitting by the top of the table, looking for signs of dominance, or weakness, or any other hint of which way things might go. So far, there was nothing.

Nate lifted one of the three forks in his place setting, feeling its weight. It had been a long time since he had eaten with silver cutlery. The elaborate array in front of him would have paid for a half decent horse. Its worth could feed a family for a month. He gazed at his hands, calloused from years of manual work, his skin weathered by the sun and wind. This place held so many bad memories, but now it didn't even feel like anywhere he knew. It was another world, one he did not recognize.

He pulled at the cuffs of his suit jacket. His new suit had been so wet when he and Daisy came down from the roof that he had been forced to change. Fortunately, Daisy had anticipated his lack of suitable attire, and several of his old suits had been hurriedly laundered the day before and made ready for him. The trousers hugged his thighs too snugly and the jacket was a little too tight around the shoulders and upper arms. But the cut allowed the revolver in his waistband to stay hidden, and fell straight down at the back so that no one could see the bulge of the large hunting knife he had concealed in a sheath in the small of his back.

The servants started bringing bowls of soup, cold cuts and more bread to the tables. The clink of cutlery on china was tentative, nervous, as people began to eat. No one had much of an appetite. Nate watched Leopold playing for a little longer, and then turned to the enormous, ancient man sitting at the head of the table.

'So, Brutus, how are you settling in to life in this new world? I expect a lot has changed since you last walked the Earth.'

'As a matter of fact, surprisingly little has changed,' Brutus responded, the turn of his head reminding Nate of one of those new-fangled gun turrets they had started installing on battleships. 'I have awoken to find the family as mired in conspiracy and back-stabbing as it always was. The same features that defined it then are equally present now. We have the warring factions . . .'

'I'd say it's been quite a while since we had any need for an all-out war, wouldn't you, Nate?' Gerald observed.

Leopold did not care for soup. He aimed his tin soldier's rifle at Nate and made shooting sounds. Then he smiled at his long-absent father, but Nate had his eyes fixed on Gerald.

'. . . we have people keeping secrets, even from those closest to them . . .' Brutus continued.

Failing to get Nate's attention, Leopold stood up on his raised chair and pushed his bread roll canoe as far as he could across the table to Daisy. She did not notice, her attention focused on Nate.

'Yes, it's remarkable what people keep from you,' Tatty said acidly, casting a sidelong look at Daisy. 'Sometimes, people aren't the friends you think they are at all.'

'And sometimes they hide a whole other side of their character,' Daisy sniped back, 'which surely is the peak of dishonesty.'

Leopold looked up hopefully at his mother. She never failed to give him attention. But now she was watching Brutus through narrowed eyes. Leopold tugged on her sleeve and she absent-mindedly summoned the servant with the violin, gesturing at him to play something to calm her restless son. As the musician approached, Nate lifted a hand to point at him.

'If you come near this table with that violin, I'll shoot you where you stand. And that goes for any other instruments you have stashed back there.'

Gerald smirked. Elizabeth rolled her eyes. Leopold's

mouth opened in an 'O' at the unfairness of it all.

'We have those whose lives are ruled by ruthless ambition,' Brutus said, paying no heed to the other goings-on at the table as he took a sip of his soup, the spoon held in his left hand.

'Why, Brutus, you almost make it sound like a negative quality,' Elizabeth remarked in a disconcerted tone. 'I would expect no less from Leopold, when he comes of age.'

'. . . and those who are blinded by insatiable greed,' Brutus continued.

'Blithering fools indeed!' Gideon barked, leaning over his bulging stomach to rap on the tabletop in agreement, with the knuckles of a hand laden with gold and jewelled rings. 'A man should control his appetites!'

Afflicted by a terrible boredom, Leopold climbed down off his chair and ducked under the table, where he proceeded to crawl around among the forest of legs, pretending his soldier was off having adventures in the Congo – whatever a Congo was – like his mysterious father.

'And finally, you have the slaves to tradition,' Brutus declared, 'and those who put the reputation of the family above all other considerations.'

'And what other considerations should be given greater priority?' Elvira demanded, aiming her listening horn down the table, having picked up on the booming voice from the other end and finding its declarations objectionable. 'Family is everything!'

'Speaking of family,' Elizabeth spoke up, and pausing long enough to be sure she had the entire family's attention, 'Gerald and I have wonderful news . . . we're going to have a baby!'

Silence descended across the dining room.

'What?' Nate and Daisy said together.

'What?' Gerald managed a moment later. 'What the bloody hell are you talking about?'

'And I thought you had a great understanding of biology,' Nate quipped. 'Looks like she's nailed you too, old chum.'

'This family gets more complicated all the time,' Tatty exclaimed. 'Will this mean you'll be getting married?'

Gerald let out a low growl, the kind of noise no one had ever heard him utter before. Nate dropped his hand under the table to the butt of his gun. All across the room, frayed nerves sparked and muscles tensed. Under the table, Leopold, trying to find a way through a wall of legs, had his soldier jab one of them with his rifle. Gideon felt a sharp point stick into his shin. Letting out a yelp, he shoved back his chair and jumped to his feet, pulling a pistol-sized, double-barrelled shotgun from under his jacket. The sudden movement caused frantic reactions up and down the table. In an instant, all of the men and a few of the women were standing, aiming firearms across the table. Hammers were cocked, warnings were shouted. At any moment, someone might fire a shot and the result would be nothing short of a bloodbath. Leopold started shrieking, calling for his mother. In the confusion of shouts, swearing and swinging of barrels, only Brutus, Nate and Gerald remained seated, though all three now had hands on weapons. Nate watched as the two points of Brutus's claws clicked together like a telegraph – the only sign that the ogre was in any way agitated. It was a gesture Nate recognized.

'*No guns at the dinner table!*' Elvira bellowed. 'Good God, have you no sense of propriety!'

'Am I cursed to be surrounded by small-minded fools and buffoons all of my life?' Gerald hissed, an apoplectic expression on his face. 'Why must you all waste your lives with petty squabbles and . . . and superstitions and . . . and selfish, clutching greed? Where is your ability to *reason*? Are you human beings or animals? Sometimes I think you're worse than both! I'm trying to change the world and you lot can't have a bowl of soup without shooting each other! It's absurd!' He took a deep breath and visibly calmed himself. 'Now . . . will you all just SIT DOWN AND SHUT UP!'

Frozen in place by his voice, the Wildensterns looked at him, then at each other, and slowly, carefully lowered their weapons. Having done that, they then took their seats, awkwardly pulling their chairs in under them as the servants who normally helped them, and who had been serving the food, had run for their lives when the guns came out. Gerald put a hand to his head, struggling to control the seething rage he felt. Daisy regarded him with cold eyes, checked the small pocket-watch she kept tucked away in her dress, and decided that the time had come.

'You tell us you're trying to change the world, but you never tell us *how*, Gerald,' she said. 'Perhaps we'll find out . . . now that the police and the army are on their way to clear out the criminals who've occupied the Glendalough mines.'

Gerald's face settled into an icy calm, his gaze fixed on her face.

'You're lying,' he said hoarsely. 'The army wouldn't make a move on our property without informing me first.'

'You never paid enough attention to the business,' Daisy told him. 'And I confess I've been a bit slow at bringing Brutus up to date on everything. Didn't you know? We sold that property last week.'

Gerald ground his teeth, staring at her with a murderous intensity, examining her face and body language for any sign that she was bluffing. Daisy, with studied indifference, looked at her pocket-watch. Brutus pushed back his chair and drew himself up to his full height. Nate resisted the urge to look up, as did Daisy. Tatty could not help but stare. Brutus was breathing slowly and deeply, gazing down at Daisy with a frown.

'I believe she's telling the truth,' he rumbled.

Gerald swore through his teeth, leaped from his chair and sprinted for the door. Everyone else stood up too. Some followed him half-heartedly out of the dining room, others joined Nate and Daisy at the windows overlooking the back of the house. A couple of minutes later, they saw Gerald on the back of his velocycle, racing away towards the mountains as fast as his mount could carry him.

'I daresay, what's down that mine that's so important?' someone asked. 'You don't suppose they've found *gold* down there, do you?'

'Do you think he might have discovered gold and not told us?' another voice piped up. 'God knows, the swine's capable of anything!'

Nate and Daisy left them to their back-biting conjecture and hurried out of the dining room. Tatty was not with them, and they didn't have time to wonder where she had gone.

'How long do you think we have before he makes it back here?' Daisy asked as they walked towards the elevators.

'That depends on how unhinged he has become,' Nate replied. 'If he thinks he can save his operation by taking on the army, and is mad enough to try, then we could have the rest of the night. But if he can afford to cut loose from whatever is down that mine, then he could decide to turn round and come back at any moment.'

There was a boy in smart livery who operated the lift. As the doors opened, Nate and Daisy stepped inside and Daisy asked for the ground floor. When the elevator came to a halt and the doors opened, Nate took a few shillings from his pocket and pressed them into the boy's hand.

'We'll take it from here, lad,' he told the boy. 'Get your-self home. And tell any of the staff that you see on the way out to do the same. Spread the word; all hell is about to break loose, and there's no need for any of you to be a part of it. Now, go . . . Go!'

The boy started walking down the hallway towards the staff stairwell, clutching the coins in his fist with a bewildered expression on his face. Nate closed the doors over and shifted the lever, taking the lift down to the base-ment. This corridor was tiled, not carpeted, and the walls were not adorned by paintings. They made their way to the end of the long hallway, where a heavy, locked door led to the outside. Daisy had given Nate a large bunch of keys to carry in his pocket, and he handed it to her.

'I knew you'd betray the family someday, boy,' a deep voice snarled from behind them. 'You have too much of your mother in you.'

Nate felt a shock run through him as he heard those words. He spun round and Brutus's engimal claw rammed into his stomach, doubling him over. Daisy fumbled with the keys, trying to fit the right one into the lock. Brutus took her head in his left hand and thumped it against the door. She collapsed to the ground, her senses reeling.

Nate tried to straighten up against his cramped stomach, pulling the gun from his waistband. But a foot caught him across the side of the head and threw him against the wall of the corridor. The gun spun away along the floor. His reflexes took over and he lunged to one side to dodge the next kick. He tried to ignore the way it hit the wall with enough force to smash the plaster, and staggered to his feet, hands raised in a guard stance. Ducking under a swinging hook, he slammed his own fist into Brutus's ribs, then delivered two more blows to the giant's body and a jab to Brutus's jaw. The strikes made no impression at all. Nate kicked the inside of Brutus's knee, knocking the bigger man off-balance. He went to sweep the ogre's other leg, but Brutus sidestepped the sweep and stamped Nate's ankle to the ground, then seized his neck with the claw.

He lifted Nate clear off the ground and shoved him against the wall. Nate kicked at Brutus's groin and thighs, but he might as well have been striking the trunk of an oak tree for all the effect it had.

'It is my fault – I accept responsibility,' Brutus said as he began to crush Nate's throat. 'I should have made a better man of you.'

'You're not him!' Nate choked, his teeth gritted, one hand clutching the claw to try and take the weight of his own body off his neck, the other flailing at the pocket of his jacket. 'You've just read his words, his thoughts. You've stolen what he is, but you're not him!'

'You're fooling yourself, boy. But you were always good at that. It was one of your mother's naïve traits . . .'

'Don't say it . . .'

'No . . . I am your father!'

'Gaaaaaaagh!' Nate roared and, lifting his knee, drove his foot hard into Brutus's chest.

Daisy was on her knees behind the huge man, shaking her head as she tried to clear it. The power of the kick took the giant by surprise, hurling him back. He toppled over Daisy and his skull hit the wall behind him, striking the plaster hard enough to leave a dent and folding his head down against his chest. Brutus groaned and tried to straighten up, his hand at the back of his neck. Nate had fallen with him, but now pulled free, leaving scrapes in the sides of his neck from Brutus's claw. He rose up onto his knees, frantically trying to get something out of his pocket. Brutus had begun to recover almost as soon as he hit the ground, and the giant was getting to his feet when Nate held up a sheet of paper in front of his face.

'Here! *Here!* If you're really Edgar Wildenstern, then this was meant for you!'

Brutus, Edgar, was about to push the sheet of paper aside when he recognized the handwriting on it. With the tentative fingers of his left hand, he took it with surprising delicacy. The giant slumped back against the wall, sitting down to read the last words his wife had ever written.

'She wrote it the day she intended to leave you,' Nate said with a cough as he stood up and rubbed his neck. 'I've been reading those words a lot. *I have spent my entire married life struggling to come to terms with the conflicting sides of your character – the implacable leader of men that is your public face, and the tender, loyal and loving husband that so few people see.* She loved you right up to the day you condemned her to an asylum. I have to say, *I* never saw the conflict in you. As far I ever knew, you were a complete bastard your whole damned life. And now you've come back to continue making our lives a misery, just as you did hers. You think *I've* betrayed the family? You've betrayed everyone who ever came close to you. Go back to Hell where you belong . . . *Father.*'

Daisy was standing now, leaning against the wall and looking anxiously at Edgar in this new, ancient form. It was just one more revelation in what was turning into a truly bizarre day. She picked out the right key and unlocked the door. Eamon Duffy was waiting at the bottom of the steps outside, with ten armed men who wore scarves around their faces to hide their identities.

'Mister Duffy . . . Eamon,' she greeted him.

'Your Graces,' he said, doffing his cap to her and Nate. 'I believe Mister Gordon has left the building?'

'That is correct,' Daisy replied. 'There's just the rest of the family to deal with. But I am certain that we might clear the building in good time and with a minimum loss of life if we can instill in them a lively terror. Is your main force on its way?'

'They'll be at the gates in twenty minutes,' he informed

her. 'Which should give us enough time to get started.'

He looked past her at Edgar, sitting slumped against the wall, the letter held in limp fingers. The giant man was rubbing the back of his neck, his eyes riveted to the words on the page. Duffy threw a questioning look at Daisy.

'Pay him no mind,' Nate grunted, studying his father's face. 'He's done.'

'These will open all of the hall doors in the house,' Daisy told Duffy, handing him the keys. 'You'll find cans of paraffin waiting for you in the housekeeping cupboards by the servants' elevators on the top three floors. That should be more than enough to get a hearty blaze going. In a building of this size, there will be no way to fight a major fire once it has set in on the upper floors. Take care you and your men do not get caught in the blaze yourself, Eamon. And remember that this building is booby-trapped throughout – you must make your way with extreme caution. The house is also full of combustibles, piped throughout with gas, and there are weapons stores containing gunpowder and live ammunition on a number of floors. Please try and make sure all the floors are cleared of people, but once you light your fires, you *must* flee the building.'

'You make a marvellous saboteur, ma'am,' he said, smiling. 'I'd hate to have you as an enemy.'

'Then it's just as well we can count each other as firm friends.'

'I'm sorry it had to be your home that got invaded, Daisy.'

'This horrible place is no longer my home, Eamon. I shall find another – one that does not turn my stomach. Burn this place with my blessing. Burn it to the ground.'

He tipped the peak of his cap.

'Yes, ma'am.'

XXXII

'POP GOES THE WEASEL'

Cathal woke to the sound of gunfire and, rolling to look at the door, immediately winced at the pain in his stump. Trying to keep his maimed arm as still as possible, he sat up and pushed off the blankets. The mines were cold and his body started shivering as he tossed the covers aside. The effects of the laudanum he had taken were wearing off and he glanced at the small green bottle on the bedside table, briefly pondering taking another dose, but decided against it.

There was no doubt about the sound – those were gunshots. His first thought was that the children were attempting another escape, or even stupidly trying to get to him. He should never have let them go on thinking that he was the Highwayboy, but it had offered them hope, even inspiration when there was none. Cathal had thought it a kind and pragmatic lie. He slowly shook his head from side to side, trying to judge how foggy his head still was after the drug. He had lied to give them hope and one of them had been shot dead, another almost killed and all of them were now sure to be punished for their transgression. And he had lost his hand.

He stood up. He was in his socks and underwear, but his clothes were draped over a wooden chair at the foot of the bed. Pulling on his trousers with some difficulty, hampered by having to do it with one hand, he tentatively pushed his bandaged stump through the right sleeve of his shirt. Moving it in any way changed the dull ache to a sharp spike of pain, and even the light fabric of the shirt seemed to drag across the bandage like sandpaper. Getting the left hand into its sleeve was surprisingly tricky. Doing up the buttons on the shirt was manageable, but when he sat down on the chair and started to push his feet into his shoes, his hands reached down for the laces on reflex. Except there was only one hand to work with. He lifted the laces of one shoe with his left hand, gazing bitterly at them, his stump poised to help. The trembling was making his teeth chatter, and he clenched them tightly shut. He finished pulling the shoes on, then pulled the laces tight and tucked them in the sides. Pulling on his jacket, he stood up, his head feeling clear enough to let him walk normally, though he was surprised to find the lack of a hand seemed to affect his balance a little bit.

When he opened the door to Gerald's cave-like study, the gunfire was only slightly more audible. Seeing Siren in its wire birdcage on Gerald's desk, Cathal walked across to it and opened the door of the cage. The engimal bird erupted from the cage in a mad flutter of wings, spiralling around the chamber, singing in a voice that sounded like someone playing a clarinet and a flute simultaneously while having a fit of the giggles. The music had a strange effect on Cathal, as if his emotions were strings and this creature was strumming them, as one would a guitar or a violin.

The sensation was like Gerald's manipulative music, but there was no sense the thing was trying to control him, merely reaching out to him instead. Siren had never had this effect on him before, and Cathal remembered what he had felt as his shape had begun to change when fighting Moby. How he had somehow unlocked some primal, natural urge. In that moment, he sensed the unmistakable shape of Siren's engimal mind in the air above him, and Siren chirped with pleasure as it felt the connection. But then it was gone, as if it were a momentary scent picked up on the wind.

Cathal hurriedly put his finger to his lips, shushing the creature, and it swooped down to him, coming to a rest on his shoulder. Cathal had spent enough time with Tatty for Siren to feel completely comfortable with him. She had even shown him some of the creature's simpler tricks. Cathal stroked its head gently, and it trilled nervously in his ear as he made his way out to the Engimal Works.

The children had come away from their workbenches and were crowded round the entrance to the tunnel leading to the surface. Two guards stood in front of the tunnel with pistols drawn. One of them was Cowen, the man Cathal had pushed head-first into the cesspit. Siren's claws tightened their grip on Cathal's shoulder, digging into the fabric of his jacket. Cowen glowered at Cathal, but kept his attention on the children in front of him.

'I'll say it one more time for the dense ones,' he rasped. 'Get back to yer work! I'm warnin' yiz!'

'What's goin' on up there, Cowen?' Cathal asked, cradling his stump carefully.

'None o' of yer business!' the guard snapped back, but he was visibly nervous.

'It's not the police, is it?' Cathal persisted. 'It's not the *army*?'

'It's nothin'!' Cowen barked. 'Nobody's gettin' in here and none of yiz are gettin' out! Mister Gordon'll be here soon and he'll sort this, and it'll all be back to normal. This place is stronger than any fortress, and we've got the power of the Wildensterns behind us! *Now get back to work!*'

He pointed his gun at one child, and then another. Pip was near the front, and they were all edging slowly forwards.

'All right,' Cathal said to them. 'Let's be careful. Do as he says.'

'But dere's only *two* of 'em, Mister Dempsey,' Pip

muttered through gritted teeth. 'Dey killed Queg, and now someone's come to get us out o' here. Dis is our chance!'

'We can take 'em!' one of the girls shouted.

'No,' Cathal said firmly. 'I have a better idea. Just come away from them. They're scared and they're likely to shoot someone in a panic. Come away there, and we'll see what we can do.'

Curious to see what would happen, the children began to back off. This alarmed the guards even further.

'Don't go cookin' up any plans, you!' Cowen exclaimed, aiming his weapon at Cathal. 'If anything happens, you'll be the first one I shoot!'

'That suits me fine,' Cathal retorted. 'Both of you keep those guns on me. Let's just keep this calm now. Nobody here's goin' to lay a hand on you.' He raised his stump. 'You have my word on that.'

When the children had backed away a few yards, Cathal murmured just loud enough for Siren to hear:

'Pop goes the weasel.'

Siren flew up from his shoulder, emitting a deep, haunting tune. The creature flew a couple of low circles over the children's heads as they watched in fascination. Then it swooped out and came in across them towards the guards. In a belated attempt to stop it, the two guards raised their guns and fired, but missed the tiny, moving target. Siren flew between them and, right at the instant when it was little more than two feet from either man's head, it let out a sound like the blast from a cannon. Both men screamed and fell away from the deafening sound, each one clutching a hand to his single burst eardrum.

The children descended on them before they could recover, and enthusiastically kicked the two men into unconsciousness.

Having securely tied up their captors, the children followed Cathal up the tunnel. Cathal had one pistol and Pip took the other. Siren returned to its perch on Cathal's shoulder. Some of the others carried lanterns, the light as low as possible, but put them out as they came into sight of the leviathan's mouth. It was open just a crack, and Red and five other men were firing rifles through the narrow gap at someone outside. Each shot was a loud, echoing detonation in the hard confined space of the mine. The rare bullet that made it through the leviathan's mouth from outside ricocheted dangerously along the tunnel.

'It'd take a cannon or explosives to get past that mouth,' Cathal said to Pip. 'And with those bloody tentacles, nobody's going to be getting too close to the end of the tunnel. If that's the peelers out there, we need to help 'em get past Red and them before Gerald gets back. God only knows what he could do if he showed up.'

'We could rush 'em,' Pip suggested, brandishing the revolver.

It was clear from the way the boy held the weapon that he had never fired a pistol in his life. Cathal did not fancy the lad's chances in a shoot-out. He shook his head. He didn't want to risk anyone else getting shot unless it was absolutely necessary.

'Can you use deh bird again?' the boy asked.

Cathal shrugged.

'Could give it a try . . . It won't help open Moby up, though. We need to let those peelers in here somehow. I don't have the whistle any more. And that trick with Siren back there was something I learned from its mistress, but I only know how to get it to make one "bang" at a time. It was a one-off thing she taught the engimal as a defence against someone attackin' her. I can't play music to it . . . give it *instructions*, you know . . . do the Pied Piper bit like Gerald can . . .'

He went quiet for a minute, listening to the gunfire and the occasional shouts from Red's men. They were scared but confident, knowing the attackers would have to get past Moby to get into the tunnel. The coves were sure that they only had to hold out until Gerald returned. They had faith in his power – either to turn back the attacking forces with his political influence, or with his music.

'Just don't go turnin' into a monster again, Mister Dempsey,' Pip muttered. 'I nearly soiled meself den – an' I only own one pair o' trousers.'

Cathal grimaced at the memory. And then he thought of the link he had sensed with Siren in Gerald's study. There had been something about his experience in the tunnel with Moby that had left a mark on him – as if a door in his mind had been opened and had not been properly shut. He wondered, could he force it open again? Did he want to?

He took the little engimal from his shoulder and cupped it in his hands, holding it near his face.

'I need you to understand me, Siren,' he said to it. 'Can you understand me? I need you to go up there and sing out whatever note opens that great big bloody mouth. Can you do that for me? Go on, now. Go open that mouth, Siren!'

With a push of his hands, he sent the bird fluttering towards the gunfight, fervently hoping it would be too small to be caught by any stray shots. He glanced down at Pip. The boy was looking a bit dubious, but obviously didn't want to say anything. Cathal was feeling more confident, however, now that he had taken the step, showing faith in this link he had with the bird.

'Give it a chance,' he said to the boy.

'Aye, right. We'll watch and see what deh little birdie does,' the boy replied, carefully looking in any direction except Cathal's. '. . . But den I'm goin' to rush 'em.'

Siren flew silently towards the men crouched inside the leviathan's jaws. The tunnel was high up on the mountainside, with only the sheer wall of a cliff visible on the far side of the valley, so there was no way for the attackers to shoot at them from a distance. Red and his men were taking careful aim at anyone who came close enough to show their head at the bright square opening of the tunnel in front of them. The leviathan's flexible metal lips were parted about six inches, allowing the defenders to shoot out, but giving their attackers very little to aim at. And bullets made little impression on hide that had, for thousands of years, withstood the most fearsome predators and the crushing depths at the bottom of the sea. Even hand grenades were of little use, the tentacles seizing any that were thrown in and hurling them back out again.

The bird flickered in and out of sight as it neared the tunnel, only visible, like the men at the mouth, when it passed in front of the three-pointed star of light shining through the narrow gap. Cathal held his breath, his grip tightening on the handle of his gun. He thought he heard a whining sound, just at the highest range of his hearing, and then Moby's three-jawed mouth snapped open. Red and his men cried out in alarm, stumbling backwards. A figure leaped into sight at the opening to the tunnel, charging forwards, firing a revolver with each hand. He roared as he ran, shooting down one and then another of the defenders. Cathal let out a triumphant shout. Siren flew straight out of the tunnel and into the valley beyond . . . And then Moby's mouth slammed shut, throwing the tunnel into complete darkness.

'Ah, shite!' Cathal swore through his teeth.

He felt Pip lunge forward and run up the tunnel, but was too late to grab him. Pip fired off two shots into the pitch darkness, wasting ammunition. Cathal cursed again and started after him. Stumbling and tripping over the sleepers and rails as he ran, he tried to catch up to the boy, who fired another useless shot, the flash illuminating him for an instant and marking him as a target for anyone who might be aiming in that direction. Up ahead, other gunshots were going off, men were shouting, someone screamed. The muzzle-flashes gave the impression of chaos, each burst of light showing men standing in different positions, acts of violence frozen in after-images on Cathal's eyes as he blinked in the darkness. He was running blind, with no idea how far it was to the leviathan's mouth, or who might be ahead, waiting for him. More shots, the sounds of a struggle. He heard Pip fall and cry out just ahead, and Cathal was nearly hit by a bullet zipping past his face as the boy hit the ground and accidentally jerked on the trigger.

'Stop shooting and point it at the bloody floor!' Cathal bellowed as he ran past.

Then, suddenly, he was in the middle of a fight. A fist brushed his shoulder in the darkness. Red's men, in their confusion, must be fighting whoever had charged into the tunnel, or else they were fighting with each other. Hearing Red swear, Cathal aimed and fired in that direction. Even as the flash of his shot faded, someone piled into him from the other side and he fell back, landing on the wooden sleepers, banging his left elbow off the rail and nearly dropping his gun. The jolt hurt his stump, causing him to yelp in pain. A hand felt for his chest, then his chin, then his face, and then bunched into a fist and struck him in the cheek. Cathal aimed over the arm and swung the butt of his gun into the man's face, but his attacker just grunted and pushed the gun aside, clawing his way onto Cathal's torso.

Cathal heard that almost inaudible sound again, and the mouth opened a few inches, enough to let in some light. Red was standing just inside, seizing a fallen shotgun from the ground. The man who was on top of Cathal pivoted and pulled a pistol from his waistband. Cathal jammed his own revolver under the man's bearded chin even as his attacker put a bullet through Red's chest before the blackguard could raise the shotgun. A second shot took Red in the head and he toppled back into the space that would once have been occupied by the leviathan's tongue.

Cathal struggled to catch his breath, his heart pumping like a steam train as the stranger stared down at him and gently pulled the barrel of Cathal's gun away from his throat.

'Now, that's no way to greet your oul' man, is it, lad?'

Cathal looked past the shabby, well-travelled clothes, the uncut hair and beard, and into the eyes of his father, crinkled with emotion.

'Pa?' Cathal gasped, his breath catching in his throat. 'Pa? Jesus, is that really you?'

'In the flesh,' William Dempsey laughed, cupping his hand to his son's face and kissing the lad's brow. 'Christ, boy, it's so good to see you! You've no idea how good it is! Thanks be to God you're alive!'

Dempsey's gaze fell on his son's right arm and the blood-stained bandages that covered the stump. A horrified whimper slipped from his mouth and he gently clasped Cathal's forearm, before pulling the boy to him in a tight embrace. Tears streamed down the man's cheeks as he held his son, and Cathal began crying, hugging him in return.

'What in God's name did the curs do to you?' Dempsey hissed, his clawed hands bunching into fists as he clutched the fabric of Cathal's jacket, trying to contain his anguish. 'What have they done to my boy?'

The shouts of officers commanding their men forward could be heard outside, and the tramp of feet running up the steep slope of the road to the mine. The other defenders of the tunnel were lying either dead or injured all around the father and son. Pip and the children were making their way up towards the light, holding their hands up to shield their eyes against the glare of the evening light. Cathal pulled himself away from his pa and scrambled across to Red's body. The white whistle lay there near his feet. Cathal blew the whistle, and Moby's mouth stretched open. From this low angle, he could see the sky. He was surprised to see that the daylight which had seemed so bright was actually only a dim grey glow through heavy cloud. Rain was falling, and he felt an urge to rush out and feel it on his face, to let it drench him.

'I don't . . . I don't understand what this thing is,' Dempsey said to his son, gesturing in bewilderment at the leviathan's mouth as soldiers and police constables cautiously entered the tunnel. 'How did it come to be here?'

'It's a giant sea monster's gob,' Cathal informed him in a dazed voice, looking out at the rain. 'Put here by a mad scientist to keep children trapped down a mine, where they pull apart the dead bodies of engimals so that he can gather intelligent particles from the children's blood and use them to give himself god-like powers . . . so he can force the world to become a better place.'

'That's the most insane thing I've ever heard,' Inspector Urskin said from behind them, staring at the monster's jaws and the horde of children standing just inside them, afraid to go near them but craving the daylight. 'You're telling us all this is down to the actions of some raving madman?'

'He's not really the raving type,' Cathal muttered. 'Though you should hear him play the fiddle.'

Patting Pip's back, Cathal led the children out through the jaws to the opening of the tunnel, past the policemen and soldiers and into the fresh air. The rain was heavy, pelting them with big drops and quickly soaking them to the skin. The men who had laid assault to the mine now came to take the children down the hill, wrapping them in blankets and picking them up, offering them water and food. Cathal felt his father's hand on his shoulder.

'Come on, son,' Dempsey said. 'We're done with this place. It's over.'

'It's not over, Pa,' Cathal replied. 'It's not over by a long way.'

Gerald pulled back on the handlebars of his velocycle, Incitatus, bringing the creature to a skidding halt. Pushing his fly-specked riding goggles up onto his forehead, he stared up into the sky, his eyes fixed on a bird flying over-head. It had a unique way of moving, and Gerald recognized it immediately. There were no other engimals like Siren in Ireland – and there could only be one reason that Siren was flying free.

The little creature soared past, making its way back to Wildenstern Hall. As he tracked it across the sky, his gaze was drawn back the way he had come. The very top of Wildenstern Hall was visible above the hills, and there was smoke rising from it. His face twisted into a knowing scowl and he nodded to himself.

'Conniving little witch,' he murmured, though not with-out a hint of admiration.

Gerald threw one last bitter look towards Glendalough, certain that there was nothing there for him now and, with a kick to the velocycle's side, he spun his mount around. Urging Incitatus into a sprint, Gerald raced back in the same direction as the bird.

XXXIII

A TOWERING INFERNO

Duffy's gang had done a thorough job. Even the rain had died down, as if nature itself was standing back to let Wildenstern Hall burn. The tower's top floors were ablaze, smoke gushing out of the windows, the building letting out a low, guttural moaning sound as the raging fire sucked air up through the elevator shafts and stairwells. The inferno ate up the family's possessions, greedily consuming the priceless antiques, the wardrobes of fashionable clothes, the furs and the silk, the rugs and the tapestries and all the other fine things. Secret stashes of paper cash blackened and curled into ash. Gold and silver melted, jewels dropped from their settings to be lost in the debris. On one side of the building, the armouries on two separate floors exploded, ammunition igniting and blasting out like deadly fireworks. Whole sections of wall were blown out, the shattered stone and masonry tumbling to the ground below. Like some giant dying, prehistoric dragon, it belched flame and pieces of its flesh. Daisy had ordered the stopcocks turned on all the gas pipes, but there was still enough gas in the lines to cause smaller detonations.

Floor by floor, the massive structure was slowly but inevitably being reduced to a burnt husk. The family had water pumps and hoses to fight any house fires, but they would have been insufficient, even if someone *hadn't* punched holes in the hoses so that they sprayed uselessly in every direction. Servants had formed a human chain in an attempt to fight the inferno, passing buckets of water hand to hand, but it was hopeless. The building was doomed.

People of a less possessive and more pragmatic nature might have by this time chosen to leave the building in a hasty fashion. The Wildensterns were made of sterner stuff – and were wary of going outside to face what awaited them.

Nate and Daisy had been searching desperately for Elizabeth and Leopold. Whatever they thought about the rest of the family, they could not leave without Nate's son. Responsible nannies had already accounted for the other Wildenstern children, their parents having long ago delegated the duty of knowing the whereabouts of their offspring. But Elizabeth would not have left Leopold out of her sight at a time like this, and Daisy had been informed that the ancient woman was still in the house and had declared her intention to 'stand her ground' there.

As they searched the fourth floor, Nate peered into the library. The smell of smoke had filled that floor already, and he knew they were running out of time. Having only recently discovered the joys of reading, he found himself dismayed that all these volumes would be lost. But he had little time to wallow in regret, for he saw a group of people at the windows who caught his attention. Neither Elizabeth nor Leopold were among them, but Gideon and his wife Eunice were. Nate's curiosity got the better of him, and he strode across the room, past the rows of shelves, to have a look out one of the windows.

A large crowd of people was winding up the driveway towards the house. At their head was a dark horse ridden by a figure dressed all in black and wearing a tri-cornered hat. Nate's eyebrows went up of their own accord.

'That's the bloody Highwayboy!' one of the Wildensterns whined. 'What's he doing here?'

'Doing a spot of rabble-rousing, I'll be bound!' Gideon replied. 'Look at the little guttersnipe, come off the hills to lead the goddamned charge, just when we're most inconvenienced! It just goes to show the lower classes have no sense of fair play.'

There had to be two or three hundred of that lower-class type out there. Most of them were peasants, some masked, others baring their faces to the masters of the estate, their expressions declaring their anger and hatred. The daylight was fading to dusk; the flaming torches the mob carried were visible from some way off, and the guttering orange flames picked out the sharp prongs of pick-axes, mattocks and pitchforks.

'What are they carrying those for?' Eunice asked in a loud voice. 'Who *are* all these people? What are they doing here? And what are they carrying *pitchforks* for?'

Realization dawned. Her jowly jaw dropped, pulling her slack, thin-lipped mouth open.

'Oh. Oh! Oh my God! Gideon, we must get out of here! Dear Lord, we must leave at once!'

'Some of the others are staying to fight, my dear. I think I should stand with them,' Gideon told her, though the tone of his voice suggested that he could be persuaded against it.

'*Stand with them?*' Eunice exclaimed, aghast. 'And . . . and what is to become of *me* when those brutes storm the house and swarm over us like . . . like . . . like vermin? You must stand with *me*, Gideon. Your duty to your immediate family must come before any . . . any honourable last stand.'

'You are right, of course, my dear,' Gideon replied after some hesitation. He held himself straighter, put his hands to his lapels, and eyed those around him as if they must recognize this fact. 'My duty must come first. Let us make haste to the train. Come along, Eunice. I will see you safely there. To the train!'

The small group of Wildensterns expressed general

approval of this strategy, and made a barely dignified rush for the door.

'Nate!' Gideon called over to him as he turned to lead his wife out. 'We must leave! Good God, man, the peasants are—'

'Yes, so I see,' Nate cut him off. 'You must make haste for the train, Gideon.'

'God, yes!' Gideon barked. 'So long, old chap!'

With that, they were gone. Nate cast a last, long look at his sister, the Highwayboy, and crossed to the door, where he met Daisy as she came along the corridor.

'Still no sign,' she said. 'We'd better go across and check the nursery. The nannies said it was empty, but . . .'

'Just so you know,' Nate told her. 'Tatty's all done up as the Highwayboy, and she's leading the tenants up the driveway in a mob armed with flaming torches and pitchforks.'

'Right . . . Well, I'm glad she's making herself useful.'

'I'm concerned they might storm the place just as we're trying to get out.'

'Then we'd best get a move on, hadn't we?'

Making for the back of the house as fast as Daisy's dress would allow, Nate felt the pressure of Gerald's absence. If there is a wasp in one's room, one wants to know where it is. Not being stung is an insufficient comfort. Knowing Gerald could be close by, Nate felt his skin itch at the thought that he could not see him. And given Gerald's knack for unpredictable strategies, Nate would much rather have kept him in sight.

'How do you think he did it?' Daisy asked breathlessly. 'Edgar, I mean. You seem convinced it's really him, though I find it hard to believe. How could Gerald have managed it?'

'Don't know,' Nate replied through tight lips. 'The original particles took over the minds of humans, so perhaps Gerald discovered how to move particles from one person's brain to another. Or perhaps he moved the *whole brain*. He obviously held onto Brutus's body, after he said he'd destroyed it – kept it frozen in those refrigerators of his. I saw Father's body in the coffin, so either he somehow swapped that out at the last minute or he must have kept Father's brain. With Gerald, who can tell how he goes about these things?'

'It seems a lot of bother just to have an assistant to run the family.'

'It's always about the thrill of discovery, for Gerald,' Nate told her. 'Though I wouldn't put it past him to have resurrected Edgar as an extra distraction, to put me off my game. He must have known I'd come back and try and stop him. Always looking to the future is Gerald.' Nate rubbed his hands together – his palms were sweating, but the hands were still steady. 'That's what's so scary about fighting the bugger. He's always a few steps ahead of you.'

The Wildenstern nursery was in the south wing, one of

the oldest parts of the house, away from the tower where most of the family's day-to-day affairs were carried out. It had once been part of the Norman keep that the Wildensterns had built when they arrived in Ireland centuries before. The room itself had once been the main hall, and it was now decorated in bright colours and equipped with rocking horses, tea sets and all manner of other, well-crafted toys. But its thick stone walls, low deep doorways and narrow windows could contain any clamorous noise a gaggle of children might make. Daisy had fought to move the nursery to a brighter, airier room, but this had been its location when all the current adults had been children, and they maintained it had done them no harm. As far as they were concerned, Daisy's attempts to move the nursery was one breach of tradition too many.

It seemed that Elizabeth agreed. As Nate and Daisy burst into the room, they found wisps of smoke already threading through the air. The roof of this wing was on fire, and they could hear the roar of flames from the floor above. Elizabeth was standing on the far side of the room, holding a crossbow. Leopold was playing with some wooden animals in the corner nearest her. He waved at Nate and Daisy and went back to his game.

'Ah, the traitors!' she said, as if welcoming some eagerly anticipated guests. She levelled the weapon at them. 'Do come in and sit down. Leopold and I were just waiting for Brutus to return, before we made our escape.'

'What if he doesn't return?' Nate asked cautiously.

The bolt loaded into the crossbow had an explosive tip – obviously intended to kill the most invulnerable Wildenstern.

'Of course he will return!' she exclaimed in a manic voice, tinged with hysteria. She raised the crossbow slightly. 'I said, sit down! My brother will be along momentarily. He would not desert me!'

No, thought Nate. But Edgar Wildenstern would drop you in a heartbeat. If he had a heart.

'Think of your son, Elizabeth!' Daisy pleaded with her. 'We have to take Leopold out of here! And you've just said you were *pregnant*, for goodness sake. Do you want your child to die before it's even born? Come with us – please!'

'Leave the castle?' the older woman sneered. 'Without the means of defending ourselves against that horde of miscreants outside? I think I shall take my chances within the protection of these walls. NOW, SIT DOWN!'

Daisy glanced down dubiously at the wooden, child-sized seats behind them as Nate wondered how traumatized Leopold would be if they snatched him and left his mother to burn. Elizabeth was sure to be an expert shot, but Nate judged the distance across the floor to be less than a dozen paces. If he threw something at her to spoil her aim—

With a creaking, snapping sound, part of the ceiling gave way and a chunk of burning wreckage the size of a travelling trunk crashed down into the room just to the left of Elizabeth. She flinched away and Nate dived across the floor. He did a forward roll, pulling his gun from under his jacket, and came up with it aimed at her chest. But the crossbow was already pointing with deadly stillness at his throat. Elizabeth tutted and shook her head. Leopold let out a cry. His frightened eyes went from the fire creeping across one side of the room, to the sight of his mother and father pointing deadly weapons at each other. Confusion, fear and panic were written on his face.

The curtains on the window nearest the blaze caught fire. More burning debris fell from the floor above, and they could hear wood crackling and breaking. Daisy rushed across to pick up Leopold and carry him away from the fire. Another section of the ceiling collapsed, pulling down flaming rafters, floorboards and furniture with it. The room was full of smoke now. A wooden rocking horse, knocked into motion by a piece of smouldering debris, caught fire, its paint igniting like paraffin and gusting into a lively blaze. The toy box next to it began to burn. Dolls made from wood, cloth or even celluloid, painted lead soldiers and wooden trains all combined to make an admirable tinder-box. The black areas of floor around the fallen wreckage were spreading, orange flickers feeding on the thick carpet and growing in size and strength. Daisy edged past the flaming rocking horse towards the door.

'Move another step and I'll shoot him through his throat!' Elizabeth shrieked over the noise, coughing as smoke caught in her throat. 'Put . . . put down my son!'

'He's going to die if we stay here!' Nate shouted at her.

'Then at least we'll all burn together!' she snarled. 'Better that we die than we be savaged by that vermin outside!'

'Get out of here, Daisy!' Nate called out, his gun still raised, his eyes fixed on Elizabeth and the crossbow she held aimed at his throat. 'Don't mind me. Take him and go!'

Daisy hugged Leopold to her, pressing his face into her shoulder. She blinked, tears welling in her eyes from the fumes. Coughs wracked her chest and she felt the choking, gritty air contaminating her lungs. The smoke would finish them even before the flames could consume them. They could not stay here any longer. She looked in desperation at Nate, then turned her eyes to the door.

XXXIV

REVOLT

Tatty waved to the mob of people behind her, calling for just a dozen of them to follow her inside. She had taught herself to mimic Cathal's voice as closely as possible, in order to pass herself off all the better as a young man. But she had always found bellowing in a deep voice difficult, and had never convinced herself that she could do so in a truly credible fashion. But people believe what they want to believe, and if her call to attack sounded somewhat shrill, that fact was overlooked as the oppressed tenants of the Wildenstern estate followed their black-clad folk hero as he rode his horse up the steps and through the front door of Wildenstern Hall. They were eager to capture as many of the tyrants as possible.

And while Tatty was sincere in her support of this angry mob, she was also intent on sparing any servants who had remained and might bear the brunt of the rioters. She planned too to limit the violence to seizing her relatives, rather than tearing them limb from limb. Whether she would succeed in restraining the mob was another matter entirely.

Some of the Wildensterns had chosen to stand and fight for their home, even as it burned down around them. Things could turn nasty very quickly. She knew for certain that Gideon kept a small cannon loaded with grapeshot in his room, and two of her cousins bred packs of savage attack dogs. And God only knew what booby-traps had been set in the hallways.

A handful of the most loyal and hard-bitten servants had also chosen to stay and defend the house. Two of these stalwart footmen were crossing the massive entrance hall as Tatty rode in, and were taken by surprise as she rode them down, kicking one to the floor as his colleague was rammed aside by her horse. Tatty jumped down from the saddle, drew a pistol with her left hand and a sabre with her right, shouting at the two men to run for their lives as she started up the wide curving staircase on the right side of the hall. Instead of the dozen she had called for, scores of the people swept in behind her, their improvised weapons held up in readiness. Some of them stopped to set fire to the priceless tapestries and wall hangings with their torches, or throw family portraits to the floor and stab them repeatedly with their pitchforks.

Checking her scarf was still firmly pulled up over her face, she tipped the brim of her hat a little lower and set off along one of the hallways, making for the staff elevator at the back of the house. It was the fastest way down to the underground train platform beneath the building. She was in no doubt that most of the family would attempt to escape by train, and it was a long way round on the surface to the trainsheds on the far side of the mountain, and the entrance to the tunnel. It took the train up to an hour, starting from cold, to build up steam, but it could be in use at any time of the day or night and there was always a crew on standby. Even now, the train could be reversing back into the mountain to the underground platform, to pick up the fleeing family and carry them away to safety. If it had occurred to any of the enraged tenants to come at the house from that side of the hill, it would be devilishly easy to derail that train as it emerged at speed from the mouth of the tunnel. Tatty wanted this wrapped up with as few lives lost as possible.

One of Gideon's sons leaned round a corner in the corridor, his rifle aimed straight at Tatty. Dropping her sword, she threw herself in through an open doorway even as her cousin's shot hit someone behind her. With her back to the door, she slid over onto her side and kicked herself back out along the hall floor, her pistol already raised. She fired three shots. One took the young Wildenstern in the leg, one missed and the third hit him in the shoulder. He spun against the wall and collapsed to the floor. The mob rushed forward, shouting curses and threats. Their fury frightened her, and as they laid into the wounded young man she came to the sinking realization that their rage could not be easily restrained.

'Don't kill him!' she cried, running out into the hallway. Realizing her voice was too high-pitched, she called again in a deeper tone, 'Tie him up and get him outside! There are more where he came from!'

But the mob would not be denied their revenge. This was the first Wildenstern they could get their hands on, and he screamed as they kicked him and beat him with the handles of their weapons.

'Stop!' she roared again.

'Stand back there!' another voice commanded – one that was used to being obeyed. 'We are not animals! Hold back and let that wretch be! You'll have your reckoning, but not like this! Stand back!'

Eamon Duffy shoved his way through the crowd, followed by his masked gang of Fenians. They hauled the attackers away from the battered form of the young Wildenstern.

'Bind him and drag him outside,' he instructed two of his men. 'Everyone else, follow me. And mind how you go, this place is a bloody death trap. Don't open any doors or take any stairs without my say-so.'

He nodded curtly to Tatty, a slight smile creasing the

corners of his eyes. She wondered if he had guessed her identity. They had met enough times for him to recognize her voice if he heard it. If Duffy suspected, he did not let it show, turning to lead the newly disciplined mob along the hallway. Snatching up her sword, she hurried to catch up with him. It was only then that she realized he was looking around, unsure of where to go.

'We need to get to the train platform,' she muttered to him, so that only he could hear. 'Left at the end of the corridor, then through the atrium to the servants' elevator.'

'Thank you, Miss . . . I mean, eh . . . thank you, lad,' he replied softly. 'I had lost my bearings there for a minute. This mob needs to be directed somewhere, or lose the run of itself. The train platform it is.'

At the T-shaped junction in the corridor, Duffy took a quick look around the corner, gently pressed Tatty back against the wall and looking around at the eager faces behind her put a finger to his lips. He nodded to another two of his men and tipped his head towards the corner. Stepping out and left, with his revolver raised in front of him, he walked slowly and carefully towards the door at the end of the hallway, with his two men close on his heels. Another fellow stood by the corner on the other side, keeping his gun trained to the right, watching for anyone from that direction. Tatty had been glad to have Duffy take command of the mob, but resented being left behind.

She rounded the corner just as the door swung open at

the far end of the corridor. There was just a second to glimpse the massive gun mounted on small carriage wheels, its ten rotating barrels fed with a large stick magazine set into the top. And then it opened fire.

The ear-piercing shots came so fast they were almost on top of each other. Duffy and his two men were caught halfway down the corridor, with nowhere to hide. Bullets riddled their bodies, punching holes through their thighs and torsos and spraying blood across the carpet and walls. Tatty jerked back round the corner as the gun swivelled and pounded bullets into the plaster and floor where she had been standing.

'What in Christ's name is that?' one of Duffy's men asked, the colour drained from his face. 'Holy Mary, Mother of God, we can't fight that!'

'It's a Gatling gun,' Tatty said through gritted teeth.

She was trying to get the image of Duffy's last moment out of her mind, but it filled her head, blotting out all other thoughts. Panic welled up inside her. What was she doing here? She was no soldier – she was a young girl, still in her teens. What was she thinking? *She* had sent Duffy down that hallway. Fear and doubt paralyzed her. This was not the first time she had experienced violence or witnessed death, but she had led them all here and now going any further would cost even more lives. What had she done?

'We need grenades,' one man said.

'We used all we had just to get down past the nutters in

the bleedin' tower,' another replied. 'Look, we didn't come this far just to get turned back now. If we rush them, we're bound to take 'em if there's enough of us firin' at once.'

'Is that right, Francie? And how many of us d'you think they'll kill before we nail 'em?'

Tatty took some deep shuddery breaths and stood up, supporting herself by leaning on the wall. In the instant before it had opened fire, she had seen the two men operating the Gatling gun. They were servants, not members of the family. There was one thing she could do. So much for her secret identity.

'You men out there!' she shouted, making no attempt to disguise her voice this time. 'This is Tatiana Wildenstern! Stand down from that weapon!'

Pulling her scarf down from her face, she turned away from the stunned men standing with her and threw her hat to the floor. Unwrapping the scarf, she undid her ruffled blonde hair and shook it free. Some of them uttered curses, or let out gasps of amazement. Others just stared, unable to believe their eyes. Remembering the tone Duffy had used to exert his will over the mob, she put all the confidence and authority she could muster into her words. It was no easy feat when her chest felt so tight it was as if it was bound with iron bands.

'Stand down, I say!' she commanded, and then stepped out into the hallway, pistol in one hand, sword in the other.

The gun did not open fire. Staring down its ten smoking

barrels, she did not shy away from its glare, walking straight towards the gun along its line of fire. Two men crouched behind it, one on the crank handle to fire it, the other with a spare magazine in his hands. They stared at her with uncertain eyes.

'Stand down!' she snapped at them again.

Still they did not move, but they did not fire either. Tatty felt her stomach clench as she stepped over Duffy's ruined body, suppressed the urge to throw up as her boots squelched in the blood soaking into the green, ivy-patterned carpet. The bore of each of the ten barrels was like a gaping mouth, ready to spit hot lead through her. The air was soaked with the smell of gunsmoke, the tang of blood.

'Stand down!'

She was only a few yards away, a few paces. Still they did nothing. Raising her pistol, she let all the wild emotion churning inside her show in her face, let them hear it in her voice as she aimed her gun at one and then the other.

'Do as you're bloody told, you ignorant swines! Stand down or I'll shoot you down!'

Their nerve broke. The two servants staggered back, away from the huge gun, and then turned and ran as Duffy's peasant army flooded into the corridor behind Tatty. Men crowded round her, congratulating her, unsure of how to treat this upper-class lady in the guise of a criminal. Some patted her on the back, and then drew back, fearing the consequences of this inappropriate contact. Others wanted to lift her onto their shoulders, but Duffy's lieutenants shook their heads discreetly. No matter how un-conventional a lady might be, seeing her manhandled onto a crowd of strangers' shoulders was a step too far in any man's book.

Tatty was a little disappointed at their discretion. Truly, even in this modern world, there were still places a woman could not go.

Leaning back against a door, she waved them on, needing to pause for a moment and collect herself before continuing. That had taken a lot out of her. Clutching her shaking hands, she let out a near-hysterical laugh, feeling a glow of triumph before a bitter grief descended over her as her eyes were drawn back to the three men lying dead in the hallway.

As the last of the mob moved on towards the servants' elevator, Tatty stood up straight. She was dimly aware of someone whistling a tune. It was a lullaby and, listening to it, she was filled with a calm, sleepy sensation, one which gave her relief from the misery she was feeling.

Then the door opened behind her and a pair of hands yanked her inside.

XXXV

AN APOCALYPTIC CHOICE OF MUSIC

The nursery was fast becoming an inferno of burning furniture, toys and curtains. Fire spread in quickly-rising flames along the carpet. Daisy took one last look at Elizabeth and Nate still locked in a stand-off, weapons pointed at each other. Both were coughing badly, struggling to breathe. They were trapped now on the far side of the room by the fire. Daisy hugged Leopold to her and made for the door.

A shovel-sized hand pushed her aside and Brutus bent low to squeeze through the doorway. Nate's newly resurrected father surveyed the scene for a few seconds, then grabbed the door and wrenched it from its hinges.

'Go,' he croaked to Daisy. 'Get Leopold out of here.'

Without looking to see if she obeyed his command, Edgar Wildenstern threw the door down over a burning grille of rafters that had fallen from the ceiling above. Using it as a bridge, he jumped across it to where Nate and Elizabeth stood.

'Brutus!' Elizabeth gasped. 'I knew you would come!'

With startling quickness, Edgar thumped her once across the head with his engimal claw and caught her unconscious body with his left arm as she slumped to the floor. He grabbed Nate's arm and shoved him ahead, towards the fallen door which even now was beginning to catch fire. Nate did not need telling twice. He leaped across, darting to the doorway and seizing Daisy's outstretched hand. They ran along the hallway, coughing and gagging, their faces blackened, their nostrils and throats lined with a coating of soot.

Edgar followed them, covering distance quickly with his long strides, Elizabeth's body tucked under one arm like an overnight bag. Behind them, the ceiling of the nursery gave way as the burning roof above crashed down into it. Flames, smoke and charred wood spat through the doorway, as if giving chase to the fugitives.

They were on the second floor, and as they crossed into the tower Nate peered out a window into the chaos outside at the back of the manor house. Pieces of burning debris were falling from the floors above. Some, like fragments of paper or fabric, fell slowly, even spiralling to settle onto the gravel and cobblestones. Others dropped like a hellish rain, bouncing off the ground in explosions of sparks. Through this spectacle rode a figure on a velocycle. Nate immediately recognized Gerald's unmistakable form. His cousin was carrying something over his shoulder – a body. A body dressed all in black, but with long blonde hair dangling down Gerald's back.

'No!' Nate shouted, hauling the window open. 'Don't you bloody dare, you bastard!'

Gerald either did not hear, or did not care to respond. He disappeared off into the darkness, in the direction of the church. Looking desperately around, Nate tore down the long drape off one side of the window, pulled out his knife and cut it down the middle.

'Nate? What are you doing?' Daisy asked, turning to wait for him.

'Go on with Edgar,' Nate said, as he tied the two halves together to make a section of material about twelve feet long. He was faced with no choice but to trust his hated father. He came up to her and kissed her hard on the mouth, ran his hand through his son's hair and then said, 'Gerald's got Tatty. I have to go.'

Daisy's expression turned to one of dread, but then she just swallowed painfully and nodded. Turning away again, she hurried off along the hall. Nate spared his father a glance, wishing he could fathom what was going on in the mind of that bizarre combination of two human beings. Edgar locked eyes with him for an instant, then strode away after Daisy. Nate shook his head and knocked out the panes of glass above the window sash, tied the fabric around it and let it fall out the window. The air was fresher, cooler outside and he realized how hard it had been to breathe, even after they'd run from the nursery. The house was slowly suffocating.

'There'll come a time,' he grunted as he sat up on the window sill and swung his legs out, 'when I'll just have to stop jumping out of windows.'

Then he seized the length of drape and dropped out into the night air.

The fabric only reached down past the first floor and part of the way to the ground floor, but it was enough. Nate slid down, let go, dropped the remaining twelve feet, hit the ground and rolled. He came up and immediately began running. The rain of fiery debris continued around him, and he had to brush off a couple of pieces as he ran. In the stables off to his left, he could hear the shrill whinnying of panicked horses. Courageous grooms were risking their lives to free the animals as the roofs of the buildings caught fire.

Sticking two fingers to his lips, Nate let out a piercing whistle. He heard a roar in response and the sound of wood shattering. A few second later, the door of the one of the stables was kicked outwards, splintering its painted boards, and Flash emerged. The velocycle spotted Nate and set off on a diagonal course away from the house to intercept him as he ran. Nate leaped onto its back without slowing down, seizing the beast's horns and tapping its sides with his heels.

The creature bunched its shoulders, tensed its flanks and

hurled itself forward, gravel spitting from under its wheels as it raced across the yard in pursuit of their quarry. Its eyes probed the darkness ahead of them, following the tracks of Gerald's mount. Behind them, Daisy and Edgar ran out of the back door of the house, each carrying their burden in their arms. Daisy called urgently to the grooms for horses. Edgar dropped Elizabeth onto the ground without any particular care, once they were a safe distance from the house, and grabbed the reins of the largest horse he could reach. As he made off at speed after Nate, Daisy called to Hennessy, who was overseeing the rescue of the horses. Pushing Leopold into the head groom's arms, she caught the reins of the only saddled horse she could see and climbed onto it. Urging it into a gallop, she set off after Edgar. She could only guess at the ogre's motives, but she was determined not to let Nate face Gerald alone.

Overhead, thunder cracked the clouds, as if a dark force lay above the cloud cover, pushing to get through. Gerald did not go far. Nate tracked him to the copse that surrounded the graveyard, and through that to the grounds of the church itself. There Nate stopped, still in the tree line, and studied the church. This was where their conflict had begun before, after Gerald had sabotaged Berto's funeral and nearly killed everyone in the previous church. It was where Nate had found out how cunning and and treacherous an enemy his best friend truly was.

Nate breathed deeply, letting his senses stretch out and take in all that they could. What might Gerald have planned? Booby-traps were not out of the question, nor were armed henchmen or even engimals driven to attack. Last time they had fought, Gerald had used his music to turn Flash against Nate. There was no question that he still intended to play that hand. After what Daisy had told him about the organ Gerald had designed – the one built of engimals' bodies – Nate knew his cousin had mastered a new level of control over the intelligent particles.

But Nate was *counting* on Gerald to use his music.

Leaning down close to Flash's ear, he whispered:

'He took your mind from you last time, but I'm not going to let that happen again.' He placed his hands on Flash's wide skull, near the roots of its horns. 'I am your master, your friend, Flash. You'll never forget that again.'

Nate opened his mind, feeling just a hint of the storm of sensation that raged beyond it. Like a door opened just a crack, with a sandstorm blowing outside, Nate braced himself against the force trying to push open that door. He reached through that narrow opening and felt around until he touched Flash's mind, feeling the raw, savage thoughts of that feral machine, many thousands of years old. He let out a gasp as he made the connection and drew the mind to him, sharing its powerful instincts, enclosing them, protecting them. Then he closed the door as far as he could, keeping hold of Flash's thoughts.

This was the final secret Nate had learned about the intelligent particles. They were designed to bond with the human mind. If you understood them, and accepted what they could do, you could control them as instinctively as you would your own limbs. You didn't need any music. It was the truth that Nate struggled to hide, the truth Gerald must never discover.

Nate was about to start forward again when he felt the ground tremble beneath his feet. Strains of music began to seep from the church. Gerald was playing the organ.

'Oh, shit,' Nate murmured. 'He's playing *Bach*.'

The staggered, rising notes of Bach's *Toccata and Fugue in D minor* lifted into the night air. It was a tune that Nate had always thought apocalyptic, and it seemed a fitting choice for this night. A jolt passed through the ground and Flash growled. Then a groaning, creaking sound erupted from the walls of the church. Ripples ruptured the earth around the building. Cracks ran like fast-growing roots up the stone walls. One of the stained-glass windows bloomed into a flower of cracks, then shattered altogether as its frame twisted. More windows burst outwards. The music rose in tempo, growing louder. Nate could have sworn there were notes going beyond his hearing range, notes that squealed high enough to hurt his teeth and others that thudded deeply in his chest. Or perhaps that last was his quaking heart as he contemplated facing Gerald. He knew any other human would have been overwhelmed by Gerald's music by this point.

With a crunching, wrenching sound, the wall over the front door of the church collapsed, the remains of its windows tinkling among the falling stone. A long snake-like shape stretched up and out, and Nate wondered if this was some new engimal he had never seen before, a serpentine over forty feet long.

But then more of the things drove through the walls of the church, planting themselves into the ground beyond its foundations. Parts of the walls tumbled inwards as the haunting music continued to play. The volume increased and the walls that contained the organ fell away. The tentacles – for that was what they were – braced themselves against the ground, and with a single powerful thrust, heaved a portion of the building into the air. A few clinging pieces of stone and masonry fell away from it, revealing the church's organ, housed in the body of some enormous engimal – a leviathan, Nate thought, one shaped like an octopus or perhaps a squid. Its body must have measured nearly thirty feet, the largest tentacles at least twenty feet longer. But where its head should have been, Gerald had transplanted a church organ, some of the pipes rising up like the smokestacks of a train, others running under the hide of the creature.

It moved clumsily at first, swaying under its own weight, its tentacles unaccustomed to carrying its massive bulk on land. But Gerald's will coursed through it, transmitted through his fingers and the keys of the organ, and the precise but powerful flow of the music.

Oval and diamond-shaped markings glowed blue along its grey-green flanks as the rain began to fall heavier again. The monster raised itself up to its full height, and Nate saw Tatty's limp form clutched in one of its eight tentacles. Gerald looked out from his seat, twenty feet above the ground, grinned maniacally at Nate and then turned the beast around and walked it right through the side wall of the church, demolishing what remained of it, and on through a gap in the trees and down the slope towards the bottom of the mountain.

Nate sat there, awestruck and terrified, for nearly a minute. Even Flash had its head low, cowed by the sight of the mighty sea creature. A leviathan – the largest of the engimals on Earth, the creatures that could make sounds no other engimal could, that could transmit them further than any modern, man-made device. There could be no denying it, Gerald had pulled out all the stops. Nate had no idea how to launch an assault on such a beast – not without getting himself killed in the process.

'That's the whole point, though, isn't it?' he muttered to Flash. 'That's what I'm here for.'

Kicking his heels into Flash's sides, he set off in pursuit of Gerald and his monstrous creation. Behind him, Daisy slowed her horse, pulling back on the reins as she saw the leviathan disappear over the edge of the hill, with Nate speeding after it. Edgar was galloping up behind her, his horse slower because of his great weight. She gazed in dismay at the scene of devastation Gerald had left behind him.

'I don't believe it,' she gasped. 'He's destroyed another church.'

XXXVI

REQUIEM

By the time Nate emerged from the trees and caught sight of the leviathan again, it had turned around. Gerald was waiting for him, gently playing scales on one of the keyboards. And there was no sign of Tatty. Nate slowed Flash's pace, coasting down the grassy slope as he cast his gaze around, searching for signs of a trap. He pulled up on a hillock overlooking a low bank, staring at Gerald's creature, which stood quietly some forty yards away. Another hundred yards behind that, Nate could see the Wildensterns' private railway line cutting down into the woods as it descended into the valley to the right.

'What's this all about, Gerald?' he called out, waving at the monster. 'The chap with the biggest organ wins?'

'One can always count on you to lower the tone,' Gerald

called back. 'But then, you never did have a good ear for music.'

'Where's Tatty?'

'I've tied her to the railway tracks, just round the curve,' Gerald told him, indicating behind him. He lifted his head and stared off to Nate's left in an exaggerated manner. 'The family will be along any minute now, on board their train. You should just have time to save her, if you hurry. But I'm afraid you'll have to go through me first. It's time we had it out, old boy. Can't have you cramping my style, don't y'know.'

Nate ground his teeth and eyed the railway line. He was sure that Flash could cover the ground faster than Gerald's beast. He could get round and hope to reach the tracks before Gerald caught up . . . but it would mean running from that huge thing, turning his back on it. He had no idea what it could do, but he knew Gerald was counting on this; using Tatty to break his focus, to distract him from the fight.

The leviathan still had a consciousness of sorts — Nate could feel it, just beyond his reach, and he knew if he reached out further with his mind, he might be able to touch it . . . but it would mean opening the door to that sandstorm that raged just beyond his awareness. It was a door he didn't know how to close.

Gerald played a few bars of *She'll Be Coming Round the Mountain*, and then tooted one of the organ pipes like a train's whistle.

Nate let out a snarl and dug his heels into Flash's flanks, launching the velocycle off the hillock and charging down the slope. Gerald began playing something lively by Haydn. As Nate made his first pass, the tentacles whipped out, snatching at him and trying to knock him from his mount. He dodged through them, Flash banking right and left through the coiling tendrils, avoiding their grasp but failing to get Nate close enough to the platform on which Gerald sat.

Nate scrambled out into rough, open ground and swung Flash's back wheel around, cutting a semi-circular slash through the bog, hearing the engimal give a rumble of satisfaction. Then they hurtled back towards the leviathan. Gerald did not wait for them to come within reach of the tentacles. The rear of the engimal opened out like a flower, diamond-shaped petals overlapping around a round, shallow hollow, complete with a cone-like stamen protruding from the centre. Nate stared as the engimal aimed this dish-shaped flower at the sky.

Gerald changed key, his music rising in pitch, and the rain began to lash down harder, soaking the ground. The wind picked up, gusting violently. Nate's heart turned cold as he saw black dots start to coalesce in the air. It was as if someone had sprinkled pepper in the sky. These were intelligent particles, swarming so thickly they were becoming visible. Gerald had found a way to communicate with the particles in the air and in the earth. Wind lashed the rain into Nate's face, blurring his sight as the music went lower. Crevasses split the ground, forcing Flash to leap to one side, then the other, lunging back and forth across the cracks in the earth as they reached out from under the leviathan.

A tentacle slammed down in front of them and Flash vaulted over it, landing solidly and then jumping again, twisting in mid-air as they passed between two more tentacles, one of them scraping Nate's shoulder, the other suffering a skidmark from Flash's back wheel. They landed harder this time, off-balance on the wet slippery ground. Nate felt his revolver fall from his waistband and hauled back on the engimal's horns to spin his mount round before another tentacle crashed down in their path, nearly crushing Flash's head and shoulders. The tentacle went to rise up again, and Nate caught hold of it as it passed over his head. He was yanked from Flash's back, barely holding on to the wet and writhing ceramic surface. But using the movement of the snake-like limb, he swung himself up through the air and over, to drop neatly onto the platform where Gerald sat.

'*Touché,*' Gerald said, working his jaw, all the expression gone from his eyes. 'I'm intrigued. How are you defending yourself from the music? How are you protecting Flash?'

'Shove it, Gerald. Let's just get this done.'

Locking gazes with his cousin, Nate was reminded of a reptile, or a shark. Gerald stood up from his chair and Nate lunged at him. Gerald kicked the chair round, jamming the back of it into Nate's stomach, then he struck the side of Nate's jaw with the heel of his right hand. Nate rode the blow, stepped round the chair, blocked a left punch and drove his left elbow into Gerald's sternum. He followed it quickly with a hook into the floating ribs, but Gerald seized the back of his neck and swung his own elbow into the side of Nate's head, knocking him straight to the floor. He pushed himself up, and Gerald kicked him under the chin, flipping him over onto his back. Nate groaned and rolled over to rise to his feet again. His cousin was much stronger, much faster than he remembered.

'It's all about making the most of the particles in your own body,' Gerald told him. 'You'd be amazed what I can do now. It's a pity we can't share it.'

Nate didn't reply. He attacked again, jabbing punches and kicks at Gerald, who evaded some, blocked others and replied with fast, vicious strikes of his own. Nate took a punch to the nose and another to his throat and staggered back. Gerald followed, but Nate planted a front kick into his stomach that knocked him towards the edge of the platform.

The leviathan had settled into stillness while they fought. Without Gerald playing music into its lobotomized brain, there were no thoughts passing through its head. Nate threw a desperate look towards the curve in the tracks, where they descended past the edge of the trees, off to the right. From his left, he heard the chuff of a steam engine approaching. The noise only distracted him for an instant, but it was enough for Gerald to spring a knife from his sleeve into his hand and stab Nate in the ribs. Nate only managed to deflect it at the last moment, the blade slitting along his right side, rather than piercing his chest. Gerald came at him again, slashing Nate's arm as he blocked this second strike. The three lamps on the front of the train were visible in the darkness now, coming round the slope of the hill, rain hissing over its barrel-shaped engine, smoke pumping from its smokestack as its pistons drove the steel wheels along the glinting hardness of the rails.

'Tick tock, tick tock,' Gerald taunted him, knife in hand. 'Here we are, Nate, on the cusp of a scientific revolution, and you have us thumping each other around the head again.'

'What can I say?' Nate grunted, drawing his hunting knife. 'I'm a creature of habit.'

'No, you're a bloody *Neanderthal*!' Gerald snapped.

Hearing a whistle, Nate glanced up at the train that was passing out of sight behind the leviathan's body. Instinctively, he looked for it to come out the other side. He had no time left. Tatty had no time left.

Gerald swept his hand across the keys of the keyboard and a tentacle swung over and down, smashing away part of the platform, even as Nate dived forward to avoid it. He rolled back again to dodge another cut from Gerald's knife and nearly fell off the small organ platform. Forced to drop his knife, he snatched at Gerald's outstretched arm, hauling himself back on, and lunged in, head-butting his cousin on the bridge of the nose. Gerald stumbled backwards, his arms flailing out. Nate grabbed Gerald's right arm and turned him, twisting the arm behind his back. Keeping a firm hold on the arm-lock, he seized his cousin's head, slamming it down hard once, twice, three times on the keyboards, knocking keys loose and forcing discordant blares from the pipes of the organ. The leviathan shuddered and tilted, confused by the signals it was receiving from Gerald. Gerald let out a pained wheeze and slumped down between the seat and the keyboards.

Jumping from the platform, Nate landed heavily on the wet, boggy ground. He had no time left. Whistling for Flash, he set off running towards the railway line. The velocycle had been waiting, and now it swept alongside, its engine growling eagerly.

Nate was about to leap onto its back when he heard some strident notes from the organ behind him. Lightning struck the ground between him and Flash, blasting them apart with a blinding pillar of light, hotter than the sun. The strike left a burnt, smoking scar on the earth as Nate ran on, trying to get back to his engimal. More lightning strikes punched the ground around them. The land shook as if in an earthquake, the ground splitting into a wide crevasse in front of him, the soil tearing open like some cavernous mouth. Nate jammed his heels into the ground, skidding gouges into the grass, stopping just inches short of the edge. But Flash could not pull round in time . . . the engimal pitched head-first into the crevasse, struck the far side and tumbled to the bottom. The crack clamped closed, cutting off the engimal's terrified shriek. Nate's link with Flash's mind was cut off like a light going out.

Nate gasped in shock, as if he had felt the impact himself. Then he looked up at the hundred yards that separated him from the railway line, unable to spot Tatty but seeing the locomotive, tons of iron and steel, rushing headlong towards where his helpless sister lay.

For a moment he was ready to surrender to utter despair. He heard and saw nothing around him, encased in a cocoon of stillness while, in his mind, he felt the sandstorm outside, pressing against the door. With a feeling of release, he let the door open, felt it torn from its hinges and smashed apart as the maelstrom outside rushed in around him and blotted out his thoughts. He staggered, clutching his head as his senses were overwhelmed, connecting suddenly with every living thing around him, with the air and earth and the water that ran through them, the fire in the lightning that threatened to incinerate him.

And among it all, he felt Gerald's monstrous engimal lumbering towards him. It gave him something to focus on, and he lifted his head and opened his eyes. The world was a different place. He could see everything now, from the tiny droplets of water in the clouds to the microscopic organisms in the earth. He could feel the forces that bound together the molecules in the leviathan's giant body.

Gerald was playing Mozart's *Requiem*; deep, brooding, doom-laden music saturating the air as the leviathan loomed over Nate, its tentacles raised to crush him. Nate gazed up at this thing, filling the sky, felt its weight cause the ground to shudder beneath his feet. He thrust his open hand into the air and clenched his fingers into a fist.

The pipes of the organ bent and buckled. With a sound like a choir shown a vision of Hell, the leviathan twisted and writhed as its ceramic hide burst open in a dozen places, its insides churning into a mass of debris, four of its tentacles wrenching loose from its body. Gerald's scream was unheard over the cacophony, as some of his bones broke spontaneously before he fell free of the dying monster.

The leviathan crashed to the wet boggy ground, twitching, its fading groans subsiding deep into its ruined body. The lifeless carcass creaked and ticked like a house settling in the chill of night.

But Nate was already running. The train had passed them by, racing on along the tracks. As he ran, he found his conscious mind struggling to maintain control. He had given away too much. As his mind was suffocated by the storm of sensation, his body could feel the soft ground under his shoes, the whip of the grass across his feet and ankles. The wind across his face and hands. The rain still fell, and it steamed and hissed on his skin. The ancient particles that had surged into awareness inside his body now threatened to take over, powered by primal urges – the human drives that were far more potent than any conscious thought. Gerald had called him a Neanderthal, and it was the primitive man in him that wanted control now. With the adrenaline coursing through his body, he was driven to fight . . . to hunt and kill.

The train, Nate's frantic thoughts shouted to be heard. *I have to reach Tatty! I must stop the train!*

But those desperate thoughts were being drowned out, lost in the maelstrom in his head. His body kept running as it revelled in the unearthly power exploding through it. Veins stood out on his neck and arms. His bounds grew longer, his feet leaving gouges in the ground. His thighs bulged, his feet burst from his shoes, his shirt and jacket split down the back as his shoulders hunched and expanded, his arms lengthening, swelling muscles shredding the sleeves. Jagged spikes of bone rose from his spine and shoulder blades. *Tatty!* a distant voice cried from inside him. *Tatty!* As if to overwhelm that desperate appeal, a joyous ape-like roar rose from his lungs. He beat his chest, charged with power, eager to find rivals, prey, lusting for violence. *Tatty!* Nate screamed as he felt himself being buried, crushed under the pressure of the beast's raw, unthinking savagery.

Then he saw her, lying no more than fifty yards ahead, with the train bearing down on her. Even from here, he could read the abject terror on her face, feel it in his own body as he shared her emotions. She was gagged, and tied hand and foot. Her neck and ankles were roped to the rails. The sight was enough to galvanize him, to throw reins on the beast. He was bounding along on all fours now, more ape than man, running on his fists, knuckles leaving dents in the earth. Nate tried to reach out for the train, just as he had done with the leviathan, but it took all he had just to steer this animal he was becoming. Trying to control its instincts was like grabbing hold of a thrashing snake.

Humans were not made to use this power. At least, not yet. Their ability to reason was not strong enough. Nate had known that all along. If he let this power loose, his own nature could destroy him – it could destroy everything. But he no longer cared. Save Tatty, he thought, that one act of resolve giving him a hold over his base instincts. I'll do anything to save her. I am not a rational man, I am an animal . . . a beast. This is not an act of reason. I'll do anything to save her. If I have to, I'll kill anyone who gets in my way. He felt a red haze cloud his mind. I'll kill the world to save her.

He ran harder, covering ground at an inhuman pace. He was galloping ahead of the train. His angle would take him into its path before it reached Tatty. There was no way he could make these brutish hands untie the ropes, even if he'd had time. And tearing her free could kill her just as surely as being crushed under the train. Could he damage the tracks ahead of her, cause the train to derail? But it would slide forward, tumble . . . it was too close to her now. Then these weak, foolish, complicated thoughts were cast aside. There was little left of the human Nathaniel Wildenstern had been. There was only the rage, the ferocity that drove him on. Tatty lay helpless, screaming through her gag as she watched the train hurtle round the wide bend towards her. The crew could not see her black clothes in the dim light. Thirty yards, twenty, ten . . . the beast let out another roar. Charging up the low embankment towards the twenty-five ton locomotive, he lowered his right shoulder . . .

With a massive impact that buckled the steel chassis, the beast's body slammed diagonally into the right front corner of the locomotive. It was if the train had hit a cliff-face. Buffers gave way, cylinders split, the barrel-shaped smoke-box that formed the face of the train crumpled around the beast, breaking off the smokestack. Pistons broke free as the train's chassis twisted and contracted and wheels broke loose. The boiler burst, spraying pressurized water and steam across the crash-site. In an instant, the train was stopped dead in its tracks, pitching sideways off the rails. The locomotive absorbed the worst of the impact from the front, only to be struck again from behind, the rear of the engine thrown forwards and to the left as the momentum of the tender car and the carriages caused them to pile up against it, the whole length of the train folding like an accordion. The engine toppled over on its side, pulling the first two carriages over with it, down the low bank on the left side of the tracks. It took nearly a minute for all the sections of the zig-zagged train to stop moving, and still the sounds of creaking metal, splintering wood and breaking glass continued as the people aboard began screaming and wailing.

The three crewmen were dead; some of the Wildensterns too, and nearly all of the rest of the family and their small cadre of servants were injured.

The beast stood over Tatty, resting the great weight of its back and shoulders on its knuckles. It felt almost no pain from the collision as it gazed down at her in curiosity. She stared up at it in astonishment, shock and disbelief. It knew on some level that this delicate creature was important to it, but it had forgotten why. She was not a mate, nor was she one of its offspring. Still, despite its ancient appetites, it had no desire to eat the meat off her bones.

When it noticed the dark grey, almost black stain creeping out along the ground from under its feet, it stepped back. Despite its brutish mind, a flicker of recognition, and alarm, crossed its broad features. Reaching down to the rail on which her neck was bound, it pulled it up, wrenching the nails out of the sleepers. It did the same with the other rail, and she was able to slide the ropes off the end. With a deep grunt, it gestured at her to run, but her ankles were still tied together. It took both loops of the ankle-rope in its thick fingers and broke them like thread, causing her to cry out in pain, but leaving her ankles free. Then it lifted her onto her feet and pushed her gently on her way with the backs of its fingers, as one might do a toddler who had fallen over. The delicate creature stumbled backwards, unable to take her eyes off the thing in front of her. The beast looked down and saw that the stain of rotten ground was spreading out in a wider circle. It had almost reached the feet of the little creature.

It bellowed at her, and she turned and fled.

'Truly remarkable,' a voice said from behind the beast. 'You've opened my eyes.'

Gerald stood there, about twenty feet away but hovering nearly thirty feet in the air. The floating quality of his hair and clothes made him seem weightless. It appeared as if his injuries had already healed. He had the expression of a man who had just experienced some divine revelation.

'I should have realized it long ago,' he added, lifting his arms and feeling the air that he could grip in his hands. 'A race as advanced as that which created the particles could naturally have made them as instinctive to use as their own bodies. And there I was, bashing out tunes like some idiot savant, not understanding the power that I held at my fingertips. Thank you, Nate.'

He regarded the beast with a critical eye and shook his head sadly.

'There's nothing left of you in there, is there, old chum? You let them release your true nature. Tch, tch. Clarity of thought and intention was never one of your strengths. And what's this mess you're leaving in the ground beneath you? Don't tell me you've gone and soiled yourself—'

Gerald was barely fast enough to react as the beast seized one of the detached train wheels and hurled it at him like a discus. He raised his hands and it slowed in mid-air a few feet away from him, then vapourized, leaving only a cloud of smoke that smelled of iron. The concentration that had taken caused him to sink towards the ground, and Gerald caught himself before he hit, willing himself to rise once more. The fat steel cylinder end of one of the train's pistons smashed him out of the air, throwing him into the wreckage of the train. As Gerald sat up, the beast raised its giant club again, the weapon nearly twice the creature's own height. Blood flowed from Gerald's nose and mouth and his head had a lop-sided shape. He stood up, staggered, and sat down again, blinking as he found his thoughts clouded by a red haze. With dull eyes, he stared down at his hands, and then gasped as an animal rage filled his body with adrenaline, that swelling seeming to change the very shape of his muscles. His neck and shoulders bulged, and he stood up and beat at his chest, wanting to let out the feeling surging up inside him.

Then the beast that had once been his best friend brought the train piston crashing down on him. Like a caveman with a wooden club, the beast battered its rival's body over and over again, until all sign of life had been extinguished. Then it stood over the corpse, its lungs heaving in long, deep breaths. From under its feet, the stain of the rotten ground spread outwards. Gerald's body was consumed in less than minute, then the steel and iron of the train parts began dissolving into rust, the rails of the track following suit, the wood of the sleepers rotting to pulp, all eaten up in the steadily widening circle of disintegration.

The beast was staring down at the growing area of rot when Daisy arrived with Edgar close behind her. They had been forced into shelter by the force of the inexplicable storm that Gerald had summoned, but had emerged from the woods in time to see Nate's collision with the train. Or at least, the thing that had once been Nate. Daisy got down off her horse, hurrying across the grass towards the railway embankment. The beast saw her and leaped into the air, landing outside the circle of rot, snarling at her but not attacking. She came towards him through the debris of the train crash. Her trembling hands were raised in front her, speaking quietly in a voice that had gone quite hoarse as tears ran down her cheeks.

'Ssshhhh,' she whispered. 'It's all right now. It's over. You can come back to me. Come back to me now, Nate. It's you, Nate. I know it's you in there. Come back to me.'

The beast settled onto its knees, a feeling of calm coming over it. It flinched slightly as her hands reached tentatively for its face, but after a few moments it let her touch it. Daisy placed her fingers gently on its cheeks, feeling how different the shape of the jaw and cheekbones were to Nate's, how tough its hide was compared to Nate's skin.

Even as she caressed them, she could feel a change in them. The beast's massive frame was subsiding, shrinking. Air was exhaled from its lungs as its chest reduced in size. The hostility faded from its eyes as the face contracted around them.

She did not notice that the rot was still eating past their feet, hissing and sizzling like fried meat as it crossed under the beast's heels. It was only when she felt a burning under the soles of her own feet that she looked down and gasped in shock. The ground underfoot was a burnt, slimy black. The stench rising from it was incredible. Whatever this was, it was dissolving her shoes. Then she remembered what Nate had told her about the prehistoric disaster.

'What the bloody hell *is* that thing?' someone shouted.

The beast looked up to see some of the Wildensterns making their way awkwardly down from the wreckage of the carriages. Gideon was at their head, cradling a broken wrist to his chest. He was staring at this monstrosity, holding his shotgun pistol in his free hand. Raising it up, he took aim at the creature. Clearly, the fact that it had rammed a train had not suggested to him that killing it might take more than a shotgun shell.

The beast let out a roar at the Wildensterns. Its body tensed, and Daisy shook her head, waving Gideon back. It was getting to its feet, starting to grow again, when she was pulled backwards, nearly throwing her off her feet. She landed outside the circle of rot.

Edgar strode past her, across the blackening ground.

'Run!' he shouted back at her. 'Run, and don't look back! RUN!'

Then he turned and embraced his son. Holding the beast down on its knees, it took all of Edgar's considerable strength to cling on to the creature. Clutching its head into his chest, he put his mouth close to its ear.

'It is my fault you are what you are, my son. This is *my* burden to bear. Let me take it from you.'

The beast twisted and writhed in his arms, but he could tell it was listening to his voice. He kept talking, kept his arms locked around it, despite the burning sensation that crept into his feet and up his calves, despite the blows it laid into his body, the claws it raked across his back. He kept talking to the beast as its cries grew more human and its blows grew weaker, though the pain Edgar felt became excruciating, and he now screamed, his own body breaking down as the rot took it. When his own strength began to fail and his legs crumpled beneath him, he kept talking, kept whispering, then gasping, then his breathing became too laboured, and he could not summon the words, and now it was the creature, his *son*, who was holding *him* up, taking *his* weight.

Nate felt the rot stop eating the ground beneath him as his consciousness returned. He could think again, the savage urges of his primal self had faded away. And with them went the intelligent particles' drive to destroy. He was kneeling on the ground, the last shreds of his clothes hanging from his naked body. His cheeks were wet with tears, his throat ragged from crying. His body ached, his muscles sent bolts of pain out when he moved, and his skin felt stretched to the point of splitting; every joint felt dislocated, and lined with gritty sand. When he opened his eyes, he looked up into the partially decomposed skull of his father. Edgar's remains fell in pieces from his arms, the bones all but stripped off their flesh. The engimal claw thumped to the ground.

Nate had nothing left in him; even his sorrow at the sight of his father's body was a dull, numbed feeling. More arms wrapped around him, warm living flesh, as Daisy and Tatty embraced him, hugging him tightly and then helping him to his feet. They supported him as he walked across the hundred yards of blackened ground, past the trees that had fallen, past the train locomotive that had disintegrated into a pile of rust. They walked out of the vast, sunken hollow of dead earth and up to the green grass where he could lie down and stare at the sky. It was a long, long time before he could bring himself to speak.

'I have to leave,' he croaked out of a horribly dry throat. 'Before this happens again.'

Epilogue

NO END OF KNOTS TO UNRAVEL

Daisy stood in the rose garden and regarded the burnt husk of a building that had once been Wildenstern Hall. A few of the older sections, further out from the tower, had survived, but most of it was in ruins. Smoke rose in a lazy cloud over it. Days had passed, and still there were parts that burned. Some of the rafters and beams in the upper floors of the tower continued to smoulder, and it was dangerous to approach as burnt debris still occasionally fell down within the walls.

Nate and Tatty were walking through the gardens nearby, talking in low voices. Nate wore warm clothes and a heavy coat, and still he looked cold, despite the sunny day. Cathal walked not far behind them, lost in his thoughts. His maimed, bandaged hand was tucked into his jacket, just as it was whenever he was out in public. Elvira had suggested that he take to wearing Brutus's engimal claw, but he had firmly declined.

Elizabeth had disappeared, taking Leopold with her. Daisy had already hired investigators to find them. Despite his faults as a father, and his own doubts, Nate was entitled to contact with his son.

A few other members of the family were around, but it was Daisy who was supervising the clean-up operation, ensuring that anything that could be salvaged from the house was pulled out before the damaged walls were demolished. She looked to the driveway that led round the stables and saw a hansom pull up. Inspector Urskin got out and waved to her. Then he helped another man out of the small carriage, one who supported himself with the help of a crutch, and Daisy saw with delight that it was Clancy, alive and clearly recovering from his injuries. Leaving Clancy to talk to some of the staff who came over to him, Urskin took his leather case from the cab and started towards Daisy. He had been a regular visitor since the assault on Wildenstern Hall.

'Your Grace,' he greeted her, taking off his hat as he approached. 'Mister Clancy was down at the Castle, helping us with his enquiries, and I thought I'd offer him a lift home, as I was coming out here myself. How goes the work?'

'Painstakingly slow, I'm afraid,' she replied. 'The place is still dangerous. It'll be a while before we can start rebuilding.'

'It is definitely your plan to rebuild, then?'

'Definitely,' she said, nodding her head, as if to reinforce her decision. 'Though I think the new building will be a little less . . . ostentatious. How goes your investigation, Inspector?'

'There is a lot that doesn't make sense, frankly. But then, how does one fathom a mind like Gerald Gordon's? The man was a genius, of that there can be no doubt, but to my mind he was an utter fiend as well.'

'He considered himself a slave to absolute and merciless reason,' Daisy told the policeman. 'Though I can't pretend to know what his goals were.' She was careful to ask the next question with a casual tone: 'Have you managed to work out the purpose of the giant engimal that was found out near the train tracks? Or how it caused the damage to the ground?'

'It's a complete mystery, so far,' he answered. 'Because of the events in Glendalough, the army were somewhat late arriving at the scene. One might almost suspect that was a deliberate ploy on the part of the late Mister Duffy. But the general believes the creature to have been a weapon of some sort. The army has experimented with such things themselves, but with little to show for it. This one seems to have suffered a catastrophic failure. The army's engimologists are intrigued by the whole matter. They say the damage to the monster seems to have been quite spontaneous – no doubt the result of Mister Gordon's tinkering.'

'Quite,' said Daisy.

'I'm here on a different matter, however, your Grace,' he added tentatively. 'Relating to Mister Gordon's . . . *factory* in Glendalough. The property was purchased by Duffy shortly before we made our assault on the mine, as you're no doubt aware.' He paused here for a second. 'The circumstances behind the deal are . . . questionable. But we found other records in Mister Gordon's office in that mine, which lead me to believe that he was involved in a number of other suspicious business dealings that might shed light on this mystery.'

'And you're here to ask me if there might be records of any other dodgy business practices going on under Gerald's management?' Daisy suggested.

Urskin shrugged and nodded.

'As you can see, the family's business headquarters, which were also housed in the main tower, burned with the rest of the building,' Daisy said, gesturing at the ruin. 'However, for the last few years, I have taken the liberty of making duplicates of all our most important documents and having them transferred to the city, for safekeeping at Leinster House. I will ensure you're given full access, Inspector. And I think I might be able to point you in the direction of one or two of the more questionable operations. There is a lot about this family that needs to be brought out into the light.'

'But nothing that would incriminate you, I trust?' the inspector asked.

'Me, Inspector?' Daisy laughed, clapping her hands at the absurdity of his question. 'I cannot sign contracts or cheques! I cannot vote or even own *property*, let alone run an empire like the North Atlantic Trading Company. I'm merely a *woman*, Inspector! A glorified secretary who even if she wanted to could not make decisions of any significance. I'm sure any court in the land would accept that the complexities of modern business are beyond my simple comprehension.'

'Of course, how stupid of me.' Urskin grinned.

Nate, Tatty and Cathal were walking towards them. The changes that had been wrought upon them were evident in their faces, and in the way they moved. They all looked older, but in different ways. Cathal was no longer a boy; his reckless, stubborn nature seemed to have mellowed some- what. Perhaps it was the loss of his hand, but he was less vocal, less contrary. Instead, he had a more solid, resolute air. There was still something of the fire in his eyes, but it smouldered rather than blazed.

Tatiana was still as bright as a button, but Daisy caught her looking towards the hills from time to time, no doubt musing about the secret life of adventurous freedom she had been forced to give up. Like Cathal, she appeared more settled, more resolved on her course in life. There was a new tone in her voice, one that expected to be taken seriously – not an expectation that Tatty would have seen a need for only a few months ago. She and Cathal had already expressed their intention to stay and help rebuild Wildenstern Hall.

Nate had spoken very little since the day of his battle with Gerald, but he and Daisy had spent as much time as possible alone together in the chaotic days that followed. He was overcome with guilt for what he had done – deserting his son and family for years, for failing to stop Gerald the first time they fought, and for the subsequent deaths his savage family had caused, including Duffy's. There were also the deaths for which Nate held himself directly responsible, including those of the train crew and, of course, his own father. But it was the fear of what he might still do that occupied his thoughts for most of his waking hours.

The strain was telling on his face, but Tatty was like a tonic to him, and Daisy liked to think that she herself was too. There were times she would catch him staring at her, and he would look away, smiling and blushing like an adolescent. It was at times like these that he did not look twenty years older than he was. He was eyeing her now as the three of them came up to where she and the inspector stood on the path that ran through the rose beds.

Urskin said hello to the others, and then excused himself, walking off to join his constables, who were engaged in the task of questioning the Wildenstern staff about the night of the fire. There were a lot of servants, and Daisy had instructed them to be completely honest with the inspector. Nothing they were likely to say would leave him any the wiser. And whether he believed them or not would be another matter. Add those stories to the colourful and invariably dishonest tales related by the family members and the detective would find himself with no end of knots to unravel. Daisy would help, where she could.

'I don't envy him his task,' Cathal muttered as he watched the policeman walk away.

'Wait 'til I show him the business files,' Daisy remarked. 'They'll send his head spinning.'

'I'm not entirely sure his head is capable of spinning,' Tatty commented. 'He is quite the most grounded man I've ever met. I wonder if he could be convinced to come and work for us? We could use a man who knows how to enforce the law. We'll have Clancy on our side, of course, but he's getting old, and I fear he's been shot once too often.'

'And Father has agreed to join us,' Cathal said. 'Though I must say, we had to do some arm-twisting. He finally said something about "testing his moral backbone". He was never one to shy away from a challenge.'

Tatty took Cathal's hand, entwining her fingers in his and looking into his eyes. He smiled back at her.

'We've been thinking about what you said,' he said to Daisy, squeezing Tatty's hand. 'And we've decided that this is what we want to do.'

Daisy exchanged glances with Nate, who nodded.

'Then I'll stay with you as long as it takes to get you

settled in,' she said. 'We'll have to inform the family, of course. This is a complete breach of the rules governing inheritance, but the family is so divided right now it won't make much difference. They're going to hate us no matter what we do.'

'Think of them as a pack of animals,' Nate said to them in a hoarse voice. 'They just need to know who's in charge.'

The following evening would be Nate's last at Wildenstern Hall. Despite the protests of those closest to him, he insisted he could not stay there. For everyone's sake, he needed to get as far from the family as possible and find a place where he could live a life free of violence. Though there was no need for the family to know the *whole* truth.

Three long dining-room tables had been found unscathed by the fire and taken out onto the lawn. They were set with white linen tablecloths, cutlery and dishes brought from Leinster House. In that warm evening, the family sat down to a relatively simple dinner, roast meat and vegetables prepared over fires made from the burnt wood and charcoal from the ruined building that stood in the background. Nate sat at the head of the main table, his rightful place as Patriarch. He took little part in the conversation at dinner, much of which was taken up by what would be uncovered by the police investigation, and what all these dramatic events meant for the future. As they were finishing off the main course, Nate stood up and tapped his glass with a knife to call for their attention.

Everyone looked to him, expecting him to raise a toast of some kind. Instead, his first words were to the servants, telling them to remove themselves from the vicinity for the next ten minutes. They promptly obeyed, leaving the family to stare suspiciously at Nate.

'As you all know, I'm leaving,' he announced. 'But I won't be going far. What you may *not* know is that Daisy will be joining me, once things have settled down here.' She reached her hand out to him and he took it, smiling sadly at her. Then he continued: 'I'm leaving Cathal and Tatiana in charge of the house, and the family business.'

There were protests and cries of outrage all down the table, but most were quickly silenced as Nate raised his hand.

'Those whelps?' Elvira bellowed, ignoring his call for order. 'Why, the boy is hardly out of short trousers, and the girl is . . . is a *girl*, by God! And a flibbertigibbet of the highest order!'

'As if you were any different, when you were my age,' Tatty muttered under her breath.

'You don't seriously think you can leave these urchins in charge?' Gideon blustered. 'I won't have it, by the Lord Harry. It won't stand!'

'They will have assistance from others we're bringing in,' Nate said firmly, 'but *you* will all do your utmost to help them. That is, those of you who are still left after the police have purged this family of its worst offenders. You might have trouble accepting their authority in the beginning, so let me make this very, very clear, in terms I know you can understand . . .'

Daisy reached under her chair and handed him a box. He set it on the table in front of him and opened the lid. Then he carefully lifted Brutus's decomposing, decapitated skull out of the box and laid it on the table in front of the box. There was a chorus of indrawn breaths. They all recognized the head, and those who hadn't experienced the battle that had destroyed the train had certainly been told about it later, in lurid detail.

'The Rules of Ascension are being consigned to history,' Nate told them. 'There will be no more attacks or assassinations . . . except by *me*. I know you have no respect for the law, so there's no point telling you that we'll call the police on you. In time, perhaps you'll learn to take the law more seriously. You obeyed Gerald well enough, and I think you know enough about recent events to be sure I won't waste time whistling or playing the fiddle to get your attention. You know how I like to keep things simple. Now, I'm going away. And for the time being, there will be one, very simple rule for you to obey without question.' He tapped the top of Brutus's head to emphasize each word: 'Don't. Make. Me. Come. Back.'

He gently placed the skull back in the box and covered it with the lid. Tatty put two fingers in her mouth and let out a shrill whistle to call back the servants, making some of the family jump at the sound.

'Who's for dessert?' she asked. 'The cooks have done up a splendid meringue, or there are marzipan fingers to have with your coffee . . .' She glanced at the box. 'They are *just* made with marzipan, nothing else of course . . .'

Nate excused himself from the table and walked away across the lawn, looking up at the ruins of the building that had been his home for most of his life.

'Where will you go?' Cathal asked from behind him.

Nate turned, surprised that he hadn't heard the younger man approach.

'Scotland first, I think,' he replied. 'Find some out-of-the-way spot and wait for Daisy. After that . . . I don't know. We'll keep moving around for a while. Don't worry, we'll stay in touch.'

Cathal nodded. He wanted to ask something, but held back, biting his lip. He still had his stump tucked into his jacket and Nate cast his gaze down at it. An uneasy look crossed his face, but then it was gone. He lifted his eyes to Cathal's.

'The worst is past, Cathal. Things will work out. Between you and Tatty, you'll make a wonderful Patriarch.' Nate smiled, putting his hand on Cathal's shoulder. 'Just mind that temper of yours. Don't lose your head. And that's not an easy prospect if you're planning on marrying Tatty.'

Cathal's ears and freckled cheeks went bright red.

'Is it that obvious?'

'I'm not *blind*, Cathal!' Nate said, grinning. 'But I couldn't ask for a better match for my little sister. I'm not sure the world is ready for your children, but you'll both do fine. I have no doubt about it.'

He turned his head to look at the sun sinking beyond the hills, and Cathal could tell that his cousin wanted to be alone. As Nate walked away, Tatty came up behind Cathal and wrapped her arms around his waist.

'You didn't tell him?' she asked, knowing the answer.

He shook his head, drawing his arm from his jacket and untying the bandage with the help of his teeth. She knew him well enough not to offer to help, but she noted that he would have to get a more presentable cover for the arm soon, now that the wound had sealed up. Unwinding the bandage, he felt Tatty's chin on his shoulder and knew she was watching as he uncovered the stump where his hand should have been.

'It doesn't have to be a problem,' she said quietly. 'We'll just tell people it wasn't as bad as everyone thought.'

Cathal wasn't so sure that would work. He looked at the stump, at the four stubby fingers and the nub of a thumb that was growing from the new lump of flesh that had sprouted from the end of his arm. There could be no doubt about it. His forearm and hand were growing back. It had been the focus of his thoughts for days, and now it was happening.

'What else can you do, do you think?' Tatty asked.

Cathal thought about Gerald's leviathan, and Nate's transformation, and the huge sunken crater of dead earth and rusted train wreckage on the south side of the hill. He twisted his head round to smile at her, and kissed her cheek.

'Isn't this enough?' he laughed, wiggling his budding fingers. 'Come on, let's get back. I don't think we should leave that lot on their own for long. God only knows what they might get up to.'

'Shame on you, Cathal Dempsey!' she exclaimed, letting him take her arm as they started back towards the dinner tables set out on the lawn. 'If you can't trust your family, who can you trust?'

Author's Note: A Bit of Background

For the sake of readers from the UK and beyond, I thought I'd provide a short note on some of the Irish cultural and historical references in the Wildenstern Saga, and particularly in this story. For the sake of clarity, I'll set them out here in chronological order, rather than in the order they appear in the story.

There is a vast and varied collection of Irish folk tales and legends that were originally passed from generation to generation by oral storytellers, but which are being gradually organized and collected into volumes by modern storytellers and historians. These range from whimsical fairy tales to epic sagas depicting god-like achievements. I mention a few characters from these legends in *Merciless Reason*:

There is Cormac MacArt, a warrior king from about AD 200. There is Fionn MacCumhaill, leader of an army of elite warriors called the Fianna, legendary defenders of Ireland (the Fenians would later take their name from this group). The further back you go, the more god-like the characters become. The Dagda featured in the oldest cycle of legends; a powerful master of all the arts, he was said to have a cauldron that could feed an army, and could regenerate the dead – though some sources ascribe this second power to the huge club he wielded in battle. Warriors in these legends were often described as experiencing physical changes brought on by their bloodlust in battle, where their bodies underwent monstrous transformations, sometimes referred to as 'warp spasms'. The most famous of these descriptions can be found in the stories of the Cattle Raid of Cooley, featuring a warrior named Cúchullain.

Ireland has suffered many famines in its history, but the one that changed the character of the country for ever, known as the Great Famine, occurred between 1845 and 1852. A catastrophic period of starvation, disease and emigration, it was a pivotal point in Irish history. About one million people died and nearly the same number again emigrated to escape the devastation. This, despite the fact that Ireland had many richly fertile and extremely pro-ductive farms. At that time, Ireland was ruled by Britain and most of the landowners (but by no means all) were British, and most of those continued to live in Britain. There was a real Duke of Leinster of the time – a major landowner – though his name was not Wildenstein, and his family was nothing like theirs, being more sympathetic to the peasants' plight. The system at the time was for the peasants to work on these farms, not for money but for the right to use a piece of their masters' land to grow their own food. These pieces of land were invariably small, so in order to make the most of what they had, the peasants chose to grow the most filling, most nutritious food available – the potato. For the poorest living in the countryside, this made up almost all of their diet. In a country whose population was as poverty-stricken as any Third World country today, the people had no means of making money to buy other types of food.

When a disease known as potato blight first struck in 1845, that year's crop of potatoes began to literally rot in the ground, before they could be harvested. The following year, the crop was destroyed again. And then again the next year.

As the peasants slowly starved to death, massive quantities of food were still being transported to Britain and beyond under heavily-armed guard. There is still ongoing debate about how responsible the government was for the disastrous years that followed, but there is no doubt that too little was done too late. Whether it was through starvation, disease, or even by drowning on the overcrowded, ramshackle 'coffin-ships' headed for America, the loss of life was unprecedented in the country's history. In the space of less than seven years, the country lost nearly a quarter of its population to death and emigration. The nation struggled for decades to recover; the Industrial Revolution that fol-lowed was slow to reach the south of Ireland, developing much more quickly up in the north. In the story, I portray Dublin as more industrialized than it actually was.

A nationalist group called the Young Irelanders attempted a rebellion in 1848, seeking an end to British Rule, but the nation failed to rise with them, as most people were struggling just to stay alive, and the rebels were easily defeated. Some of the survivors later joined others to create the Irish Republican Brotherhood. A very different organization to the likes of the modern IRA, it had major public support among the Irish people. Part civil movement, part guerrilla army, it had ties to another group, the Fenian Brotherhood, in the United States. The members of both groups eventually became known as 'Fenians', though the term would later be used by the British authorities to refer to any nationalist sympathizer. From the 1850s right up to the twentieth century and the 1916 Rising, the IRB remained the dominant rebel group in Ireland.

Apart from the fantasy/science fiction elements of the Wildenstern Saga, such as the family itself, the engimals and the intelligent particles, the life of ordinary people in Ireland is depicted as accurately as I was able to within the confines of the story.

Oisín McGann

ANCIENT APPETITES

Oisín McGann

Nate Wildenstern's brother has been killed, and the finger is pointed at him . . .

After nearly two years, eighteen-year-old Nate returns home to the family empire ruled by his father – the ruthless Wildenstern Patriarch. But Nate's life is soon shattered by his brother's death, and the Rules of Ascension, allowing the assassination of one male family member by another, means he's being blamed. He knows that he is not the murderer, but who is?

With the aid of his troublesome sister-in-law, Daisy, and his cousin Gerald, he means to find out. But when the victims of the family's tyrannical regime choose the funeral to seek their revenge, they accidentally uncover the bodies of some ancient Wildenstern ancestors, one of whom bears a Patriarch's ring. The lives of Nate and his family are about to take a strange and horrifying turn . . .

SHORTLISTED FOR THE
2007 WATERSTONE'S BOOK PRIZE

978 0 552 55499 2

Are you being watched?

STRANGLED SILENCE

Oisín McGann

*Ivor is convinced he's
being watched . . .*

Amina Mir is doing work
experience with a newspaper
in London when she meets
Ivor McMorris. Ivor served in the war in Sinnostan and
believes that someone interfered with his memories while
he was there. He's afraid that if he tries to do anything
about it, the watchers might make him disappear.

Chi Sandwith investigates conspiracies. He has spoken to
soldiers who, like Ivor, are haunted by their experiences in
Sinnostan. They speak in fearful tones of a covert operations
group known as the Scalps. People who ask too many
questions about the Scalps tend to suffer 'accidents'.

Tariq is Amina's teenage brother. He's taking part in
a new school programme, run by the Army. They are
using action-packed computer games to teach parts of
the curriculum . . . and he's loving it. But he starts to
suspect that the games have another purpose.

Some questions are better left unanswered.
Some mysteries are best left unsolved.
The truth is out there – but it could get you killed . . .

978 0 552 55862 4